In West Mills

In West Mills

A Novel

DE'SHAWN CHARLES WINSLOW

BLOOMSBURY PUBLISHING

NEW YORK · LONDON · OXFORD · NEW DELHI · SYDNEY

BLOOMSBURY PUBLISHING
Bloomsbury Publishing Inc.
1385 Broadway, New York, NY 10018, USA

BLOOMSBURY, BLOOMSBURY PUBLISHING, and the Diana logo are
trademarks of Bloomsbury Publishing Plc

First published in the United States 2019
Copyright © De'Shawn Charles Winslow, 2019

ISBN: HB: 978-1-63557-340-4; eBook: 978-1-63557-341-1

Library of Congress Cataloging-in-Publication Data

Names: Winslow, De'Shawn Charles, author.
Title: In West Mills / De'Shawn Charles Winslow.
Description: New York : Bloomsbury Publishing, 2019.
Identifiers: LCCN 2018034737 | ISBN 9781635573404 (hardback) |
ISBN 9781635573411 (e-book)
Classification: LCC PS3623.I66425 I5 2019 | DDC 813/.6—dc23
LC record available at https://lccn.loc.gov/2018034737

2 4 6 8 10 9 7 5 3 1

Typeset by Westchester Publishing Services
Printed and bound in the U.S.A. by Berryville Graphics Inc., Berryville, Virginia

To find out more about our authors and books visit www.bloomsbury.com
and sign up for our newsletters.

Bloomsbury books may be purchased for business or promotional use.
For information on bulk purchases please contact Macmillan Corporate
and Premium Sales Department at specialmarkets@macmillan.com.

To the reader.

Part One

ONE

In October of '41, Azalea Centre's man told her that he was sick and tired of West Mills and of the love affair she was having with moonshine. Azalea—everyone called her Knot—reminded him that she was a grown woman.

"Stop tellin' me how old you is," Pratt said.

"Well, I thought maybe you forgot," Knot retorted. She was sitting at her kitchen table, pulling bobby pins from her copper-red hair. She picked up her glass and finished what was left in it. She had barely set it back on the table when Pratt picked it up and threw it against the wall. He then packed all his clothes in the old suitcase he'd brought when he moved into her little house a few years back.

"I'm gettin' outta here," he affirmed.

"Need some help packin'?" Knot shot back, and she laughed. It wasn't the first time Pratt had packed that ragged bag. He stared at her, frowning.

"Drink ya'self to death, if that's what you want to do."

"Go to hell, Pratt."

"I'm *leavin'* hell!" he yelled.

A few days later, Knot came home and found a folded note peeping out from under her door. First, she looked down at the signature. When she saw *Pratt Shepherd* at the bottom, she took a chilled glass from her icebox, poured a drink, and sat down to look over the message. She read most of it. It said that Pratt was at his sister's house, just across the lane. Knot wasn't surprised. Pratt's sister and her two little girls were the only family he had in West Mills.

In the letter, Pratt reminded her that he still loved her, still wanted to marry her, and still wanted to start a family with her. He wrote that he would wait around for just one week. Then he was going back home to Tennessee. That's where Knot stopped reading. She laughed out loud, tossed the paper onto the table, and set her glass down on it. Funny—it was usually the books she used to teach her pupils that got the wet glass.

Knot would be lying if she told anyone that Pratt wasn't a good man. He didn't mind hard work, he picked up after himself, he kept his body nice and clean, and he knew how to give her joy in bed. But the truth was Pratt wasn't much fun to her otherwise. He didn't have much to talk about. And he couldn't hold his liquor to save his life. After two drinks Pratt was laid out, spilling over, or both. Knot liked men who could match her shot for shot, keep her mind busy when they weren't drunk, and still do all the other things Pratt could do. Aside from all that, her father—she called him Pa—wouldn't like Pratt. If she were ever going to be married, it would have to be a man her pa loved just as much as she did.

Pratt's threat to leave West Mills could not have come with better timing, because Knot's twenty-seventh birthday was a week around the corner. When the weekend came, she walked down the lane—two houses to the left of her house—to tell her good friend Otis Lee Loving all about her newfound freedom. And since Knot visited him most Saturday mornings, and knew he would be in the kitchen, she didn't bother knocking.

"You need to go on over there and fix things up with Pratt," Otis Lee said. "Otherwise, he gon' be on the next thing headed west." Otis Lee set a cup of black coffee on the table in front of Knot; his face was angry-looking and peach. He didn't sit down. Just then, his wife, Pep, showed up at the table with a boiled egg and a biscuit, all inside the cracked, sand-colored bowl Knot wished they would throw away.

"Pratt can catch the next thing to hell," Knot replied.

Pep pushed the bowl in front of Knot, next to the coffee. She didn't sit down, either. Knot looked up at them and wondered what the day's lecture would be about.

"Eat," Pep commanded. Even at seven o'clock in the morning, her round face looked full and healthy, as though she had slept on a pillow made of air. Not the rough, feather-stuffed pillows Knot used.

"I thought I left my mama in Ahoskie," Knot scoffed. "Y'all got anything I can pour in this coffee? Something 'sides milk, I mean."

"Why you so set on bein' lonely, Knot?" Otis Lee asked.

Pep looked down at Otis Lee as though he had gone off script. And he looked up at Pep as if to say, *I couldn't help myself.* The way he and Pep stood there, side by side, made them look more like a boy and his mother than a husband and his wife. Why the two of them behaved so much like old people, Knot never understood. They were only five years older than she was. For Knot, it was Otis Lee's being happily married, being too short, and old-man ways that ruined the handsomeness she'd seen on him when they'd first met. And that handsomeness, as striking as it was, had never caused the feeling Knot got deep in her stomach when she met a man she wanted to touch, or be touched by, in the dim light of her oil lamp.

"Y'all know he tried to beat me, don't ya?"

Otis Lee and Pep both sighed, at the same time. Knot wondered if they had rehearsed it.

"You sit to my table and tell that tale?" Otis Lee reproached. Then he began with his *You know good'n well* this and *You know good'n well* that. At times like these Knot had to work hard to keep her cool. Because if she didn't, she might tell Otis Lee that if he spent more time worrying about his own life, and his own family, he might know that the woman he knew as his mother, wasn't; she was kin but not his mother. *If his real mama is anything like mine, better for him if he don't know. Ain't none of my business anyhow.*

"Tell me one thing," Knot said. "Why y'all always take his side?"

"It ain't just about Pratt's side, Knot," Otis Lee insisted. "You need to be nicer to everybody 'round here." Knot heard bits and pieces of what Otis Lee recounted about how her drinking had gotten out of hand; how she seemed to want to be by herself more than anything nowadays—unless she was at Miss Goldie's Place, of course. Knot started nibbling on the biscuit and then on the egg, trying not to hear all the things she already knew about herself.

Otis Lee turned to Pep and mused, "You remember when she used to go see the children and they mamas, Pep? Used to visit people just 'cause she had time. People used to talk so nice about that, Knot. Thought the *world* of it. Didn't they, Pep?"

"Yes, they did," Pep replied.

Knot dropped the egg back in the bowl and asked, "Ain't I sittin' here, visitin' with ya'll right now?" Knot was certain they'd both heard her question, although neither of them responded.

"Now folk say you show up to that schoolhouse smellin' like you bathe in corn liquor," Otis Lee went on. "That's 'bout all they sayin' 'bout you now."

"What people you talkin' 'bout, anyhow, Otis Lee?" Knot said. She took a sip of the coffee. It was weak.

"What you mean, 'what people'?"

"Y'all ain't got but three or four hundred folk 'round here," Knot pointed out. "And most of 'em is white folk who don't know me from a can of bacon grease."

"Some days you talk like you don't live right here in this town," Pep remarked. Knot couldn't think of anything to say back.

She knew that some if not all of what Otis Lee was saying was true—about people whispering. Many times Knot had noticed how some of the women stopped talking when she came near them at the general store. And at the schoolhouse, she'd been a bit hurt by how some of the people had seemed as if they didn't want to be seen speaking with her too long when they came to pick up their children. They'd ask how their little ones were doing with their lessons and then hurry off as though Knot had a sickness they didn't want to catch.

Knot did her job. As much as she hated it, she did it well. No one had complained about her teaching. They couldn't.

So many of the ma's and pa's had themselves thanked Knot for the little rhymes and games she'd taught their children to help them divide a number quickly—without using paper and pencil. Or the funny ways she'd taught them odd facts. She remembered asking one of the boys one day, "Sammy Spence, what's the capital of Iowa?" And once he'd answered correctly, she'd asked, "How you remember to keep the *s*'s silent?" and Sammy had responded, "My name got *s*'s, and they both make the *s* sound. But not for Des Moines, Miss Centre!" And Knot had said, "So you *were* listening, weren't you?" And she had rubbed his head. When Knot had first arrived in West Mills, there were some eight-year-olds who couldn't write their names. Her pa would have been just beside himself about that if she ever told him.

Otis Lee was still lecturing.

"You ain't gettin' no younger," he cautioned. "Pratt love you to death, gal."

"He left," Knot said. "I ain't throw him out."

"This time," Pep remarked, and she walked to the basin.

"You got somethin' to say, Penelope?" Knot shot back before realizing that her question would only bring on the second part of the Loving lecture.

Just three months earlier, Pep reminded Knot, she had thrown Pratt out for trying to do something nice.

"All he wanted you to do was stay home from that ol' juke joint for one Friday night," Pep recalled.

"But I felt like going," Knot grumbled.

"He cooked a chicken for ya, child," Pep said. "This one"—she pointed at Otis Lee—"can't even boil eggs."

"I can *too* boil eggs, Pep," Otis Lee said. "You know good'n well I—"

"If I come home to a cooked hen," Pep continued, "I'm gon' sit with my man and eat."

"He ask her to read to him, too," Otis Lee informed his wife. "She tell him, 'No.'"

Pep looked at Knot with shame.

Knot couldn't deny any of it. It had been his request that she stay home and read to him that irritated her most.

"I read to folks all goddamn week long," Knot had said to Pratt. "You crazy if you think I'm stayin' home to read to yo' big ass."

"Selfish and stubborn," he'd called her, shaking his head. And Knot had said, "I'm twenty-six years old. I can be selfish if I feel like it." And Pratt had said, "Naw, you can't, neither." And Knot had yelled back, "Well, get the hell on out my house! Right now! And don't you come back to my door." He was back at her door, in her house, and in her bed in less than a day.

Otis Lee's four-year-old son, Breezy, came scooting down the stairs on his butt. His little face was mashed flat on one side and his hair was full of white lint. He looked as though he'd been working in the cotton fields Miss Noni had told Knot all about. Breezy went and stood between his parents. Pep rubbed his head and pulled him against her thigh.

"Say good morning to Miss Knot," Otis Lee nudged. And the boy did. Knot was glad Breezy was there to draw some of the attention away from her. She was done picking at the egg and biscuit, and done being picked on.

"You hear anything we just say to you, Knot?" Otis Lee asked.

Knot wiped her hands on the damp rag that was on the table.

"I thank y'all kindly for the breakfast. I'll be goin' on home now."

"Go on over there and make things right with Pratt," Otis Lee demanded. "You hear me?" He was looking at her as though she were a daughter or a sister he couldn't control. Knot looked at Pep, and Pep turned and went to the icebox.

"The hell I am," Knot said.

"Ma!" Breezy exclaimed. "Knot say a cussword!"

"I'm *Miss* Knot, lil boy," Knot corrected. She couldn't resist giving the boy a quick tickle on the neck. And she realized that she might be missing her nephews back in Ahoskie. "If yo' ma and pa don't let up, I'm gon' let you hear some more cusswords."

On her way out, she heard Breezy say, "Pop, Miss Knot got our bowl!"

KNOT FINISHED EATING the egg and biscuit when she got back to her house, while she read a chapter of *The Old Curiosity Shop*. It was her pa's favorite book, by his favorite author. And because he had read those big books to her with such joy, Dickens had become her favorite, too. Her pa had read that book to her more than twenty times when she was a small child. He used to sit on the floor next to her bed two or three times a week and read. Sometimes Knot saw specks of his patients' teeth and blood on his shirts. It would make her mother angry.

"I ain't got time to worry 'bout keepin' shirts pretty, Dinah," her pa would say to her mother. "Them folk be in pain when they come to see me. Half the time, they already tried to snatch the teeth out theyself."

Knot's pa shared with her his love for reading, no matter how tired he was. And each time, Knot would hold on to his long, rough goatee so that she would know when he got up. As hard as she would fight sleep, it won the battle every time.

On the night of her birthday, Knot spent close to an hour looking at the only five dresses she had liked enough to bring with her from Ahoskie. She modeled each of them for the little mirror on the wall. She had to stand far away from it to see her whole body. And when she walked close to it, most of what she saw was her pa's V-shaped jaw. *He couldn't deny being my pa even if he wanted to. How many people in Ahoskie got a jawbone like Dr. G. W. Centre?*

Knot ruled out the black dress and the white one. The pink one with the white bow, the green one with the blue trim, or the plain yellow one had to be the winner. Finally she chose the yellow one. She liked the way it looked next to her skin. Pratt used to tell her it made him think of peanut butter and bananas—something he loved to have on Sunday mornings. The dress was over ten years old, but that worked in Knot's favor. It showed whatever curves she had, which Pep claimed were starting to go missing.

When the sun went down, Knot dressed up and bundled up. She walked the short distance—less than a quarter mile—to the dead end of Antioch Lane, to Miss Goldie's barn house juke joint, where Knot knew people would be throwing away the money they should have been saving to buy their Christmas hams if they didn't have a hog of their own. But with the Depression just behind them, and war hovering, *ain't nothing wrong with folk havin' a drink or two in the company of other folk who want to have one or two.*

GOING ALONE TO Miss Goldie's Place reminded Knot of her first few weeks in West Mills, and on Antioch Lane, back in '36. How nice it was to not have a nagging man looking over her shoulder, counting her drinks, or running off the friendly men she had met since moving there to take the teaching job her pa had arranged for her.

When Knot pulled open the big heavy oak door and stepped inside, the first thing she looked for was Pratt sitting at the piano, playing his tunes. He was nowhere in sight. *What am I lookin' to see if he here for? It's my birthday.* She would have stayed either way.

It wasn't long before the friendly men started asking Knot unfriendly questions: *You done put Pratt down again, Knot?* And: *Knot, is it true you plum' put a piece of glass to Pratt's neck?* To some of the questions, Knot declared, "That's a damn lie!" To other questions she replied, "That ain't none of yo' goddamn business."

Knot left their tables and found company with the few men who didn't know her name yet. And there was one, a young one, standing at the end of the counter. He was tall, just the way Knot liked them. *He just might be the tallest man I ever stood close to.* Pratt had held the record for the tallest and the stockiest. But this fellow was tall and slim.

Valley, Knot's buddy who poured drinks at Miss Goldie's Place, told Knot he was too busy to help her court. If she wanted to know who the young fellow was, she had better go and ask him herself, Valley said.

"And if he don't seem interested in you, s—"

"Send him over to you?" Knot finished, knowing Valley's taste in men.

"Yes, ma'am," he whispered, and smiled.

"You ain't gon' be satisfied 'til you put yo' mark on every man west of the canal," Knot said. She and Valley laughed. Then he reminded her, first, that he hadn't had any luck thus far and, second, that she'd promised to make him one of her famous Antioch Lane bread puddings before he was to leave to go out of town again. "Don't start in with me about that damn puddin', Val. If I *do* make it, I want my dollar—*just* like everybody else gives me for it."

"I *always* pay you," Valley said. "I don't know what ya talkin' 'bout."

"You want me to go home and get my ledger?" Knot countered. Valley smiled and rolled his eyes.

Miss Goldie was sitting about midway along the bar, wearing overalls and a man's shirt. She was smoking a pipe. Unlike most pipes Knot had seen the people of West Mills puffing on, Miss Goldie's didn't look as though it had been carved out of wood by a five-year-old. It was a nice pipe. *Probably ordered it from Europe or somewhere.*

Next to Miss Goldie was Milton Guppy, sitting there glaring at Knot as he always did. Knot never understood how he had gotten such a strange last name. The glares, however, weren't a mystery to her. The teaching job her pa had set up for her had belonged to a Mrs. Guppy. And when Mrs. Guppy had been dismissed, she also dismissed herself from her marriage, taking her and her husband's four-year-old son with her. No one knew where the two of them had gone, since she was rumored to have had no family to speak of. The mean looks Mr. Guppy gave Knot whenever she saw him—sometimes Knot thought he was even growling— were enough to let her know he hadn't gotten over it. She sympathized. *But it wasn't my fault! I ain't make her run off.*

After a few months of Guppy's glares, Knot had walked up to him once, up-bridge at the general store, and said, "If you got somethin' to say, go 'head and say it and get it over with. I probably done heard it from other folk, anyway." And Guppy had said, "I don't b'lee I will, Miss Centre. Don't want to make ya late for yo' *teachin'.* Wouldn't dare keep the good teacher 'way from the good *teachin'* job she come here and steal." And Knot had said, "I'm gon' tell you the same thing I tell everybody else who got a problem with me being up at that schoolhouse." And after she did, she'd told him, "Now you can go to hell." She had left the general store without the hard candy she had planned to buy for the children.

Tonight, at Miss Goldie's Place, Knot gave Guppy a *Don't look at me* stare. She could tell by the evil look on his face that he must have already lost his week's pay at the dice table.

Miss Goldie looked irritable, studying Knot and Valley. Finally, she cleared her throat in a loud *This is for y'all to hear* way. Knot knew Miss Goldie was watching every move in the building, and she didn't like it when her workers carried on long conversation when they should have been refilling jars and glasses and collecting nickels and dimes.

Knot finished her first drink—it was her third, if she counted the two she'd had at home—and she danced over to that young man at the end of the bar.

"Tell me one thing," Knot said to him. He was standing there in a suit. *Lord, the man wore the whole suit to the juke joint.* Whether it was navy blue or black, Knot couldn't be sure. "You think yo' people know you snuck out they house yet?"

"Well, if I *had* snuck out," he replied, standing straight and putting his hands in his pockets, "they wouldn't be able to find me. I'm a long way from home." He didn't sound anything like she would expect from a man of his height. He sounded as if nature had gotten tired and quit working halfway through his change of voice when he was a growing boy.

"I figured that part out already," Knot said. And it wasn't just the sharp suit that had given it away. *His haircut can't be more'n a day old. And he got the nerve to have a part shaved there on the side. Menfolk in West Mills don't wear parts in they heads.* Knot said, "I hear the North on ya' tongue. Where's home?"

"Wilmington," he answered. "Wilmington, Delaware."

"I know where Wilmington is, thank you," Knot retorted, and she wondered how she'd had all that schooling without learning there was more than one Wilmington—one other than in North Carolina.

She looked at him for as long as she could without feeling simpleminded. With teeth as straight and white as his, and with him not having a single razor bump on his chin, she was sure he wasn't more than twenty years old.

"You can't be more than nineteen, twenty," Knot guessed aloud. He showed her a sly smile. *I'll be damned if he ain't got dimples to go 'long with that grin. Shit, I don't know if I ought to slap him or kiss him.*

"People usually ask me what my name is by now," he said.

Knot was about to tell him that she didn't care what people usually wanted from him, but his eyebrows caught her attention. His eyebrows were so thick and neat against his smooth, black forehead, Knot wondered, *If I stick the edge of a butter knife under the corner of one of 'em, would I be able to peel it off whole?*

"Well, go 'head and tell me your name, then," Knot said. He came closer to her, and she looked up at him.

"It's William. And you guessed my age pretty close. I'm almost twen—"

"Buy me a drink, Delaware William. It's my birthday." Knot turned toward Valley and shouted, "Pour me what I like! This here fella's gon' give you the nickel."

"William," Delaware William corrected.

"Forgive me," Knot said to him. And to Valley she said, "Delaware William's gon' give you the nickel." When she looked back up at Delaware William, he was smiling again and shaking his head.

Valley came to the end of the bar where Knot was standing. With his finger, he signaled Knot to lean in. "Ain't you got somewhere to be in the mornin'?"

"You ever hear tell of me not showing up?" Valley sucked his teeth. Knot said, "I didn't think so. And I'll thank you kindly to get me my drink. My damn birthday'll be over, foolin' with you."

Valley fanned his bar rag at Knot. "You just as crazy as you can be, Knot Centre."

"What was that he just called you?" Delaware William asked.

After Knot decided she wasn't going answer him, she looked him up and down.

"My name's Azalea." And after he showed her a confused look, she said, "What's ya business in West Mills, Delaware William?"

"I'm just William," he said politely. "William Pe—"

"What's ya business here in West Mills, is what I asked," Knot interrupted.

"We just stopped to rest. On our way back up from Georgia. Played some gigs down there for a few months."

When she asked him to explain the *we*, he pointed to another young man who sat at a table with the pastor's daughter. Knot was certain the girl had snuck out of the house. Without a doubt, it wouldn't be long before the girl would give the young man what he wanted. Knot could tell by the way she was giggling. If the girl was anything like Knot was as a teenager, Knot knew how the night would end. And that young man would be leaving town soon after.

Knot, figuring she didn't have more than a few hours with Delaware William, finished her drink in three swallows. Then she and Delaware William left, kissing and feeling on each other the whole walk back to her house. Between the heavy petting, she caught a few glimpses of the full moon. It was like an usher leading the way down an aisle.

"Looks like we're in some damn slaves' quarters or something," Delaware William remarked. Knot couldn't argue with him about that, even if she were sober. She had thought the same thing when she first moved to West Mills and rented the little house from a man named Pennington. According to Otis Lee and Miss Noni, Riley Pennington—Otis Lee's boss—was a descendant of the line of Penningtons who had once owned the whole town, which, in those days, had been called Pennington, North Carolina. It didn't change names until a man from Maine named Leland Edgars Sr. and his two sons—Miss Noni said they were both tall and handsome with long, pitch-black ponytails—moved to town with a bunch of Northern money. They bought up a bunch of land with trees and opened a mill on the west side of the canal, causing people to refer to the whole town as West Mills. And now, aside from the one large farm, the Penningtons owned only an acre here and an acre there.

"Used to be," Knot said, and that was all she felt like telling him. "Now that you got ya history lesson, shut up and kiss me some more."

When they arrived in front of her house, that same moonlight that had led them there showed her that Pratt Shepherd was sitting on her porch. He sat there as though he had been one of the first Penningtons.

"Young fella," Pratt called out, "best if you turn around. Head on back up the lane so I can talk to Knot."

Delaware William had his arm around Knot's shoulder, and she felt it slide away. Knot leaned into him—she might have fallen over otherwise.

"Well, sir," Delaware William said, "I didn't hear her say she wants to talk to—"

"I used to know a boy that look something like you," Pratt cut in. He stood to his feet. "Got his face cut up for walkin' another man's wife home. They cut that fella's face up real bad. Right here on this lane."

Knot didn't get a chance to tell Delaware William that Pratt was no one to be afraid of; he had turned around and hightailed it back down the lane toward Miss Goldie's Place. When Knot turned back around to face Pratt, he was sitting again.

"I'm gon' count to ten . . . or eleven," she slurred, steadying herself in front of the porch and placing her hands on her hips. "When I get through countin', you best be off my damn porch or I'm gon' have to hurt ya."

"What? You got a gun, or somethin'?" Pratt taunted.

"Did you hear me say I got a gun?" Knot shot back. "I might, though."

"Sit down, Knot. Sit on down here 'fore you fall and crack that lil head of your'n?" He patted the porch two times.

Knot spit on the ground and said, "My new man'll come back and crack *yo'* head open to the white meat."

"Who?" Pratt asked. "The one that just run off? He ain't even stay long enough for me to tighten my fist."

Knot turned and looked down the lane. Delaware William may as well have been a ghost. Pratt, she discovered when she turned to him once more, looked as though he would die if he held his laugh in any longer. And once he let the laugh go—he slapped his knees, too—Knot said, "Go to hell, Pratt."

She sat on the porch next to him and their shoulders touched.

"Happy Birthday, darlin'." He leaned over and kissed her on the cheek. She swatted him away, but she was so glad he was there; something was stirring around inside her and she was in the mood for a man's company.

Pratt pulled her close to him. She liked the way her ear felt against his fleshy chest. A whiff of his clean breath relaxed her. Pratt's breath smelled as though he had chewed on mint leaves all day instead of just after dinner, as he usually did. Knot figured she would let him kiss her, knowing he'd happily join her inside the house, where he would make her feel good under the quilt. *Hell, it's my birthday.*

In the doorway, Pratt kissed her face and neck. And before she knew it, they were on the bed they had been sharing, off and on, for two years. She didn't know what it was, but it seemed as though his touch was different, better than before.

"Feel like you grew some more hands," she whispered in his ear before softly biting his earlobe. *Did he put butter on his lips?* She had never known his lips to feel as soft as they felt tonight. She enjoyed their new softness even more when Pratt kissed the insides of her thighs and moved up to her shiver spot.

Pratt laid his large body on top of hers. She imagined a giant pillow. As big—with just the right amount of heavy—as he was, that night he was a nice cloud hovering over her, making love to her. Knot knew she would certainly be hoarse in the morning.

Lord, have mercy.

When they were done, Knot lay there wishing Pratt would fall asleep so she could have one more drink. *That jar is whistlin' for me.* But after all Pratt had just done for her, she didn't want to spoil it.

The Dickens book was on the floor next to her headboard, so she decided to read for as long as her eyes would allow. *But it sure would be nice to have a cool glass with a splash in it while I read. Damn!* Pratt was wide-awake on the other side of the bed, picking with his toenails.

The next morning when Knot woke up, she lay there thinking about how she hadn't gotten to do what she had wanted—*in my own house.* She nudged Pratt until he was awake.

"What is it?" he mumbled. He had one eye open, one eye shut.

"Get up!" Knot exclaimed.

"What for?"

"Get up and get the hell on outta my house." And after he was dressed and about to walk out, she said, "And don't darken my doorway. *Never* no mo'."

"Azalea!"

"Gone!" she yelled, before slamming the door and making the drink she had wanted the night before.

TWO

After slapping hogs' butts all day at Pennington Farm, Otis Lee returned to Antioch Lane to attend to his own small backyard farm. He and Pep had chickens, a lot of chickens, more than anyone else on the lane. One neighbor had said, "Otis Lee Loving, I swear it's more chickens in yo' coop than it is people here in West Mills. Is you raisin' *them* for to be ate, or for them to eat *us*?" Knot happened to be visiting Otis Lee at the time, and she'd snapped, "Just buy the damn eggs or shut up." Otis Lee had secretly gotten a kick out of that.

It was time for the chickens' second feeding; Pep was in charge of the first. One thing Otis Lee loved to do was to feed his chickens. He called them *cluckers*. There was something about the way they came running when they heard him reach his hand into the pail and pull out a handful of dry corn. It made him feel needed—it was a different kind of need from Pep's and Breezy's. All they needed was the love he showed from just being there. Other people, and the cluckers, might not fare as well if he weren't around, checking in, warding off danger, or steering them from it. After he threw a few handfuls of the feed onto the ground, he looked around and noticed that something wasn't the same as it had been the afternoon before. It seemed as though the cluckers weren't as loud, or there weren't as many of them. Otis Lee stood looking around his feet—not counting, exactly, but studying them.

First, he scanned the birds to see if he could find Ruby, his pet hen. He spotted her and let out the breath he didn't realize he had been holding.

"Pep!" he yelled toward the house. He looked back down at the cluckers and around the coop. No reply from Pep. And again: "Penelope!" When Pep finally came to the window and raised it, he asked, "You let somebody come in the coop and steal some of my cluckers?"

Pep sucked her teeth and went about shutting the window.

"You hear me talkin' to you?" he said.

"Ain't nobody stole nothin', fool," Pep replied. "I sold three this morning, and they's one in my stove, and your mama and grandmama got two back there in the stove." Pep pointed past the coop to the other house—a smaller one—in their yard.

"Ain't I told you I don't sell chickens?" he retorted. "I sells eggs." He wanted to throw one at her.

Without saying a word, Pep just looked at him with the face she often made when the queue at Manning's General Store moved too slowly. Otis Lee looked at the other house, trying to understand why in the world his mother, Rose, and his grandmother, Ma Noni, needed two cluckers. *Takes Ma Noni two days to eat one drumstick.* And Rose seemed to eat only enough to stay alive. *She eats more of her fingernails than food,* Otis Lee thought. "I get tired of y'all messin' with my—"

"Why won't you hush that fuss and brang your lil self upstairs for a few minutes," Pep said. "Need you to come see 'bout me." She gave him half a smile and shut the window. *She think I'm gon' come runnin'. But I ain't just yet.*

He wanted to go running to her, though. Pep was his everything. As much as he loved other people and other things, Pep came in first place. It didn't matter to him that she hadn't been his first lover. She hadn't even been his best lover, but she believed she was, and he wanted her to continue believing it.

Back in 1929, when Otis Lee and Pep went to bed together for the very first time, he had told her she was the only woman he had been with. After he had told her the lie, it had seemed as if she was trying to claim his body. She had wanted to make love every day—and many times a day. How they hadn't had one hundred babies, Otis Lee couldn't comprehend. But they figured God wanted them to have just one.

Pep was the second woman Otis Lee had slept with. She was, however, the first woman he hadn't paid to sleep with. But as far as he cared, Pep might as well have been the first and only one. She was the only woman he wanted. And now Otis Lee felt a little smile taking over his face. He was ready to go upstairs and see about his wife as she had told him to do.

But just as he was about to go inside, Pratt came from around the house. He looked quite sad, moping, as though he had been sent to the yard to get a switch for his own spanking. By the looks of it, Pratt had gone home and put on clean clothes before he had come across the lane.

Much to Otis Lee's irritation, Pratt talked in circles for a few minutes; it was Pratt's way of leading up to bad news or asking for a loan.

"Out with it, Pratt," Otis Lee said. "Pep's waitin' on me."

"It's 'bout time I move on. Goin' in the service."

"Goin' in the service for what, Pratt?" Otis Lee said. "Did they *ask* you to come?"

"Yeah," Pratt said. "They need me, probably."

Otis Lee looked at his friend.

"What in the shit you gone and done, Pratt?"

Recruiters had already come through West Mills and selected the men they thought most fit to serve. Otis Lee and Pratt had both been passed over; Otis Lee was too short, and Pratt had quite a limp. Both men had been glad about being rejected. It was a truth they had shared only with each other.

"How you get 'em to take you?"

"I just tell 'em I want to be useful any way I can," Pratt replied.

Otis Lee thought it was an awful idea, and he said so. What sense did it make to sign up to go get hurt, or killed? Especially with Pratt having a good job and all.

"What's the 'and all,' Otis Lee?" Pratt asked. "What else I got? The mill?"

The two of them stood quietly for a moment. Then Otis Lee decided he might as well pick up his pail and go back to feeding his cluckers.

Pratt added, "Onliest reason I stayed this long is 'cause of Knot."

Pratt had come to West Mills in '38; he had only planned to stay for one month—to take care of his sister Pleasant's two little girls while she was in jail. Pleasant had taken her last beating from her husband, Bo Frost. One day, while he was beating her, he had made her say, "Yes, sir," over and over.

And when she said it, he had said, "I can't hear ya." So Pleasant had decided, she'd told Otis Lee, that she wanted to make sure he didn't hear much else for the rest of his natural life. Pleasant had waited for her little twin girls, and Bo, to fall fast asleep. She had only meant to teach Bo a lesson, but the knife had gone so deep into Bo's ear that he choked on his blood and died. Pleasant had run over to Otis Lee's house and banged on the door. How Pep had slept through the loud knocking, he couldn't understand.

"He dead, Otis Lee," Pleasant had said. The hard, fast knocking didn't match the way she had given him the news. It was as if she had just said good morning to him.

"Who?"

"Bo," Pleasant had answered. "Just as dead as he can be, and I killed him."

She didn't need words to ask Otis Lee what she should do, because her eyes had already done so.

"Where the twins?" Otis Lee had asked. After she told him that they were asleep, and that they hadn't seen or heard anything, he said, "Thank God."

Otis Lee had put on his coat, wrapped a quilt around Pleasant's shoulders, and walked her back across the lane to her house. He told Pleasant to sit in her kitchen while he looked in on her girls; they were both snoring quietly. Otis Lee couldn't bring himself to go into the room where Bo's body lay, but he could smell it. Years of working on Pennington Farm had made it hard for him to miss that distinct odor of new death. *Probably a pond of blood in there.* So he took a seat at the table with Pleasant.

"Tell me what happened, Pleasant," Otis Lee had said, and she did.

"I'll sit here another minute or two," Pleasant had said, "then I'm gon' pack up me and the girls and go from this place." She said she'd change her and the girls' names and run away "like Mrs. Guppy did."

Otis Lee had told Pleasant that, since everyone on Antioch Lane knew that Bo Frost hadn't been kind or even decent to her—Otis Lee couldn't imagine that Bo had ever treated any woman with kindness, based on the way he'd often spoken of his family in South Carolina—she would be better off turning herself in.

"Goin' on the run with them children won't be easy," he had cautioned.

Otis Lee had begged Pleasant to think of her whole family back in Tennessee. And after what felt like a couple of hours, though it had only been one, Pleasant decided to take Otis Lee's advice. The judge rewarded her honesty by sentencing her to only thirty days. And since Bo had cut ties with his family, Otis Lee and Pep made arrangements for him to be buried. Otis Lee, the reverend, one deacon, and the undertaker were the only ones to attend.

Once Pratt had met Knot, going back to Tennessee after Pleasant's release was the last thing on his mind, he had told Otis Lee.

Now Otis Lee turned to Pratt and said, "Me and Pep seen you run a fella off the other night. So I was sure you and Knot was gettin' on all right again."

"Me too."

"Y'all ain't making good sense for my understandin'," Otis Lee said.

"Mine either. She tell me she don't want me. She meant it, too. She was sober as yo' hen when she say it."

Otis Lee picked Ruby up and sat on the wooden bench he had installed just outside the coop. Ruby had a twisted beak; Otis Lee could only feed her by hand with the soggy corn-meal that he kept in a cup inside the pail of dry corn. He used to be afraid that he'd accidentally choke her, but after three feedings he'd gotten the hang of it.

Before he began feeding her, he rubbed her soft, tangerine-colored feathers. She lowered herself onto his lap as though she were warming eggs.

Pratt went on and on about how he wanted Knot to be his wife.

"I want us to be like you and Pep."

Shit! I'm s'pose to be in there with her right now!

Otis Lee listened to Pratt while he tried to feed Ruby. She usually kept still while Otis Lee pushed the meal into her mouth. But today she flapped her wings and struggled. Pratt was still going on and on about Knot. After a couple of tries, Otis Lee let Ruby get down and roam with the other cluckers. She looked satisfied.

"Stubborn," Pratt remarked. Otis Lee wasn't sure if Pratt was talking about Ruby or about Knot.

"Knot don't know what she want half the time," Otis Lee said. "You know that. You ain't got to run off like you doin'."

"I done told ya what she say to me, man. She know her own mind. And I ain't on it no more. She love them damn books of hers more'n she love me."

"Nooooo," Otis Lee denied.

"It's the truth," Pratt said. "Corn liquor, the books, them letters from her pa, and then me. Maybe."

Pratt was right. Knot knew her own mind, and she knew it well—drunk or not. And the truth was, Otis Lee knew exactly how Pratt was feeling. *Try to steer somebody from a harm they love, but seem like the more they get steered away, the more they want the harm.*

Otis Lee had tried to steer Knot, just as he had tried to steer his older sister, Essie, who had left home to go north. She was in New York passing for white. Who Essie's white father was, Otis Lee never knew, and he didn't care. He had known his own father and he still missed him dearly. He'd drowned in the canal when Otis Lee was a child.

Essie was living a life Otis Lee couldn't get his head around. It seemed as though she put herself in harm's way every day. At any minute, if her truth were uncovered, she could be beaten or something worse. Otis Lee didn't know Essie very well. His mother had told him that Essie was already grown and gone before he could even turn over on his own. But it didn't matter. From the time Otis Lee was old enough to understand that he had an older sister, and old enough to understand her circumstances, he cared about her.

In '24, when Otis Lee was sixteen, he'd gone to New York, and with the help of his aunt—the aunt who had adopted Valley—he found Essie. New York City had proved itself to be all the things he had heard about it: nothing like North Carolina, never resting, plenty to offer, and plenty to take away. So Otis Lee was pleased to find that Essie lived in what he thought of as a calm part of town.

Even so, he had wanted so badly to help her and protect her—even knowing of the bad thing she'd done to the family. Ma Noni had told him that Essie had sold her land dirt cheap, for pennies on the dollar, so that she could have money to run away and pass. According to Ma Noni, Essie had caused him, Rose, his father, and Ma Noni to be homeless for a while because of what she had done. Neither Otis Lee's father nor Rose ever spoke of it. And when Otis Lee once asked Rose about Essie and the land, all she had said was "The past is the past, baby boy. Everythang turn out all right."

While living in Brooklyn, in Essie's brothel, Otis Lee often thought of all the things Ma Noni had told him, and he imagined killing Essie. But mostly he just wanted to protect her, lead her away from the danger she was courting. Finally, after some time living with and working for Essie and her crooked policeman husband, Otis Lee saw that she was no longer the Essie his mother often secretly spoke so fondly of. She had become Ellen O'Heeney. And for Ellen O'Heeney, there was no turning back.

That's what she had told him as he was leaving her house on that cold day in '27. Otis Lee remembered the sweet look in her eyes when he walked away from her back stoop. That sweet, sad look—a look he wouldn't understand for several decades, after receiving a bundle of letters—was all he was going to get from his sister, because she didn't make a move to hug him or even shake his hand. But it had seemed to Otis Lee that she had wanted him to see that sweetness.

Now fourteen years had come and gone since he had returned to West Mills, married Pep, and, years later, become a father. Otis Lee hadn't heard from his sister. No one had.

Essie knew her own mind, just as Knot knew her own. Otis Lee decided he would be misleading Pratt if he stood there trying to convince him to stay in West Mills for Azalea Centre. So he didn't.

When Otis Lee came back from his thoughts about Essie, Pratt was picking at a piece of wood from one of the pen's posts. Ruby had made her way back over to them. He thought she might be ready to eat some more, but when he tried to pick her up again, she flapped her wings and made her fussing sounds. Otis Lee let her be, and he and Pratt bid each other a good evening.

A few days passed and Pratt came to Otis Lee's house dressed in his only suit—a black one—to say his good-byes. Pratt rubbed Breezy's head, fluffing up the boy's halfway-curly hair.

"When you see Miss Knot," Pratt instructed the boy, "give her a hug and tell her it's from me. Hear?"

"She ain't gon' let me give her no hug," Breezy said. His face wore a tight frown. Otis Lee smiled, fighting back tears.

"You has to hug her quick," Pratt explained to Breezy. "When she sit down, you has to get close up on her and just do it. Fast, like. Understand?"

Pep was busy crying. She had fussed Pratt out for days for enlisting himself, and she had fussed Knot in and out, high and low, for being part of the reason he had done so.

After they had done all the handshaking and hugging, Otis Lee watched Pratt walk out of his yard and up the lane toward Busy Street, where there would be a bus to take him to the train station in Norfolk. Pratt's walk was a hesitant one. If there had been anything Otis Lee could have said to get his buddy to stay, he would have. *Going off to war*, Otis Lee thought to himself. *I don't believe I'll ever see Pratt Shepherd again.*

"You know something, Pep?" Otis Lee said, standing next to her, his left arm wrapped around her ample waist. "Pratt's probably the best fella Knot'll ever have."

THREE

In December of '41, Knot accepted the fact that she had a baby on the way. *That goddamn Pratt*, she thought to herself.

Knowing that she would not be able to visit her family in Ahoskie for a long time—having them know she was to be an unwed mother was never an option—she sat down to write a letter to her father. Knot wrote that she would soon be going north for six months or so, for more training as a teacher—which was what she would have done to hide the pregnancy from the people of West Mills if she hadn't drunk and gambled away so much of her money at Miss Goldie's Place. She wrote that, since she did not yet know the address of whatever rooming house she'd be living in, he should send a reply to Penelope Loving. And her pa did just that.

He wrote that he was proud of her, that her two sisters were just as proud of her as he was, and that they all loved her very much. *My smart, sensible little Knot*, her pa had written. She needed a drink after reading that part. The letter had been written in his handwriting, and Knot noticed that it didn't have any of the fanciness—her full name written out, the sentences lined up on the paper just so—that it would have had if her mother had written it. So she wasn't at all surprised that her pa's letter had no mention of her mother.

As scared as Knot was of being someone's mother, she was more scared of dying on some old woman's kitchen table, trying to avoid becoming someone's mother. She would have to get used to the reality of what her life and body would be like for several months to come. Finding someone reliable and willing enough to take and raise the child was another challenge.

Otis Lee and Pep would have been her first choice if she hadn't grown so close to them. She needed the two of them for herself. And with Pep constantly trying to convince Knot to keep the baby, the Lovings would probably keep the child for only a week or two before coming up with some reason to bring him or her back.

And there was the freedom—the freedom Knot would certainly lose while the child grew inside her. But the thought of the freedom she'd lose if she couldn't get anyone to take the child off her hands was far more terrifying. *Damn*, she thought, *I'll never see the inside of Goldie's again if I got a young'un in tow.*

Unsure as to whether the god her pa prayed to was real, and remembering Matthew 19:14, Knot wanted nothing to do with bringing a sick baby, or a dead one, into the world. She drank far less than she had before—which wasn't hard, since, for a while, she could barely stand the smell of liquor. For many weeks Knot could barely stand the smell of anything. Sometimes, just looking at the jar of corn liquor sitting on the shelf in her pantry would turn her stomach.

"You better live, goddamnit," Knot said to the twitching she felt inside her belly. "You better live."

FOUR

Otis Lee told Phillip Waters, and Phillip's wife, Lady, that there was a young woman in town who was going to have a baby she couldn't keep.

"My Lord," Lady said. She stepped away from the table and put her hands over her mouth. "It's Reverend Walker's oldest daughter, isn't it?" She tapped Phil's shoulder twice. "Didn't I tell you this would come to pass? I saw that girl coming from Goldie's many a night. Many, *many* a night. Lord, have mercy."

What in the devil Lady doing on that end of Antioch Lane that late at night? Goldie didn't open the doors to her juke joint until nine o'clock, Otis Lee had heard. Before he opened his mouth to ask the question, he remembered Phil mentioning Lady's recent idea to try to minister to Goldie's customers as they were leaving in the wee hours. *I wished she'd gone 'cross the lane and try that ministerin' out on Knot.*

"It ain't our place to judge, Lady," Phil told her. "Folk make mistakes."

"I don't think I was passing judgment," Lady said. She sat back down. "Not one bit. Just telling you what I've seen, is all." She put her elbows on the table and propped her chin on one wrist.

Lady was older than Otis Lee and Phil—nearly ten years older. Phil and Lady had met in New York City. Before Otis Lee had found Essie, he, Phil, and Brock Manning were all working in a hotel in Lower Manhattan. Lady wore two hats at that hotel: some days a cook, and other days a cleaning lady. Otis Lee had already known how to clean a house because Ma Noni and Rose had taught him to do almost everything they knew how to do. But Phil's mother hadn't shown him much about housekeeping, so Lady showed him how it was done. Before long, Phil was telling Otis Lee that he loved Lady and he'd decided to ask for her hand in marriage. Although Lady had been born and raised in Harlem, she had told them many times how much she loved the calmness of the South—despite its problems. And now Otis Lee looked at the two of them and was glad to see them together and still in love.

"I didn't mean nothin' by it, darlin'," Phil said to Lady. "You ain't mad at me, is ya?"

Lady said she wasn't mad, and they smiled at each other. Otis Lee always admired, and was often confused by, how Phil and Lady's arguments were so quiet and peaceful—the ones he'd witnessed. He and Pep had at least one twenty-minute argument each day. Most of them were loud. And they enjoyed them.

"Is it Reverend Walker's girl, brother?" Phil asked.

When Otis Lee told them it was their across-the-lane neighbor, Knot, who was in the family way, Lady asked if Milton Guppy was the child's father. And when Otis Lee asked Lady why in the world she'd think that, she replied, "Well, I saw him coming outta her yard one night. So, I just thought maybe—"

"Noooo," Otis Lee said. "Milton ain't got no parts of this. Pratt left somethin' behind and don't even know it. And now the fool's gon' off to get himself killed in the war."

"Knot don't want to write to his people?" Phil asked.

"She say she ain't able and wouldn't if she was," Otis Lee answered. "Knot don't want to be a mama. And she serious 'bout it. That's why I'm here talkin' to y'all."

Otis Lee wondered what reason Milton Guppy would have to be in Knot's yard. *Maybe they friendly now, and she got him bringing her liquor.*

"But wait a minute," Lady said. "I thought Knot's taken poorly with the pox. Will that child live?"

"No pox," Otis Lee promised them. "Just a baby comin', is all."

FIVE

Mornings became Knot's enemy, so she stopped teaching. After she had made amends with mornings, afternoons became the bully. For as long as she could hide herself, she took on part-time house cleaning. Those earnings were stuffed in her feather bed along with the little money she hadn't blown at Goldie's. That took care of the rent for the three-room railroad house she lived in—if she counted the pantry as a room—and it kept her fed until she could get back to work. When her stomach began arriving at places before the rest of her body, she didn't leave her house, except to step out onto the porch for fresh air—something she did only late at night. The only people Knot believed needed to know of her condition were the two people who were going be there when she gave birth, and the two other people who had agreed to raise the child.

One day in March of '42, Knot lay across her bed reading and fighting off the urge to rub her stomach. She heard three hard knocks on the back door. *Can't be Otis Lee or Pep. They know the code.* She had told Otis Lee and Pep that they were to call out to her before they knocked. She supposed it could have been someone from the lane wanting to order a bread pudding. But since she had told people she was ill, she thought anyone would be foolish to want anything from her kitchen.

Knot waited a minute to see if the person would say anything. They didn't. But they did knock three more times.

"Come on and open the door, sweetie."

It was Miss Noni. Knot wondered how such a tiny person like Miss Noni had such a strong knock. *Is she throwin' her whole damn body 'gainst the door? And what the hell she want?*

"Knot," Miss Noni called, "come open the door, sugar."

"I can't let you in here!" Knot yelled toward the door. "You might catch it!"

"I done had it. Open this door, child."

Knot got up off the bed and grabbed a pillow to hold in front of herself. Before going to the door, she stood in front of her mirror and shuffled her hair around a bit. She hadn't combed it in days, so it didn't require much effort. She noticed that the copper color of her hair seemed to be fading. Pregnancy was turning her hair brown. She didn't like it.

Knot opened the door, and Miss Noni stood there wrapped in coats and scarves. It looked as though she were wearing three of each, in various colors. *It ain't even cold out there. Shit!* Miss Noni had a wicker basket hanging from the bend of her right arm. The basket looked new, as though it had never been set on a floor or the ground.

"You gon' welcome me in?"

Miss Noni walked past Knot and straight to the kitchen, where she set the basket on the table. The table wobbled under the basket's weight. Then she turned to Knot and quipped, "Or is Otis Lee and Pep the only two that's 'lowed to visit?" She began unwrapping herself, and talking.

While Miss Noni talked about the weather and how she had made sure that she and Rose had plenty of firewood,

Knot concentrated on keeping the pillow in front of her large belly.

"I see *you* got enough firewood," Miss Noni said. She pointed to the corner of the kitchen. "You drinkin' plenty water, Knot? And milk? Drink plenty milk. Hear?" Now Miss Noni was moving around the kitchen and talking. *Have mercy.*

Knot didn't know Miss Noni's exact age, though she was sure the woman had to be at least eighty-eight or ninety. But she looked much younger; her skin shone. Were there wrinkles on Miss Noni's brown face? Yes. But they were shallow. *And she gets 'round like she's my age.* And what was that nice smell coming off Miss Noni? *Smell like limes, or maybe lemons.*

"I got ya some lemons, sweetie," Miss Noni said, echoing Knot's guess. "I done cut 'em for ya, honey."

Using both her hands, she unpacked the basket, which held a lot more than lemons. There was bread, a jar of preserves, and eggs that Miss Noni had probably taken from Otis Lee's coop while he was at work. Or she may have gotten them while Pep was up-bridge at the general store and Otis Lee was in the front yard talking to a neighbor. Miss Noni set some things on the table; others, she took to the pantry.

"Lemons for what, Miss Noni?" Knot already knew the answer. The older woman told Knot to suck on the lemon to soothe her sour stomach if that was still a problem. She unwrapped the white cloth filled with lemon wedges and handed one to Knot.

"Take this," Miss Noni commanded. Knot took the whole bundle from the older woman's hand and set it on the table. "Pep ain't tell you 'bout the lemons?" Knot didn't get a chance to answer the question, because Miss Noni had gone back to talking about other things. "When I was a just a lil thang, the ol' woman who looked after us when our mamas was in the fields, her place used to be just 'bout in the same spot as this house you livin' in."

Knot sighed. "I know, Miss Noni."

"I told you 'bout her?"

"Yeah."

And in unison Knot and Miss Noni said, "Aunt Buddy."

"Aunt Buddy lived to see me have my own first child," Miss Noni went on. "And she was 'bout ninety-five then." She counted her fingers, clapped her hands and said, "Six years older'n I is right now! Ain't that somethin', Knot?"

Knot sucked her teeth. It was at that moment she figured she might as well move the pillow she had been holding. *All this damn talk about babies.*

After tossing the pillow against the closest wall, she sat at the table, which was half covered with food. She must have had a look on her face to go along with the mad feeling she had.

"What's the matter, love?" Miss Noni asked.

"They promised me they wouldn't tell," Knot grumbled. She was now craving a drink—her first craving for anything in a couple of days.

"Nobody tol' me nothin', puddin'," Miss Noni said. "Well, just that you got the pox. That's what y'all young folk call it nowadays?" This time Knot didn't try to answer the question. She wouldn't have been able to, because Miss Noni was talking about her own pregnancies.

Knot watched Miss Noni as she went to the icebox and put the lemons in next to the block of ice. She then revealed to

Knot that she had seen Otis Lee and Pep's comings and goings at Knot's house.

"They was even walkin' like they got secrets," Miss Noni said. Knot would have loved to know how Miss Noni had been able to see all of what she'd just described from far back in Otis Lee's yard. But Knot didn't want to know right then. She'd had enough of Miss Noni's talking already.

Miss Noni's visit lasted just under two hours. She cleaned a little and changed the linens. Over and over, Knot said that she appreciated the help but that she was able to do those chores herself. Miss Noni looked around the rooms, shook her head, and continued her work.

Knot thought of ways to get a sip of liquor while Miss Noni was there in the house. She believed that if she could get just one swallow, she might be able to handle the old woman until she got tired. *And when's that gon' be? She look like she might go home and clean her own house when she get through with mine.*

Miss Noni went in the bedroom to sweep. That was Knot's chance to tiptoe to the pantry, and she took it. She counted four swallows before closing the jar of moonshine. Those four swallows helped Knot ask a question that had been worrying her mind from the time she had let Miss Noni see her belly.

"I ain't gon' tell nobody 'bout yo' pox, sweetie," Miss Noni said. "You think I'd do that?"

Knot didn't know what to say, but she wasn't going to apologize.

"I don't mean no harm by it. Just need to know," Knot explained.

Miss Noni told Knot there was no need to worry. "Just 'cause I talk 'til I'm tired don't mean I can't hold a secret. I got secrets in here"—she pointed to her left temple—"that'll make folk hate me if they got out. My own flesh and *blood*. Hear?" She went into the pantry and began straightening things. Knot thought that part of their conversation had ended. "But you know somethin', Knot? Sometimes it's best to keep 'em locked inside. Secrets. Best for everybody *sometimes*."

You mean secrets like you really Otis Lee's great-grandmamma, not his grandmamma? Knot just shook her head and said, "Yeah."

When Miss Noni was done with all the cleaning, and done with all the storytelling about her days as a young wife and mother, she rewrapped herself in all those garments, kissed Knot on the cheek, and told her to take good care of herself.

"Lots of water!" Miss Noni shouted on her way out the door. "And milk! Hear?"

LATER THAT WEEK, Otis Lee and Pep came to check on her. Miss Noni had gone to their house and told them she knew everything. Pep said Miss Noni cursed them for not having trusted her with Knot's secret. Knot didn't care to hear any of that.

"The Waters ain't changed they minds, have they?" Knot asked.

"Naw," Otis Lee replied. "Don't worry 'bout that." He reminded her of how many years the couple had been praying for a child of their own. "They figure the Lord must not want it to go that way. But like I say, I know they got plenty love to give to anybody, 'specially a child."

When Knot had first told Otis Lee that she was expecting, and asked him for help finding adoptive parents, she had assumed that he would ask the Mannings first. He'd told her that even though he knew they had the same love to give, plus more, he also knew their business—the general store—was like a child to them.

While Otis Lee spoke about what a good choice Phillip and Lady were to raise the soon-to-come baby, he picked his teeth with a sewing needle. Knot wondered why Pep sat there and let him do that in front of people. When he finished picking, he set the needle down on the plate Knot had just served him bread pudding. He'd done this many times before, but now that Knot was pregnant, it annoyed her. And Pep had a habit of rubbing one hand with the other. That irritated Knot even more. She didn't understand why these things bothered her so, but they did. And as if those things weren't enough, her feet and legs ached. She tried her best to reach down and rub them, but her stomach would no longer allow it.

Pep moved her chair in front of Knot's, and then, to Knot's surprise, one of her own legs was on Pep's lap, being rubbed and squeezed. It was the best thing Knot had experienced in days.

"You worryin' 'bout Lady and Phil changin' they minds," Pep said, "but it's liable to be *yo* mind that gets changed when that baby come."

Knot slid her foot off Pep's lap and replied, "No, my mind ain't gon' get changed. And I wish you'd let up 'bout that, Pep."

Knot and Pep rolled their eyes at each other. Pep motioned for Knot to put her swollen foot back on her lap and went back to rubbing and squeezing.

IT WAS ON a Saturday afternoon in July of '42 when dull pains forced Knot to pace two rooms of the little house. A shot of the clear elixir only helped her a bit. Knot, being as no-nonsense as she was, knew she had a long day (or longer) ahead of her—a long day of pain. She would not allow herself to be fooled into believing otherwise. She had seen her older sisters, Mary and Iris, giving birth. They had cursed and screamed as though Satan were standing next to their beds. The rooms had smelled as though someone were cleaning fresh game. Mary, Knot's oldest sister, had asked the midwife to end her misery.

"I can't take another fuckin' minute of it!" Mary had screamed. And after they had pulled the second round of shit-and-blood-covered rags from under her, she said to her mother, "I'm dying. Y'all might as well smother me and get it over with."

Knot remembered having to turn away from Mary because she herself was about to die—from laughing.

Knot's mother, speaking most eloquently, had whispered, "Quiet, now, Mary. Every woman feels like she's dying when there's a whole other person coming out of her. It'll be over before you know it. Breathe." Now Knot knew Mary's pain.

At least two hours passed before Knot felt something warm moving slowly down her leg. When it slid from her ankle onto the wooden floor, she bent over to examine it. It looked like snot. And when she stood back up, what seemed like a river of pee fell from between her thighs. She felt the weight inside of her move lower.

"Breezy!" Knot yelled from her bedroom window. "Come here a minute."

The boy came running and grinning, just as he did when Otis Lee or Pep sent him to tell or take Knot one thing or the other. He was holding two kittens. He held them tenderly, one in each arm, as if they were babies. *Damn if he ain't got to have two of everything.*

"Is Pep home?"

"Yes, ma'am!" Breezy answered.

"What you hollerin' for? I'm right in front of ya."

Breezy shrugged and stood still. Knot realized even her own voice sounded too loud.

"Well, take them cats back to they mama, and run tell yours that my time's come. Tell her just like that. Hear?"

"Yes, ma'am," he whispered this time. But when he ran from her window, it seemed as though the sound of his shoes hitting against the dirt was too loud, too. Everything was so loud. And everything was aggravating. The sun was shining too bright, the wind was blowing too hard, the sweat on her lips was too salty.

Knot kept pacing until Pep, Otis Lee, and Miss Noni all arrived with their arms full of this and that. Knot wondered who had gone and gotten Miss Noni.

"Why in the hell y'all got Noni wit' y'all?" she exclaimed when Miss Noni went to the bedroom to do God knew what. "Do I look like I got patience for her right now? Shit, I ain't even got patience for *me* right now."

Knot sat on a kitchen chair, and Pep rushed to her. Pep told Otis Lee to put his bundle of supplies on the table and get out.

"You in good hands," Otis Lee said to Knot on his way out. He smiled. "Pep's gotcha." Once he was gone, Pep told Knot to slide to the edge of the chair.

"You doin' good, Knot," Pep reported after lifting Knot's slip and looking between her legs. "Things is goin' just like they s'pose to. Get on back up and walk a lil more. That'll help ya later on."

As Knot expected, the pains became much fiercer. Some of the sounds and words that came from her own mouth frightened her. And there was the sound of Miss Noni's mouth running.

"Well, you lucky you still young," Miss Noni said. "I was a young girl when I had Gertrude. But that Rose snuck up on us. I was over forty when I got big wit' her. And I tell you, honey, that was a hard day. I—"

"Miss Noni," Knot cut in. She was lying on her side.

"Yes, darlin'?"

"You know I love you, don't ya?" Knot said.

"I know it, sugar."

"Good," Knot replied. "Now, will you please hush all that goddamn talkin'?"

Miss Noni laughed, clapped her hands, and said, "Yes, ma'am."

For a moment Knot worried that something might be going wrong: the pains had slowed. But Pep assured her that it was normal for the body to take breaks. And Knot trusted her words. Pep had delivered many babies, colored and white.

She came from a long line of midwives. Pep had given birth to her own son with no help at all. Knot had listened to Otis Lee tell the story at least a hundred times. Otis Lee had helped Pep to the bed so that she would be comfortable while he'd be away getting help. But before he could get his boots laced up, Pep had Breezy in her arms, clearing his mouth with her finger. Then the boy had let out the loudest cry either of them claimed they had ever heard from a newborn. "It all happen quick as a breeze, Knot," Otis Lee'd said. Knot hoped she would have the same luck Pep had.

Knot wanted to ask Pep if Otis Lee was nearby. As much of a meddler as she believed him to be, he was also the most peaceful person she knew on Albemarle Lane. If he could just sit out in the kitchen while she labored, she might feel even safer than Pep and Miss Noni already made her feel.

"Pop," Knot heard Breezy say outside of her bedroom window, "what my mama and Ma Noni doin' with Knot?"

"Knot ain't feelin' so good right now," Knot heard Otis Lee say. "They gon' sit with her a while, 'til she feel better. She'll be all right. You go on and play with yo' buddies. Go on. Leave them cats alone, 'fore that mama cat scratch yo' face up."

Hearing her bossy friend's voice gave Knot more comfort. Then she thought about how her pa would be worried crazy if he were there. *Mad and worried.*

AN HOUR LATER, Pep tried to lay the plump, angry, minute-old girl onto Knot's chest. "Lay her in the other room, Pep," Knot ordered. She couldn't bring herself to look at the newest person in the room, so she turned her face away from them all.

"She got to be fed, sugar," Miss Noni protested.

"Not right this minute," Knot said. She felt an exhaustion she'd never known was possible.

The baby made those sweet sounds that caused people to want to hold and kiss them. Even Knot had been tempted by those sounds when her nephews were born.

"Please take her away!" Knot yelled. She wished she had pulled the sheet, or one of the pillows, over her own face, because before Pep was all the way out of the room, Knot looked up and caught a glimpse of the child's face. Her eyes were wide open, taking in the world. It was the prettiest, and most dangerous, glimpse Knot had ever taken in her life.

Knot heard Pep ask Otis Lee to go and tell Mr. and Mrs. Waters that the baby had arrived and that it was a healthy girl. "And tell 'em to get they bottles and milk ready," she heard Pep say. And although Otis Lee didn't say anything in return, she knew he must have been disappointed in her.

With the going down of the sun came Lady and Phillip Waters. Knot hadn't seen so much smiling in her life. They came to her bedroom doorway to wish her good health and to thank her for what Lady referred to over and over as a gift. Secretly, Knot was happy to see their joy.

Lady was dressed entirely in white, like a nurse. And her eyes were spilling tears. To Knot, she looked as though she wanted to take the baby and fly away. And Phillip, he looked like he was ready to fly off behind his wife and new child. *If Heaven's a real place*, Knot thought to herself, *them two is surely goin'.*

From her bed, Knot watched Miss Noni wrap the baby carefully. Then she passed the bundle to Lady, who headed for the door, cooing and thanking God, her arms filled with baby. But before Lady and Phillip were off the porch, Knot called up all her strength and called out, "Mr. and Mrs. Waters!" They stepped back into the house. "I just want to know one thing." And she held up one finger.

"Yes, ma'am," Phillip said. "Anything."

"Whose baby is that y'all got there?" Knot asked.

Lady squared her shoulders. She looked as though she were going to give a speech to soldiers.

"I got a niece over in Moyock," Lady answered, "and this here's *her* baby."

Phillip put his hand on Lady's shoulder.

"See," Phillip said, "Lady's niece ain't ready to raise a child just yet. She ain't much more'n a child herself, ya know. So me and Lady decide we gon' raise her baby."

"We'll love her just like she's our own," Lady reassured everyone. "We already do."

Knot rested her head on the pillow and dozed off.

Later that evening, Knot was awakened by the smell of fresh-baked biscuits, and she heard something thick being mixed in a bowl with a wooden spoon. She lifted the sheet to peek at her stomach. It looked the same as it had earlier that day. But when Knot shifted herself around to sit upright on the bed, she could feel the difference she couldn't see. The truth was, Knot missed the extra weight. She missed that seven or eight pounds that had gone out the door in Lady's arms.

"Hey, in there," Knot half shouted, as loud as her tired body would allow. Pep came into the room beating cake batter. She asked Knot how she was feeling. "Thirsty."

"I'll bring a glass of fresh water in just a minute."

"I don't want no more damn water. Look in my pantry and bring—"

"It's gone," Pep said. She told Knot that the corn liquor had been knocked over. "On accident."

"That's a lie and you know it." Knot wanted to be angry, but that required energy. Pep kept her eyes on the bowl she was holding, still beating the batter. Then Knot asked, "Where's Otis Lee? I know he's got a lil bit at y'all's house. Please go get it, Pep."

Knot begged, and Pep refused.

"You crazy?" Pep shot back. "I give you that and you sure to bleed to death right where you layin'." Pep left the room and Knot slid back down in the bed. Just like a small child who had been sent from the dinner table for misbehaving, she began to cry.

Knot wasn't sure if she was crying because Pep wouldn't allow her to have her favorite thing, or because of the aches that were left over from all her body had gone through that day, or because she had sent a baby—her baby with those wide eyes—across the lane to stay forever.

Knot couldn't seem to stop weeping. No matter what good times she tried to conjure in her mind, she could not stop weeping.

Pep came back with a glass of cool water and a hot biscuit that looked like it could be melted down and used to make a necklace and a pair of matching ear bobs. Knot watched Pep set the food and water on the nightstand that her pa had built for her when she was a child. Otis Lee and Valley had, separately, spruced it up some since she had moved to West Mills, but she had warned both of them that if they made it look too different from the way her pa had made it, she'd use the nightstand to beat them.

Pep picked up *The Old Curiosity Shop* and flipped through its pages.

"How many times you done read this same book, Knot?"

"Find me a sip of what I like and maybe I'll tell ya."

Pep began to read from the first page. She read it smoothly, the same way a longtime teacher would read at a schoolhouse. Then she closed the book and set it back in its place.

"Tell me one thing," Knot said. Pep sat on the bed, and Knot saw how tired Pep must be. *She can barely hold her eyelids open.* "How come you ain't taught yo' husband to read?"

Pep looked at Knot as though she had spoken in tongues.

"He *can* read," Pep retorted. "Enough to get by, anyway." Pep rubbed her own left hand with her right one. "It ain't all that important to him."

"Well, it ought to be. He's a worrisome sumbitch, but he smart. My pa always said, 'A smart Negro can go a long way. But a smart Negro with book learning can go *all* the way.'"

"All the way where?" Pep asked.

"Up, I guess." Knot said, and she yawned. Pep giggled. Then she yawned, too.

"He got his reasons, Knot."

"Who?"

"My husband," Pep clarified. She stood from the bed and stretched her arms above her head. Knot asked what his reasons were. Pep fluffed Knot's pillows and said, "He say readin' ought to be something folk do 'cause they *enjoy* it. Not 'cause they scared of what might happen to 'em if they can't." *I don't know what in the hell she talkin' about, and I don't feel like askin' no more questions*, Knot thought.

"Eat that biscuit and drink that water," Pep said. "I'm goin' home for a lil while. I might have me a drink of moonshine."

"I knew y'all had some."

"We do," Pep said. "Yo' moonshine."

Knot rolled her eyes at Pep, at the glass of water, and at that pretty golden biscuit. But she was grateful to have all three.

FOR TWO WEEKS Knot drank, cried without trying, and stuffed cabbage leaves in her bra to stop the milk. If the thought of leaving her bedroom wasn't enough to piss her off, the thought of leaving her house was.

Otis Lee and Pep were the only two people who could convince her to open her door. Pep came to be sure Knot was healing properly. Otis Lee, often with Breezy trailing behind him, came to bring plates of hot food, of which Knot ate little. On other days Otis Lee came just to make sure she had gotten out of the bed. After that, Knot stopped letting him in. But she wasn't able to refuse him entry for more than a couple of times.

"Azalea Centre!" Otis Lee had yelled from her porch one day. She had drunk so much, she could barely walk. "I gots my sledgehammer wit' me. I'm gon' give you a few minutes to come open up this here door. And if you *don't*, there ain't gon' *be* no door for you to come and open. I mean ev'ry word of it, too!"

Knot had somehow made her way to the door, and she opened it. She remembered collapsing into Otis Lee's arms. He had dragged her out onto the porch for air and sunlight. He had told her the next day. She had not remembered that part.

ONE AFTERNOON KNOT lay across her bed, miserable—but not from a night, or a morning, of drinking. She did not know why she was miserable. One hour she was crying, the next hour she was angry. So angry, she threw dishes around the kitchen. Then she'd broken into a strange laughter that she later felt embarrassed about. If anyone asked Knot to list all the feelings and thoughts she'd had that day, she'd be afraid of being taken to one of those places for the insane. So she lay down. *Best if I just lay here.*

There was a tapping on her door. She decided to ignore it. Then she heard someone walking outside of her bedroom window.

"Miss Knot!" It was Breezy.

"What?" Knot said.

"Can you please come to yo' window, Miss Knot?"

"For what?"

"My pop say he want me to see yo' face and he say for me to keep talkin' to you 'til you come to the window so I can see yo' face."

Knot went to the window and raised it. To her surprise, she enjoyed the coolness that came in.

"You seen me," Knot said. "Now go on."

"My pop say for you to come to suppa at half past six," Breezy relayed. After delivering the summons, he told Knot things she hadn't asked to know. He told her he had learned to write his whole name and that he had helped Pep bring in the eggs. "I ain't drop a single one of 'em, Miss Knot!" Then he told her all about how he and his grandma Rose played catch with a pinecone. "And, Miss Knot, my hands was hurtin' and my mama put some saff on 'em, and I—"

"Tell Otis Lee I'm too sick," Knot interrupted. *I damn sure hope he outgrows all that damn yappin'.* "I'll come another night."

Breezy ran home to deliver the message, but he was back at Knot's window in less than five minutes. Knot didn't need to look at her clock to know that.

"Miss Knot!" Breezy shouted.

"Lord Jesus," Knot whispered. She had lain back across her bed. If the empty liquor jar had been closer to her, she would have thrown it at the window. "What, child?"

"My pop tell me to say you best have yo' hind parts at his table at half past six." Knot got up from her bed and went to the window. Breezy was not alone this time; a posse of kittens was around his feet.

The mother cat stood nearby grooming herself. But she looked up every few seconds. And the kittens looked at her. It was as though they knew she was there if or when they needed her.

Knot looked back at Breezy. He had been waiting patiently for the next message to take home.

"Seem like yo' pop think he's my pop, too."

Breezy shrugged. Knot thought of Otis Lee and his sledgehammer.

"Okay," she said. Breezy walked back toward his house, and his furry friends followed.

Knot heated water and sat down in the bath. It was the second tub bath she'd had since giving birth; the first one was a week after. And it was the memory of that first bath after the birth that reminded her of the birth itself. And recalling the birth reminded her of the precious, dangerous glimpse.

Knot sat in the tub until the water was nearly cold. At one point she was sure that it must have been the warm tears that dripped from her chin that kept the bathwater from freezing.

It ain't so bad, Knot, she wished someone would say to her. Maybe her pa would say that if she had written to him and told him the truth about everything. *You just not ready for motherhood yet. And I think it's mighty smart of ya to know that 'bout yourself.* Knowing she wasn't ready didn't mean she liked not being ready. But it felt safe to her—the only kind of safe Knot felt all right with. Safe by not having to worry about hurting a child's feelings, the way her mother had hurt hers. Safe by not becoming someone's wife just to figure out, years later, that she didn't want him. Safe to get a bit of joy from the moonshine—something that couldn't hurt her or be hurt by her.

SIX

After supper, Otis Lee helped Breezy into his light jacket, gave him a small lantern, and told him to go and visit Ma Noni and Rose. Breezy was happy to go, because Ma Noni always had a treat there for him. Otis Lee knew Breezy would come back with crumbs around his mouth. And there would likely be a piece of something else, wrapped and tucked into his coat pocket, to take to the schoolhouse the next day.

Otis Lee stood on the back porch and watched the lantern move through the big backyard, en route to the other house. He remembered the day Breezy was born. *Five years old. Old 'nuff to carry his own lantern.* A hint of sadness moved through Otis Lee. *Time don't wait on nobody.*

When Otis Lee saw that Breezy had made it to the other house safely, he went back to the table where Pep and Knot sat, neither one of them saying a word. Pep got up and cleared their plates.

Otis Lee told Knot that he had run into the schoolmaster earlier that morning, and he had given Otis Lee a message for Knot—a message Otis Lee was more than happy to deliver.

"He say if you all healed up from the pox, and if you through drankin'," Otis Lee said, "him and the children want ya back at the school. He say the lil ones miss ya a whole lot, Knot. Ain't that what he say, Pep?"

"I wasn't there," Pep replied. Now it was her turn to go off script, he supposed.

"Well, that's exactly what he say to me, Knot," Otis Lee said. "And I think it's—"

"I ain't goin' back to the schoolhouse," Knot announced. And Otis Lee could tell that she meant it. Her eyes looked dead, which was far different from the way her eyes looked when she was drunk.

Knot looked away from him, and she began fingering the hem of her dress—the black dress.

"I thought you enjoyed workin' wit' the young'uns," Pep said. "You used to tell me how quick they learn. You loved it."

"Never loved," Knot said. "Didn't even like."

She had told Otis Lee that before, but he hadn't really believed her. She'd said that she had become a teacher only because her father told her that she would be good at it, since she loved to read and work out math problems.

"I just did it to get the hell outta Ahoskie," Knot had told him a few years ago. "Pa made me teach his patients. I got tired of that shit."

Otis Lee looked across the table at Knot. She was still fiddling with her hem and looked as though she'd burst into tears at any moment—or fall asleep.

"Well, we got to find you some work," he affirmed. Knot showed no interest.

Otis Lee knew that if Knot were well, she would have told him that she could find her own work. She would have told him to go to hell and to mind his business.

While Pep spoke to Knot about things she had missed on and off of Antioch Lane, Otis Lee sat thinking and worrying. He'd seen what could happen to people who let sadness get locked inside of them for too long. When he was seven years old, his father drowned in the canal. An accident. Rose had taken it awfully hard. Ma Noni had let Rose sit in her sadness for a long while.

"People got to feel it and get it out," she had said. But she believed that Rose had fallen too deep into the grief. She used to make Rose get out of bed and out of the house. That's where Otis Lee had gotten the idea with Knot. Ma Noni had told Rose to come to work with her in the fields, even if she cried half of the time they worked. And that's what Rose did. Cried and picked. Over time, Rose cried less and less, but she was never quite the same again.

When Otis Lee lived in Brooklyn, working in Essie and her husband's brothel, he would often see Essie sitting in a corner of a room, crying. And when she'd see him, she would hold her handkerchief over her face. One day he'd seen her weeping, and he walked around the brothel to make sure her husband was away. He made sure everyone else in the house was gone or busy. The coast was clear, so he went to Essie and kneeled in front of her. She had looked nervous until he told her it was safe for them to speak.

"Sista, you ain't got to stay here if it's hurtin' ya," he had said. "You got a whole mama, and a grandmamma that loves you. Even with runnin' off like you did, we still love ya, and we be mighty glad to have you back. Let's go on home, Essie."

Essie had sat up straight in her chair and looked as though she wanted to thank him. All the weeping had turned her face as red as a rash. Her long, shiny, pitch-black hair hung almost to her knees.

"I wish it was that simple, baby," she had said to him. Essie moved as though she were going to cup his chin with her palm, but she stopped. She stood up, smoothed her dress, and tossed her hair behind her shoulders.

"Go on back to your work now, Otis Lee," she had said softly as she dabbed her eyes with the handkerchief. "Please."

It seemed to him that Essie was choosing sadness. And now, here Knot was, sitting at his kitchen table, looking sad about something he knew she had a choice in.

"If you want your baby back, just go on over there and get her," Otis Lee said. "She's your'n!"

"Otis Lee!" Pep shouted. She gave him the same look she gave Breezy whenever he passed gas in the kitchen.

"That's why she sad, ain't it?" he asked.

Otis Lee looked at Knot, hoping she'd look back at him with something happy in her eyes, something alive in those eyes of hers. Anything to let him know she would be all right if she just went to the Waterses' house and told them she wanted her baby girl. But Knot only stared at the table. Pep mumbled something, but Otis Lee kept his eyes on Knot, still hoping. *Make her want that child, Lord. It'll be all fixed up if you just make her want that child.*

Finally, Knot looked up from the table, but she didn't turn her gaze to Otis Lee.

"I thank y'all kindly for the nice meal," Knot said. "Both of ya."

After Knot had put on her shawl, she touched Otis Lee's and Pep's shoulders. It was the closest thing to a hug Otis Lee knew he would ever get from Knot. He wondered what she might do if he just stood up and hugged her.

"What I'm gon' do 'bout her, Pep?" Otis Lee asked after Pep had seen Knot out and sat next to him.

"Nothin'," Pep said. "Knot ain't yo' wife." And in the sultry, soft voice she used with him when she was feeling frisky, she said, "Whole lot of woman sittin' right here beside ya. Need to be reminded? 'Cause I will. Right now. At my kitchen table." She placed her hand on his groin. "This oughta get yo' mind off her."

"Always, baby," he agreed.

"You sure 'bout that?" Pep teased.

"Course," Otis Lee told her. "And you know it." He kissed Pep's lips, her neck, and he squeezed part of her ample thigh. "This here's what I like. Knot ain't got *none* of this. Blind man can see *that*."

Pep laughed. And they kissed the way they had when they'd first met. She lay her head on his shoulder and said, "Knot ain't Rose, Otis Lee." She put her hand on his and she rubbed the top of his thumb with her own. "She ain't Essie, either. Ain't yo' place to do nothin' 'bout Knot. Worr' 'bout me and our boy, if you want somethin' to worry about."

"But y'all doin' better than I am," he said. He saw a serious look on Pep's face, so he smiled.

"Then be satisfied with us bein' all right, and turn Knot and ev'rybody else's mess loose."

Breezy came through the door with something wrapped in a cloth. Otis Lee knew there would be at least two things, because Breezy always liked to have two. Two apples, two baby chicks to have as his pets, two chicken legs on his plate at supper. *That boy always wanting two.*

"Where's the lantern?" Otis Lee asked. Before Breezy answered, Otis Lee guessed that Ma Noni wouldn't let Breezy carry the lantern by himself. And he was right.

Breezy took off his jacket and dropped it onto the floor. Pep made him pick it up and put it on the back of one of the chairs. Then she asked him, "What's that you got there?"

"Ma Noni give me some cake," he said. "Look!"

Otis Lee watched his son unwrap the cake. Breezy went about it carefully, as if there were a sleeping kitten or puppy in it that he didn't want to wake. In the cloth, there were two pieces of pound cake with something spread between them.

"What she put in the middle?" Otis Lee inquired.

A frown appeared on Breezy's small, round face. It was clear to Otis Lee that the boy had grown tired of answering questions. Breezy sighed and replied, "Zerves!"

Otis Lee and Pep glanced at each other and smiled. Breezy rewrapped the cake sandwich just as carefully as he had unwrapped it, and set it in the middle of the table.

"Don't eat my cake, Pop," he warned.

"I'm gon' eat it all," Otis Lee joked. Breezy whined, before giggling and running up the steps. Pep told him to slow down so that he wouldn't fall again.

Otis Lee and Pep sat quietly, still holding hands. Otis Lee said, "What he say that is spread in the middle?"

Pep took a deep breath, just as Breezy had. "It's zerves!" The two of them were bent over in laughter.

Then Otis Lee asked, "You still ain't sad 'bout us not havin' more?"

And Pep said, "More what?"

"More babies."

"You crazy?" One was enough, she said. And Otis Lee was glad to hear her say it. *One's enough for me, too.*

"Ma Noni and Rose gon' rotten that boy down to the core," Otis Lee mused. "We ain't gon' be able to do nothin' with him."

Pep reached behind her head and released her ponytail from the light blue piece of ribbon that had been holding it. She scratched her scalp and said, "I ain't too worried 'bout that. *We* can handle him. I feels sorry for the one who marries him, though."

Otis Lee grunted in agreement, and he thought about Knot. He hoped she would come out of her sad spell soon enough.

SEVEN

Knot sent a letter home saying she had returned to West Mills from Pennsylvania and that she was going to visit Ahoskie as soon as she was settled back in and rested. Knowing her mother would recognize fresh motherhood on her if she visited too soon, Knot wrote that it would probably be a few months before she'd have a chance to make the trip. Just thinking about the ride gave her a headache and a backache.

"I wonder what it'd be like if I move back," Knot said to Otis Lee one day. He had come to pick up the bread pudding Pep had ordered.

"Back where? Back to ya people?"

"Yeah," she replied. And she watched Otis Lee turn the question over in his head. If she knew Otis Lee as well as she believed she did, she knew he would say it might be a good idea for her to return to the place she knew best, with her family around.

"I don't think that's the place for ya. Not now."

Well, I'll be damned.

Knot knew there was no way she could go back to Ahoskie to stay. Everyone knew her family, which would get in the way of how much she enjoyed drinking, playing cards, and so forth. Her pa was one of the few colored men in Ahoskie—a dentist—whom the other coloreds and Indians looked up to. He had managed to polish his reputation after he had become sober. *I ain't goin' to let my drinking set him back.*

"Listen to me real good, Mary, Iris, Knot," he had said to them one day. He lined them up in the parlor. He sat in his chair and twisted his long goatee. "There ain't a whole lot of thangs I'm scared of. But one thang I'm real scared of is that one of y'all might take up drankin'. That'll do me in. Hear?" They had all said yes and they gave him a hug, all three of them at once. Knot hadn't been old enough to remember her pa as a drunk. But Mary had, and she had told Knot she was lucky she didn't know that side of their pa.

Fifteen days later, Knot received a reply to the letter she had mailed home:

September 1942

Dear Azalea,

I pray God will see fit to get this letter to you quickly. Your father has been in bed for more than a week with fever like I've never seen in all my days. He has lost all control of his body's doings, and as you might imagine, we expect he won't recover unless the Lord our God performs a miracle. Your sisters and I are just beside ourselves with worry.

Come as soon as you possibly can, child. He's asking for you.

Please travel safely and with haste.

With love,

Mrs. Doctor George Washington Centre

Knot only had one drink that Wednesday night. She was afraid that if she had more, she might oversleep and miss the bus that passed through West Mills every Monday and Thursday, en route to the state capital. The bus would stop close enough to Ahoskie that Knot could get off and hitch a ride to her family's house. Or, since fall temperatures were still mild and bearable, she would be able to walk from the station.

After packing a bag—she refused to pack the black dress—she sat on her bed Indian-style. The house was quiet enough that she might hear an ant trying to lift a bread crumb.

"Listen up," Knot said, looking at the ceiling. "If you real, and you care anything 'bout good people, I'll thank ya kindly to heal my pa from whatever it is he done caught." She felt a lump forming in her throat.

"I don't ask for much. I don't hardly ask you for nothin', matter of fact. But for my pa, I'm askin' you to fix it."

Knot didn't look away from the low wooden ceiling of her bedroom. Even to wipe the tears from her cheeks, she did not look away.

The next morning, before the sun was up, Knot tapped on Otis Lee's door twice and walked in. Pep was in the kitchen having tea, and she was boiling two eggs for Breezy, who was still in bed. Otis Lee had already left for Pennington Farm, Pep said. He wanted an early start.

"Where you goin' with that?" she asked, looking at Knot's valise. After Knot told her that she was going to Ahoskie, Pep asked if anything was wrong.

Knot had made the decision to remain strong until she arrived in her hometown and saw her pa. In order to do that, she needed to get there without speaking to anyone about what her mother's letter had said.

"Nothin' that won't be over soon, I guess," Knot said. "Tell Otis Lee for me?"

Pep didn't reply with words. An odd silence stood between them until she stepped closer to Knot and kissed her on the forehead.

"Be safe. We'll look after yo' house."

On the bus, Knot made many attempts to read some of the novel Valley had sent to her from Washington, D.C., *Bleak House*. When it had arrived in the mail, Knot had read the title and said to the book, "Val couldn't choose a different one? Shit. My house is bleak enough."

With many of the British novels she had read before, Knot had found herself completely taken—so much so that she'd go nearly an hour without taking a sip from a drink she'd poured. She brought the new novel along with her, hoping it would distract her from the possibility that she might be going home to see her pa's cold body set up in the parlor. *He might pull through it, Knot. You know how Dinah is. Fret over a cough.*

At a quarter past eleven o'clock, Knot stood before the double doors of the two-story homestead. The late morning breeze was cool, but the short walk from the station, the bright sun, and the one shot from her flask gave her reason to tie her sweater around her now wider waist.

She put two mint leaves in her mouth and chewed vigorously. *Why take the chance at gettin' found out 'fore I even set foot in the damn house?*

First, Knot tried opening the door on the right. It was locked. After trying the one on the left, she knocked and then walked around the porch to one of the large windows to see if anyone was coming toward the door. She saw her mother, Dinah—Knot had been raised to call her Mother, although Knot and her sisters secretly called her Dinah Bright—look out the parlor window.

She still looked just as Knot imagined she would—just as she had two years back, when Knot had last seen her: dressed as though she were going to noon tea with the mayor's wife. Dinah's hair was smoothed back and up to form a bun that sat firmly at the top of her head. *Her skin*, Knot noticed— even through the window, Knot's eyes were drawn to her mother's enviable skin. She had once heard her pa say, "Dinah Bright Centre, you look like God done rolled ya 'round in ground nutmeg. And you know I loooove me some nutmeg." Her mother had smiled, waved him off, and said, "Don't speak that way in front of the girls, George." But it hadn't been often that Knot witnessed her parents engage in playful banter.

Through the window, Knot could see that her mother was sad, maybe even mad. Was it unusual for Dinah to look that way? No. As far back as Knot could remember, her mother had never been one to show joy, which was odd, since Dinah had been one of the most pampered colored women in Ahoskie. But the mad, sad look on Dinah's face today was different.

He dead already, Knot thought.

Knot ran back to the door and waited for her mother to open it. Although the two of them had not always gotten along, Knot was prepared to embrace her mother, rub her back, and do what a person was supposed to do when her whole family needed her most. So Knot couldn't have expected that her mother would open the door, walk up to her, and grab ahold of Knot's left breast. She gripped it firmly and squeezed.

At some point Knot's knees had made contact with the porch, but she could not remember when. She hadn't felt that much pain since the day Pep cut her to make it easier to birth the child Lady Waters had named Frances.

Still kneeling and looking at her mother's ankles, Knot felt as though a heat wave had traveled to Ahoskie and singled her out. She thought she would faint from the vicious throbbing in her breast. The one that had not been squeezed began to throb in sympathy with the one that had been assaulted.

Knot stood to her feet and looked into Dinah's deep-set brown eyes.

"Bitch!"

"Call me all the names you want to call me, Azalea Marie."

Knot tried to go around her mother and into the house to see her pa. From what the letter had said, every minute counted. And she wouldn't waste it by standing on the porch with Dinah Bright Centre.

Dinah shoved Knot away and blocked the entrance.

"Move!" Knot yelled. And then, as loud as she could: "Pa! I'm here! I'm here, Pa!"

"You show up at *my* home full of milk, with no husband by your side and no child in your arms, and I'm supposed to just let you in? With all the work I put into raising you to be something?"

Knot tried again to walk around her mother.

"Iris! Mary!" Knot shouted toward the door. "One of y'all come get her out my way!" One of them or some other relative had to be inside sitting next to her pa's bed, dabbing the fever sweat from his forehead, she thought.

"No one's in there," Dinah said. It was her sinister laugh that explained to Knot why no one else was in the house. Knot would do anything for her pa. Everyone knew it. Dinah Bright Centre was no exception. "I had to get you here somehow, to see if it was true."

Knot's heat wave was on its way back to her. *That goddamn schoolmaster.* "Who told you?"

"*That's* what you have to say to me?" Dinah asked. "*That's* your concern?"

"I had a baby, Mother!" Knot screamed.

She wanted to take it back. *I had a baby, Mother!* She wanted it back. Not because it wasn't true, or because she hadn't come to terms with it. It was the way she'd said it—in her mother's style of speaking, the way Dinah had forced Knot and her sisters to speak—that angered her now. Proper. Elegant. Things always had to be proper and elegant for Dinah, Knot remembered. Well, it had to look that way to other folk. Because if everything in the Centre household looked proper and elegant, the people in town would never believe that Dinah almost never hugged her three daughters. People would never believe that Dinah hardly ever told her girls that they were smart and beautiful. She rarely had kind words for them, or for Knot's pa—unless they were in the midst of company.

So Knot wanted her words back so that she could say it again her way. But since the moment had passed, she said instead, "You act like I killed some-damn-body! Shit!"

"Maybe you have. I can't be sure of anything where you're concerned, Azalea Marie."

Having no intention of acknowledging her mother's snide remark, Knot used the quiet moment to collect her thoughts. Someone had told her mother things that most people in West Mills didn't know.

"I just want to know one thing," Knot said. "Who tol' you?"

"I couldn't say even if I wanted to," Dinah replied. She told Knot that she had gone into downtown Ahoskie to pay their household accounts. A man—his head and face had been wrapped in a red wool scarf—had approached Dinah. "I should have known right then that he was bringing bad news. It was so hot that day, Azalea."

Dinah leaned against the closed front door. Her calm storytelling caused Knot to forget that the two of them hadn't been that far off from coming to blows just minutes ago.

The man with the red wool scarf had said only three muffled words to Dinah: "'Bout your daughter." The note he'd handed her before he had run off was short and sweet:

Knot got a baby. She gave it away. They both alive and well. Your daughter want to come back to you. Take her back, Miss Centre. West Mills no good for her.

"Let me see it," Knot demanded of Dinah.

"Oh, dear daughter," Dinah said, peering sullenly at Knot, her head cocked to one side. "I threw that thing inside the cookstove the moment your father and I were through reading it."

Pa know she tricked me? I don't believe it.

"I always knew you'd be the one to hurt me, Azalea. On the day you were born, when I saw all that dark red hair slicked down around your head, I knew it. As pretty and precious as you were, I knew you'd give me trouble. You can't help it."

"You tried like hell to get rid of my red, too," Knot shot back. "The hours I sat, tied to a chair in that shed like a dog, with that goddamn coal mush caked in my hair."

She wanted to scream *Bitch!* again. But there was no need. The mention of the coal mush seemed to have gripped Dinah by her shoulders and shaken her.

"You'd be wise to watch your tongue, girl."

"Thought I forgot, didn't ya?" Knot said. Tears ran down her face. "Oh, what I'd give to forget it. I forgive you, though."

"I think you should leave," Dinah told her. "Right now!"

"You won't get no argument from me on *that*," Knot retorted. She wiped her face with her hands, readjusted her bobby pins, and smoothed her dress. With her valise in hand, she said, "I'd thank ya kindly if you tell me where Pa is. Somebody who got sense 'nuff in his head to know that just 'cause his daughter ain't perfect, it don't mean she evil."

"Leave your father alone," Dinah said. "Go back to whoever wrote me that note."

"Never mind," Knot said. She began her walk toward the dirt road that would take her into town.

"If you don't have a husband or a child with you," Dinah shouted, "there's no sense in going to see him! Save yourself the trouble, Azalea!"

"I'm *Knot!*" she said. She kept walking.

"You always preferred that backwoods pet name your father gave you to the sweet, decent one I gave you!"

Knot turned her head toward the house just enough to return her mother's sinister laugh like an unopened gift. "You don't know shit 'bout sweet and decent!"

Would Miss Noni tell my secret to the schoolmaster?

"One of these days you'll thank me for the talk we've just had, Azalea Marie!" Dinah declared. "Once you've raised children of your own, you'll thank me!"

Ah, go to hell.

ON THE WAY to the church where her pa had a back room to practice dentistry—it would not be more than a twenty-minute walk, especially at her current pace—all Knot could think about was Dinah. She did not want to, but her mind seemed to be giving her no other choice.

Why in the hell she so mean? Shit!

Had Mary's suggestion, years ago, that Dinah was grumpy because her marriage to their pa had been arranged been correct? Every so often, Mary's story came to Knot—especially when Dinah showed anger toward one or all of them:

"Before you two came along," twenty-year-old Mary had said to Knot and Iris, "I heard Dinah Bright telling Mr. Barco that she'd been forced to marry Pa."

"Forced?" Iris, twelve at the time, asked.

"She didn't have a say in it, is what I mean."

"Who Mr. Barco?" nine-year-old Knot asked.

"You mean '*Who's* Mr. Barco?'" Mary corrected. "You're both too young to remember him. He was Dinah Bright's best friend since they were tiny children." Mary leaned closer to Knot and Iris and whispered, "He was . . . a *different* kind of man."

"What that mean?" Knot asked.

"He liked men the same way men like ladies," Iris answered. Mary looked stunned, and asked Iris how she knew about that. And Iris said, "*You* told me." Mary denied it, but Iris would not relent. "You even said the Bible says Mr. Barco will go to hell when he dies. And—"

"Enough, Iris!" Mary broke in. She had covered her own face with her hands.

"If we dig a deep, deep hole in the yard," Knot said, "can we see hell?"

"No," Mary told her. "It doesn't work like that."

"I don't understand," Knot said.

Mary sighed and continued, "So, anyway, Pa's father used to have tobacco fields, and he had sharecroppers."

"Can I have a definition?" Knot asked.

"It's '*May* I have a definition?'" Iris replied. Knot sucked her teeth.

Mary gave the definition. "Dinah Bright told Mr. Barco that Pa's father treated them like they were his slaves."

"Ooooooo," Knot said. She was brushing her hair. Iris offered to do it, and Knot allowed her. It was something Knot enjoyed, and Iris often said she couldn't wait to grow up and have daughters of her own. Knot sat on the floor, between Iris's knees, eager for the rest of Mary's story.

Me and Iris used to be so close, Knot now thought to herself.

"Dinah Bright and her pa were sharecroppers, too, and—"

"What was Dinah's pa's name again?" Iris asked.

"John Quincy Bright," Mary said. "Or John Quinton Bright. One of those. Well—"

"And what was Pa's pa's name?"

"Shut up, Iris!" Knot said.

"I give up!" Mary exclaimed. And they never spoke of their parents' arranged marriage again.

THE CHURCH KNOT had gone to for as long as she could remember—long before her pa and Dinah had been named head deacon and head deaconess—was half a mile from the house. If anyone had asked her whom she had seen on the road during her walk there, she would have been able to say. But when the church was in sight, she realized that she didn't remember the walk at all. Because after thinking about Mary's story, Knot's thoughts had shifted back to her mother—strangely, her mother's way of speaking. She recalled Dinah reprimanding her pa for his own way of speaking.

"In the name of all that is holy, George," Dinah had said one evening during dinner, "I can't understand why you insist on speaking that way. After all the schooling you've been so blessed to have."

"This the way I spoke 'fore I went to school," Knot's pa said, "and it ain't spoil my education nary a bit. You talk how *you* want to talk, and I'll talk how *I* want to talk." He mixed his field peas with his mashed potatoes while he said it. "I remember a time when you didn't talk the way—"

"Pass the salt, please, Iris," Dinah interrupted. Knot remembered that her mother had not looked up from her plate again until the end of the meal, when she stood to clear all the dishes. But this wasn't the first time Dinah had brought up the topic with George, and it definitely wasn't going to be the last.

KNOT FOUND HER pa in the room he had built onto the back of the church. The door was ajar and she saw him sitting at his desk, reading a book. There was no one there to have a tooth pulled or to have patches of rotting gums cut out of their mouths.

Knot stood in her spot quietly, watching him. Up until seven weeks ago, he had been the person she had cared about most of all. *I woulda kept that child if I didn't care 'bout her.*

Knot's pa was now sixty-two years old, with a full head of cloud-white hair that looked as though it hadn't been near a pair of shears in several months. His goatee matched his clean white shirt.

After they hugged, he used his rough thumbs to wipe the tears from Knot's cheeks. His expression was serious, the one he used when he used to look into her and her sisters' mouths, searching for cavities. Knot told him about everything that had happened at the house with Dinah. She told him everything. The truth. He leaned on the front of his desk and clasped his hands together like a dead man in a box made of strong cedar. Knot put one of her hands on his as if she were testing to see if it was still warm.

"I'm sorry to hear 'bout ya troubles, Knot," he told her. "Folk say it's an awful, *awful* thing to see ya child go before you do."

"Pa"—she touched his shoulder—"the baby ain't—"

"That child's in the hands of the Almighty," he said. "Okay? Make ya peace wit' it, Knot. Make ya peace wit' it."

The pain she saw in his bloodshot eyes was almost enough to weaken Knot's knees, but she stiffened her legs. *I already kneeled enough for one day.*

"Do this for me," her pa said. "Go visit wit' Iris. I'll talk to ya mama and see if I can't make things right 'tweenst y'all. She ain't the only one that's vexed by yo' doings, though. I need you to know that."

"Pa, I ain't mean to hurt—"

"Well, what *did* you mean to do, Azalea?" he asked. The same bloodshot eyes seemed to be piercing hers, searching for anything to help him understand where he'd gone wrong.

"Pa, please listen to me. I made a—"

With a clenched first, he pounded the stack of large dentistry books that sat in the center of his desk. "Go to ya sister's!"

He called me Azalea, she thought to herself on the way to Iris's house. She was too stunned to cry about it. *I don't know when the last time was he called me that.*

SHE WAS ONLY a year old when her pa had given her the nickname. He had told her of how she would often reach up to one of Dinah's whatnot shelves to get ahold of some small ceramic ornament. Whenever anyone else tried to get the ornament from her, she would hold it as tightly as she could with both of her small but fat hands. He had said that Knot would ball her little body up almost into a knot so that they couldn't get Dinah's ornament.

"You'd just giggle 'til ya got tired," her pa had told her. "We had to wait for ya to get tired 'fore we could get stuff from ya. Wouldn't be long 'fore you'd be *right* back at that shelf, messin' with ya mama's whatnots."

TWO DAYS PASSED and Knot hadn't heard or received anything from her pa. The waiting was torturous, as was Iris's lecturing, which began on the second day. Iris did not say a word to Knot on the first day. If it had not been for the brandy Iris's husband Leonard kept at the back of a kitchen cupboard—his rule was that the brandy could be sipped only on Thanksgiving, Christmas, and New Year's—Knot was sure that she would have lost her mind.

Leonard and their four sons were in Edenton for the week, visiting Leonard's family. Knot couldn't have been happier about that. The children and their *Aunt Knot* this, and *Aunt Knot* that. Leonard and his *Don't say this* and *Don't say that in front of the boys.* With all that was going on, Knot wouldn't have lasted even an hour in their home if they had all been there.

"Pa'll forgive me, right?" Knot asked, pacing back and forth in front of Iris's butcher table. The two of them had eaten dinner in silence: tomato stew with chicken. Knot hadn't had much of an appetite, but she forced down one bowlful.

Iris did not look up from the yellow quilt she was knitting. "I don't know, Knot. You'll have to wait."

"'*I don't know, Knot. You'll have to wait,*'" Knot mocked in a very high-pitched voice. "Ain't you got nothin' to say besides that? Shit." Iris kept knitting.

Knot felt like she did back when she was a little girl waiting for Dinah to decide what her punishment would be for kissing boys behind the church during worship services. Even then, when Knot would ask Iris what would happen to her, Iris would say, "You have to wait, Knot." And she would wait. The punishments came, went, and it would all be over.

With elegance and poise, Iris worked the yellow yarn and the two wide silver needles. Although Knot had never taken up arts and crafts—reading had always been her passion—she had enjoyed watching her sisters' hands working fabrics and thread. As a young girl, she sometimes fell asleep watching the rhythm of their hands' movements.

Iris was still as petite as she had been when they were teenagers. If Knot hadn't seen the four pregnancies with her own eyes, she might not believe they'd occurred. *And that chin.* Mary, Iris, and Knot all shared their pa's V-shaped chin. But only Knot had the copper-red hair.

Just as Knot was preparing to ask Iris once more what she imagined their parents had discussed, there was a knock at Iris's front door, followed by a "Yoo-hoo!"

KNOT WONDERED IF Mary and Iris had, like the scriveners in the British novels, sat to write two copies of the same fire-and-brimstone sermon. The difference was that Mary hadn't made eye contact with Knot while she preached. And, having spoken to their mother, Mary had more to add.

"The B-word," Mary said, looking at Iris. "She called Mother the B-word."

Knot noticed that Mary hadn't called their mother Dinah Bright, and it annoyed her. She also noticed how much weight her eldest sister had gained since she'd last seen her.

"Anybody ever grab *yo'* sore titty before?" Knot said to Mary.

"I refuse to speak to her," Mary told Iris.

"Mary," Iris scolded. "Please behave like the grown woman you are."

"I most certainly will *not*," Mary shot back.

"Then carry yo' big ass back up the road where you come from," Knot retorted. The three sisters were silent for a minute. "I ain't mean to call her a bitch."

"Knot!" Iris shouted. Her yarn and needles landed in the center of the table. The needles chimed.

"I was mad and it just come out! Shit!"

"That's no excuse," Iris said. And after she picked her knitting back up: "Well, new motherhood *will* make you say and feel strange things. On *many* a day I've wanted to—"

"Iris!" Mary exclaimed. She took a deep breath, held it, and released it dramatically. "Where's your child, Knot?"

"Oh, you back to bein' a grown woman now?"

"She gave her baby boy to strangers, Mary," Iris said. "To strangers!"

I couldn't tell Iris the truth. Bad as she wants a daughter, it'll surely kill her to know I gave mine away.

Mary's swift approach reminded Knot too much of Dinah's grab-and-squeeze earlier that week. Going to her nephews' bedroom, where she'd been sleeping and drinking the stolen brandy, was the right thing to do, she decided. So she went.

"What in God's name have you done, Azalea?" she heard Mary say from the bedroom. And then: "Why has she always had to be so damn different?"

"Mary!" Iris said.

"Right down to the hair," Mary went on. "You know, our grandfather had that copper-red hair."

"Which one?" Iris asked. Knot could tell that Iris was tired and that she was just humoring their eldest sister.

"Pa's pa," Mary replied. "You two are too young to remember him. But he had that copper-red on his head. I'm so grateful I didn't get it. So grateful."

It was her powder-dry mouth that convinced Knot to get out of bed. Having drunk what was left of Leonard's holiday-only brandy when she'd run away from Mary and Iris, and after all the crying and sweating throughout the night, Knot wondered if there was even enough water in Iris's well to quench her thirst.

In the kitchen, she dipped out and drank three cups of cool water before sitting at the table. She was tired. If she had to bet on how many hours she'd slept, she'd put her money on two. *If I thought maybe Iris would let me lay 'round a while, I'd go right back to bed.*

"Knot!" Iris called from her garden, just off from the back porch. "Come out here, please." Knot sat on the edge of the porch, waiting for the day's oration.

"Leonard's going to be awfully upset when he finds his brandy all gone," Iris said. Gently, she separated tomatoes from their vines. "I hope this is just something to get you through this . . . other problem."

And because Knot had already told Iris one of the biggest lies of her life, she thought she might as well tell another.

"Just to get me through, Iris."

As Knot stood to go back into the house, Iris said, "I imagine you don't want to talk about this, but—"

"But you want to anyway."

Iris was smiling now. She looked up at Knot, and the bright sun bounced off the greased part she had combed in the middle of her head. She said, "I am Dinah Bright Centre's daughter, aren't I?"

Iris asked Knot how her labor had gone. Had it been easy or unbearably hard? Of course it was hard, Knot told her. But had Knot felt as though it would be the last thing she did on earth, as Iris and Mary had described it? No.

"Yeah," Knot said to Iris. "I just knew for sure God was callin' my number."

THIS TIME THE knock at the door was not Mary. It was not anyone Knot knew. It was a young fellow with a mouth full of gauze.

"You Knot Centre?" he said as best he could.

"I am."

"Doc Centre send me with this," he said, handing her a piece of paper, folded and sealed with a dime-size drop of red wax. And when Knot told him to come inside while she looked for a nickel, he said, "No need, ma'am. Doc Centre jus' pull my tooth out my head for free!"

In her sister's yard, with the fall sun warming her, Knot read her pa's letter.

Our Dear Azalea,

We were truly sorry to hear of the illness you suffered in recent months, and we are most grateful to God that you have survived and are now doing well. However, we must not ignore the fact that you brought the infirmity upon yourself by dishonoring the laws that God set forth in his Holy word. In doing so, you have brought us great pain. We have indulged your inclinations toward rebellion far too many times. And for that we must ask you to depart from us.

When the Lord instructs us to welcome you back into the fold, we will write to you. Please do not come to our home until you have received an invitation signed by me, or by your loving mother.

We do this because we love you, and because we love our Lord and Savior Jesus Christ. We pray that you will take care of yourself for your continued good health and growth.

Love,

Dr. George Washington Centre and family

The yellow quilt that Iris had been knitting looked nice lying on the healthy grass. It looked as though it had been made for that exact purpose.

"It's pretty," Knot admired. "But all that work just to lay on the ground?" *Damn. I sound like Dinah Bright sayin' that.*

"I won't tell you who you sounded like just now," Iris said, echoing her thoughts. And after she read their pa's letter, she said, "They're just making a point, Knot. You'll see. Give it a month or two. I promise you, in a month or two, they'll be—"

"Shut up and sit here with me a lil while, Iris," Knot interrupted. And when Iris tried to hug her, she pulled away. "Just sit with me."

On Monday afternoon, with her valise in one hand and the yellow quilt tucked under the opposite arm, Knot walked to the store where she would catch the bus back to the place she now thought of as home, where she knew Otis Lee Loving would tell her she always had family as long as he lived.

There were two benches in front of the store. Neither of them had *White* or *Colored* written anywhere on them. But since there was a white woman—she looked to be around Knot's age, red-haired, smoking a long cigarette and wearing a white dress (*after Labor Day?*) that fit her like an apple fits in its peel—sitting on one of the benches, Knot sat on the other.

In her mind, Knot played eeny meeny miney mo to help her decide whether or not to reread her pa's letter. Maybe she'd find something tender, more forgiving, in her pa's words if she gave it another once-over. Miney mo told her to read it again. So she did. The second read was only another spear in Knot's side. Oddly, it made her think of Pratt's last letter (*that goddamn Pratt*), the one announcing that he'd leave if she didn't take better care of herself and love him more. Her pa's letter asked her to go away and take better care of herself.

Dinah say she burned the letter she got that was 'bout me. Good idea. That white woman might have a match.

If Knot had had any idea that in order to borrow the red-haired white woman's matchbook, she'd have to hear about her failed marriage, she would have never gone over to what she assumed was the White bench.

"Those are *my* fucking children!" the woman said to Knot, pointing north. She took a drag from the long cigarette. They hadn't formally introduced themselves, but Knot had secretly nicknamed her "Fancy." "That's the part she keeps fucking forgetting."

Fancy was waiting on the Raleigh-bound bus. She had arrived in Ahoskie the same day Knot had, to visit her children who lived temporarily with Fancy's mother. Fancy put emphasis on *temporarily*. Knot had already gotten the match. *But I ain't gon' stand here and light the letter in front of her. She'll be wantin' to know my business.*

"Well, have a safe tr—"

"Those rascals barely listened to a fucking word I fucking said all weekend long!" Fancy shouted. "But she's got them hanging off her every word."

"How many you got?" Knot asked, noticing the woman's black high-heeled shoes for the first time. She and Fancy were standing a few feet away from the White bench. Fancy, unable to answer with words because she was taking a drag from her cigarette, held up two fingers. She turned her head to the right, in the opposite direction of Knot, and blew the smoke out. Because Fancy had called her children rascals, Knot assumed they were boys.

"Two girls," Fancy said. "Redheads, both of 'em. Like their mama." She smiled and ran her fingers through her own hair, which was cut short; it hung just below her earlobes. "I fucking love them from head to toe. Don't exactly have a choice. But I'm sure you know that feeling. How many do *you* have?"

"None," Knot said. She felt as though she'd seen someone looking for something precious, valuable—and she'd been the one who had stolen it. "Just nephews."

Fancy looked at Knot's bosom and then her own. "Lucky woman, you."

At least another twenty minutes passed before Knot's bus arrived. By that time she had heard Fancy—her real name was Joanne, but she went by Jo—say *fuck* and *fucking* enough to last a lifetime. And Knot now knew more about Jo's estranged husband than she'd ever known about Pratt. *Pratt Fucking Shepherd.*

Jo had quoted First Corinthians 13:11 when she spoke about her husband.

"He was *my* childish thing, Miss Centre," she had said. "I had to fucking put that childish thing away."

With her pa's letter still crumpled in her hand, Knot thought of the line about how he'd indulged her for far too long. If she were honest with herself, he was right. She'd believed her pa would always accept any and everything she did, even if *she* didn't accept all she did. Childish, maybe. But it was her right, she believed. Her right to do something differently from the way Dinah Bright, Mary, or Iris would do them. And Knot still felt—and couldn't imagine herself ever feeling differently—that letting that baby girl go was the most grown-person thing she'd ever done.

"You goin' to have another one of yo' cigarettes?" Knot asked. And when Jo was about to light it, Knot said, "Here."

She struck the match against the White bench and lit Jo's cigarette. Then she lit her pa's letter.

Pa'll come around soon. I know he will. This lil note'll be good as trash.

BACK IN WEST Mills, Knot found housework on both sides of the bridge. Two households, three days a week at both, paid her more than teaching ever had. And now that people had heard that she was well again—free of the pox and with no scars, the rumor went—they began requesting her bread puddings. She had Valley to thank for speaking so highly of them. And to thank him, on the weekend after Thanksgiving, she invited him out for a drink at Miss Goldie's Place.

"Valley!" Knot shouted across the table. The man at the piano was playing heavy-handedly. "Now, I know I been drinkin', but I'm pretty sure you the only man at this table who ain't told me how nice I look tonight."

"It won't do me *or* you any good if I said it," Valley quipped, shaking the dice.

Their eyes met, and they both bent over in howling laughter. The other men at the table looked at each other and shook their heads. By the looks on their faces, one would think they smelled boiled eggs.

"You know what, Knot?" Valley asked. "I look good tonight, too, damnit. *You* ain't said a word 'bout that."

"I got a good reason for that, too," Knot answered. Valley and the others at the table all looked at her, smiling and waiting. "The Bible say, 'Thou shalt not lie'!"

There was raucous laughter at the table. Valley laughed so much that he had to stand up to breathe, bringing a smile to Knot's face. While she had been happy to be back near old-faithful Otis Lee, Valley was the one with whom she had the most fun. He had always accepted Knot just as she was, and she offered him the same courtesy in return.

While Knot had met a few men like Valley—men who shared their beds with other men—he was the only one she'd ever been close to. Soon after Knot had moved to West Mills, she'd met Valley at the schoolhouse, where he had been hired to build a new set of steps for all three entrances.

One day the children had all gone home for supper, and Knot had sat on one of the windowsills eating a cheese sandwich and sipping from the flask she had brought in her cowhide book sack. The first thing Knot had noticed about Valley was his height—six feet three inches, she'd estimated. His pretty face was the runner-up. It looked as though he had never frowned in his life. But when she'd seen how carefully he handled the building materials, and how he had so diligently aligned the steps with the doors, she knew he was also smart. *It might take some time for me to get used to them damn cornrows, though.*

"Valor's my real name," he had said after Knot insisted that he eat her extra cheese sandwich. "I like for people to call me Valley, though."

Valley, she thought. *I think I like the sound of that.*

She told Valley her names, real and preferred. Then she said, "Well, Valley, I guess you know I'm new 'round here. Won't you come by my place this evenin'? I'll cook, and you can tell me what I need to know 'bout this lil town y'all got here."

Valley looked up at Knot from the new steps where he had sat down to eat, and he smiled.

"Try this idea on for size," he said. His voice so raspy, it sounded as though he'd had his first cigarette at the young age of three and hadn't been able to quit. "You come to *my* house this evenin'—since I probably cooks better than you, anyway. And when we get through eatin', we'll have us a drink and talk about things that's usually for just women-folk." He winked at her. Knot could have been knocked over with a dry leaf.

She'd had to settle for Valley's good cooking and good company. But even that had proven to be hit-or-miss: Valley had a lover in Washington, D.C., and was often gone for months at a time, to which Knot eventually grew accustomed.

A couple of weeks after meeting Valley, Knot asked him about her neighbor, Otis Lee Loving.

"We cousins," Valley said. "Well, he ain't my *real* cousin, but his aunt Gertrude's been like a mama to me. Brought me here to West Mills with her when she got tired of New York City. I was still a boy." Valley told Knot that Otis Lee's a good guy. "He on the straight and narrow, though, Knot. Loves his wife and all."

"I ain't askin' 'bout him in *that* way, Val," Knot said. Otis Lee wasn't her type. She wanted there to be no mistake about that. "What I'm gon' do with that short man?"

When she'd first moved onto Antioch Lane, a couple houses away from Otis Lee, he had come over with his little boy on his hip. The welcome he'd extended was sincere, Knot had decided.

"If you need anything, anything at all," Otis Lee said, "you just tap on our door. Me and Pep is there." Knot could tell, on that very day, that Otis Lee was a good man indeed. *A good man and a goddamn stick in the mud.*

One evening, not long after Valley had misunderstood Knot's question about Otis Lee, he told Knot that Otis Lee didn't like him, and it wasn't just because Valley liked men. It had something to do with Otis Lee's aunt Gertrude. Otis Lee had always suspected his aunt of having part in some illegal business. She had come back to West Mills a while before the Depression with so much money, she had been able to buy a piece of land for Miss Noni, Rose and her husband, and Otis Lee to live on.

"The same land they live on now," Valley said. "Them and all them goddamn chickens Otis Lee got. You know he steals them chickens from Pennington's, don't ya?" Knot could have cared less about those chickens.

Gertrude had also bought herself a separate piece of land, where she'd had her own house built. About that, Valley said, "All the land in this town and Gertrude had to buy herself the piece with red clay on it, knowin' it was gon' ruin every shoe she got." Valley had a knack for adding details that Knot believed to be a waste of breath.

When Valley had become a teenager, Gertrude put him up in a rented place on Busy Street—an apartment above the general store.

"Well, how'd Gertrude make all that money?" Knot asked.

"Blackmail," Valley said. "Plain and simple."

He explained to her that in '23, when he was ten years old, he had gone with Gertrude to Brooklyn to see Essie. It was not just an aunt going to visit her niece. Gertrude needed Essie's help because her own small brothel, which was in Queens, had been suffering. The constable was hounding Gertrude for his weekly hush money payment. Essie's brothel in Brooklyn was doing quite well, he said.

"Knot, I'm tellin' ya. They had a big business goin'," Valley went on. "Women, and numbers, and gamblin', and liquor. You name it, Essie and her husband had it."

Gertrude knew Essie and her police officer husband would have plenty of money to spare. Essie had secretly helped Gertrude before. When Gertrude asked for more help, Essie told her that if she couldn't run a whorehouse, maybe she ought to try her luck with something different.

"Essie gave Gertrude forty dollars," Valley said. "I was standin' right there." He told Knot that it all happened on Essie's back stoop. Gertrude had dressed up in a maid's uniform, to make their meeting look as normal as possible. "Essie told Gertrude that the forty dollars was to pay off the policemen, and that was all she had. So, when we got 'bout halfway down the block, Gertrude said, 'Come on,' and we was headin' back to Essie's. I was scared, Knot, 'cause Gertrude could be a piece 'a work when she wanted to be." Gertrude threatened to tell Essie's white police officer husband that his wife was a Negro. Gertrude was also prepared to tell the officer that Essie had a little Negro son.

"Otis Lee," Valley said.

"What about Otis Lee?" Knot asked, confused.

"Otis Lee's the lil Negro son."

"No!"

"Yes!" Valley shouted.

"Otis Lee never tell me that Rose ain't his mama," Knot said. Valley stared back at her, silent.

"He don't know, Val?" Knot asked. Valley shook his head no. "Val, you lyin'!"

"I wish I was," he replied.

He swore her to secrecy.

Valley visited Knot a few times during her pregnancy, before he was to leave for one of his long stays in Washington, D.C. She tried the pillow-holding trick with him, too. Valley looked at her and said, "This pox bullshit you got Otis Lee and Pep tellin' people ain't hittin' on nothin'. I lived with womenfolk most of my life, Knot." He lit a cigarette. The smell almost made her sick. "So you can drop that damn pillow when I visit. You kept the secret I told you 'bout Otis Lee's real mama, so I'll keep yours."

Before Valley left for his long trip, he told Knot to write down the name of the author she liked so much. He promised to send her a new book. Maybe two, he said. Now Valley was back in West Mills, and they were at Miss Goldie's Place having a good time, as though the past year hadn't happened.

"We glad to see you back in here, Knot," Valley said. He shook the dice, called out a number, and dropped them on the table.

"Speak for yo'self," one of the other men at the table teased. Knot couldn't remember his name. *He's a lot of fun to drink with, though.* "I saved up a whole heap of money while you was sick and shut in." Everyone at the table, including Knot, laughed.

"Well," Knot said, "since you got so much saved up, go buy me a drink. You know what I like."

More laughter.

When the man whose name Knot couldn't remember returned to the table after getting Knot's fresh drink, he told her that he, too, was glad to see her alive and well. They clinked their glasses together. She still couldn't remember his name.

There must have been eight or ten dice rolls before Milton Guppy came in and stood next to their table.

"Well, if it ain't the good teacher," Guppy said. There was no question in Knot's mind—which was foggy by now—that Guppy had had more to drink than she. "Beat the pox, did ya?"

Knot did not care for his tone—especially the emphasis he had put on *pox*.

Motherfucker. He wrote the letter, Knot thought. *But how the hell he know?*

"I made it through," she replied. She sat up straight in the chair and squared her shoulders—just as Dinah did when someone was being disagreeable.

"You did more'n make it through," Guppy shot back.

I'm gon' put this drinkin' glass upside his head tonight. I can already see it. Knot looked around the table. Everyone was sitting quietly, frowning.

"Look to me like you come out of it *better*," Guppy went on. A bit of saliva ran from his mouth. "Better off than you was 'fore the pox got to ya."

"Nice of ya to stop by and speak, Mr. Guppy," Knot said. He laughed a dark, mean laugh. "Now go on. I ain't in the mood for it."

"Oh, come on, now," he said. "No need to be like that, good teacher. We go way—"

"They got another game goin', Milton," Valley cut in, "over there at the corner table."

Guppy took a step toward Valley. "Well, I don't reckon I *asked* to know where the other game's at," he said. "But thank ya. What I do want to know is this here, Knot . . ."

And for every step Guppy took toward her, her fist drew tighter around the drinking glass she was holding.

". . . What make you think you can up and quit the job you took from my wife?" he finished.

"Okay, now, Guppy," the man whose name Knot couldn't remember said. "That's enough."

"Naw, it ain't enough, Max," Guppy declared. "I lose my wife and my son 'cause she got that teaching job. And she got nerve to *quit*? I oughta knock her—"

Knot drank the last of what was in her glass, ready to throw it at Guppy. But before she could feel the warmth of that last swallow move down her throat, Valley had jumped on Guppy. She could hear the blows, one after another.

She tried to stand, but she stumbled back into her chair. And the juke joint spun until she closed her eyes. When she reopened them, Miss Goldie had appeared with her club. Valley and Guppy were both dealt a lick on their behinds— hard enough to stop them from fighting.

"Go on up the lane with this shit, boys!" Miss Goldie shouted.

Neither man looked into Miss Goldie's eyes. It was as if they had turned into little boys listening to their mothers yell threats of punishment.

"I want to hear some 'I'm sorrys' right now!" Miss Goldie said. "To me! And to one another! And to my other customers! Or y'all can get out and stay!"

Guppy turned and walked toward the big, heavy door. Knot was certain he was going to call Valley a sissy-fag. So it came as quite a surprise to her when he screeched, "Fuck you and yo' run-down joint, Goldie."

Miss Goldie tapped her club on the floor twice, and her sons-in-law came from their corners. They escorted Guppy out by his arms.

"Walk him all the way home, y'all," Miss Goldie instructed.

Before the heavy door had closed all the way, Knot heard Guppy yell, "Fuck you, too, Miss Centre for comin' back here! A good fuckin' teacher, you are!" Knot could hear him beginning to cry. "My family's gone 'cause of you and that damn teachin' job."

At the bar a few minutes later, Miss Goldie said to Knot, "I wonder if it ain't time for him to move away from here." She was sitting on her stool, smoking a cigar, legs crossed at the knees. Knot sat next to her, on the stool where Guppy often sat.

"Maybe *I* oughta be the one to go," Knot mused.

"He been in here talkin' to me 'bout yo' pox, Knot," Miss Goldie told her. Discreetly, she pointed at Knot's stomach. She had never been one to beat around the bush. "I don't know who else he mighta told."

"My people," Knot said. "Went there and took 'em a letter."

"How you figure that?"

Knot told Miss Goldie all that had happened while she was in Ahoskie, including the wrapped-up man who had passed Dinah the note before running off.

"You hear what he say to me?" Knot asked. "Said, 'Fuck you for comin' back.' That's how I know. He gon' be on my case 'til I'm gone, I believe."

Miss Goldie now sounded even more certain that it was time that Guppy leave West Mills. "They's a lot of things I hate in this world, Knot. But I *really* hate to see a man try to bring a woman down. Now, that shit there, that gets me real mad." She put the cigar out. "Whole lot o' these bastards 'round here got mad at me when I opened this lil shack we sittin' in right now. Told me it should be my husband 'stead of me." She stood up to demonstrate for Knot how she had stood up to one of the men. "You know what I say to that fucker, Knot? I tell him, 'My husband likes that I make my own money so I won't bother his.'" Miss Goldie laughed. "Don't worry yo'self about Guppy, child. Goldie'll 'tend to it. We womenfolk has to stick together, ain't we?"

Knot wasn't sure what that meant, so she didn't say yes.

"You ain't gon' hurt him, is ya?"

"No, child," Miss Goldie reassured her. "I ain't in *that* kinda business." She looked offended. "Guppy owe me a favor or two. Anyhow, if he don't want to listen to me, I know somebody he *will* listen to." She picked a piece of lint from Knot's collar. "I'll 'tend to it."

For reasons Knot couldn't put her finger on, thanking Miss Goldie didn't seem like the right thing to do. And Miss Goldie didn't appear to expect gratitude. Whatever she was planning to do would be done. *Miss Goldie don't beat 'round nobody's bush.*

Knot watched as Valley plunged his right hand into a silver pail half filled with iced water. The pail was much like the one she'd seen outside of Otis Lee's chicken coop, half filled with corn.

"This shit's cold," Valley said, clenching his teeth. He looked as though he were smiling. Then he averted his gaze from the pail, which made Knot wonder if there was something nasty in it—something aside from his puffy fist.

"Hold it there for at least two—three minutes if ya can," Max told him. "Then you be ready for ya next match." He patted Valley on the back.

Valley and Max would not stop talking about the fight, so Knot went to the bar, ordered a drink, and sat there to enjoy it. Alone. The whiff of familiar cologne interrupted her second swallow of brandy, a drink she'd grown to like more than she'd expected. The arousing scent made her think of Pratt.

Why, though? Pratt ain't wore a drop of cologne the whole time I knew him. Goddamn Pratt Shepherd.

Knot asked the man tending the bar—his was another name she'd forgotten—if he would open another window to let more cool air in. It was steaming hot in there, she said.

"Look around, Knot," he said. And she did, but it was the people talking, laughing, dancing, and drinking she noticed more. Not the windows. "They's all open. Every last one of 'em is open to ya."

THE NIGHT'S COOL fall air met Knot at the door, kissing her on both cheeks. The danger she'd always been warned about all her life—*You'll catch your death, child, going outside damp*—was for those who didn't spend time in small juke joints. Knot sat on the one chair Miss Goldie allowed people to bring outside. She closed her eyes and aimed her face toward what stars might be looking down on her.

"I would escort you home," a man said, "but your husband might not take too kindly to it." Knot opened her eyes. Delaware William stood there with his hands in his pockets, that nice familiar scent standing there with him.

Knot looked him over and wondered if he lived in a barbershop or a tailor shop. *Got to be one of the two.*

"I ain't got no damn husband," she replied, trying to get up. Delaware William helped her to her feet. Without thanking him, she turned and walked toward her house. When she didn't hear him following her, she said, "Come on, if you comin'."

KNOT WAS FAMISHED.

In her kitchen she sat across the table from Delaware William, her eyes transfixed on his beauty—a beauty she'd forgotten, though he had not forgotten hers, he said.

"You a pretty woman, Knot."

"How you know to call me by that?" she asked.

"I listened, that's all."

They shared the Granny Smith apple Delaware William had cut into two unequal pieces. Knot used the smaller chunk as a spoon to scoop the custard she'd made earlier that day— she was tired of making bread pudding—into his mouth. He rolled his eyes toward the back of his head, causing Knot to smile, unable to pull her lips together. With the other apple chunk, Delaware William returned the favor.

Now on the same side of the table as him, Knot strad-dled him in a way she didn't even know she could. She wrapped her arms around his wide back and pulled his chest against hers. Her breasts were no longer sore and she liked their new size.

Delaware William pulled away slightly and began to unbutton her dress. For every button he unfastened, Knot felt tiny tremors all over. Once the top half of her dress was around her waist like a belt and he had tilted her back, Knot felt his warm mouth on her left nipple, his tongue swiveling. The breast quivered on the inside.

Don't let no man in yo' bed for a good while, Knot remem-bered Pep saying to her a few weeks after she'd given birth to Lady Waters's baby. *You'll be big again, easy.*

"You know what to do when ya love comin', don't ya?" Knot said to Delaware William. He nodded his head yes and they went to bed.

Knot had her way with Delaware William, and she allowed him to have his way with her. He fell asleep smiling.

In the morning she heard him stirring around in the kitchen. He was humming, too. He hummed and sang as though he knew she was enjoying it. When she kissed the crease in his back—he hadn't heard her approach—he stopped. He was spreading butter on pieces of white bread.

"What ya stop for?" she asked. "You don't sound half-bad."

He laid the butter knife and bread on the table, turned to face her, and sang a beautiful melody she'd never heard. She backed up into the bedroom, leading him, and he sang all the way.

Delaware William was Knot's guest for almost a week. As much as she enjoyed his company, she was not unhappy to see him go. And she loved the good-smelling scent he had left on her sheets.

EIGHT

In mid-November of '42, Otis Lee invited Brock and Ayra Manning over for dinner. By mistake, he had mentioned the upcoming gathering to Ma Noni. She tried to invite herself, but he told her he wanted to talk to the Mannings about a private matter, which only made her more persistent.

"You just as well to go 'head and tell her," Rose advised from her rocking chair. She was rocking and biting her nails. "She'll just worr' ya half to death 'til you do."

"Shut up, Rose," Ma Noni said. And when Otis Lee told them what the private matter was, Ma Noni said, "Well, I s'pose I'll make you a lil pound cake for yo' guests. Y'all gon' need somethin' to sweeten them up."

"Knot gon' be there?" Rose asked, rocking.

"I think I oughta talk to 'em first, just me and Pep," Otis Lee said.

Later that evening, after the plates were cleared, there they all sat bunched around the small, rectangular table: Otis Lee, Pep, Brock, Ayra, and Breezy. Everyone had had a piece of Ma Noni's pound cake, and it was time for Otis Lee to send Breezy upstairs to write his name and his numbers. He promised Breezy that he would give him two pieces of candy if he wrote everything nice and neat.

"I'll come help ya," Pep said to Breezy.

"Penelope," Otis Lee said. Pep went up the steps with her son. It was as though she hadn't heard Otis Lee call her name. Before the Mannings had arrived, Pep had warned Otis Lee that he'd be on his own after dinner.

Brock and Ayra sat looking at Otis Lee as if he were a pastor and they were waiting on the Word.

"Y'all get enough to eat?" Otis Lee asked.

"Uh, if I know you good as I think I know you," Brock began. He had picked up the habit of saying *uh* when he spoke. "I b'lieve you, uh, got some, uh, bad news for us or something."

"Depends," Otis Lee said. Brock asked Otis Lee if he needed a loan. "You know damn well I don't need no loan, Brock."

"Well, uh, how I know that?"

"What's the problem, Otis Lee?" Ayra asked.

"Another baby's comin'."

The Mannings both smiled, and they congratulated Otis Lee.

"Noooooo. Not *us*," Otis Lee corrected. "Knot's got another one comin', and I—well, she was wonderin' if—hell, y'all already know what I want to ask. Same thing she wanted from Phil and Lady."

Brock pulled a handkerchief from his shirt pocket and wiped his forehead and the rolls on his neck. Then he rested his hands on his large stomach, which Otis Lee felt Brock was far too young to have. Otis Lee was ready for the many questions and the many *uh*'s Brock would have for him.

"Uh," Brock said. "What I, uh, want to know is, uh, why do Knot—"

"Hush, Brock," Ayra broke in. Otis Lee couldn't be happier with Ayra at that moment. Of Otis Lee she asked, "When?"

Ayra was a straight-to-the-point kind of person, which Otis Lee respected, but sometimes he wished she'd allow a conversation to take what he believed to be its natural course. She was a self-made businesswoman, Brock often said; Otis Lee never quite understood what that meant, especially since Ayra—born and raised in West Virginia—had grown up as a sharecropper, much like him and Brock. Many times he'd heard Ayra say, "Time's money, and money's lost when time's wasted."

Otis Lee had always hated that expression.

Like Knot, Ayra had been taught to read at an early age, and she was even better at arithmetic. Ayra's father hadn't cared much for Brock at first, Brock had told Otis Lee and Phil years ago. But when Brock had convinced Leland Edgars Jr., a white shopkeeper, to sell him the general store, Ayra's father had changed his tune.

Otis Lee felt confident that Ayra would be a great mother, especially to a child who would likely be born smart.

"Pep say the baby'll be here 'round the end of April, early May, by the looks of things," Otis Lee told them.

"Tell Knot my answer's yes," Ayra said, and she got to her feet.

"Uh, uh, Ayra," Brock said, looking up at her, "we gon' need to discuss this, ain't we?"

Otis Lee didn't know how much discussing they would do, because Ayra seemed to have already made up her mind when they left his house, which did not surprise him. When Breezy was born, Brock had told Otis Lee—and he'd made

Otis Lee swear on his life that he'd never tell a soul—that Ayra was of two minds about motherhood.

"She, uh," Brock had said, "she don't want to ever be in the family way. Said she wish the baby'll just show up without it needin' her body to get here."

Otis Lee, having heard Pep tell several stories about her line of work, hadn't pressed any further and just replied, "Yeah."

Brock had also said, "Yeah."

AN HOUR AFTER the dinner with the Mannings, Otis Lee sat downstairs in the kitchen, thinking about Knot. He would walk over to her house soon to tell her that her second baby would have a home.

I can't make good sense of any of it. What she want? Pep had told him time and time again that Knot's wants were just that—Knot's wants. And he agreed. *But she my neighbor. She my friend. And her people put her down and all. I got to look after her.*

He heard a knock at the door. He thought it might be Knot coming to ask how the meeting had gone with the Mannings. But it wasn't Knot; it was his mother.

"Get a coat on and come walk with me," Rose said.

It had been so long since she had invited him, or anybody, to join her for a night walk. When Otis Lee was a little boy, he would hear her get up in the middle of the night, three or four times each week. He'd ask where she going, and she would tell him to go back to sleep. It wasn't until he was seven years old that she first let him bundle up and walk with her. On the night of one of Otis Lee's birthdays—he could not remember whether it was his eleventh or his twelfth—she had cried quite a bit while they walked.

"What's the matter, Mama?" he had asked. She didn't answer him, but he figured that it had something to do with a note that had come in the post earlier that week. Otis Lee remembered that Rose and Ma Noni had fussed about it. He had heard Ma Noni say, "I don't want to hear nothin' 'bout you scared. You ought to never went 'long with that lie from the first!"

Otis Lee never got a clear understanding of the argument. He had asked Rose about it, in the days after that birthday, but she had said, "Grown folks' business, baby. You not s'pose to ask about grown folks' business. Let that be the last time you do. Hear?" So, all these years later, when Otis Lee's mother knocked on the door that belonged to him—a grown person—he still felt it wrong to ask: *What's the matter, Mama?*

"I think what you doin' to help Knot is real good of you," she told him, "but you got to let her look out for herself, and her own business. She a grown woman that do grown woman thangs." She rubbed her hands together and put them in her coat pockets. "You don't want to be caught up in other folks' lies and secrets. Ain't a good feelin' to keep stuff in ya."

She reminded him of the pain he had felt when he went off to New York to find Essie. Otis Lee had cried to his mother because he felt as though he had failed her. Rose had asked him how he could fail her at something she hadn't even asked him to do.

"If Knot stay in West Mills to see them babies grown," Rose said, "people gon' be mad with her, and maybe mad at you, too." *But, Mama, why you never say nothin' 'bout your daughter runnin' off to pass and leavin' us like she did?* "Secrets don't stay that way forever, Otis Lee."

Otis Lee tried to remember a time when he had heard his mother speak so much at once, but he couldn't; he could not recall a single instance.

"Faithful Otis Lee," she called him before she kissed his forehead the way she had when he was a boy. "You still my Faithful Otis Lee. Your daddy'd be proud if he was here to see you."

From his mother and grandmother's house, he walked toward Knot's. But before he arrived, he stood on the lane's shoulder thinking. *She ain't said nothin' about my daddy in years.*

In May of '43, Otis Lee sat on Knot's porch and waited for her second child to be born. When he heard the healthy cries, he felt his shoulders relax. Otis Lee did not ask for Pep's permission to enter the house. From the porch, he'd heard her cooing along with the newborn.

"Boy or girl?" Otis Lee asked, his back turned toward Knot's bedroom door. He heard Pep coming toward him with the baby.

"Another lil woman," Pep answered. "Here. Hol' her while I go finish up with Knot."

"Ev'rything's all right, ain't it?"

"Yeah," Pep reassured him. "She just got to do the last part. Sit down there." She pointed at a chair in Knot's kitchen. "You can finishing cleanin' her." And a minute later Pep brought Otis Lee a pan of warm water and a clean rag. "Wipe her gentle, now. Not too—"

"I remember," Otis Lee said. "I sure do remember."

This baby girl was smaller than Frances, but she was strong. Her arms and legs moved as though she were trying to leap from the blanket and run away.

"You got yo' mama's chin, lil gal," Otis Lee whispered.

He heard Knot grunt. Then a sigh of relief.

"Well done," he heard Pep say.

Now walking slowly around Knot's kitchen table, he said to the baby, "Did ya mama see that chin she give to ya? Hmm?"

Pep bathed Knot, and when the room was back in order, Otis Lee went in. Knot looked much better. Not as tired and sad as she had the first time. If she'd said she was happy, he'd have believed it.

"Bring her," Knot said.

Otis Lee didn't understand. But Knot had asked for her baby. *Thank you, God!*

"I say bring her," Knot said again. But he couldn't move. *Why can't I move?* Had the happiness caused his knees and legs to lock?

In disbelief, Otis Lee watched his wife as she laid the baby next to Knot and covered them both with a sheet. Otis Lee heard the child feeding. But when she was finished and had belched—she belched on her own—Pep picked her up.

"Go get Ayra and Brock," Pep said. Otis Lee almost gasped for air. "This lil woman's ready to go home."

"Knot?" he said.

She slid to the edge of the bed and looked at him. If she had blinked, he'd missed it, but he was almost certain that she hadn't. The assured look on her face made it difficult for Otis Lee to swallow.

"You got somethin' to say?" Knot asked.

Damn right I got somethin' to say, Knot! You can be a good mother. I know you can! You got all the help you need, right here in this room, and in ya heart.

He looked at Pep and thought about what his mother had said to him on the night he'd had the Mannings over for dinner.

"Naw, Knot," Otis Lee replied. "I ain't got nothin' to say."

Up-bridge at Manning's General Store, Otis Lee found Brock sweeping glass from the porch. Another window had been shattered.

"You, uh, you don't look like you come with good news," Brock said.

"Look to me like *you* the one got bad news," Otis Lee retorted. "What happened here?"

Two teenaged boys had come into the store to buy candy that wasn't sold on the east side of the bridge. One of them, a Pennington, told Ayra one too many times that she was beautiful. The boy said that if he were older, or if Ayra were younger, he'd visit her store every day of the week.

"So, I, uh, tell the boy to take the candy, and his money, and go on somewhere 'fore he start somethin' I got to finish," Brock said. The boy who had not been flirting with Ayra told the Pennington that they had better leave, Brock told him.

"Course he, uh, called us 'nigger' a few times on their way out of the store. And, uh, 'bout ten, fifteen minutes after that, a pop bottle come right through this window." He shook his head. "Some of 'em still mad 'cause Leland Jr. sell me this place. If they ain't breakin' the window 'bout one thing, they, uh, break it 'bout somethin' else. Comes 'long with the territory, I guess."

Otis Lee thought it awfully sad that a fifteen-year-old flirting with a man's wife, calling that man and his wife niggers, and disturbing their business "came with the territory."

"What ya know good?" Brock said.

"They's a strong lil girl waitin' on y'all," Otis Lee announced. He wished he could say it with a little more joy.

"It's here!" Brock shouted, leaning the broom against the wall. It fell and made a popping sound on the porch. "Ayra!"

Otis Lee heard Ayra running through the store, her shoes' heels sounded as if they would break through the floor. She flung the screen door open and it hit Brock on the knee. Neither of them seemed to care. Brock took both of Ayra's hands in his, and the two of them danced in a circle just like small children. The customers came out and stood around them.

"Didn't I tell you them two crazy?" one customer said to another. Otis Lee heard that and it made him smile.

"Y'all gon' dance all day, or we goin' to the lane?" Otis Lee asked. They ignored him. He didn't bother them again for a few minutes. Seeing his two friends hopping and skipping around gave him more joy. And he hoped that his other friend, Knot, would soon find the thing or person to give her joy.

NINE

If cleaning houses, selling bread pudding, and reading long novels and the occasional letters she received from Iris took up half of Knot's time, drinking and watching the two baby girls grow took up the other half.

Did she watch because she wanted to? *No.* Why, then? *Because it's West Mills.* Every once in a while she invited a nice, handsome man to her home after an evening out at Miss Goldie's Place. But fearing a third pregnancy, she'd asked Pep for advice.

"Sleep in yo' own bed *by yo'self*," Pep had told her. "That there's my advice."

The two arm babies, Frances and Eunice, quickly grew into hip babies. Then they were walking babies. And before long the two walking babies became schoolgirls. *I'm glad I ain't workin' at the damn schoolhouse. Shit.*

When Knot heard people say that six-year-old Frances—Phillip and Lady called her *Fran*—could play the piano as though she'd had lessons before birth, she remembered Pratt sitting at Miss Goldie's piano and playing until he'd nearly fall asleep or until his hands began to hurt. He would ask Knot to rub and squeeze them for him. *That damn Pratt. Seem to me like he'd at least write to the Lovings and let 'em know something, if he's livin'.*

After hearing that five-year-old Eunice Manning sang hymns just as well as Gertrude Ward, she knew why. *Course she can. Delaware William hummed or sang me to sleep every night that week.*

I done right by them lil girls, she thought to herself one night on her way home from the juke joint. *Who gon' argue with that?*

Sometimes, when Knot happened upon the Mannings' up-bridge on Busy Street, she'd see Eunice jumping rope or reading a book outside on the store's porch. On one occasion Knot walked close enough to Eunice to see her own chin on Delaware William's face. Knot laughed quietly—or so she thought. It turned out to be loud enough for Eunice to hear. The girl had given Knot a mean stare. *That's Dinah Bright right there.* Since Knot lived close to Fran, she saw her several times a week—every day, almost.

"Hey, Miss Knot," Fran often said when Knot passed the house. Knot tried her best not to draw the girl's attention, but Lady and Phillip had raised Fran with good manners. The little girl greeted everyone she saw.

Pa would have loved her.

ON A SUMMER afternoon in '48, a few days after Knot had received yet another RETURN TO SENDER-stamped envelope from her pa—it had been the thirtieth, or the thirty-first, she'd lost count—she and Valley lay in her backyard on the yellow quilt Iris had given to her. They shared a glass of the red wine that Valley had brought home from D.C. Knot only had one flute, and Valley refused to drink it from a jar.

On a whim, when Valley had arrived in her yard earlier that day, Knot decided to tell him that another returned letter had arrived. Just as he had years ago, when returned letter number twelve had come, he'd said, "It'll be all right. You watch and see. He'll get his senses back together. You gon' always be his baby girl." Otis Lee had said the same, which made Knot think it was sad that he and Valley were so estranged.

As much as she appreciated their condolences for the continued loss of her relationship with her pa, she wanted them to stop. The lashing out at little Breezy for talking back to his pa, the drunken lectures she'd given up-bridge about how her father did every little thing Dinah Bright told him to do, and the ripping up of letters from her sisters—who still had daily contact with her pa—had stopped. Knot just wanted to move on from that pain. So today, already regretting that she had even mentioned the returned mail, she thanked Valley and asked him to kindly shut up about it. And he did.

"This here's good wine, Knot."

"Go 'head, Val. Say it a third time."

"Well, it is," he said. "Like what the rich folk drink."

"Says who?" she asked.

"Says the man I got it from, for a dollar." Valley laughed at his own joke.

While the warm grass tickled her feet, Knot endured Valley's chatter about the war, of which he seemed to know very little. And if his war chatter wasn't offensive enough, there was his sneezing. Pollen.

"So you all right, you say?" he asked.

"I'm fine," Knot insisted. "Please don't ask me again. *Please.*"

"I'm gon' ask as many times as I feel the *need* to," Valley told her. "He's ya pa. You got to have some kinda feelin' about it. Hell, *I* would. All them damn envelopes."

She had more than a feeling about it. There were three: confusion, betrayal, and guilt. They weren't new. Just back, like old friends you didn't miss.

But if Knot had been asked to name a winning feeling, it would not be confusion, betrayal, or guilt. *Hurt. Hurt is the winner.* The same hurt that urged her to spend less time with Valley, less time visiting the Lovings, less time talking with the friendly people in town who had shown her nothing but kindness. To spend more time at her kitchen table with a bottle and a chilled glass.

"I *do* wish you'd let up 'bout me and my pa, Valor."

"Well," he said as if he hadn't heard her, "at least ya sistas still nice to ya." Then he sneezed. They lay there silently for a few minutes, passing the flute back and forth. "You know what, Knot? I think I'll join the service. Air Force."

Knot rolled her eyes at him and said, "Boy, please. You ain't joinin' shit. Hand me that glass."

"It's a flute," he retorted. Before he handed it to her, he examined it closely. "Where you get this flute, Knot? It look like—"

"Yours," Knot affirmed. She had taken it from his apartment the last time he'd written and asked her to go and make sure he had emptied all the food from his icebox. Then she said, "Don't be a fool like Pratt. With this *service* talk, I mean."

"Military ain't foolish," Valley shot back. Then he sneezed.

"We probably live in one of the few places in this whole damn country that live our lives the same, war or no war. Why can't folk live well enough alone?"

"See, now *you* the one talkin' foolish," Valley said. "We all takes a hit some kinda way when there's war." He sneezed again, then took the flute from Knot's hand.

There had to be some truth in what Valley had just said, she imagined. But since he'd said he didn't want to discuss it any further, which was fine with her, she decided not to tell him.

Just as Knot was about to turn onto her back and close her eyes, she looked up and saw Fran coming toward them. *She probably heard his loud-ass sneezin'.* The child came with a purpose. Knot could see it in her walk.

"Miss Knot!" Fran shouted. She had on a cute pair of overalls to match the ones Phil wore when he worked in his garden. And Lady had put two pretty ponytails on both sides of Fran's head. White ribbons on each. "I got a idea."

"Well, hurry up if you gon' tell it," Knot told her. "Me and Valley talkin' grown folk business. And he don't feel good. Don't you hear him sneezin'?"

Fran narrowed her eyes at Knot and Valley and sucked her teeth.

"Never mind," she said, walking away.

Valley laughed and sneezed.

On any other day Knot would have let the girl go back home without a word of protest. But there was something about the way Fran didn't seem to need Knot to hear the idea that made Knot want to hear it. She found herself wanting to hear it badly.

"Don't 'Never mind' me, lil woman," Knot said. "Tell me your idea."

Fran turned around, but it didn't look as though she planned to walk back over to them. Her two ponytails were swinging just enough for Knot to notice.

"Let's us be best friends," Fran suggested. "Like you and Mr. Valley."

When Knot glanced over at Valley, he was looking at Fran as though he wanted to pick her up and kiss both her cheeks. *Where'd the sneezing go?*

No one had asked Knot to be their best friend since she was a small girl herself—around Fran's age. Even Valley hadn't proposed best friendship to Knot.

At least half of Knot's childhood flashed before her as she lay there looking at the first little girl she had carried inside her, pushed out, and given to the neighbors.

"Tell me one thing," Knot said. "How many grown womenfolk you know that's got a lil girl for they best friend?"

Fran looked at Knot as though she were waiting for a point to be made. Valley covered his face.

It was evident by the little girl's frown that she would not be leaving until she'd heard Knot's decision.

"Listen," Knot said. "If I'm still livin' when you get to be grown, and if you stay outta my business, maybe we'll see about bein' friends. How's that?"

Fran propped her hands on her tiny waist and declared, "That's too long."

She skipped away as though she had better things to do.

Valley passed the flute to Knot. There was enough for one more swallow. "She got her own mind, don't she?" he remarked. "Just like somebody else I—"

"Go to hell, Val," Knot said. Valley laughed and sneezed again.

The cool soil felt wonderful beneath Knot's toes when she dug them past the warm grass. *Seeing that girl mighta been what I needed today*, she thought.

"What you got goin' on in yo' head, Knot?" Valley asked. He had lain flat on his back and put his hat over his face. Knot didn't answer him. She had lied enough for one day.

That's too long, Fran had said to her. But Knot knew it wouldn't be very long at all, with the way time passed so quickly.

As SURE AS the sun rose in the morning and fell in the evening, twelve years later, in 1960, on a day that seemed to have gone by too fast, Knot sat on her porch and wondered how on earth she had lived long enough to see her girls become young ladies pretending to be grown women. Eunice was seventeen, singing in and directing three choirs. Fran was eighteen, the pianist for two of those same three choirs.

Lord, have mercy.

"There's trouble," Valley said to Knot one evening as she sat at the counter at Miss Goldie's Place. "And since you ain't mentioned it, I'm guessin' you don't know."

"I wish you'd stop with the damn preamble and tell me, Val," Knot said.

He had heard that Fran and Eunice's cordial childhood camaraderie had come to an abrupt end.

"Why?"

"You mean to tell me you ain't heard *nothin'*?" Valley asked. "Not *one word* of it?"

"Valor!"

"Well," he whispered, "you ain't gon' like it one bit. But it's over a boy."

The idea that Fran and Eunice had reached an age for falling in love made Knot feel old. But hearing that Fran and Eunice had fallen in love with the same tall, slim, gingerbread-skinned man with eyes that looked like watered-down black tea made Knot hold her head.

All the boys in this town, and they both want Robert "Breezy" Loving.

Knot felt as though there were a Jane Austen novel being played out there on Antioch Lane. She went back to reading Dickens.

Part
Two

TEN

On an unusually cool day in June of 1960, Otis Lee, while at work, thought about how grateful he was that he and his family lived in a fairly peaceful town. He'd heard stories about the young colored people in Greensboro who had organized a sit-in a couple months earlier. "A terrible thing," he'd lamented to Pep one evening, "the things that got said and done to them young folk. They 'bout Breezy's age, you know?" And Pep had said, "I know, love." Otis Lee hadn't been called a nigger to his face since he was a teenager living in Brooklyn, New York.

While he knew his son had not completely escaped the harsh tongues and glares of some of the whites on the east side of the canal, Greensboro hadn't come to them yet. And Otis Lee hoped things would get better so that it wouldn't have to.

That day Otis Lee also thought a lot about getting home. It was his birthday, and Pep had told him that she would make him a very special meal.

"Got us some new seasonings from Ayra," she had said that morning. "She say we gon' want it on everything we eat after we try it." She would use them on a hen, she said. She also promised him a bit of birthday loving, which he was most excited about. Pep had not required, nor had she seemed interested in, much bedroom time from Otis Lee in the past few years. So when she mentioned the birthday loving, he smiled so much that his cheeks were sore by the time he arrived at Pennington Farm.

"Mind if I knock off a lil early today?" Otis Lee asked Mr. Pennington. "My birthday."

"I can do you one better, Otis," Pennington said. Otis Lee had told Pennington many times that Otis Lee, for him, was like a first name, not a first and middle. "I'll give you a ride right to your very door, if that's what you need."

During the ride, Pennington asked Otis Lee his age.

"I made it to fifty-two, sir," Otis Lee answered.

"Well," Pennington said, "If you'd waited just one more week to be born, you and me coulda been twins. I'm a '08 baby, too."

Pennington began talking about how they were both getting on in age and how much times, and West Mills, had changed since they were boys. Although they had been born and raised within a mile of each other, Otis Lee had never met Riley Pennington until the day Big Riley hired him in 1927, just after Otis Lee's return from New York.

"Otis," Pennington said, lighting a cigarette and using his knee to steady the steering wheel, "you remember when West Mills had just one general store?"

"I certainly do. Leland Edgars's store."

"Yeah," Pennington said. "He gave it to that boy and his wife."

"He sell it," Otis Lee corrected. His legs became restless.

"He do what?"

"Leland Edgars *sell* it to my friend *Mister* Brock Manning and his wife, *Missus* Ayra Manning." Otis Lee kept his eyes on the road. But more than once he could see Pennington glance over at him.

"I suppose you're right, Otis," Pennington agreed. "Nobody gives away a business, do they?"

Pennington spoke about the handful of small businesses that had opened on the west side of the canal in the past four or five years: a new gas station for coloreds with a pool hall in the back, a bakery . . . The Mannings had changed the store's name to Manning's General Store, and the old schoolhouse had been enlarged. Otis Lee remembered that there was somewhere he needed to go before heading home, so he asked to be dropped off at the church.

"No problem at all, Otis. No problem."

When Otis Lee was out of the truck, Pennington said, "I don't mean to be rude, Otis, but can I ask you why you comin' to an empty church on a Tuesday afternoon? And on your birthday?"

Otis Lee pointed toward a bevy of headstones set off in the back corner of the churchyard.

"Well, I wouldn't be here to have a birthday if it hadn't been for some people back there in them graves."

Pennington and Otis Lee shared a look of understanding, and they shook hands.

Though it could not have been more than ten yards, the walk from the church's front yard to the cemetery felt like a mile to Otis Lee's tired legs and feet. First, he visited his father's grave. Then he stood between his mother's and grandmother's graves. *Time don't belong to none of us. Don't love us, neither.*

Rose had been dead five years. An enlarged heart, the doctor had said. By that time, Ma Noni no longer knew who Rose or anyone else was. Going to the corner of his sitting room—which was where Ma Noni's bed was set up when he and Pep had moved her in with them—and telling her that another one of her children had died before her would have been a waste of sadness, best saved for someone who could feel it.

A month before Ma Noni died, Otis Lee watched Knot feed her the bread pudding she had been asking for. After only one teaspoon, Ma Noni gripped Knot's wrist and said, "Essie."

"Now, I know you ain't forgot me that quick, Miss Noni," Knot said. "It's me: Knot."

"That ain't Essie, Ma," Otis Lee added. "This here's our friend Knot. Remember Knot?"

Ma Noni stared at Otis Lee. She stared into his eyes as though they were speaking words that only she could hear.

"Come get this baby, Essie."

Otis Lee could see that her hold on Knot's wrist was tight. Knot was struggling to pull her arm away.

"Essie, come on here and get this baby. Hear?"

Once Knot had pried herself from Ma Noni and handed Otis Lee the bowl of pudding, she left his house without a word.

"Ma Noni," he said. "That was Knot. You helped Knot wit' her first baby. I think you remembers a lil of it today."

Ma Noni looked off at the wall. "Tell Essie come get her baby."

Soon after Rose was buried, Otis Lee received a sympathy card from Essie. The envelope read *O'Heeney*, with the address below. How she had learned of Rose's passing, Otis Lee never figured out. Essie had written a brief note inside, simple enough for him to read on his own. *She was the best mother in the world*, the note read.

The two hundred dollars she'd placed inside the card infuriated Otis Lee, and he planned to return it. But Pep said, "You crazy? That'll pay off most of the bill we got up there at Hobson's. Caskets ain't made outta flour and water, Otis Lee."

Otis Lee wondered what Essie had told her husband about her family life. He had never asked her that question on their occasional quick talks when he worked in her house. He imagined that Essie must have told O'Heeney that she had been orphaned or something similar.

One morning in Brooklyn, Otis Lee was sweeping the brothel's front stoop and O'Heeney came home from wherever he had been all night. O'Heeney rarely greeted Otis Lee, but when he was in a good mood he would do more than greet. He sometimes gave Otis Lee an earful about things Otis Lee did not understand. *Senator So-and-so*, and *Congressman This-and-that*.

"You know, boy," O'Heeney said, "I swear I know you from somewhere, but there's no way. I've never had much dealings with you all." By then Otis Lee had been living in their brothel for more than six months.

OTIS LEE LOOKED down at the headstones. He missed his mother and grandmother more than he could ever put into words, even to himself. *What I'd do to have me a piece of Ma*

Noni's pound cake and to hear Mama complain 'bout how Ma Noni made pound cake too much. Otis Lee closed his eyes and whispered a prayer, thanking God for another year.

Otis Lee held two fingers to his lips, kissed them, and touched all three headstones. With his handkerchief, he dried his face of sweat and tears before turning toward Antioch Lane and walking home, where he'd find Pep, the only girl his mother and grandmother approved of. If Pep had decided not to bake a single crumb for him, and if she had decided not to touch him for another year, he would not mind. He simply wanted to get home to her.

When he got closer to the house, he heard Pep inside. She was not practicing "Happy Birthday to You." He heard her say, "Boy, what's ailin' you?" He hadn't heard her speak with such anger in all the years they'd been married. "And you best tell it right the first time!" Pep yelled to Breezy. "Why'd you have both of 'em in my yard, anyway?"

"What's wrong in here?" Otis Lee asked. Pep was standing eye to eye with their son. As broad-shouldered and strong as Breezy looked, he appeared boyish in front of his mother.

"I ain't have *them* in your yard," Breezy replied.

When Otis Lee heard how Breezy had said *them*—with far too much timbre in his voice, and with his chest poked out a little too far—he knew Pep's open right hand would soon find Breezy's left cheek.

A few minutes after Pep's slap, Breezy said, "I just invited *one* of 'em, and Eunice showed up startin' trouble."

Pep said she was sure it was him who had started the trouble.

"You always got to have two," she accused. "Two of everything."

"But, Ma, I ain't—"

"Shut up!" she shouted. "Never thought I'd ever come home and see folk fightin' in my yard like they crazy."

When Otis Lee heard the part about a fight, he asked, "Who was fightin'?"

"The girls," Pep replied. She hadn't taken her eyes off their son.

"What girls, Pep?"

"Fran and Eunice," Pep said. "Fightin' out there in my yard over this one here." She pointed at their son. She whacked him on the shoulder, and he winced.

Otis Lee looked at Breezy, not knowing what to say to the young man at first. Then he did. "Boy, is you lost yo' damn mind? Ain't you tol' me all them dealings was done wit'?"

"He better put a stop to this mess right now," Pep said. "'Cause I won't have—"

"Hush up a minute, Pep, would ya? Please?"

Breezy tried to speak, but Pep told him to get out of her sight. And when he had gone out the back door, Otis Lee said, "How you know I ain't want to ask him a question or two?"

"Ought not be no questions," she argued. "Ought to be orders."

Her voice was trembling now, and Otis Lee knew she was more hurt than mad. He knew because he was hurt, too. Two girls whom he loved like nieces had been fighting. And they'd been fighting because his only son hadn't learned to make a decision like a grown man.

When Otis Lee went outside, he saw Breezy sitting on the porch steps, looking as though he had been wronged. Otis Lee picked up his pail and began tossing corn to his cluckers, and Breezy came over to him, ready to explain, it seemed. It reminded Otis Lee of one of his last talks with Pratt. *I damn sure wish Pratt was here. Maybe he'd 'tend to his daughter.*

"Well," Otis Lee said. "What you got to say for yo'self?" Breezy had folded his arms across the same chest he had poked out toward Pep. "Unfold ya damn arms when I'm talkin' to you. I ain't one of the fellas." Breezy put his hands in his pockets. Then Otis Lee went on, "You walk 'round here like the world's yours just 'cause you a lil bit pretty. Lot more things goin' on in the world 'sides bein' pretty and havin' women."

"Pop—"

"You know it's young fellas your age fightin' for rights? Gettin' hot coffee poured on top they heads? Young ladies, too!"

"That's what you want me to do?" Breezy countered. "Go piss off some white boys so they can pour coffee on me and spit in my face?"

"Naw," Otis Lee said, "but open your eyes, boy. This world ain't gon' always give ya everything you want."

Breezy said he hadn't done anything wrong, which caused Otis Lee to set the bucket of feed on the ground.

"I love both of 'em," Breezy professed.

"That don't matter, Breezy. Whole lot of men love more'n one woman. Can't have both the women you love."

Otis Lee went back to throwing feed to his cluckers, and for a moment he wondered how his own father—who never got to see Otis Lee as a young man—would handle this.

When Otis Lee looked back up at his son, he found that Breezy had his arms folded across his chest again and was looking at Otis Lee as though he had caught him stealing.

"What's wrong wit' you?" Otis Lee said.

"So I can't have everything I want, but you can?"

"The hell you talkin' 'bout, boy?" He stepped closer to Breezy.

And Breezy said, "Knot."

ELEVEN

Among the pastimes Knot had taken up recently, there was daily apple eating while reading the newspaper. Most days she did that inside, but today she sat on the edge of her porch. There was an article on the front page about a bank that would break ground on the east side of the bridge within the next month. The write-up said that all would be welcome at the bank and that all would be treated equally. On the other side of that page was an article about the sit-ins. Knot shook her head and took a bite out of her apple.

Carefully, not wanting to rip the paper, as she had the day before, Knot turned the page, hoping to find something that might make her laugh: a comic strip, a crime report of a foolish perpetrator, something like that. But before she was able to run her eyes across A-2, she looked up and saw Otis Lee coming her way. *What he got in that potato sack today?* It was probably a chicken that he'd ask her to cook and to bring him and Pep a taste of once she had. It was his way of making sure she was eating more than apples, she had decided. Or his way of making sure Knot wasn't trading the chicken for something strong to wet her whistle, as he sometimes put it. "I ain't doin' no such thing, gal," he had said when she confronted him with her theory. "You grown. I ain't yo' father."

Today, Otis Lee was approaching with a frown. It had rained almost all day, which had surely made his work difficult. And now she would have to hear all about it. Otis Lee handed her the sack and said, "A goose in there for ya."

Wondering why he had come to her with a goose, Knot said, "What the hell you bring me a goose for?"

Otis Lee told Knot that he had first asked Pep if she wanted the goose. He went on and on about making sure Pep had what she needed and wanted first. To Knot, he was talking about Pep as if he had been married for only a week.

"'Cause Pep's my wife. The one and only," he proclaimed.

Knot chose not to interrupt. Years ago she had noticed that he sometimes talked in circles when he was tired or frustrated about one thing or another.

"What's that got to do with you bringin' me a goose?" Knot wanted to know.

He reminded Knot that she had mentioned months ago how much she would love to have a pot of goose and dumplings. Dinah's goose and dumplings had been the last she'd eaten. That was the last meal she'd had with Dinah just before moving to West Mills to accept the teaching job.

"I got up this mornin'," Otis Lee said, "and that damn goose was in my coop, worryin' the hell outta my cluckers. Troublesome damn thing, that goose."

"Oh," Knot said. "So you decide you'd bring it here to trouble me, I guess."

The angry look, and the heavy sigh he gave, led Knot to say, "Sit down awhile and rest yo'self. You want a drink?"

"You know I don't want no drink," Otis Lee replied. But he did accept the offer to sit. He lay the sack on the ground near Knot. "And you don't need one, neither."

"Well, you can go on home if you gon' start up with that kinda talk," Knot said, and she took a bite out of her apple. He asked her if she had another one, and when she came back out onto the porch, she called his name and tossed an apple to him.

"How you gon' sell cobblers if you eatin' all the apples?" Otis Lee asked.

"People ain't half buying my cobblers," she explained. "I don't like makin' them no how."

As Knot waited for Otis Lee to tell her about whatever had caused his bad mood, she surveyed the brown sack moving next to her foot.

"Val's back in town," she announced. "You seen him?"

"What I need to see him for?" Otis Lee told her, crunching on his apple.

"You ought to be nicer to him," Knot said. "He yo' cousin."

"Not blood, though," Otis Lee reminded her. "That's why he . . . well, you know that he is."

"Ain't you ever seen a man you liked before?" Knot asked. "I see pretty womenfolk all the time. Every day I—"

"I ain't in the mood for jokes, Knot."

"I ain't jokin'," she said.

"Two of the same ain't—"

"Lord, have mercy," Knot interrupted. "Ain't you got a birthday comin'?" She threw the apple core out into the yard.

"Was yesterday," Otis Lee said. "And you forgot. Again."

"Oh," Knot said, "Well, happy birthday. I'll make you a cobbler sometime this week. I—"

"Pep come home from up-bridge and found Fran and Eunice fightin' in my yard," he blurted out. "In my front yard, Knot!" He stood up and stiffened.

Once he'd told Knot the whole story, she didn't know what to do first. Would she laugh at the thought of Breezy standing there, looking foolish, or should she cry because the girls were fighting over a man? She never liked to see or hear about women coming to blows over a man. Fran and Eunice had both been raised to behave better; she knew it for a fact. That had been one of Knot's biggest concerns during both her pregnancies: making sure they would be raised by people who would bring them up to be halfway decent. *And Breezy, what's wrong wit' him? Shit!* Breezy was like a nephew to Knot, and she knew he was a good young man deep down. *A little spoiled. A lot spoiled, to tell the truth. But he a good fellow.*

Pep had already told Knot some weeks ago that Fran and Eunice had been coming to her house to see Breezy. Pep had turned them away. She didn't want to risk playing favorites, she said.

Breezy was now working on Pennington Farm with Otis Lee. And Otis Lee had told Knot that the girls had gotten to the point of bringing Breezy lunch. Not on the same days, which Otis Lee said he'd found peculiar. "It's like they got some kind of schedule that all three of 'em wrote up, Knot," he said.

The Lovings, the Waterses, and the Mannings had talked it over, and they all agreed they would have to put their feet down with Breezy and their daughters. There were too many young men and women in West Mills for them to share, Pep said.

Knot sat quietly, using her tongue to loosen apple from her lower front teeth as she listened to Otis Lee fuss about their children. She was glad Otis Lee had something else to focus on besides how much she drank and what visitors she had.

"Well, what y'all gon' do?" she asked.

"Damn if I know," he replied.

Knot looked at her friend. He seemed tired and worried.

"Tell me one thing, Otis Lee," Knot said. "Don't Breezy got sense enough to know he can't have 'em both?"

By the new look he gave her, Knot wondered if, without realizing it, she'd said something nasty about his deceased mother or grandmother.

"Course he got sense enough! How you ask me somethin' dumb as that? You think I raised a nut?"

Knot hadn't had a drink in several hours—not since the gin on the rocks she had drunk with Mrs. Reynolds, the mayor's wife, after she finished cleaning the guest rooms for a big to-do they were having. So Otis Lee had picked the wrong time to yell at her.

"This ain't the right time to jump hot with me, you lil high-yella sumbitch!" Knot shot back. She snatched the sack from the ground and walked toward her backyard. Halfway there, she figured it was the right time to say something she had wanted to say to Otis Lee for years. And since he was already in a testy mood, why not seize the moment? "Maybe you *did* raise a nut!" she shouted, walking back toward him. He hadn't moved. "He's damn sure one *rotten* mothafucker!

Always has been!" And then: "This shit ain't *my* fault! You hear me? It ain't my fault!"

"Did I say it was *your* fault?" Otis Lee asked.

Why did I say that part—the part about fault?

"You just as well had said," Knot retorted. "I didn't raise them girls! So don't come over here blamin' me, goddamnit!"

Otis Lee just stared at her, his eyebrows pulled together.

Now she was ready for a drink. The one she'd had with Mrs. Reynolds had been out of boredom. The drink she needed now was out of necessity.

She didn't know what else to say. And she understood perfectly why Otis Lee was still sitting there looking at her as though she had spoken in a language neither of them knew. She wanted to be alone. Of that she was certain.

Returning the sack of goose to Otis Lee was the right thing to do before saying, "Just get out my goddamn yard, Mr. Jaggers."

"Who?" Otis Lee asked.

"Go to hell!" she yelled. "You, and the Waterses, and the Mannings. All y'all!"

"You crazy, Azalea. Plum' crazy!"

She watched him march out of her yard.

Knot let the screen door slam behind her when she went inside the house and to the pantry. There was no time to get a cool glass from the icebox. She needed firewater in her quickly. She drank it straight from the jar. The little bit she spilled was of no consequence. After another swallow, she sat at her kitchen table.

That shit ain't my fault. Ain't my fault at all!

Knot picked up the plate she had used that morning for the one piece of toast and the one boiled egg she had eaten before she went to Reynolds Landing. She threw the plate against the wall—the same wall Pratt had thrown her glass at almost twenty years before. *Goddamn Pratt. And that goddamn boy from Delaware.*

A few days went by before she bent down to pick up the three shards of white ceramic plate.

TWO DAYS AFTER Knot swept up the pieces of broken plate, she felt an overwhelming craving for pecan pie, which Pep had shown her how to make. Although she had all she needed in the pantry, Knot convinced herself that she needed to go up-bridge, to the general store, for more sugar. And on her way back, she would stop to see the bootlegger.

At the store, she bought the sugar and a few other items, just to make the trip more worthwhile. Ayra and Brock spoke to her when she went to the counter to pay. They asked her how she had been doing and how her baking business was going. The Mannings were always kind to Knot, just as they were with all their customers.

"Thank y'all, hear?" Knot said after Ayra passed her the paper bag. "I really appreciate all y'all done and all y'all do."

On her way out of the store, startled by the bell they had tied to the doorknob, Knot saw Eunice coming up the walkway. *Well, shit. I guess I can't run back, can I?*

"Afternoon," Knot said when she and Eunice passed each other. She did not expect the young lady with the V-shaped chin to respond, especially since Knot and everyone else knew Eunice could be as coarse as a hairbrush, even with her parents' customers. So the town drunks didn't have a chance with Miss Manning.

Before Knot turned her eyes from Eunice, she saw Delaware Williams's thick eyebrows. It was the eyebrows that caused Knot to drop her groceries. Sugar and cornstarch covered her shoes. And the tomatoes she had gone to so much trouble to pick out were now covered in dirt and rock pebbles.

"Got everything, Knot?" Eunice asked.

Her voice. Even to hear Eunice speak—she hadn't been close enough to Eunice to hear her speak in at least three years—was like listening to opera. She'd only said three words, but to Knot they were a song. Otis Lee had said Eunice sang beautifully, like a bird, high-pitched but not squeaky. But he didn't mentioned that Eunice spoke beautifully, too.

"I got it," Knot said. "Thank ya, though."

Eunice moved closer to Knot. She smelled like lavender, but she looked as though she had just finished cleaning out an attic. Loose ponytail. Overalls. And there was the ill-tempered expression she was known for.

"Good people, aren't they?" Eunice remarked. She folded her arms just as Dinah Bright would. "My mama and daddy. They good people."

Strange thing to say to somebody while you standin' there, watchin' them pick up the groceries they just dropped, and ain't lift a finger to help.

"Yeah," Knot agreed, holding the bag in front of her chest like a shield. "They are. They better'n good." Eunice drew in a deep breath, turned around, and went into the store.

Making a pecan pie was now the furthest thing from Knot's mind. How could she concentrate on anything after seeing a little bit of her pa and Dinah Bright and Delaware William and even a bit of herself all at once on the steps of Manning's General Store? The little bit that was new, however, was the lovely voice. *I swear that girl got a pretty voice.*

The next day Knot made two pecan pies. One of them would be a peace offering to Otis Lee, an apology for throwing him out of her yard earlier in the week. When she got close to the Lovings' house later that afternoon, she saw Otis Lee in the coop feeding his chickens. In her mind she played eeny meeny miney mo to decide whether to go to him first or whether she would be better off going in the house to see Pep first. Miney mo told her to go to Pep first. But Knot had never been a fan of being told what to do.

"What ya know?" she said, standing at the edge of the coop.

When Otis Lee turned to see her, he was smiling.

"Was your ears burnin'?" he asked.

"Naw," Knot said. She set the pie on the bench. "What you say 'bout me?"

"Eunice got on the train this mornin'," he announced. "She gon' to New York. She tell Brock she want to go try her luck with the sangin'. Begged him to buy her a ticket and let her go." Otis Lee was glowing almost. Relieved, it seemed. "It ain't even been five minutes ago that I tol' Pep I need to go tell you the news."

The relieved look on his face set Knot at ease, too. But while Otis Lee went on talking about his conversation with Brock, Knot slowly felt something other than relief.

Something familiar had begun to butt up against the feeling of relief. Knot couldn't say anything to Otis Lee because she was busy trying to remember where she knew that feeling from. It was sadness. Sadness with a hint of happiness mixed with it.

"Knot," Otis Lee said, "you hear any of what I just tol' you?"

"Yeah," Knot replied. *Only God and them chickens of yours heard anything you just said, Otis Lee.* "I heard ya."

"Ev'rything's all worked out, Knot. Eunice gon' be just fine. *Just fine.*"

And it was then, as swift as a mosquito bite, that Knot remembered the day she'd brought Eunice into the world. Recalling it as though she were watching it at a picture show. Knot saw Brock and Ayra leave her house with her second baby girl bundled in beige blankets.

"It all sounds real nice, Otis Lee," Knot said. "I think we oughta drink to it."

Otis Lee laughed and said, "You know I don't want no drink." He went back to feeding his chickens, smiling the whole time.

KNOT NEVER MADE it inside to see Pep that afternoon. Eeny meeny miney mo told her to go home and try to drink that familiar feeling away. And she obeyed.

TWELVE

Early fall of '62 brought a lot of rain to West Mills. The sky poured buckets of it on the day Pep asked Otis Lee to go across the lane to buy her a jar of Lady Waters's town-famous cha-cha. Otis Lee, for three days in a row, heard her talk about how badly she was craving it. If Pep had been younger, he would have sworn she was expecting a child.

"Why don't you go on over there and get it?" Otis Lee said. "Lady'll be happy to hear you say you longin' for some of her food."

"I ain't goin' out in that rain," Pep retorted.

"You tryin' to send *me* out in it," he grumbled. Pep gave him one of those kisses that always calmed him down. "Well, if I go, I ain't comin' right straight back. I'm gon' sit and talk with Phil awhile."

"Good," Pep said. Breezy had gone out, and she said she wanted some time to herself anyway. "Seem like I can't never get this place to myself on Saturdays."

Otis Lee was on his second helping of Lady's chicken and dumplings and a second helping of Phil's opinions on what he thought the civil rights leaders ought to do. To Otis Lee, it sounded as though he didn't want them to do anything. In the middle of the lecture, Phil looked out the living room window and asked, "Whose fancy car is that, brother?"

"Where 'bouts?"

"In yo' yard," Phil said. Lady went to the window and looked out. "Lady, darlin', step aside so brother can see the car." If she heard what Phil had just said, Otis Lee wouldn't know it. She didn't budge.

"Somebody's sittin' in it," she reported. And once Otis Lee was ready to head out the door and into the drizzle, she said, "Here. Don't forget Pep's cha-cha. Tell her I want to know if it taste like I left something out. Don't forget, hear?"

Otis Lee took large steps, careful not to slip in the mud. Now closer to the new-looking brown Cadillac, he noticed the mushy red clay on the tires and felt sorry for the person who would have to clean it off. Then he saw the colored man sitting behind the steering wheel. The man seemed to have no interest in rolling down the window—not even a little.

Standing next to the driver's door wasn't enough. So Otis Lee tapped on the window with his knuckle. With the window now rolled down a few inches, Otis Lee could see that the driver was young, twenty-two at the most.

"Good afternoon," Otis Lee said, noticing the sandwich on the passenger's seat and the bottle of pop in his hand. The fellow looked at Otis Lee and continued to chew. *Well, is he hard o' hearin' or just got bad manners?* "Can I help you?" Otis Lee asked.

"No. But thank you. I'm fine," the fellow replied. His way of speaking was unmistakable. He was from the North. "I'm just the driver. My boss lady's inside."

There were two reasons Otis Lee didn't have to ask the fellow for his boss lady's name. First, not a single white person in West Mills had a driver anymore. Even the wealthiest families who lived on the east side of the canal drove themselves around. They had to. The colored men who had been drivers went back to working in the mills. They made more money that way.

Second, the moment the fellow spoke the word *driver*, Otis Lee's mind left his body for a journey back to the 1920s and it visited him as a young man in New York City. Essie's husband—his name was Thomas, but Essie called him "Thomas Dear"—had hired a driver. Based on what Otis Lee had overheard, Thomas had actually hired the driver because one of the other police officers had hired one for his own wife. "I'm happy to drive myself around, Thomas Dear," Essie insisted. And Thomas said, "If Elis Foley has a boy taking her to those afternoon coffees or teas or whatever the hell it is you all do, you'll have a boy driving you, too."

Now Otis Lee felt something like warm cooking grease moving through his bowels. He nodded at the driver and ran to the backyard. In the old outhouse, he pulled his trousers down just in time to sit on the cool, damp wood where the hole had been cut many years ago. As his body relieved itself—he had very little to do with it—Otis Lee pulled spiderwebs from his face and hoped an angry snake wouldn't come out from a crack.

Essie? In West Mills, North Carolina? In my house?

Who else can it be, Otis Lee? Shit and get out of the outhouse.

While in New York City, Otis Lee often went to the Municipal Building on Centre Street to shine shoes for extra money. He was certain there were more people walking around on that block and in the lobby of that building than there were in West Mills and the two neighboring towns. Everyone had somewhere to be and they acted as though they only had ten seconds to get there. And they all had something to sell: newspapers, candy, mismatched jewelry, lost or stolen pens. What they all—blacks and whites—seemed to be running low on most, both in Manhattan and in Brooklyn, were "Hellos," "How ya doings," and "Come agains."

Otis Lee only went to Centre Street on days when he didn't have to work at Essie's. He hadn't told her or anyone else at the brothel about his side hustle. But one day, kit in hand, he ran into her.

"Don't you get tired of workin'?" she asked him. Otis Lee remembered that she spoke in her southern accent when she felt safe, which was usually when he went with her to run errands.

"What I do when I ain't at yo' place don't concern you," Otis Lee shot back.

"No need for the sass," she said, and he felt a hint of guilt for having snapped at her. "Just thought you might want to rest, is all. More to life than workin', baby. Had anything to eat?"

"Essie, you ain't got to do all this pretendin'," Otis Lee told her. He looked down at the pavement while he spoke to her, but his focus shifted to her glistening black shoes. "Our mama's in West Mills, missing us both. And soon as I get up enough money to go back—enough to have a head start down there—I'm goin'." There was a brief silence. And when he lifted his eyes to meet hers, they looked as though they would spill over any second. She walked to the car O'Heeney had purchased especially for her to be chauffeured around in. The driver, a middle-aged colored man, opened the door for her. Otis Lee turned and walked away, not wanting to see her ride off that way. That night at the brothel she was sitting in the parlor with one of the customers. Essie gave Otis Lee a familiar look—the same look Rose had given him when he was a little boy and not feeling well—as if she was suffering because he was suffering.

Now, sitting at the kitchen table with Pep and Breezy, Essie greeted him with that familiar look. Seventy or seventy-one years old by now, not a single strand of her once pitch-black hair had been able to resist time. It was silver—all of it. But Otis Lee would recognize his sister anywhere. And to him she looked whiter now than she had all those years ago. He wondered if the thought of being white made the body follow suit.

Essie stood and walked to him. She moved quickly for a woman her age, he thought. It reminded him of Ma Noni.

"Otis Lee," Essie began. Her voice was much higher-pitched than he remembered. "I know I—"

"I know you been in the North a long time," Otis Lee cut in, "but down here, when we gon' visit somebody we ain't seen or heard from in God knows when, we sends a note or somethin' ahead of us."

"I thought—"

"I don't want to hear nothin' from you, Essie," he said.

Essie lowered her eyes for a moment, which gave him enough time to notice the green brooch on the lapel of her dark blue blazer—the same brooch he had seen her wear almost every day when he lived with her. He would never forget that brooch.

What Otis Lee had forgotten, however, were the eyes. When Essie looked back up at him, he saw his mother's eyes. *They 'bout all Essie got to prove she's my mama's daughter. She probably ain't never even wanted them brown eyes.*

"I think she ought to leave," Otis Lee said to Pep.

"Sit down a minute, Otis Lee," Pep suggested.

"Don't 'sit down a minute' me, Penelope," he argued. "What she want?"

"I want to know you," Essie told him, touching his hand. He would have snatched it back from her, but he would never have snatched his hand away from his mother if she had been there. *Them's Rose's eyes lookin' at me.*

"Pop," Breezy said. Otis Lee felt his son's wide but light hand on his shoulder. "She want to talk to you. She ain't come to cause us no trouble. She just want to talk." Otis Lee looked at Breezy, and he felt hot tears running down his own face.

Wet-cheeked, Otis Lee stared at his son, because he could not look at Essie while saying what needed to be said; her eyes—his late mother's eyes—would make it too hard if not impossible.

"I want her out," Otis Lee declared. "I think it's best she don't come here no more." Essie walked back to the table and picked up her purse. "I'm sorry to have intruded," she apologized, and headed for the door.

"Just a minute, ma'am," Breezy said. He stood in front of Otis Lee, but Otis Lee wouldn't look up at him. "She's ya sister, Pop. The only person in this world you shared a mama with. Sit and talk to her. She's ya blood."

"She run off and left us!" Otis Lee shouted. "Left her mama, grandmama, and me. Left us with not a damn *thing*! And wouldn't come back wit' me when I went to help her!" He could not remember the last time he'd cried so much or yelled so loudly. "Sit and talk to her for *what*, Breezy? 'Bout *what*?"

Otis Lee heard Essie's heels coming back toward him. Breezy made space between them. And Otis Lee saw that her cheeks were wet, too.

"*Sent* off, Otis Lee," Essie corrected. "I didn't run off. She *sent* me off."

WITH PEP AND Breezy gone to visit Knot, Otis Lee and Essie sat across from each other at his table. Essie told Otis Lee that she had wanted to come when Rose died, but she hadn't been able to work up the nerve, not having made an effort in all the years that had come before.

Otis Lee had paid close attention to only three-quarters of what his sister had been saying because he was thinking about his son. He was proud that Breezy had seemed concerned about something other than his own needs and wants. *Finally becomin' a grown man with some sense in his head.*

"So what made ya come now?" Otis Lee wanted to know. "You sick or somethin'?

"I'm all right," Essie reassured him, "as far as I know. But I'm no debutante." Otis Lee did not know what that meant, and his frown must have said so. "I'm no longer a spring chicken."

He hadn't been to the chicken coop. *Did Pep or Breezy feed my cluckers?*

Essie said, "Ma Noni used to say, 'No man knows the day nor the hour.'"

Easily, Otis Lee could have flipped the table over when his sister recited the quote. Instead he took a deep breath.

"What reason did Ma Noni have to want you gone, Essie? I can't understand that."

Essie told him everything she'd been told about Rose and Leland Edgars Jr.

"I can't remember a single day that woman was kind to me, Otis Lee," Essie said. "Ma Noni, I mean."

"But you was her daughter's child, Essie," Otis Lee said. "I just can't underst—"

"Look at my face, Otis Lee," Essie broke in. "I came along in 18 and 91. Can you imagine what it was like for Ma Noni to see her daughter with a white-looking baby on her hip? A baby that was *hers*? In 1891? I'd probably been sent away the day I was born if there was anywhere to send me. I was probably fourteen or fifteen before Leland Jr. even acknowledged to Mama that I was his."

Essie said she didn't know what Ma Noni had said to Leland Edgars Jr. to convince him that Essie needed to be sent away all of a sudden. But he had given her money—it had been far more than the twenty-five dollars Otis Lee had heard about—to help with the journey. Essie said she always assumed there must have been some vicious lie, or a threat, to make things happen so quickly.

"There something I need to—"

"So you ain't sell Ma Noni's land behind her back?" Otis Lee said.

"She didn't own any land," Essie told him. "If she had, what would I know about selling land? I was just a young girl."

Otis Lee thought about what Essie had said over the course of the past few minutes. *She can say anything now, with Ma Noni and our mama gone on.*

"Otis Lee, I need to—"

"Why you ain't tell me this stuff when I found you, Essie?" Otis Lee asked. "You coulda—"

"I wasn't ready," Essie replied quickly. It was as if she had prepared to answer that question before he asked. "You wouldn't have believed me anyway." She reminded Otis Lee of how ornery he had been with her when he showed up at her back door, pretending to be looking for work. She had thought he was there to blackmail her, she reminded him. So she had offered him a real job. "Even with you hating me, I wanted you around. You're my blood, Otis Lee. Just like your son said—what's his given name again?"

"Robert," Otis Lee answered.

"After—"

"After my father," Otis Lee affirmed.

"I see," Essie said. And she slid to the edge of her chair. "There's so much more I need to tell you. I need you to hear me out because—"

"I don't need to hear no more," he interrupted.

She ain't got but one nephew, and she don't know his name. She don't know any of us. She ain't wanted to. Otis Lee decided then and there that everything Essie had said was a lie. Ma Noni had not lied to him all those years. He was certain. *She ain't have no reason to! It don't add up. She lyin'!*

Otis Lee looked across the table at his sister, the kin he hadn't seen in thirty-five years, the kin who hadn't cared about their mother, who wasn't there when their mother was sick and asking for her. He got to his feet and looked down at her.

"I want you to leave, Essie. Right now, please."

"Otis Lee . . ."

He walked over to the door and opened it. Essie stood slowly, looking at him. She went in her pocketbook and pulled out an envelope.

"Here," she said, holding it out to him. "Some things I wro—"

"Take whatever it is, and yo'self, and get on, Essie, or Ellen—whoever the hell you is."

"Please take it."

"Get out, goddamnit!" Otis Lee shouted. "Now!"

WHEN ESSIE'S CAR was gone, Otis Lee sat and cried until his sides were sore. And once he'd wiped what he decided would be his last tear for his sister, he wanted to get out of the house.

"Where she go, Pop?" Breezy asked. He and Pep were walking into the yard.

Otis Lee hugged his wife and pulled his son's head down so that he could kiss his forehead.

"Don't worry 'bout Essie, son," Otis Lee reassured him. "She all right. Always gon' be all right. We will be, too." He patted Breezy's arm and said, "I'll be back later on."

"Where you off to?" Pep asked.

Without turning around, Otis Lee said, "Goin' to Knot's. Think I'll have me a drink."

THIRTEEN

The morning after Otis Lee's real mother had visited him, Knot went to be sure he had survived the night of drinking, and to allow Pep to curse her out for letting him drink beyond his limits.

"You sat yo' lil behind there and let him, Knot?" Pep scolded. "I had to clean him up twice last night."

"Spit up that much?"

"Spit up, peed, and shit," Pep said. "All at the same time."

Knot turned her head so that Pep wouldn't see her holding in the laugh.

"I see ya," Pep told her. "And I don't see nothin' funny 'bout it. He just find out his grandmama coulda been lyin' to him all them years 'bout Essie runnin' off, and all you can think to do is hand him your jar?"

Pep went on for three or four minutes, and Knot didn't stop her. *She'll run outta breath soon, I s'pose.*

"You ain't care, though. Did ya?" Pep asked. "Gave *you* a reason to drink."

"See, now you gon' piss me off, Pep," Knot shot back. She stood up and walked to the door. "I don't need nobody to give me a goddamn reason. When I get ready for a taste, I gets my taste."

"Get on outta here," Pep ordered. "I ain't in the mood for it."

"I ain't, either," Knot replied. "I come to check on him and you want to fuss."

"Bye, Knot," Pep said, and she nudged Knot out the door and closed it.

Knot was just about to tell Pep to kiss her ass and to go to hell, but it dawned on her that Valley had probably had a hand in all of it, since Essie had known exactly where to go.

Knot stood near the ditch in front of the Lovings' house and waited for anyone who might be headed in Valley's direction.

"Where you goin', Knot?" Max asked, coming to a complete stop in front of her. He, his wife, Johnnie Mae, and their two grandsons—who were both staring at her from the back seat of the black Nova—were dressed in their Sunday best.

"Y'all drop me at Val's right quick," Knot said. "I'll give you a quarter."

"Ain't got time to go that far," Johnnie Mae protested. "We already 'bout late, and these boys gon' usher today. They real excited 'bout it, and—"

"We coulda been halfway there by now, Johnnie. Shit," Knot said.

"We got to go, Knot," Max insisted.

"Johnnie Mae," Knot said, "you learn how to make bread puddin' yet? Or pecan pies?"

Johnnie Mae sighed and said, "Get on in here, girl."

Knot climbed in back with Max and Johnnie Mae's grandsons.

★   ★   ★

DREADING THE PROSPECT of having to clean red clay from her shoes, Knot went around to Valley's back door. Two minutes after she had knocked, he showed up at the window.

"What is it?" he asked. Her knocks had forced him out of bed, which explained why he was only wearing underpants. They were so thin that when Knot glanced down, she was able to see the length and girth of his private parts. *A goddamn waste.*

"I'm surprised you was able to sleep at all," Knot said. "You sneaky sumbitch." She shoved him out of her way and went inside.

In the kitchen that once belonged to his adoptive mother, he asked Knot if she wanted a cup of tea.

"You had something to do with Essie comin' to town?"

"Says who?" he asked. Coming from Valley, that was a yes.

"You shoulda let Otis Lee know she was comin' to his house, Valor," Knot scolded. "Shoulda let me know, too. Shit. He damn near drank all my liquor." Before Otis Lee had told Knot anything about his talk with Essie, the two of them had knocked back a few shots. They knocked back a few more after he'd told her about Essie's visit.

"I want coffee," she said, pointing at Valley's stove. "Black."

"I got Earl Grey," Valley replied. "No coffee."

"Well, excuuuuuse me, Your Royal Highness," she grumbled. "You need to stay outta folks' business. Why won't folk leave well enough alone? I just don't under—"

"It was time, Knot."

"Why?" Knot said.

Knot was of the belief that some secrets, if not most, should remain as such. Sometimes the not knowing was a hell of a lot better, she told Valley. She wished Miss Noni were still alive to concur.

After Valley put the kettle on the stove, he rummaged through his cabinets.

"Looooong time ago," he said, "somebody shoulda tol' him who is mama is."

Well, I'll be damned, Knot thought to herself. *Otis Lee ain't said a thing 'bout findin' out Essie's his mama. Said lots 'bout Miss Noni, though. A whole lot.*

"Well, I'll be damned," Knot said to Valley, joining him in front of the stove.

"What's wrong?" Valley asked.

KNOT AND VALLEY grew tired of repeating *Well, I'll be damned*. So they each had a cup of Earl Grey—straight up, no chaser.

"She come all the way down here and ain't tell him she's his real mama?" Valley remarked. He lit a cigarette.

"Good," Knot said, having thought about it. "It's for the best. And I ain't have enough for him to drink after gettin' that kinda news anyhow."

"Be serious, Knot."

Learning that Miss Noni may have been gravely dishonest had hurt Otis Lee enough. Knot was confident that any more news—especially the news that Essie seemingly hadn't delivered—would have shattered him. She explained all of that to Valley impatiently.

"I see yo' point," Valley said.

"I'm *so* glad you do," Knot scoffed. Valley picked up on her sarcasm, and he rolled his eyes. Now it was time for her to ask a hard question. "You had a mind to blackmail Essie, didn't ya?"

"Course not!"

"Tell the truth, Val."

"I am!" he insisted. "You sharp-chinned heifer!"

He swore that he had not gone to Essie with blackmail. He said Essie's police officer husband was dead and gone and that she didn't care as much about people knowing she was colored.

"I asked her for some help!" Valley exclaimed.

"Help?"

"Just help," he said. "With my gamblin' tab. That was it! She said she'll help me, long as I help her fix things up with Otis Lee—if you must know."

"All right, all right," Knot said.

If Valley were lying, he'd be scratching his chin. He was, however, scratching his head quite a bit. He had recently put a relaxer in his hair, and he'd left it in too long.

"You gon' tell him Essie's his mama?" Knot asked.

"Naw," Valley said. He took a pull from his cigarette, blew out the smoke, and slurped his tea. "Hell, I did my part. Through wit' it now." Another pull and slurp. "You ain't gon' tell him, are ya?"

"Nope," Knot reassured him.

Otis Lee's done a whole lot for me. I won't see him hurtin' no more'n he need to hurt. Guess I owe him that much. Knot took a sip of the bitter tea while Valley smoked and scratched his head.

"I know one damn thing, though," Knot said. She held up one finger. "You try some blackmail shit with me, I'll—"

"I just tol' you I did not go to that woman with blackmail, Knot," Valley broke in. "And to tell ya the truth, you kinda hurtin' my feelings, thinkin' I'd do somethin' like that. I done a lot of shit in my day, but not blackmail." Slurp and scratch.

"If you say so, Val."

"I do say so. And ain't nobody studdin' you and them ol' secrets you got," he said. "Them babies is grown women mindin' they own business."

He was right. After Eunice moved north, Fran and Breezy went steady. Everyone was happy. And later that year, Fran had a baby girl. Pep and Otis Lee were so happy to have a grandchild, Knot hardly heard the two of them talk about anything else. She saw them going back and forth from their house to the Waterses' house, grinning from temple to temple.

Otis Lee had tried to get Knot to join them.

"I'll get 'round to it sooner or later," Knot told him.

ONE DAY, ABOUT two weeks after Fran's baby had been born, Knot was passing by their house. She was heading up-bridge. Knot saw Lady and Phillip in their garden pulling up collards she assumed would be on their Christmas dinner buffet. They both waved at her and smiled.

"Knot!" Fran yelled from the upstairs window. "You ain't been over here to see my baby! And I don't quite like it!"

"Otis Lee tell me you give him a pretty grandgirl," Knot said. "I'll come see her later on. Get yo' rest."

"We ain't been doing nothing *but* resting," Fran told her. "Come see her while she got her eyes open. I just got through feedin' her. She'll be sleep in a few minutes."

Shit! Fuck! Damn! Fuck! Shit!

Unable to come up with a quick excuse to not go and see the newborn, Knot decided it was time to get the visit over with. She would go in, see Fran's baby, and everything would fine. *Nothing to it.*

When Knot was inside—it was her first time in their home in many years—she felt the way she had when she was a young girl, being led into Lilly's Millpond to be baptized by her pastor. She had been so afraid. Knot remembered him telling her to have no fear. He had said, "These here waters may be cold, but when you come up outta here, you sure to feel the fire of the Lord shut up in your *bones!*"

Knot saw the staircase to her right and followed it to the upstairs hallway. She heard the baby make one of those sounds—the sounds they make in preparation for wailing. After turning the corner and seeing Fran in a chair with the little person resting on her chest—the little head was bobbing this way and that—Knot froze where she was.

"Well," Fran said, "come close enough so you can see if she look more like me or like Breezy."

Knot took a couple of steps closer—only a couple. Her heart was already trying to beat her and leave her for dead.

"I don't know," Knot said. While she looked back and forth between Fran's face and the baby's, the sunlight showed a hint of copper-red in Fran's hair. It was the first time she had seen that. And then, somehow, she had an answer to Fran's question. "Like you. She look like you, I think. And she's a big ol' healthy baby, too." Fran smiled and kissed the top of her baby's hairy head. "What's her name again?"

"Cedar," Fran said. "Cedar Marie Loving." Then she told Knot that she and Breezy were going to be married.

"We ain't in a big rush, though. We'll do it sometime next year."

There were a few things Knot knew when she left the Waters house. The first being that she would not be able to get the sight of that beautiful baby out her mind for at least a month. Second, Knot needed a drink. *Cedar Marie.* Third, she was confused to hear that Breezy and Fran were planning to marry, because a few months back, the North had chewed Eunice up and spit her all the way back to West Mills. Knot had gone to Otis Lee and said, "What in the hell is she doin' back so soon? Ain't nobody *that* damn homesick."

"She ain't visitin' this time," Otis Lee had said. "Breezy tol' me she came back to stay."

"How he know?" Knot had asked. Otis Lee had stood there looking at her, shaking his head.

Not long before Fran's little girl took her first steps, Eunice was up-bridge on Busy Street rocking a colicky baby of her own. A boy. Except for the middle name, Eunice had named the child after Breezy. Robert La'Roy Loving.

Knot had been expecting to hear about wedding plans between Fran and Breezy. Instead it was Breezy and Eunice who got married, and they moved into the apartment over Manning's General Store—the same one in which Valley had lived before he inherited and moved into Gertrude's house.

The part that baffled Knot most—it kept her awake for more than one night—was that Fran didn't seem to care about Breezy and Eunice's union. *I can't make head or tails of it to save my life.*

★ ★ ★

ONE DAY, GIRLS, Knot's pa once said to her and her sisters, *y'all gon' find yourselves walkin' behind me slowly. Everything I ever tried to tell you three, you'll remember it. Every last word. Y'all'll be walkin', but I'll be layin' down. Just live long enough. You'll see.*

ON THE FRIDAY before Christmas of 1964, Knot was sweeping balconies at the Penningtons'. Lady Waters was there, too. She was inside polishing silverware and ironing tablecloths. She had told Knot she wanted to make some extra money to travel north for New Year's Eve to visit people she'd kept up with in letters but hadn't seen in decades.

"If you don't get somewhere and rest that cold off, you ain't gon' be well enough to go nowhere when the new year gets here," Knot had said earlier that week. Lady had been coughing a lot, and she got tired just from walking from the dining room to the kitchen.

Having left her sweater inside, Knot planned to give the second-floor balcony a quick hit, as she called it. Once the cool wind hit her harder than she'd expected, her plan changed. *Half a quick hit.*

Just as Knot was about to go back into the house, she saw an unfamiliar green Buick drive up. Curiosity won the battle against the December chill. So Knot stayed on the balcony and swept until the Buick got closer.

The passenger side door opened and Otis Lee got out.

Otis Lee?

"Well, I'll be damned! Otis Lee Loving! What you doin' ridin' up in that shiny string bean?"

Mary, Knot's older sister, and Mary's oldest son, Onslow, got out of the car. The way they got out of the Buick so slowly, both dressed in black, made Knot think of oil. She went downstairs, but not hurriedly. *No sense in runnin'. Not with all that black they got on.*

"We weren't able to wait, Knot," Mary explained. Her breath smelled of Premium Soda Crackers, coffee, and lies. "Pa had to be buried as quick as we could manage."

Mary said that Ahoskie's only colored undertaker—who was also a Centre, though he was of no traceable relation to them—had sold all his supplies to the white undertaker for cents on the dollar and had skipped town. No one knew why, Mary said. The white undertaker had quoted them an unfathomable price to embalm their pa's body.

"Everyone thinks Pa was a rich man," Mary said. "He gave most of it to that no-count church." She said the majority of what was left had been used to send Onslow to Shaw University. Thank God there were no liens against their parents' property, Mary said.

Knot did not speak. She only listened, deciding which parts to believe and which parts she'd hurl back at her sister.

"We just didn't have a choice, Aunt Knot," Onslow said. "We just didn't."

Mary once again opened her arms and tried to hug Knot. The first time Knot had taken a couple of steps backward. But this time she held her hand up. *Stop.*

Knot didn't doubt her sister's remorse. Mary's tears had already done the vetting. It was the fact that she and Mary had exchanged two letters in the past five months, neither of which had noted that their pa's health and finances had been failing for well over a year. It was that fact that caused Knot to wonder what it would feel like to knock Mary's and Onslow's heads off their shoulders.

But it would hurt him some kind of bad to see that.

Hurt who, Knot? Yo' pa's dead.

I know. But Otis Lee's standin' right here with his arm 'round my shoulders. It'll hurt him to see me fight my sister.

"I'm *so* sorry, Knot," Mary said, tilting her head to one side in a way Knot recognized. And it all became clear to her—as clear as the jar she now longed for.

"Dinah Bright," Knot realized.

She could almost see the weight rise, like steam, from Mary's slumping shoulders. Knot said the name again, and she took both of Mary's hands into hers. Knot had to hold them firmly, because that was the only way Mary would understand that all was well.

Mary shook her head no. Her tears took up the same speed. When she rested her damp cheek on Knot's shoulder—like a small child who had been fighting against an oncoming nap—Knot heard her sister whisper, "Dinah Bright."

Onslow joined their embrace and said, "We're real sorry, Aunt Knot. Sorry things happened the way they did."

Knot had heard about people going into shock. But she had never been able to imagine how it might feel.

This must be it, she thought to herself. *When you know you hurtin', but there ain't no pain. When you know you sad but you don't feel like you gon' cry. I want to say a whole lot of stuff, but I don't want to talk. This must be it. Got to be what shock feels like.*

Mary and Onslow offered to drive Knot and Otis Lee back to Antioch Lane. Knot declined and walked back toward the

Penningtons' wraparound porch, where pumpkins lined the right side of the steps, and where Lady Waters stood in the doorway. Once Knot was almost to the porch, she heard Otis Lee say, "She'll be all right. A good walk is what she need for now. My mama used to always go for long walks when she got hol' o' some bad news. They helps things, ya know?"

"Yes, sir," Onslow said.

"I'll walk wit' her," Otis Lee reassured them. "Y'all best get back on the road. Be dark 'fore ya know it."

"Mother," Onslow said to Mary, "we'd better get going."

The last thing Knot heard before going back inside was her sister's voice.

"Thank you, Mr. Loving," Mary said. "I'm glad she has you here."

Me, too, Knot thought.

TWO WEEKS LATER, soon after Christmas, pneumonia had worn out its welcome with Lady Waters. Finally it decided to leave, and it took Lady along with it. That afternoon Fran came over to Knot's house to tell her. Knot was still in bed when she heard the knock on the door.

"Anything you want me to do?" Knot asked. Fran sat down at the table and put her face in her hands.

"I just had to get outta there for a few minutes, Knot," Fran explained. She had taken Cedar to the Lovings. "Daddy over there givin' them people a hard time. Won't let them take mama out o' the room."

"Jesus," Knot said, hard-pressed to imagine what that scene must have looked like. Knot couldn't understand exactly, but she had some idea of what Phillip was feeling. She knew what it felt like when somebody walked out the door with something—or someone—that she had gotten used to having with her every day. Even when she hadn't wanted the something or someone with her every day, she had still gotten used to it.

Why Fran had come to her, Knot didn't know. But the truth was, she kind of liked that Fran had. It made Knot feel like a person—a regular person. More and more, Knot had found herself wondering what the ladies on the lane did together when they piled into cars and drove off on Saturday mornings; what they talked about when they walked while pulling their grandchildren in red wagons. *Is it too much to ask for me to live my life the way I want and have folk treat me regular?* How often was it that anyone came to Knot during hard times? Almost never. Yes, sometimes Valley came to talk about his lover in D.C., and the new lover in Chesapeake. One man wanted Valley all the time, and the other man didn't seem to want Valley enough.

Yes, Otis Lee had sought Knot out when Essie had visited and turned half of his world upside down. *I'm glad Essie left the other half of his world alone. Shit.*

Having Fran come to her, especially at a time like this, meant something. Knot wasn't entirely sure what that was, but she thought she might be able to get used to it.

With her face still buried in her hands, Fran sat quietly, just as Knot had done when Mary and Onslow came to West Mills with the news about her pa's passing. Knot thought about that sad look her pa had when she spoke to him in his office the day he told her to make peace with the loss of her child—the child who was sitting with her right now.

THE PEOPLE OF West Mills New Nazareth Missionary Baptist Church knew how to send someone home. That was how the pastor had put it several times that week at the Waters house.

At Lady's service, during the viewing, voices sang, hands clapped, and tambourines were beaten against hips and palms. Some members alternated the tambourines between hip and palm. All of this Knot saw from the tenth pew, where she sat with the Lovings on her right, Valley and the Mannings on her left.

Knot was in the center.

Ayra Manning wailed as though Lady were her sister or a best friend. The two of them had never been close.

Why folk act so crazy when they go to funerals?

Eunice directed the choir. She looked regal, professional, and content while doing so. Her thin arms moved in ways Knot thought were peculiar, but the choir members seemed to know what every strange, quick movement meant.

On one of the front pews with Phillip's sisters and his one brother, Fran rocked from side to side, backward and forward. She had gone and bought a wig. It had a part in the middle, and the hair fell past Fran's shoulders.

"I ain't feelin' like sittin' in Anna-Faye's shop this week," Fran had said the night before.

The matching dresses that Fran had bought for Cedar and herself were lovely. They were black with sailor collars.

Phillip had wanted them all to wear something new and pretty to Lady's funeral. He believed a funeral was just as important as a wedding or an Easter Sunday service.

From where she sat, Knot could see Fran's shoulders bouncing. A controlled bounce, and her cry was a quiet one, fighting to get out. Knot had become so distracted watching Fran, she hadn't felt Otis Lee reach over and take her hand. And when had Valley put his arm around her shoulders?

Knot kept her eyes on Fran, the woman who had, on a hot day in '42, become her new favorite person. Keeping her eyes on Fran, Knot figured, was probably the best she could do for her, because the sympathetic tears that Valley had just blotted from her face would not be enough.

Phillip Waters sat on the same pew as Fran. He had held her and rocked with her for a while before succumbing, briefly, to his own grief. That was before his nieces had gone and sat on both sides of Fran, fanning her and rubbing her back. Then he sat as still as a statue. Knot didn't see him move again until the undertaker escorted him to Lady's casket for a final good-bye.

But when Phillip turned to walk back to the pew, he dropped to the floor. Every usher—and the two deaconesses who were still young enough to move with haste—ran to him with their fans. It looked as though a swarm of paper butterflies had run to his rescue.

Three days later, there was a small graveside service for Phillip Waters next to Lady's fresh grave. And while the pastor gave the last prayer, Knot looked out into the distance. She could have sworn she saw two butterflies chasing each other playfully.

At the repast, Knot saw Fran struggling to hold her sleeping child and eat at the same time. Many of the women at the table—women from Antioch Lane—offered to hold Cedar.

"I'm fine," Fran said. "But I thank you." The same had been said to Pep and Otis Lee. Breezy had gone home.

Knot saw one of Phillip's sisters leave her chair, which was next to Fran's. So she went and sat in it. Without any planning, Knot held out her arms. It was as if something had taken control of her body and her mind. And if that wasn't enough for Knot to wonder about, Fran placing Cedar in the bend of Knot's arms was. Eunice was the last small child Knot had held.

Fran didn't say a word. Instead, she laid Cedar in Knot's arms, turned back toward the table, and ate.

THAT EVENING AT the house that now belonged to Fran, Knot sipped the hurriedly made corn liquor she had bought when the news of Lady's death gripped her heart the same way Dinah Bright had once gripped her sore breast. After everyone had left the house, Knot and Fran wrapped the many cakes, pies, rolls, chicken legs, and hams that neighbors had brought. Knot had made four pecan pies and two large pans of bread pudding. The puddings hadn't lasted very long. Plenty of pecan pie remained.

The Lovings had taken Cedar home with them for the night, since they would also have La'Roy. They urged Fran to try to get some sleep.

"Won't you sit and rest a minute?" Knot asked. "And take a swalla of this here. Take two, three swallas." Even bad moonshine had been hard to come by. So Knot was surprised by her own offer to share.

Fran drank from Knot's glass, coughed, and set it on the table.

"I don't see how y'all drink that shit," Fran said. She made a funny face.

"Good," Knot replied. "Leave it right where it is."

In the middle of swaddling half of a Bundt cake, Knot heard Fran begin to play the piano. It startled her a little, because she hadn't heard Fran walk into the living room. Fran played a tune Knot didn't recognize, but she was certain that it didn't sound like anything anyone played in church. It reminded her of Miss Goldie's Place and the '40s, when she would sit at her favorite table swaying her head from side to side while Pratt played some of the most beautiful sounds she had ever heard. People would dance all around the room, holding their drinks up and away from their clothes.

Goldie's got a lot of damn nerve. Just up and decide to close.

As far as Knot knew, no one had heard anything from or about Pratt. Pep and Otis Lee would have let her know if they had received any word from him. And since Pratt's sister Pleasant and her twin girls had moved back to Tennessee shortly after Pratt had left town, there was no one around to ask. Knot figured Pratt Shepherd had moved on with his life and was probably happy, with a wife and children. *Might even have grand-young'uns. To tell the truth, I don't think I'd mind seeing Pratt. Just one time, maybe.*

Knot decided to have a slice of pound cake and asked Fran if she wanted one, too. Fran stopped playing the keys and sat still, but did not reply.

"Do that mean no?"

Even if Knot had received a warning card from the mailman two days in advance, she wouldn't have been ready for what Fran said next.

"Did you drink while you was pregnant with me?"

Like a draft sneaking through the space under a bedroom door, the question had come cool and easy. Knot didn't look in Fran's direction right away. She couldn't. She was afraid of the look she might find on the young woman's face. So Knot kept her eyes on the white-from-too-much-flour pound cake that Johnnie Mae had brought. She thought about Fran's other questions, the ones that hadn't been asked, like: *Is it true that you didn't even keep me a whole day?* Knot would have said, *Yeah, but you see I ain't fit, don'tcha?* And: *Who's my father?* To that, Knot would have answered, *He don't know nothin' about you and I ain't seen him since before I even knew I had you on the way. So what difference do it make?* Where were the cries and the cursing out? Just one time, if it ever came to it, Knot would have stood listening to every hot word. For Fran and for Eunice, she would take it just one good time. She'd let them say whatever they needed to say.

Still unable and unwilling to look up from the slice of pound cake, Knot pinched pieces of it and set them aside. Little pieces, the size someone might give to a baby who had recently begun eating table food.

"I ain't drink as much," Knot replied, also cool and easy. Now she was ready to look at Fran—her daughter—in the eyes. And when she did, she saw Pratt looking back at her. "I ain't gon' sit here and lie to ya. Pregnant or not, I was still me. So I drank."

Fran looked up at the wall in front of her—a wall covered with family photographs. Faces of people who had replaced Knot's family: Phillip's nieces, his sisters, the one brother, and many others. She went back to playing the piano, and the tunes were different. Much slower, with more church in them than the tunes she had played before.

Knot pinched pieces of cake until the whole slice was two little piles on the napkin. She wondered how long Fran had known the truth. She imagined Lady must have told her very recently, while her lungs were wracked with pneumonia.

Eunice. Fran ain't said nothin' 'bout Eunice. Do she know 'bout Eunice, too? Do Eunice know 'bout everything?

Since there was a spirit of asking and telling in the house that evening, Knot thought she might as well ask a few questions of her own.

FOURTEEN

It was twenty minutes past six o'clock in the morning when Otis Lee heard someone downstairs knocking at the door. He knew it wasn't Knot because she rarely knocked. That was something he and Pep had gotten used to and had come to find comical, years ago.

Pep, Cedar, and La'Roy were all snoring. Otis Lee had been awake for at least an hour, lying there thinking about the previous day. It had been a terrible sight: his most dependable neighbor and longtime friend, lowered into the ground. *Phil and Lady, both of them, gone too soon.* They had all looked forward to getting old and doing a bunch of nothing together.

The knocks were getting louder, so Otis Lee moved quicker. He got up and noticed that his grandchildren had somehow gotten tangled together and La'Roy's arm was just inches away from Pep's chin. Otis Lee had told Pep to put the children in Breezy's old bedroom for the night and to line the edges of the bed with pillows to keep them from rolling off. But she had refused. She had said they still might fall off the bed, break a limb, and that she and Otis Lee wouldn't know a thing about it until morning.

It *was* Knot at the door, after all.

"Where's Pep?" she demanded, once she was inside.

"Where's yo' coat?" Otis Lee asked, closing the door. "I seen enough death for one week." Knot stood in his kitchen wearing the dress she had worn to Phil's service—the same one she had worn to Lady's funeral. Her red hair was standing straight up on her head. It seemed to Otis Lee that every day the hair closest to Knot's scalp looked more and more like fresh milk.

"I said, where's Pep, goddamnit!" Knot shouted. She looked as though she were about to head for the stairs, but Otis Lee reached out and tugged on her arm. She snatched it away from him. He was so glad he and Pep had put all their dishes away before going to bed. From the look of things, if there had been a cup or saucer on the table, Knot might have thrown it.

"She still in the bed," Otis Lee whispered. Pep liked to sleep late on Sunday mornings, especially if she had decided to skip church. And he was not ready for Cedar and La'Roy to be awakened. He would need two cups of coffee first. "What in the devil is wrong with you, gal?"

"Got somethin' I needs to say to both y'all no-good Judases," Knot said. "I might as well get it out in one shot."

"*Judases*?" Otis Lee asked. "Now, you hold on just a min—"

"Y'all told 'em!" Knot yelled. "Y'all tol' 'em everything. Maybe I got a thing or two to tell, too!" She looked like she wanted to spit in his face.

"Talk sensible," Otis Lee pleaded. "Who told who what?"

"Y'all told the girls I'm they real mama," Knot said. "And nary a one of ya parted yo' lips and said a word to me about it. Ain't I got a right to at least know?"

She pulled out a chair and dropped herself onto it so hard the legs squeaked against the wooden floor. And before she had even settled into the chair, she was back up on her feet. It was as though she didn't know what to do with herself.

Otis Lee was certain that he hadn't said a word to Fran or his daughter-in-law about Knot being their birth mother. He and Pep had not even told Breezy.

"Knot," Otis Lee began. He gently touched her elbow and led her back to the same chair she had sat in for less than a second. "Sit and catch ya' breath, Knot. Please. Catch ya' breath and then we'll talk about it. Want some water or somethin'?"

She declined the offer of water but sat. His plea seemed to have calmed her some. But her eyes still bored into him as if she might slap him at any moment, which was why he placed his chair near hers, but not too close.

"The day of that fight they had," Knot said.

"Eunice and Fran's fight?" Otis Lee asked. "Knot, that's been four, five years ago. Why you—"

"That's when Pep tol' them," Knot explained. "And you ain't said nothin'."

"'Cause I—"

"Fran ain't got no cause to lie, Otis Lee," Knot broke in. "What she gon' lie for?"

He could hear the pain in her voice. It reminded him of hearing that her father had returned the letters she'd written. Otis Lee knew this was a time for him to be quiet and listen. So he asked Knot to tell him all that Fran had said.

After Pep had pulled Fran and Eunice apart by the collars, escorted them to the back of the house, and slapped them both because they had nearly knocked her over trying to get to each other again, she made them sit down on the back porch. Pep lined Eunice, Fran, and Breezy up as if they were little children at school, Fran had told Knot.

"Fran said Pep spit it right out," Knot told him. "Said: 'Y'all sisters. Knot's y'all's mama.' " Knot got to her feet again and pointed toward Busy Street. "That's why Eunice left town quick like she did."

If even a soft breeze had come through the window, it would have knocked Otis Lee from his chair.

"And y'all two," Knot accused, her voice shaky now, "y'all two look me right in my face damn near every day, and neither one of you opened yo' mouths to tell me that the girls know! I didn't *want* them to know, Otis Lee. That's the best thing I coulda ever done for 'em. Ain't I got a right to that?"

Otis Lee was about to tell Knot that he was hearing all of it for the first time, but he heard Pep's voice behind him from the stairs. Her voice startled him because he hadn't heard her moving around upstairs in their bedroom.

"Whole lot of nerve you got, Miss Centre," Pep said, now standing in front of them, looking only at Knot. Her tone reminded Otis Lee of the Sunday, back in the '40s, when Pep had walked up to one of the neighbors—Johnnie Mae—in the churchyard and fussed her out for spreading the silly rumor that Pep was letting Otis Lee lay with Knot. And when he'd made the mistake of telling Knot what had happened, he had to pull her away from Johnnie Mae's front porch. "Otis Lee Loving's like a *brother* to me, you buck-toothed cow!"

Now Otis Lee had to wonder if Pep saw him sitting there. She hadn't offered him so much as a glance. And as cold as it was in the kitchen, Pep was wearing nothing except her thin nightgown.

"You come in my house talkin' 'bout yo' rights? Yo' rights to any of what them girls get to *know* and *don't* get to know was gone when Lady and Ayra went home with them babies in they arms."

Otis Lee looked up at his beautiful wife of thirty-three years, then at the woman he cared for as if she were a blood relative, like a sister. Knot had become just that to him. A sister. That's how he loved her. How could he not?

Now the trouble was that he didn't know which of them—Pep or Knot—to be most upset with. Was it the one who had kept such a secret from him for the past three or four years—*and she musta tol' our boy to keep the secret, too*—or was it the one who had come into their home, angry to no end, as though someone owed her something? *As good as me and Pep been to her?*

"You made me a promise," Knot reminded them. "Right here in this room, y'all made me a promise. And ya made it again at my bedside. Twice!"

"But listen to this here," Pep began. She stepped closer to Knot. "I made another promise to somebody else. To my *son*. The day I reach 'tweenst my own legs and pull him outta me by his shoulders, I made a promise to him that long as I draw breath in and out of my body, I was gon' look out for him. Do whatever I got to do that's good for *him*."

Pep said she had believed with all her heart that if Breezy knew Fran and Eunice were sisters, he would stop causing them so much pain with the back and forth. She said she thought she was killing two birds with one stone. "'Specially since they had got to fightin' and carryin' on. I'm his mama, Knot Centre," Pep went on. "I did what I thought was best for my boy. Best for all *three* of 'em, I thought. Nobody else was doin' nothin' to fix it."

Otis Lee had been looking down at the floor, but he looked at Pep when she said the last part. And their eyes met. La'Roy's whines and whimpers were the relief he needed. So Otis Lee stood and headed for the stairs.

"Come back," she said. "I'll 'tend to him. You stay down here and talk to yo' *friend* 'bout her rights. And when you get through with that, you get her out o' my goddamn house."

"Penelope!" Otis Lee shouted. He watched her disappear up the stairs toward their grandson's cries.

From upstairs Pep said, "They's more to worry 'bout in life than drinkin' and readin' them damn books, Knot." She didn't say another word. And when Otis turned back around, Knot was halfway out of the door.

He hadn't liked the way Pep had said *friend*. She had spoken the word in the same way she would when she meant one thing and said another. Their many years of marriage had taught him to know the difference—although sometimes he needed a direct answer from her. In any case, he liked neither the way she had said *friend* nor what she had implied.

Had he spent too much time worrying about Knot and her doings? Yes. When Knot was younger and new to Antioch Lane, had Otis Lee stayed up and waited until he'd seen her get home? *Yes. That's just the right thing to do for any neighbor who don't know her lay of the land yet. Right?* Had the eggs, the chickens, all the things he had stolen from Pennington Farm and given to Knot to be sure she ate well—especially with all the drinking—had it been too much? *Some folk might say so.* Had he shown all of his neighbors as much care and attention as he had shown Knot, and still offered her?

Knot ain't like the rest of 'em, damn it! She different!

How so, Otis Lee? How's she different?

She different from them, and she just like Essie.

Had Pep really believed that Breezy would stop wanting both Fran and Eunice simply because they had the same mother? She couldn't have, he thought to himself. *That there's why Breezy loved the two of 'em so much. They got the same blood movin' warm through they veins.* Eunice and Fran looked nearly nothing alike, but to Otis Lee there was plenty that made them similar: they went after whatever and whomever they wanted, and neither of them had ever been shy with their words.

Otis Lee sat at the kitchen table with the first cup of coffee, of which he had only taken a few sips. Pep came down the stairs with Cedar on one hip and La'Roy on the other. She placed both children on Otis Lee's lap and got them both a slice of white bread, a dollop of pear preserves spread evenly on each.

Otis Lee watched her every move. Watched and wondered. She went about the tasks as if nothing out of the ordinary had happened just ten minutes ago.

"Bacon, sausage, or both?" Pep said to him.

"Why you tell them gals—"

"I ain't gon' talk 'bout that all day." She put the frying pan on the left front burner.

"It won't be all day, Penelope," Otis Lee said. "But we gon' talk about it right now."

She got some bacon from the Frigidaire. They had run out of sausage.

Without pause, Pep told Otis Lee that it wasn't fair. And when he repeated, "Fair?" he said it louder than intended. Both grandchildren turned their heads to look up at him.

"It ain't fair," Pep whispered. "Ain't fair that Knot get to live her life any way she want and ev'rybody else got 'tend to her business, keep her children alive and well and happy." The bacon sizzled. "Knot needs to hurt, Otis Lee. I know that ain't right to say, but she need to feel *some* hurt."

"Don't you recall Knot sittin' at this table, near 'bout crazy from sadness when she had them babies?" Otis Lee asked. He helped Cedar and La'Roy tear their slices of bread into smaller pieces. "She *did* have some hurt, Pep. A whole lot."

"That's what her problem is," Pep said. She cracked brown eggs one by one against the side of the cookstove and she let their insides drop into the hot skillet. "She *did* have it. Other people's *still* got it. Might *always* have it. But like I said, it ain't fair."

Otis Lee felt as though he were talking to a stranger.

After having told Fran and Eunice the truth, Pep had, for a short time, felt guilty, she admitted. "But when Essie came here and tol' you 'bout how she got sent off, as hurt as you was 'bout the lies you got told all your life, you was freed up some. You might notta known, but I saw it. You was better when Essie left here."

"Stay on the track, Pep," Otis Lee said. "We talkin' 'bout—"

"I thought I was doin' the right thing. And now I'm through wit' it."

"Why you keep it from *me*, though, Pep? And got my son lyin' to me, too."

"He ain't got nothin' to do wit' it," Pep said. "And I say I'm through wit' it. Ya hear me? What's done is done."

The two of them sat at the table quietly. Pep fed Cedar, and Otis Lee fed La'Roy. The children began to refuse the bits of eggs being held in front of their mouths, so Otis Lee and Pep fed themselves.

"Lord," Otis Lee sighed. La'Roy was now playing with Otis Lee's nose. "She probably over there 'bout to drink herself to—" He did not want to finish the sentence. "She ain't want them girls to know, Penelope."

He waited for a response from his wife. A sign of remorse, he hoped.

"Well, I forgive ya," he said, finally.

"Forgive *me*? For what?" Pep asked, slowly laying her fork on the table, out of Cedar's reach.

Otis Lee turned his head to release his bottom lip from his grandson's clutch.

"You got nerve enough to ask me that? After you done kept somethin' serious as that from me for four years? You oughta be *glad* I forgive ya."

Pep's laugh was coated in anguish.

"Maybe I got some things I need to forgive *you* for, too, then," she said. "Me and Breezy *both*."

"Well, I'm listenin'," Otis Lee told her, "'cause I ain't done nothin' but *loved* y'all, and worked *hard* to keep both of y'all happy."

"Not half as much as you love Essie and Knot, though," Pep insisted.

"Now, that some crazy talk, there, Pep," he said. "Ev'rything—ev'ry single thing I *ever* done for Knot—you got told 'bout it beforehand. *Always* beforehand, Pep. And you always gave yo' blessin'!"

"*Course* I gave my blessin'," Pep replied. "Wit' my words, I gave you my blessin'. But don't you know me, Otis Lee? Sometimes you ain't got to say a word and I know what you feelin' and thinkin' in yo' head. Can't you do that for me? I guess not."

Pep stood up, put Cedar on Otis Lee's other thigh, and went upstairs.

"Penelope!" Otis Lee shouted. "Penelope, come on back."

FIFTEEN

Burning the books, and using liquor to do it, had crossed Knot's mind several times between the time she left the Lovings' house and now. But to whom, or what, would she turn when people—real people—let her down? And even though her pa—the person who had shared her love for the written word—had become one of those real people, the books were all she had left of the Pa she had known before he abandoned her.

Life is funny, ain't it? I got two grown children—even got two grand-children—and I'm sittin' here, thinkin' about bein' somebody's child.

Knot heated a pot of water for a washup. And after she had mixed it with a few jars of cold water, she added the last bit of perfume oil that Pep had given to her before Lady Waters's funeral. She stood in front of her barely standing vanity and scrubbed herself from head to toe. The funeral dress lay draped across the chair next to her bed. She thought she had tossed it haphazardly when she'd taken if off. Instead, it looked as though someone had laid it out carefully for her to wear again.

Now dressed the way she might if she were going to inquire about an advertisement for employment, Knot stood far back from her mirror and looked for anything that might cause offense.

All right, Knot. Just as well go on and get this over with.

Knot hadn't been to the apartment since Valley had moved out of it. Although she hadn't made it inside yet, she could tell it would look far different from how she remembered it. The staircase leading up to it was new. The wood used to build it reminded her of the schoolhouse. And there were potted plants—she was not able to identify them, but Dinah Bright might have—on the right end of every other step.

The door opened and Breezy came down, running almost, looking around as if he were dodging a loan shark.

"Hey, Knot," he said. "What you need?"

"You ought to have somethin on yo' chest, boy," she scolded.

He asked again, "What ya need?"

"I come to talk to yo' wife," she said.

Breezy told Knot that she didn't need to worry about apologizing to Eunice about the past. "She got a good life," he said.

"I know she do," Knot said. "But I figure she might want to say somethin' or ask me somethin'. No better time than the pres—"

"She don't, Knot," Breezy cut in, his nostrils flaring.

It was not fear that forced Knot to take two steps back; it was concern. "Eunice made peace with you bein' her real mama years ago. She fine. *We* fine. But if you go up them steps, it might bring on trouble ain't nobody lookin' for." He looked up toward the door nervously. "Eunice said she grateful it had all happened the way it did. Good for everybody."

"And you don't think she got nothin' to get out?" Knot asked.

"No, Knot," he replied. He glanced up at the door again. "Trust me on this. Let the past stay where it is."

"Well," Knot said, having studied Breezy long enough. "I'm goin' home. But don't you ever forget I tried and you got in my way. Hear?"

"I won't forget," he reassured her. "Thank ya, Knot."

Before turning to walk away, Knot looked at him once more. This time she saw the eyes that had looked up at her the day she had gone into labor and sent him to get his mother. And she had called on him again, just hours before his wife had been born. *Two times. Breezy always wanted two. Two of everything.* His big, tea-brown eyes had been full of wonder in those days. But now they seemed to be full of worry.

JUST AFTER NOON, Knot was back at her house. She pulled off the brown-and-white dress and tossed it in the corner of her bedroom. She poured a drink—a short one, just enough to loosen the tension she had been carrying in her neck all morning—and opened the letter that had come from Valley a few days earlier.

December 20, 1964

Dear Knot,

I'll be glad when you folks get some telephone lines on Antioch Lane. I'm tired of writing these damn letters. I'm in New York. Been here about a month. I don't care much for it anymore. I thought D.C. was busy and loud. NYC is nothing but noise. I must be getting old. I know because noise never got on my nerves so bad. I got some loose ends tied up though.

You know I turned 51, don't you? Anyway, I'm writing to tell you I'll be heading to West Mills in a couple of weeks. And

I want you to make me a bread pudding when I get there. I'll be there around the 10th or 11th. Planning on staying a good while.

Knot, if you don't mind, will you go to Gertrude's house to sweep and dust a little bit for me? I'm bringing somebody with me. His name is Mitchell. From England. He's around my age. Well, that's what he claims, but I swear I think he's 60 or 65. He looks nice though so I'm ok with it. He's nice and he wants to see North Carolina. You going to love how he talk, Knot. You'll get to hear what the people in them books you read talk like.

Anyway sister, do that for me, please. And I'll pay you when I get there. See if you can get your hands on a jar of the good stuff for me. Check with Max first. He made a nice batch before I left. It was not half bad for it being his first time at it.
Ok. Love you. Bye.
Valor

Reading the letter made Knot feel good. And she was glad he would soon be home. *Course he want a bread puddin'*, Knot thought to herself, smiling. Before Mary and Onslow had shown up in West Mills, dressed in all black, Knot had been trying her hand at making various types of new cobblers. Peach. Cherry. She had made one with peach and cherry. The cobblers had turned out well enough for her to try again.

Knot thought she might make one for Valley and his new friend—to go along with the bread pudding, of course. But what she wasn't going to do was go and clean up the place he still referred to as "Gertrude's house." Many times, Knot had told Valley that she would never go into that house alone again. Because the last time she had agreed to have it ready for one of his homecomings, she could have sworn she smelled sassafras in the air. Otis Lee and Valley had once told her that Gertrude had loved sassafras tea and other uncommon root teas. Valley had always hated them. And after Gertrude died, he purged the cupboards. So when Knot thought she smelled it, she left the cleaning bucket where it sat. It was Otis Lee who went back to make sure she had locked the doors.

"Valley can sweep his own damn floors when he get here," Knot said to Fran a week later.

"What loose ends Valley got in New York?" Fran asked.

"Probably somethin' to do with Es—" Knot began but stopped herself. "Ain't no tellin', and it ain't none of my business."

Knot was glad she hadn't spit Essie's secret out at Otis Lee when she had gone to his house, mad, the morning after Phillip Waters's burial service.

Fran offered to go along with her to Valley's house, but the day before they planned to go, another letter from Valley came in the mail. Mitchell from London had invited Valley to travel back to England with him—just for a few months, Valley's letter said. And Valley had said yes. He assured Knot that he would stay there no longer than three months—even less if Mitchell got on his nerves. *Write me back, Knot,* he had written above his signature. Mitchell from London's address was a curious-looking stack of numbers and words penned at the bottom of the paper.

Now Knot felt a twinge of loneliness. She was happy to receive more regular visits from Fran. And Otis Lee made his rounds. Whether Pep knew or approved, Knot didn't know. But Knot missed Valley more than she had realized. And when she replied to his letter, she was sure to mention it.

Filling Valley in on the recent deaths, the betrayal she had suffered from Pep, and about Fran and Eunice knowing the truth about their births would not be right for this letter. His knowing would not change any of it. She wanted him to enjoy himself. *The dead rest with the dead*, she thought as she got toward the end of her note to him. And as a postscript Knot wrote: *Bring me something signed by the Queen*.

SIXTEEN

On a Saturday afternoon in January of '66, Otis Lee walked across the lane to Fran's house. He needed a laugh. For that, he could count on Cedar. Much like both of her parents had been, Cedar was a happy, agreeable child.

While on the floor playing with Cedar and the lettered blocks he and Pep had bought her for Christmas—Sears, Roebuck had offered the most affordable price—he noticed that Fran's belly looked round and hard. She must have seen him when he'd taken the fourth glance because she gave him the answer to a question he had been taught never to ask a woman unless she was his wife or his daughter.

"You didn't know?" Fran asked. "Pep gave me a piece of her mind about it last week."

Lecturing Fran about her ongoing affair with his married son would have been a waste of his time. He had done that already, to no avail, it would appear. *The more you try to steer 'em from somethin', the more they go to it. They ain't gon' be satisfied 'til they drive me crazy!*

Damp-chested from the sweat of frustration and from the overbearing heat of Fran's woodstove, Otis Lee marched home to confront his wife about keeping yet another secret. She knew how he felt about her keeping things, important things, from him. He had made himself clear about that. Who had Pep become? he wondered.

The faster he walked, the farther away his house seemed.

There was a new-looking, shiny black car driving by, and it slowed down in front of him. Otis Lee waved the driver down.

"Yes?" the driver, a middle-aged colored man, asked.

"Essie send you to spy on me?"

"I'm sorry?" the man in the car said.

"Ellen," Otis Lee corrected. "Ellen O'Heeney. She send you to spy on me, ain't she?"

"I don't know what you talkin' 'bout, brotha man."

The gentleman rolled his window back up and drove toward the dead end of Antioch Lane, where Miss Goldie's Place stood empty. Otis Lee watched the car turn around and head back up the lane, toward up-bridge. Otis Lee went inside and looked out the kitchen window. He was sure the shiny black automobile would come by again.

"Otis Lee Loving," Pep said, "what's ailin' you?"

And then he remembered what his mission had been when he had left Fran's house, before he had seen the car. He turned to her and declared, "I ain't tellin' you *nothin'*!"

"Fine," Pep said.

"When you start tellin' *me* stuff, I'll start tellin' *you* stuff. How ya like *that*?"

Pep walked to him and held his face in her soft hands.

"We got grandbaby number three comin'," she told him, smiling. "Happy now?"

Otis Lee felt himself relax, though against his will.

"What we gon' do with that boy of ours, Penelope?"

"Nothin'," she replied. "Tol' you years and *years* ago that I felt sorry for whoever was crazy enough to marry him."

Otis Lee felt sorry for Eunice, too. But it didn't seem to him that Eunice was feeling sorry for herself. Now it was Fran for whom Otis Lee felt the most concern. *She love Breezy that damn much?*

Otis Lee could not help but think that maybe Knot could talk Fran into moving on, finding love elsewhere. Surely there were other men in West Mills whom she could have—if only she wanted anyone else. Now a second baby was coming. *What's done is done.* But he thought, just maybe, if Knot might speak with her daughter, they could prevent a third Breezy-Fran baby. He would have to at least ask Knot. *She gon' sure as hell say no*, Otis Lee thought, *but I'm gon' ask her.*

So Otis Lee was surprised when, the following day, Knot said, "Well, what you want me to say, exactly?" She was standing in front of the counter Breezy had built for her, rolling out dough for a cherry pie order.

"I don't know," Otis Lee said. "You her mama. Ain't you got some kinda gut feelin' or somethin' 'bout these things?"

Knot rolled her eyes. And as she sprinkled flour over the dough, she said, "Go to hell, Otis Lee."

"You gon' talk to her or what?" Otis Lee asked. "Fran's gon' be the one hurtin' behind all this mess. Breezy ain't gon' leave Eunice. I can tell you that right now."

"Why you so sure 'bout that?" Knot said.

"'Cause he's mine," Otis Lee answered. "And I know him. Know him well."

Knot went about her work as though he were not there. He was thinking about their conversation when he noticed a book on the corner of the kitchen table.

"*The Old Curi . . . Curi-oh—*"

"*Curiosity*," Knot said.

"*The Old Curiosity Shop*," Otis Lee read aloud.

SEVENTEEN

Later that year, in June, Fran brought forth another little girl. Knot decided to wait almost two weeks before visiting. Since Fran had not sent for her—nor had she complained to Otis Lee about Knot's absence—Knot felt certain that Fran understood.

But Fran must have grown tired of understanding, because she showed up on Knot's porch one day, one daughter in her arms, the other standing next to her. Cedar held a fat pencil in one hand and a notepad in the other.

"I needed to get out o' the house awhile," Fran declared. "And don't you think it's time you meet my new baby?"

"Otis Lee say you named her Lady," Knot said. "Bring 'em on inside. The heat."

Once they were seated, Fran said, "Lady Sequoia Loving. Cedar done started callin' her 'Coy,' though." Knot looked at the sleeping baby, then at Fran's pretty smile. The new child looked like Breezy. So much so that Knot wondered if Fran had had any part in it at all.

"Lady Coy," Knot said. "This one's gon' be moufy and uppity. I can see it in her lil frown. I think I'll call her 'Lady Coy.' Y'all call her what ya want to call her."

Fran smiled and yawned. Then she said, "Show me yo' new room. Finished now, ain't it?"

Knot had forgotten that Fran had not seen the finished room that had been added to the back end of the house. Clara Pennington, Riley's youngest daughter, had come to Knot's house one day to pick up the ten pies she had ordered. Knot hadn't seen Clara survey the rooms, but she knew Clara Pennington well enough to know it was happening.

"Miss Knot, I'm just gon' be right honest with ya," Clara said, "and I hope you won't take offense, but I just don't know how in the *world* you do it."

"Do what, Clara?"

"Live in such a cooped-up ol' lil place such as this."

"Well," Knot said, biting her tongue, "I *like* my lil ol' cooped-up place. Nobody livin' here but me. I'm fine."

"Okay," Clara said. "Well, I sure do hope my granddaddy sold it to you cheap all them years ago. Should've just *given* it to ya."

That's exactly what he did, Clara Pennington. I told him he won't get no more money outta me for this shack. So he gave it, and this lil block of land, to me. I ain't paid nothin' but taxes. But that ain't nobody's business but mine and his—God rest his soul.

"He gave me a fair price," Knot said instead.

About a week after that, Clara came to Knot's house again—this time, not to pick up baked goods. And her brothers had joined her. They were holding pencils, small notepads, and measuring tape.

"Now, Miss Knot," Clara Pennington began, "don't cuss us out." She wanted to have an addition built on to the back of Knot's house—"For all your service," she explained. "Please let us."

At first, Knot did want to curse Clara Pennington out. But another idea came to her mind.

"Naw, I don't believe I want y'all to build me no room," Knot had said. "I thank ya kindly for the thought, though. Now, y'all go on home or somewhere."

That evening Knot went into her pantry and pulled down the old tin can where she kept her money. She counted it twice.

Well, Clara do make some sense, don't she?

Knot asked Valley and a few men with whom he got along to build her a new bedroom. The old bedroom would be her living room, she told them.

"Looks *good*, Knot," Fran admired. She had propped Lady Coy on her shoulder. "Looks *real* nice. I'm proud of ya."

She say she proud of me. Well, I'll be damned.

Now back in the kitchen, Fran yawned again.

"Felt like the walls was closin' in on me over there," she said. "And these two want every lil bit of energy I got."

Knot's saying that she understood would not have been the right thing, though she did have some understanding of what Fran was going through. The difference was that Knot had gone through it without the children, which was the reason she had decided several months before, when Otis Lee asked her to have a talk with Fran, that she would not get involved. *I ain't got the right.*

Knot opened a bottle of pop and poured some for Fran and a little bit for Cedar. "Since when you start drinking pop?" Fran asked, smiling mischievously.

Knot took Fran's meaning and she didn't like it.

"Look here," Knot said. "Don't start. You want it or not?"

Fran took the glass and drank the cola without pausing to breathe.

Just a week earlier, Valley had taught Knot a trick to make her brandy last longer. The brandy-pop mixture had taken her by surprise. Now she made sure to have a few bottles of cola in her pantry at all times.

Cedar did not take a single sip of hers. The child was not keen on sweets, Otis Lee had once told Knot. She had forgotten. Cedar was the only child Knot knew who loved to drink water and eat raw carrots.

There was a perplexing look on Fran's face when Knot looked at her. Fran looked tired as she rocked the infant. But Knot also saw something that resembled peace. Cedar was on the floor, on the yellow quilt Knot had laid down for her, writing capital letters and naming them out loud. She moved her legs as though she were swimming, her hair divided to form three ponytails: one on the left, one on the right, one in back.

Let me go 'head and get this over with.

"Tell me one thing," Knot said. Fran rolled her eyes. "Is you gon' give Breezy any more young'uns?"

"I don't know," Fran snapped. She didn't seem to have taken even a second to think it over. It was as though she had known the question was coming. "But I might if I feel up to it."

"Lady Waters got to be spinnin' in her grave," Knot remarked. "Lady and Phil both got to be spinnin'."

"We come over for a nice visit," Fran grumbled, "but if you gon' chastise me, we'll just go on back home." But she did not get up.

Knot could hardly stand moments like these—moments when she saw and heard just how much she and Fran were so much alike.

It was Knot who was spinning. Her mind was spinning with madness and sadness. She was sad for Fran. Mad for Eunice. Sad and mad for both of them. But, years ago, Knot had promised herself—a promise she was unable to keep—that she would no longer worry about the Eunice-Breezy-Fran saga. They were three adults with children of their own.

"You know what?" Knot shot back. "Do whatever the hell you want to do. Go on home if you want. I don't care."

That was the first lie Knot had told Fran in a long time.

After a long sigh, Fran said, "Who had a baby from him first, Knot? Huh? Breezy got his reasons for marrying Eunice."

"You said you ain't want to talk 'bout it," Knot reminded her, "so I don't want to hear nothin'."

That was the second lie Knot had told Fran in a long time. And Knot wondered if even Lady Coy knew it was a lie, because she started fidgeting and whining. Fran pulled out a breast and began to nurse. Then Fran reminded Knot that Pep and Otis Lee had lost income.

"Ain't nobody called on Pep to deliver a baby in God knows when," Fran said. "Women want doctors and things now. Younger people." And Otis Lee's knees had become a hindrance. Just twenty minutes of standing required BC Powder. His hours at the farm had been cut, Fran said.

These were things Knot already knew. She and Pep had only recently reconciled their differences, and that was when Pep told her all about it. Knot didn't want to think about it.

If she thought about Otis Lee and Pep's aging, she would have to think of her own.

"Why you sittin' there tellin' me all this like I just come to West Mills this mornin'?" Knot said.

Fran sighed again and moved her limp bangs away from her face. "How you think Otis Lee's Frigidaire stays stocked full of food? Where you think Breezy got the money to buy stuff to put that new roof on Pep and Otis Lee's house?" Fran listed the many things Breezy had done, and for each she asked Knot, "Where you think he got the money? You think he makin' *that* much money from changin' oil in folks' cars? Or from trimmin' folks' shrubs?" She switched Lady Coy from one breast to the other.

"C-E-D," Cedar spelled, talking to her sheet of paper. Her legs were still swimming over the yellow quilt.

"That's enough now, Fran," Knot said. "All I know is that Breezy got a wife, and you—"

"I don't care nothin' 'bout Eunice standin' in front of the pastor with Breezy," Fran declared. "Shit. I'm the one told him to go 'head and marry her. For the money. That lil marriage they got ain't hittin' on *nothin'*. It ain't *never* been hittin' on nothin'."

Knot went to the pantry and poured a splash of cola and three splashes of brandy. That was not what Valley had shown her.

But what about Eunice? Knot almost said to Fran. But as far as she knew, Eunice hadn't made threats to take La'Roy and leave again. Had Eunice stopped caring? Was she so busy, now that Brock and Ayra had retired and put the general store in her charge—not to mention the choirs—that she had stopped caring about her marriage?

Knot stood on the threshold between her kitchen and pantry looking at Fran, Cedar, and Lady Coy. Her daughter and two granddaughters. That was who they were now. She knew it would be foolish to think of them simply as her neighbors.

Knot quickly finished her drink. Fran had Lady Coy up on her shoulder again, patting her back, trying to get her to belch.

Cedar came over to Knot and said, "Look, Knot! Look what I can write!"

"I ain't got my glasses," Knot told her. "Can't you read it to me?"

Knot imagined her own pa sitting in the corner of the room. He would be smiling if he were there. And he'd tell everyone in town that Cedar was suited for teaching.

Cedar seemed more than happy to give a lesson.

"It's my *other* name," she announced. With the fat pencil she pointed at each letter.

"L-O-V-I-N-G."

EIGHTEEN

Otis Lee and Pep sat on their couch, shoulder to shoulder, watching the midday news. Walter Cronkite was talking about the Vietnam War, which Otis Lee was glad had—just a few weeks ago—come to a close. Getting their first television had made Pep what he called a newsaholic. If she was not watching soap operas, she looked for news. When King was shot and killed seven years ago, in '68, Otis Lee and Pep spent a great deal of time at Breezy and Eunice's apartment, watching the coverage. After King's funeral, Pep said she never wanted a television in her house. They were terrible things that brought sadness, she said. But when Breezy showed up with one four months ago, Otis Lee had to threaten to cut the power cord to get her to turn it off.

While Cronkite spoke, Otis Lee wondered what his life might have been like had he gone into the service. A handful of men from West Mills had gone to fight in various wars. Those who had come back with their right minds sat up-bridge and told their stories. Those who had lost their right minds sat up-bridge trying to tell their stories. Otis Lee remembered when the draft office in Norfolk, Virginia, had written and told him to report for an examination. Rose, Ma Noni, and Pep had been sick with fear. As was Otis Lee, but he had hidden it and cried in private. In Norfolk they took his measurements. He was to go home and wait for further instruction, if there would be further instruction.

"You mind if I change the station?" Otis Lee asked.

"I *do* mind," Pep replied, dragging a comb slowly through her salt-and-pepper hair.

"Is that my comb?" he said. And then: "Pep, you sit there and act like you don't hear me talkin' to you?"

"Leave me alone, Otis Lee. You sat up-bridge all mornin'. You think 'cause you decide to come home you can run my TV set?"

It would be a losing battle. "Hand me my comb," he said. She pushed his hand away and kept her eyes on Cronkite.

There was a knock at the door, and when Otis Lee opened it, there were two Mahalia Jackson–looking women with big hairdos standing on his porch. They were both smiling at him.

"Can I help y'all?" he offered.

The one wearing all denim spoke first. "You don't remember us, do you, Mr. Loving?"

He looked at them closely—one and then the other. They looked familiar, but not familiar enough.

"I'm sorry to say I don't," he confessed.

"I'm Vera," the one in denim said.

"I'm Vic," said the one in black pants and an orange blouse. "Victoria. We're Pl—"

"Pleasant's girls?" he exclaimed. "Great day in the mornin'! Get in here!" He opened the door and yelled for Pep.

Once Pep had hugged them several times—she also kissed both their faces—Vic said they had a surprise. She would be back in just a minute, she said.

Otis Lee, Pep, and Vera sat in the living room. Pep asked Vera to bring them up to date on her and her sister's lives. Otis Lee wanted to ask about Pratt, but he figured Pratt had likely died in the service, since he hadn't written or visited. And there was always the possibility, Otis Lee thought, that Pratt had simply decided that West Mills and everyone in it were a part of his past, just as Essie had.

While Vera talked, Otis Lee looked at Cronkite, waiting for the perfect moment to mention Pratt.

"Damn if y'all ain't got old," Otis Lee heard coming from behind him. The voice was rough and smoky—a man's voice.

Otis Lee stood and turned to find Pratt Shepherd, still tall, smiling with large bright dentures.

"Great day in the mornin'!" Otis Lee exclaimed once more.

He and Pratt embraced like long-lost brothers. Otis Lee didn't know when the tears had come. So he was surprised when Pratt pulled a tissue from his pocket and handed it to him.

"Look at this ol' crybaby here, y'all," Pratt teased.

Otis Lee tore the tissue into two and he gave half back to Pratt. "That makes two of us." Then he looked around the room at the other four faces. "Five of us, really."

They laughed and hugged again.

Otis Lee and Pep made tuna sandwiches for their guests. Once the sandwiches were eaten, Otis Lee and Pratt went down and across the lane to the old house where Vera, Vic, and Pleasant had once lived.

"The girls gon' have what's left of this ole place torn down," Pratt told Otis Lee. "Gon' try to sell the land."

"Smart," Otis Lee said. He asked Pratt how he'd been.

"Livin' a plain ol' life," Pratt answered. "Was married for 'bout fifteen years."

"Yeah?" Otis Lee said. "What happened with that?"

"Grew apart, I guess."

"Oh," Otis Lee said. "Any children?" He wished he could pull the question back into his mouth and swallow it.

"Naw," Pratt said, and he chuckled. "I had my nieces and nephews 'round, though." He told Otis Lee that when he'd gotten back to Tennessee, after being honorably discharged, his brothers and Pleasant had children enough for everyone.

"Breezy was enough for us," Otis Lee said. "He's got three, and that *still* ain't stopped him from being enough for us, Pratt. I swear!"

"He still like two drumsticks on his plate?" Pratt asked.

"Same Breezy," Otis Lee affirmed. "Still want two of ev'rything."

They walked through Pleasant's old house, stepping on and over loose floorboards and talking about how well some of the wood had held up over the years.

"I see Azalea's house is still there," Pratt remarked.

Otis Lee was wondering when Pratt would mention her. Otis Lee hadn't mentioned her because he was still trying to decide how much of Knot's past he should tell Pratt and how much Knot ought to tell him herself—if Pratt planned to see her at all.

"Yeah," Otis Lee said. "It's still there. She still there in it, too. Slowin' down a lil, like the rest of us. But Knot is still Knot—you can believe *that*."

"She ain't got married?" Pratt asked.

"Nooooo."

"She got children?"

"Sorta," Otis Lee admitted.

They looked at each other.

"Vic and Vera ain't gon' get much for this land," Pratt said, looking out of the cracked bedroom window. He told Otis Lee that the twins had only recently learned that the lot belonged to them. Pleasant had always believed that the land belonged to a white man and that they were merely renters. But as it turned out, Bo Frost had owned the land. So, the twins were next in line for it, although they had little to no interest in owning property in the town where their mother had so horribly suffered. It was Pratt who had urged them to come to West Mills and start the process of selling it.

"It's so small," Pratt said, "might not even be able to sell it at all."

"Yeah," Otis Lee agreed. "Well, maybe somebody'll buy it to put one of them mobile homes on. One of them'll fit nice on it."

In Pleasant's yard, Otis Lee and Pratt stood and talked about this thing and the other. Otis Lee was consumed by curiosity about Pratt's time in the military, but he thought about the veterans who sat up-bridge. *I'll wait for Pratt to tell me whatever he feel like tellin'*.

"Tell my nieces to sit tight a lil while," Pratt said. "I'm goin' over there and see 'bout Azalea for a few minutes. She live by herself?"

"Yeah. Mostly," Otis Lee said. "Valley's there with her half the time, though."

"Ain't much changed at all, is it?" Pratt asked.

"You in West Mills," Otis Lee reminded him.

Otis Lee watched Pratt until Knot came to her door and let him in. He would have loved to have heard what she said when she opened the door. Otis Lee was happy to see his old friend again, but he couldn't help but wonder if Pratt's visit would be good or bad for Knot. Otis Lee thought it might be good for Knot to see someone who had once loved her so much that he'd left town to make the love stop. But Pratt had a daughter who he did not know existed. And if he found out, it might send Knot deeper into the bottle over something so far in the past—all of their pasts.

An hour passed, and Pratt's nieces told Otis Lee and Pep that they were going to check into a motel. They would come back for Pratt in a little while. Pep insisted that they leave Pratt's suitcase with her and Otis Lee. Pratt could sleep in Breezy's old bedroom, she said. She wouldn't have it any other way.

The twins had been gone for only a few minutes when Pep mused, "Maybe we oughta walk over there and make sure they all right. Remember how they used to argue and carry on?"

"I ain't forgot," Otis Lee said. "Let's give 'em 'til mornin'. He'da been back a long time ago if they was arguin'."

OTIS LEE HEARD Pratt come in early the next morning, just after the sun had begun to show the crown of its head. Otis Lee met him in the kitchen. It reminded him of when Breezy used to come home past his curfew.

Otis Lee could have been toppled over by a twig when Pratt said, "You know, I was thinkin' 'bout what you said yesterday."

"What's that?" Otis Lee asked.

"I do believe I want to look into how much them mobile homes cost."

For many days after saying his good-byes to Pratt, Vera, and Vic, Otis Lee felt a heavy burden.

"I let him leave this house without him knowin' he had a daughter," he lamented.

"Listen," Pep said, climbing in bed next to him. "Pratt was right there in Knot's house last week and she ain't tell him. It ain't for you to worry about no more." She lay down and turned her back to him. Then she sat up again. "I know you don't think I do, but I loves Knot, too. But I ain't goin' back down this road wit' you again 'bout her secrets. I just ain't."

STRANGELY, IT WAS his wife's whispers that woke him up in the middle of the night. It was not until he was downstairs in their living room that he was able to make out what she was saying.

"Forgive me, Lord," Pep pleaded. "Please forgive me."

"Pep?" Otis Lee asked, kneeling in front of her. They were in the center of the room. "Pep, what's wrong? Talk to me."

She was not crying. She rocked and whispered. Whispered and rocked.

"Forgive me, Jesus," she prayed. "Please forgive me, Father God."

Otis Lee took Pep by the shoulders and shook her gently. She opened her eyes and said, "I need forgiveness."

"For what, Pep?"

Now there were tears.

"I'm the one who wrote that letter," she admitted, lying on the floor. It was as though all the strength she had had escaped her body along with the confession. "It was me."

"Pep," Otis Lee began, trying to pull her up. "Pep, sit up and tell me what you talkin' 'bout. Come on, now."

"Her people shun her 'cause of me," she said. And when the wail had passed, she confessed, "I wrote it and I paid Guppy to take it to 'em."

Part Three

NINETEEN

If anyone had told Knot that in summer of '76 she would have Pratt Shepherd's foot on her knee, and be clipping his toenails because he could no longer reach them on his own, she would have advised them to see a doctor and have their head checked.

In the living room of Pratt's new mobile home—he had purchased it when he'd moved back to West Mills in March, but he didn't move into it until April—Knot watched *All My Children* and clipped his toenails without looking.

"Don't cut too deep, Azalea!" Pratt shouted, sitting in his green pleather recliner. He was naked, and he had put a sheet underneath himself so that he wouldn't stick to the chair. "Will you *please* look at what you doin' so you don't take my damn toe off my foot?"

"Hush yo' fuss, Pratt," Knot replied. "That's probably exactly what I need to do."

Pratt suffered from gout, and he was just coming off of a weeklong flare-up. She clipped the last nail and slowly lowered his foot to the floor. He had been in such pain. In bed, he had held Knot's hand and trembled. And she had rubbed his chest and told him, "I got ya, Pratt. I got ya."

A few months after their reunion, the one she hadn't been in any way prepared for, Pratt called her and said, "Guess what?" He had not said hello, nor had he asked how she was doing.

"Tell me or hang up, Pratt." She was in the middle of helping Cedar write short sentences.

"I bought it from 'em," Pratt announced.

Frustrated with the partial information, she hung up on him. But he called back immediately.

"Why you hang up?" Pratt asked.

"I told you to tell me, or don't."

"I bought Pleasant's old land," he explained.

And after a brief mull over, Knot said, "That's foolish. If they weren't able to sell it to nobody 'sides you, what make you think you gon' sell it?"

"I want to live on it," he answered.

The next mull over was longer. Then she said, "For what? You ain't got no family here."

"What you mean?" he replied, "You and the Lovings gon' be my family there."

"I ain't studdin' you, Pratt Shepherd."

"That's what your mouth say," Pratt had countered. "But I know you love me, Azalea Centre."

"I'll be goddamned," Knot said before hanging up the phone.

Now she was with him, in his mobile home, grooming his feet.

"Thank you, Knot," he said.

"I'm goin' home awhile," she told him. He asked why, and she told him she wanted to watch more of the soaps. It didn't make sense—she could watch them there, he said. "I want to watch my stories in peace," she replied.

"Peace, huh?" he said.

Pratt's feelings about her drinking had not wavered. She drank far less than she had before his permanent return to West Mills—there were stomach problems—but she still enjoyed a few nice pours per week. Pratt raised a great deal of hell about those, too. Knot told Pratt that she would be damned if she were to give up the two weekly drinks, especially since Pep had persuaded her to accompany her to church twice a month. She even put money in the collection plate.

"What is it 'bout them soaps you like so much?" Pratt asked. "I remember a time when it was always a big ol' book on your lap."

"They pass the time," she answered, putting her slippers on and heading toward his door. "I'll be back over after the—"

"Oh!" Pratt exclaimed. "I knew it was somethin' I was s'pose to tell you. You'll never, in your whole life, guess who I seen up-bridge yesterday at the fillin' station."

"I ain't gon' try to guess," Knot said. "Who?"

"Guppy," Pratt said. "Him and his son was at the fillin' station. That man is still strange. Just old and strange now."

Every muscle in Knot's body locked. That was the form fear had chosen for Knot today. It locked itself inside her. She could neither blink nor swallow.

What in the fuck is Mr. Guppy doin' in West Mills?

Guppy's son hadn't remembered Pratt or West Mills, Pratt said. "They was on they way back to Maryland. Comin' from visitin' some people down in Charlotte. That's what the son said. Ol' Guppy ain't say too much."

The day after Miss Goldie had run Guppy out of town, she summoned Knot to the juke joint in the middle of the day. She was sweeping when her son-in-law escorted Knot inside.

"Me and Guppy come to an agreement," Miss Goldie told her. That day she was dressed in a way that reminded Knot of a grandmother—not a woman who owned and operated a juke joint. "We thought it best he move on."

"Where to?" Knot asked.

"Far from here," Miss Goldie replied, working the broom in one of the corners of the big room. "He won't be back. Not while I'm livin'."

Knot went back and forth as to whether to ask Miss Goldie how she had managed the Guppy problem. Finally, she decided it might be useful to know the details, if Miss Goldie would share them.

"I'll put it to you like this, Knot. And this is how you'll put it to Guppy if he ever comes back here botherin' you. Me, Guppy, and Reverend Walker had some dealings."

"Dealings?" Knot repeated. "I don't take yo' meaning, Miss Goldie."

"Oh, come on, now, Knot," Miss Goldie had said, smiling. "You take my meanin'." And after Knot had shrugged, Miss Goldie put her hands on her hips and clarified, "In my bed, Knot. The dealings was in my bed. The three of us. Many times." She resumed with her sweeping. "Guppy couldn't get enough of Reverend Walker. Couldn't get enough. I never seen nothin' like it in my life. I enjoyed it, though."

"Oh," Knot had said. "I see."

Now Miss Goldie was no longer around to protect Knot from Guppy. She and Reverend Walker were both in their graves. Now Guppy was here in West Mills. Old, with nothing to lose, Knot imagined.

"He ask me how you doin'," Pratt said. "I tell him you doin' just fine. And he tell me to ask you 'bout the pox you had. Pox got hold o' ya?"

KNOT WATCHED PRATT come back to the living room with underpants on, and he stood in front of her. Where was the limp that the gout had given him? He had come down the hallway so quickly. And it seemed as though he looked younger—as if the anger had dialed his age back forty years. She remembered, just as clear as crystal, the last time he had packed his old suitcase and left her house.

"When was you gon' tell me I got a daughter, Azalea?" Pratt asked. "A daughter that's a grown woman! A grown daughter that's got two young'uns her own self!"

Knot said the first thing that came to her mind: "Fran say she ain't need to know who her daddy is!"

"I ain't ask you what Fran need to know, Azalea," Pratt said. He paced in front of her. The muscles in his legs rippled with every step.

"We thought you was dead!" Knot shouted, and she picked up a magazine from the coffee table and threw it at the wall. "Even Otis Lee and Pep thought you was dead. You ain't write or nothin'!"

"But when I came back with Vic and Vera, you couldn'a thought I was dead!" he said. "Why ain't you tell me then? Or the first time I asked you who your girls' daddy was?"

He asked if Otis Lee and Pep knew. But before she could answer, he said, "Never mind. I don't even want to know right now."

Knot stood up and hastened toward the door. Her hands shook, and she felt as though a swarm of butterflies had taken up residence in her stomach.

"You betta not walk out that door," Pratt told her. "We gon' talk this here thing out!"

But Knot had already run outside. She missed a step and fell hard into the warm grass. How Pratt got down the steps so quickly, she could not imagine. But he was there, helping her up. And he held her.

"You coulda tol' me, Azalea," he said. He pulled her closer into his chest.

Knot let her arms drop to her sides. And she heard a loud cry. After hearing it three times, she realized it was coming from her own mouth. It was as though the hot sun, or Pratt's loving grip, was drawing the sound out of her.

"I got ya, Knot," Pratt said as he rocked her from side to side.

"I'm so sorry," she said as best she could. "I'm so sorry, Pratt."

"It's all right. I gotcha."

Knot put her arms around Pratt's wide waist, and she surrendered to his tender embrace. He whispered and rocked. Rocked and whispered.

In the kitchen, Pratt handed her a glass of ice water. He had wrapped the cold glass in a dishrag—just as she would have—and sat next to her.

Who was Eunice's father? he wanted to know.

"You don't know him," Knot said. He said he might. "You don't. *I* ain't even know him."

ONLY ONCE HAD Fran asked who her father was. The man who had played the role had not yet been in the ground twelve hours. To Knot, it had seemed that Fran's question had been more about breaking the silence that had fallen on them in Fran's kitchen than it was about getting an answer. If Knot had known how genuine Fran was being when she had once said she didn't care who her real father was, Knot and Pratt might have been far less nervous when they sat her down an hour later.

"I kinda thought he was," Fran said. Ten-year-old Lady Coy was sitting between her legs as she greased the child's scalp. Knot had asked Fran if she didn't think Lady Coy ought to go upstairs or outside to play while they talked. Fran said she didn't keep secrets from her children. "But like I told you a long time ago, it don't matter a whole lot to me," she went on. She would be lying if she claimed to have never wondered what her father might look, act, and sound like, she said. But it had never been something she thought a lot about.

"Ma," Lady Coy said. "Is my daddy my *real* daddy?"

"Be quiet, Coy," Fran scolded.

That's why you oughta send her outdoors, like I tol' you from the first.

Knot glanced over at Pratt, who now donned a somber expression. He looked as though he had been the one who'd grown up without knowing his real father.

"It's nice having you around," Fran told him. "You already got my girls spoiled." Pratt smiled like the Cheshire cat and leaned back in his chair.

If Fran wondered 'bout her real pa sometimes, Eunice probably wondered 'bout hers, too.

Feeling relieved, Knot leaned back in her chair as well. She might feel a little more relieved if she knocked on Eunice's door and said, *Yo' real pa's first name is William and he's from Wilmington, Delaware. I called him Delaware William 'cause I didn't want to know his whole name. Didn't need to. And he could sing like nobody's business. That's all I know 'bout him. I'm sorry.* But Knot trusted Breezy to know his wife.

BACK AT THE mobile home, Knot and Pratt ate Spam sandwiches on Wonder Bread and shared a beer.

"A glass of water'll be stronger than this," Knot said, sliding her half glass of beer toward Pratt.

Pratt had cut the sandwiches diagonally. They tasted better that way, he had insisted. *Goin' the same place, no matter how ya slice it.*

Sandwiches eaten and beer flattened, Pratt looked across the table and asked, "What else I miss while I was gone, Azalea? You ain't got no husband under the floorboards or nothin', do ya?"

Well, Otis Lee's sister ain't his sister. She's his mama. He don't know it, but I do. I knew it 'fore I even met you. And I ain't gon' tell him, or nobody else who don't already know. 'Cause it'll hurt him some kinda bad. And it ain't none of my business.

"We in West Mills, on Antioch Lane," Knot said. "If I tell ya anything else, I'll have to make it up."

Knot was right. Two years later in '78, getting house numbers excited just about everyone in town. "We a real city now!" people said to one another. In '80, West Mills's first nursing home—privately owned—was built. The Penningtons and the Edgars were its primary investors. And in August of '82, just a week after Knot returned to West Mills after having gone to Ahoskie to help Iris attend to the business of burying Leonard, Knot had to slap Eunice Loving.

"I need to go up-bridge," Knot said to Valley, who lay on her couch as if he owned every thread of its upholstery. He had been staying in her house because there was a possum family living under his, and one of them had found a way inside. Until he could get someone to go out and close the possums' passageway, he refused to stay there at night.

"Them fuckers act like they payin' me rent or something, Knot," he had grumbled when he came with a bag of clothes. He was more than welcome in her house, she said—especially since she was now spending most of her time at Pratt's.

Valley told Knot that it was too hot to walk up-bridge and that he would not be going with her. He had made two mistakes: assuming she wanted him to come along, and assuming she planned to walk up-bridge while the day's temperatures were in the high nineties.

A few minutes later, Knot stood in front of Fran's porch and yelled, "Hey, in there!"

"Yeah!" Fran hollered back.

"What ya know?"

"Nothin'," Fran replied.

"Take me up-bridge."

"When?" Fran asked.

Knot made her way up the porch steps. She knocked twice with a knuckle and walked in. From the strong smell of pine-scented cleaner, Knot figured Fran had just mopped the kitchen floor. The smell reminded Knot of all her years as a domestic. She knew it had to have been Fran who had mopped because she had never seen Cedar or Lady Coy holding so much as a dustrag.

"Can't you take me now?" Knot insisted.

Fran lay stretched out long on her couch. She wore a T-shirt and a pair of cut-off denim shorts and was smoking a cigarette. And since she was not wearing her wig, her short-cut hair was sticking in every possible direction. Fran was busy watching the game show Knot couldn't stand. *They just got married and they foolish enough to go on TV so everybody can see how much they don't know one another?*

"You hear me, Fran?"

"Ain't got time to go up-bridge right now," Fran told her. "I'm gettin' ready to get supper goin'. Pratt can't take you?"

"You getting' forgetful," Knot said. She reminded Fran that Pratt had left that morning to go to Chesapeake for his great-niece's third wedding. "You gon' take me or what?"

"Later on, Knot. Shit." Fran smashed her cigarette in the ashtray.

Knot heard Cedar and Lady Coy talking in the room upstairs. She looked at the ceiling, then back at Fran.

"Well, can't Cedar drive me right quick?" Knot heard Lady Coy say, "Nope." *That's one sixteen-year-old who got enough mouth for us all.*

Knot was surprised to find the girls at home. Since they had gotten their driver's licenses—they had gotten them on the same day—the two of them had been taking the hour-long drive up to Norfolk two or three times a week to go to the shopping malls. According to Breezy, he was nearly going broke because all three of his children were constantly at those malls.

Figuring that no one in Fran's house seemed likely to hurry and give her the ride, she let herself drop onto the felt tangerine armchair that matched the couch Fran lay stretched out on.

"Well, I'll rest here awhile and talk to ya 'til ya ready, I guess."

A minute later Fran had on the red wig that made her look like the woman from *The Facts of Life*, and the two of them were headed to Fran's old Chevrolet pickup.

Knot heard a car speeding up the lane, kicking up rocks, the engine revving. It was Eunice. And she turned into Fran's driveway. *Lord, have mercy.*

"What in the devil do she want?" Knot said.

Fran opened the truck door and tossed her keys and pocketbook on the seat. Then she put her hands on her hips. Eunice parked her shiny burgundy Datsun close behind Fran's truck. She slammed her car door so hard, Knot wondered how the driver's side hadn't caved in.

"Fran Waters," Eunice said. "We need to have a word."

"No, we don't need to 'have a word,'" Fran told her, "'cause I ain't in the mood for nothin' you got goin'. So, you can get back in your lil car and—"

"Trying to get me voted out, aren't you?" Eunice accused. Knot was glad that Eunice had the good sense to stand where she was. *I ain't got the strength to keep Fran off her if she say the wrong thing.*

"Voted out of what, Eunice?" Fran asked.

"Don't play dumb with me," Eunice snapped. "I already know what you're plotting. And all I have to say is, if y'all can find somebody who'll do as much for those choirs as I have for *free*, then help yourselves."

Knot almost burst into laughter when she heard what Eunice had come there to discuss. Instead, she giggled. She was sure Eunice had come because Breezy had, again, begun to spend a lot of time at Fran's house—something Knot had decided, years ago, not to mention. *Waste of my breath.*

"I don't know nothin' 'bout it," Fran insisted. But since Eunice had come there about choir business, Fran reminded Eunice that she had, for the past five months, asked that Eunice put in an order to have the piano tuned. It still hadn't been done, Fran pointed out.

"And for that you want me out?" Eunice asked.

"Didn't I just tell you I don't know nothin' 'bout no votin'?" Fran said. Her job was to sit at the piano on Thursday nights for rehearsals, and for Sunday morning worship services. "I don't know and I don't *care* about nothin' else y'all do."

"I should've known you wouldn't own up to it," Eunice scoffed.

Knot saw Valley come out of her house and onto her porch, his hands on his hips. But before he could take the first step down, Knot waved her arm and fanned her hand, signaling him not to come.

Knot stood and listened as Fran and Eunice repeated the same foolishness over and over: "You want me voted out," one daughter said. "I don't care 'bout no choir president," said the other.

Eunice ain't offered me so much as a glance since she hopped outta that little car of hers.

To expect a hug or a conversation from Eunice would have been ridiculous, Knot well knew. *But, shit, a lil head nod or just a lil look-over woulda been just plain civil, Eunice.*

Over the years, these thoughts about Eunice had passed through Knot's mind many times, and she had mentioned them to Otis Lee more than once.

"I wouldn't worry 'bout that too much if I was you," Otis Lee had advised. Breezy and Eunice had been married two years. "I'm her father-in-law. And before that, I was just like a uncle to her. But sometimes I *still* catch her lookin' at me like she scared I'm gon' steal her china dishes."

From somewhere around a corner, Pep had yelled, "She ain't got no china dishes! I seen real china plates on the east side of the canal. And them plates Eunice Manning got ain't it."

"She's Eunice Loving now, Pep," Otis Lee reminded her.

Knot remembered feeling an urge to defend Eunice against Pep's words, but she couldn't. Pep and Otis Lee knew Eunice far better than she did.

While Fran and Eunice argued back and forth about the choir business, Knot had a chance to look Eunice over. If only Eunice behaved as beautifully as she looked and dressed, Knot thought to herself. Seldom did Eunice leave home without wearing a skirt suit. Arguing with Fran, Eunice wore a baby blue one. *But for what? Just to run an errand or two or to go sit with Brock and Ayra?* She looked as though she were en route to an office job, maybe at West Mills Savings and Loans. But Knot and everyone else knew that Eunice hadn't worked anywhere since she sold the general store three years earlier, in 1979.

Just as Knot was about to walk over to Fran and ask if she was going to ever get a ride up-bridge—the store's owner was known for closing for lunch—Cedar and Lady Coy came out onto the porch. Cedar lit a cigarette that was longer than the ones Fran smoked. She wore an A-shirt and a pair of white shorts to match. Four straight rows of pink hair rollers covered her head. All Lady Coy wore was a black slip. No rollers.

"I swear," Lady Coy remarked. "Y'all be fussin' over some of the dumbest shit."

"Go back in the house, please, Coy," Cedar ordered.

"Why you tellin' me to go back in the—"

"You don't help things," Cedar cut in. "Won't keep yo' mouth shut. Go!"

Lady Coy went back inside, letting the screen door slam behind her. Knot wondered where they had learned to do all of that door slamming. *They didn't get that from me. Everybody know I throw dishes.*

"That sounds like choir meeting business to me, Eunice," Cedar said. "Not something that oughta be talked about in our yard." She stood tall on the edge of the porch.

Dinah Bright.

"What do we need a choir meeting for?" Eunice said. "I'm meeting with the ringleader right now."

Then Fran said, "I'm gon' say it one more time and then you best go: I don't know nothin' 'bout what you—"

"She just needs to leave," Cedar interrupted. "That's all. And I mean it."

"Who do you think you're talking to?" Eunice asked Cedar. "I know you haven't had much of a decent raising with *her* as a mama"—she pointed at Fran—"but you won't talk to me any kind of way."

When Knot and her sisters still lived at home, Iris and Mary got into the occasional push and shove, for which their pa would shame them. He told them that they looked like crazy people and that he would not have it.

"Stop this mess! Hear?" Knot yelled, walking toward her daughters. Fran took a step back; she looked shocked. "Y'all too old for this shit!"

"She's full of the devil," Eunice argued, pointing again. "All of you are! Breezy, too!"

"Leave my yard, Eunice," Fran commanded.

"Eunice," Knot said, "I think you best lea—"

"Shut up!" Eunice shouted. "Drunk bitch!" She sucked her teeth and made a face as though she wanted to spit. "Nobody wants to hear you."

Knot had not meant to do it. And after Eunice made that sound—the whine—Knot wanted to take back the open hand that had landed on Eunice's lips.

Fran and Cedar were now a statue of two goddesses holding hands.

Eunice yelled, "Bitch!" once more before bursting into tears and leaving in her Datsun.

Knot, Fran, and Cedar sat on the top step of Fran's porch, Knot in the center. Cedar and Fran both smoked fresh cigarettes.

"Ain't y'all got anything to say? Besides sittin' there puffin' on them things," Knot scolded.

Cedar sucked her teeth and went inside shaking her head.

Fran looked over at Knot, frowning. She asked, "You all right?"

"I ain't mean to hit her," Knot said. "God knows I didn't, Fran."

"Eunice'll live," Fran reassured her, rubbing Knot's back.

They sat quietly—until Lady Coy yelled from the upstairs window.

"Ma!" she said. "Y'all still going up-bridge or what? I got the taste for a cold pop."

Knot looked up at the window. Lady Coy didn't wait for Fran to give an answer before disappearing back into the house.

On the drive up-bridge, after they'd been flagged down by Valley and picked him up, Knot asked Fran to stop by Eunice's house so that she could apologize. She wanted to say sorry for more than the slap.

"Don't do it, Fran," Valley said. Knot was sitting between the two of them. She wouldn't be able to get out at the stop sign if Fran refused to stop.

"I ain't takin' her there," Fran snapped, "Eunice'll call the law quick as that." She snapped her fingers. "She ain't have no business talkin' to you like that. No business comin' to my house the way she did, either."

Fran must think I'm slow in the head, Knot thought.

"You know damn well that ain't what Eunice really come to fuss about," Knot said. "You heard what she said 'bout Breezy, just like I heard."

"Leave that alone, Knot," Valley said. Knot told him to shut up.

Fran sighed and they rode the rest of the way in silence.

On the ride back to Antioch Lane, Fran asked if they wanted to be dropped off at Pratt's or at Knot's house.

"Pratt's," Knot answered. And to Valley she said, "You go on to my house. I ain't in the mood for you right now." Fran dropped Valley off first, which made no sense, but Knot said nothing.

Now in Pratt's driveway, Knot began, "I just want to know one thing." She held up one finger.

"I don't want to hear it, Knot," Fran grumbled.

"Will you *please, please* leave Breezy alone and let her have him?"

"Get yo' bags and close the door, Knot," Fran said.

"Nope."

"Eunice still got Breezy," Fran pointed out. "She's his wife."

"Eunice ain't got him all to herself, though."

"Get yo' bags, Azalea Marie Centre, and close my door."

"You think I care 'bout you callin' out my whole name?" Knot asked. She collected her two brown bags but she did not close the door. "Breezy and Eunice is husband and wife."

"I just said that," Fran said.

"Well, since you know it so goddamn good, leave him alone."

"It's *your* turn to tell *me* one thing," Fran countered, holding up one finger. "When you gon' stop drinkin' like that doctor been tellin' you?"

If the question hadn't stunned her, the look on Fran's face did.

"Go to hell, Fran" was all Knot could think of to say. And now it was her turn to slam a door.

On Pratt's sofa, Knot sat with the unopened bottle of rum in her hand.

I got Fran tellin' me what to do and lookin' worried 'bout me. I got Eunice callin' me a drunk bitch. And I got Otis Lee thinkin' he can trust me.

Knot drank only one shot of the rum. She lay on the couch, wishing Pratt were there. Otis Lee would force her to take the hug she needed, but he'd just lecture her the second he released her from his embrace.

Knot tried as hard as she could to get that sound out of her head—the sound of Eunice's whine. She was grateful for the knock at the door. It was Valley.

"Get up and open this door," he demanded.

"Didn't you hear me tell you I ain't in the mood?" Knot asked, still lying on the couch. Valley seemed to know she wasn't going to get up, so he came in without being invited.

"Knot," Valley began, sitting in Pratt's chair, "I think it's nice of you to worry 'bout the girls. They yours. But you just as well turn it loose. They been doin' that dance for a long time. Probably don't even know how to do it no different." He stood up again to turn on the television. "They all right, Knot."

Knot lay there looking at the television, knowing Valley was right and refusing to tell him so. She felt a little at ease. But now that the sound of Eunice's whine was gone, it was the image of Fran's sad eyes that haunted Knot when she closed her own and tried to sleep. And again she heard her Fran say, *When you gon' stop drinkin' like that doctor been tellin' you?*

TWENTY

Ice water poured in a jar. That was what Otis Lee wanted to take outside with him. Not a bottle of pop or the small bottle of prune juice Pep had set out for him before she left the house. Breezy had given her a ride to the hospital to visit Knot and Valley. Otis Lee had gone to see them both the day before. Visiting Valley was the easy part. Valley hadn't known Otis Lee was there. It would have been the same if he had been awake.

Knot was in better shape—alert and ornery. She wanted to go home. But her doctors said it was too soon. Knot was weaker than he'd ever seen her, and there was a gurgling cough. Otis Lee had been tossing and turning with worry since Knot had been admitted. And his appetite was hit or miss. But for the past couple of days he had had other things on his mind—things that took up almost as much space as his worry for Knot.

Outside, under the shade tree that Cedar, La'Roy, and Sequoia had helped him plant ten years ago, in '77, Otis Lee sat and enjoyed the morning peace and quiet.

He hadn't been there five minutes when he looked up and saw Pratt coming his way. Usually, Otis Lee liked to have some just-Otis Lee time under the tree, but today he was glad to see his friend coming to join him. He imagined Pratt needed the company, too.

Once Pratt was seated, Otis Lee said, "I got butterflies."

"What ya say?" Pratt asked. He used his finger to push his ear gristle in Otis Lee's direction.

"I say I got butterflies." Otis Lee kept forgetting he had to speak loud for Pratt. That little microphone they had put in Pratt's ear didn't seem to be up to its purpose. *Money down the commode.* "I'm gettin' on the airplane in a few days. Goin' to New York to 'tend to some business."

"Well, is the butterflies 'bout the plane or is they 'bout the business?"

"Both," Otis Lee said. And since Pratt was taking too long to ask, Otis Lee added, "You want to know what the business is 'bout?" Pratt said yes, and Otis Lee swore him to secrecy.

"Don't y'all get tired of secrets?" Pratt wanted to know.

Otis Lee told Pratt about a letter that had come a few days back, from a lawyer's office in Brooklyn. The letter said that Otis Lee had inherited two houses—side by side—and there was some money in the bank. Essie had died a couple of months earlier, and she had left it all to him.

"Good gracious!" Pratt exclaimed.

Otis Lee said he was shocked because he imagined Essie had died a long, long time ago, since he hadn't heard from her since her unannounced visit in the early '60s.

"Now, if I'm seventy-nine, that mean Essie live to be ninety-five, ninety-six." They both used folded paper towels to wipe sweat from their foreheads as they talked about how few people live that long anymore.

When the mailman had come to deliver the letter, Otis Lee was sitting outside, watching Cedar's four-year-old twin boys throw a football around.

"And the twins, they run over and ask him if he got a piece of candy. Them two don't forget nothin', do they, Pratt?"

"They smart," Pratt affirmed.

"Smart, and bad as shit," Otis Lee said. And Pratt agreed.

"Long story short, the letter say I got 'til September the fifteenth to respond. And I ain't gon' drag my feet on it."

Pratt agreed with that too, and he said so.

Cedar had told Otis Lee that she thought it best if she and her husband drove him to New York.

"But I say noooo. I'm gettin' old. I want to fly one time 'fore y'all stand 'round a hole and throw dirt in my face. Cedar laugh and tell me I was talkin' crazy."

"You gon' live a long time, Otis Lee!" Pratt said.

"Already been a long time," Otis Lee replied.

Pratt asked Otis Lee if it might be best to take Breezy to New York along with him. "People in the North is crazy," he said.

"No!" Otis Lee said. He hadn't yet told Breezy or Pep about the lawyer's letter. Breezy, Otis Lee believed, would be after the two houses in Brooklyn. And Eunice would be after much more, he said.

"Well, sit down, man," Pratt said. "You gon' work yo'self up."

Otis Lee looked down at his feet and tried to remember when he had stood up. He had lost his cool, and he didn't like it. *Get yo'self together, Otis Lee.* He leaned back in his chair and tapped his fingers on the armrests.

"Goin' to New York without tellin' Pep?" Pratt asked.

It had all been worked out. Cedar would pick Otis Lee up once Pep had gone to visit the sick and the shut-in, and they would leave a note for Pep saying they were safe and attending to something in Brooklyn. They would call her once they arrived safely.

"What if Pep don't go visitin'?"

Otis Lee almost stood up again. He shouted, "Don't jinx me, Pratt!"

Then, Pratt asked about Otis Lee's plan for the houses he was to inherit.

"Ya know, Pratt, I'm gon' tell you the funniest thing. After I read the letter from the lawyer's office, I was watchin' the twins play. The biggest one come runnin' over to me and say, 'PawPaw, can you take us up-bridge. We want a icy.' And I say, 'Naw, Mackum. Cedar put ice cream in my Frigidaire for y'all. I ain't goin' up-bridge today.' Then he and the lil one—"

"Robert," Pratt said.

"Yeah. Robert," Otis Lee said. "They start to laughin' and fallin' all out in the grass." Pratt looked confused, so Otis Lee held one finger up and continued. "Mackum say, 'PawPaw, my name is *Malcolm.*' And I say, 'Well, ain't that what I just say, Mackum?' And they fall right out and laugh some more. I keep sayin' the name wrong so they can laugh and fall out."

"They funny, ain't they?" Pratt said, and he smiled. He wasn't wearing his dentures.

"Pratt, I'm gon' tell you the truth. Seein' them boys laughin' and havin' a good time like that really made me feel good. They ain't got a care in the world, and I don't want 'em to *never* have to worry 'bout the kinds o' stuff we had to when we was young." The two side-by-side houses in Brooklyn would go to Malcolm and Robert, Otis Lee told him. "That way they got a head start in the world."

"That's smart," Pratt said.

"I worry 'bout them boys, though, 'cause Robert say to me, 'PawPaw, can we *pleeeeeease* have a icy from up-bridge? I don't want no ice cream.' And he wouldn't let up, Pratt. Steady tellin' me he want the icy, not the ice cream. And Mackum, he ain't put up no fuss. He was happy to have the regular ice cream from the Frigidaire."

"What's yo' worry?" Pratt asked.

"I don't know which one of 'em to be worried 'bout the most—the one who take the first thing that get offered to him, or the one who always want what he want." They looked at each other and nodded. "Either way, I'm leavin' Essie's houses to them. But when I get up to New York, in that lawyer's office, I got to remember not to go in there callin' her *Essie*, 'cause the letter calls her Ellen O'Heeney, and that's what I'm gon' say. She change her name when she went up north. She was passin' for white. You remember me tellin' 'bout all that, don't ya?" Pratt said he remembered some of the story.

They sat quietly. For men their age, to speak of passing was akin to speaking ill of the dead.

"I don't mean no disrespect, Otis Lee," Pratt said. "But how yo' mama get two young'uns from white mens?"

"It wasn't no *mens*," Otis Lee corrected. "Only Essie got the white father. My father wasn't white. Not one bit white."

"I ain't mean nothing by it," Pratt said. "I just . . . well . . ."

"What?" Otis Lee asked.

"You yella," Pratt pointed out. He whispered it.

Otis Lee told Pratt that some Negroes are just born light, but it didn't mean they had a white mother or father.

"Maybe my pa had some light-skinned folks in his family or somethin'," Otis Lee mused. He had never met his father's family. They had lived somewhere in the islands. "You want some of this ice water, Pratt?"

"Naw. I'm all right."

"Go on and have some," Otis Lee said, "'cause if you pass out, I can't help you up."

Pratt took the large jar and drank. Otis Lee did the same before reminding Pratt about Essie's brothel and all the ways she and her husband made their money.

"Hard life, though," Pratt remarked, and he belched.

"Yeah," Otis Lee said. He belched, too. "And that O'Heeney, he was somethin' else, Pratt. When I was there workin' in they house, he would stand at the top of the steps and holler, 'Ellen!' I could hear him all the way downstairs in the cellar. I'd be down there polishin' shoes that belonged to the johns." Otis Lee slid to the edge of his chair. "Essie would say, 'Yes, Thomas Dear?' I never heard her call him just plain *Thomas*. Was always *Thomas Dear*. And he would say, 'Send the half-breed up here with his shaving kit, would ya? I can't go out with a chin full of stubble.' I don't think he ever did know my name." O'Heeney, who believed Otis Lee was the son of one of the runaway girls who once worked at the brothel, also called Otis Lee a nigger. Otis Lee never figured out how O'Heeney decided which awful term to use. All the while, Essie would just say, "Yes, Thomas Dear."

"Well, Pratt," Otis Lee said, "things a lil better now, I guess. Times of folk being called niggas and half-breeds is done. It's 19 and 87!"

"That's right," Pratt said. They glanced at each other and looked out at the yard. A neighbor passed by and blew her truck horn. Otis Lee and Pratt both waved. "You lucky your sister loved you, Otis Lee," Pratt said. "Shit. You couldn't mess with folk when they was tryin' to pass. They'd kill ya."

It was something Otis Lee had considered before going to Essie's house, back in the '20s, he said. He had told her that two of his friends, Phil and Brock, were in New York with him and that they knew the truth, too. But it was a lie. Phillip had returned to West Mills with Lady, and Brock had returned even sooner, Otis Lee said.

"Brock was workin' in Edgars's general store. He put all his money together and bought it off him when Edgars took his business on the other side of the canal. All that was long, long 'fore you moved 'round here, Pratt."

Pratt nodded and they sat and let the occasional breeze blow across them. A stray cat that lived under Otis Lee's porch came and sat with them. The cat had taken to him much like the hen Ruby had decades ago. Otis Lee did not know whether the cat was male or female. It didn't matter.

Pratt asked if Valley was doing any better.

"No change," Otis Lee said. "You ain't say nothin' to—"

"Naw," Pratt said. "Naw." Otis Lee said he believed God was making Valley rest from all the traveling he had done over the years. They both shook their heads and looked out into the yard.

"How you and Phil and Brock decide on the North?"

"We wanted us some better work, decent work," Otis Lee explained. "Somethin' 'sides diggin' ditches and that kinda thing."

Otis Lee had told Rose and Ma Noni that he was going north. They hadn't had much to say about his plan—at first. "They ain't think I meant it."

Otis Lee had not been able to get work at the one lumber mill that was in business at the time, he said. For a while he had worked in the fields with Rose and Ma Noni. And sometimes he had even joined them in their domestic work on the east side of the canal.

"Got tired of that, though. Quick. One day I say to Ma Noni, 'I'm through cleanin' houses with y'all. That's women's work.' She was sittin' at the table, mixin' stuff up to make cornbread. She say, 'Come here and taste this, see if it's sweet enough.' And, Pratt, when I bent over to taste the spoon, she went upside my face so fast—great day in the mornin'!" Otis Lee held the side of his face as if he still felt the sting.

"She got ya, ain't she?" Pratt asked.

"Yeah," Otis Lee said. He relished the memory. Essie's visit had almost ruined all his memories of Ma Noni. Otis Lee knew most of what Essie had told him was probably true, but Ma Noni had never shown him anything but love.

Ma Noni had told him to never again say *women's work* in her presence. She had dared him to try and imagine the things she had done when she was a young woman to keep a roof over her head and over the heads of her younger brothers and sisters. Ma Noni had said that cleaning up after people had been a breeze in comparison.

"Pratt, after that wood spoon went upside my jaw, I ain't say that shit 'round her no more."

Otis Lee had waited two weeks after Ma Noni hit him to tell her and Rose that he and Brock were definitely heading north. Rose objected and worried. "She said, 'People act like the North is heaven or somethin',' " Otis Lee told Pratt. "I believe she was sad 'cause she was tired of losing folk she loved."

"Who she lose?" Pratt asked.

"What you mean, 'who she lose?' " Otis Lee said. "She lost Essie, she lost my father, and she was gon' lose me 'cause I was movin' away." He looked at Pratt and saw that he was working his mouth around. "You want some more water, Pratt?"

"I'm fine."

"You ain't fine," Otis Lee said. "Here." Otis Lee passed the jar of cool water to Pratt, and he watched him drink two gulps before he start talking again. "Ma Noni was cookin', sweepin' the floor, or wipin' somethin', seemed like." Ma Noni came around to the idea of Otis Lee going off into the world, and she trusted Otis Lee with Phillip and Brock. "Ma Noni say to me, 'Them is good boys you want to go 'long with. Y'all been taught to look out for one and each.' "

But Ma Noni hadn't liked his plan to find Essie.

"Ma Noni flew *hot*! She come walkin' to me quick. I step back 'cause you never know what she was gon' do. Ma Noni was swift, man. Great *day*!"

"She go upside your head again?" Pratt asked.

"Nah," Otis Lee said. Ma Noni had asked him if he was crazy. "She look at me and say, 'What you think Essie gon' do if you turn up talkin' 'bout 'Essie! Essie! Big Sista Essie!'? Think she gon' invite you in and hug ya?'" The memory of Ma Noni's anger when speaking about Essie reminded him of the talk he'd had with Essie at his kitchen table.

Otis Lee told Pratt that it was his aunt Gertrude who had told him that Essie was in Bedford-Stuyvesant. Pratt said he remembered Gertrude and that he had always thought she was strange. Pratt said he'd once thought Ma Noni and Gertrude were sisters. It had been a common error, Otis Lee said. "Ma Noni had Gertrude when she was real young. Fifteen or sixteen. Somewhere 'long that age."

And when Pratt asked how Gertrude knew where Essie was, Otis Lee was reminded of the fact that he never knew the truth about that. "Gertrude ain't tell me. But I know she come back to West Mills with a whole lot of money. And I mean a *lot*, Pratt." He held his hands apart, as if he were holding a big pot of gold. "But my mama tol' me that Gertrude used to tell folks lies 'bout they future, and they paid good money to know. She made a killin' from it, too."

Gertrude had advised Otis Lee to go north, make money, and come back. *Think of your future, and the children you might have one day*, she said. She thought his plan to look for Essie—who she referred to as being blood but not family— would only lead him to troublesome times. But Otis Lee should do what felt right for him, she said. Then she poured him a cup of a strange-looking tea. It would clean him out before his journey, she said.

"Looked like some ol' ditch water to me," Otis Lee recalled. "But I drank it, and I was back and forth to the outhouse all *night*!"

Pratt roared with laughter.

"Well, Pratt," Otis Lee said, "I'm goin' on indoors. It's time for my before-lunch nap."

They shook hands, and Otis Lee walked toward his porch. The cat walked in front of him as if it thought Otis Lee had forgotten the way.

When Otis Lee was about to step inside, Pratt called out to him.

"What you gon' do Thursday mornin'?"

"What ya mean?" Otis Lee asked.

"'Bout them butterflies?"

Otis Lee looked at Pratt for a second and said, "I ain't got the butterflies no more."

TWENTY-ONE

It was the thirteenth day Knot had been in the hospital, if she'd counted correctly. One thing was certain: she'd been hooked to the dialysis machine five times. Five times she had felt as though she were freezing to death—it was summer— while her burgundy blood moved out of one arm, through the clear wide tubes, into the machine, and back into her body through the other arm. *Five times.*

The doctors had managed to get her stomach working well enough that she could eat solid foods, and the fever had subsided. *But if I could just lay in my own bed, breathe in the smell of my own house, my own stuff, my own self, I'd be a lot more comfortable.*

"When y'all gon' let me outta here?" Knot asked the brunette nurse who was there taking her vitals. Those were the first words she had spoken in hours. She was surprised by her own whisper.

"We'd have to get your strength up quite a bit first, Miss Centre," the nurse said. "Not to mention your kidneys. Those kidneys of yours are misbehaving. Dr. Taylor is going to want to see some improvement with them before he—"

"Dr. Taylor can go to—"

"May I have one of your arms?" the nurse asked. Knot used the little strength she had gathered from breakfast to pull her left arm from under the top sheet and the store-bought quilt Pep had brought to her a couple of days after she was admitted. She had asked Pep to bring the yellow quilt from her closet. Pep had also purchased a new book for Knot—a gift. On the front cover there was a half-naked couple looking into each other's eyes.

"Why you bring this?" Knot asked.

"'Cause I ain't seen you read like you used to."

Knot thought about asking Pep if she remembered what she had once said to her years ago about reading, and life. But instead she said, "Thanks, Pep."

Knot felt a tightening around her arm as the nurse squeezed the black rubber ball. Four squeezes, pause, four more squeezes, pause.

"Y'all keepin' me here for the money. I ain't gon' get well. Shit. I can die at home."

A couple of days after Fran had brought Knot into the emergency room—Fran had carried her just as a groom carries his new bride across a threshold—the doctor told them that Knot's kidneys weren't pulling their weight, which explained why she often went more than half a day without urinating. The coughing had taken its toll, too. It was one of the coughing spells that had caused her to faint. When she had come to, Fran was lifting her from the bathroom floor.

"If I hadn't walked over there to take you a plate," Fran remarked an hour after Knot had been admitted, "ain't no tellin' what would've happened."

"Well," Knot said, "what was on the plate?" Fran rolled her eyes. Pratt told Knot to be quiet and rest.

Knot didn't want to hear Fran's account of how the ambulance took too long to get there, forcing her to take Knot to the hospital herself, worried sick all the way there. Knot didn't care to hear Fran say how limp Knot had been when she'd lifted her. Knot had heard it three times too many. But it was the terrified, serious look Fran had on her face that haunted Knot most of all. Pratt sat next to her bed, showing her the same terrified, serious look. It was the same look Pratt had given her when she told him to get out of her house, that morning in '41, after they had made Fran.

It was a good thing, Knot thought, that Fran had Pratt—that they had each other. The two of them got along well—so well that Knot had become jealous. She had felt that same jealousy when Fran took her to Ahoskie during the week of Leonard's funeral. Iris showed Fran more attention than she showed her own grandchildren.

Since Knot had been admitted, it seemed to her that everyone who visited sat around with serious looks. Fran, Pratt, Otis Lee, Pep, Valley, Breezy, Cedar, and Lady Coy. Even La'Roy had been by to see her for a few minutes; he brought the look too, as well as a friend.

"I must not have but a few minutes left to live if *you* come to see me," Knot said to La'Roy as he stood at the foot of her bed.

"You'll outlive all of West Mills, Knot," he replied. The red roses he'd bought for her were pretty. She didn't care a great deal for roses. *But these here roses come from La'Roy*, she thought. He looked a lot like what Knot could remember of Delaware William.

La'Roy hadn't visited Knot at home more than six or seven times in his entire life. And those visits only happened when he came with Breezy to fix a pipe or to patch up a soft spot on the floor. But Knot hadn't expected visits from La'Roy. *Ayra and Pep are the grandmas he know.*

Knot glanced over at La'Roy's friend.

"You can come away from the wall, young man," she said. "It ain't gon' fall in on us." The friend and La'Roy looked at each other and smiled. She saw La'Roy gesture with his eyes for the friend to come closer to him, but the friend did not move.

"Y'all got girlfriends?" Knot asked, having already decided what the true answer was. She wanted to have a little fun. *It's borin' in here. Shit.*

Knot had asked La'Roy how his schooling was going. He was enrolled at the college—mathematics. He'd said it was all going well. The news made Knot feel proud. She knew her pa would feel proud, too.

"Do as the doctors tell you, Knot," La'Roy advised after sitting with her for half an hour. He kissed her on both cheeks and then on her forehead, all while he held her hand. He said he would visit again in a couple of days. And on his way out of her room, he said, "My mama sends her get-well wishes, Knot."

That might have explained the dreams. In a couple of Knot's dreams, Eunice, too, had come and stood next to the bed with a serious look. That dream reminded Knot of the slap. She never got a chance to apologize, face-to-face, for that, or for anything. If it had not been for Otis Lee getting

Brock to talk to Eunice, and getting Eunice to agree to a brief phone call with Knot, there probably would have never been a talk at all. Eunice was quiet on the phone. She told Knot she was sorry, too, for speaking to an elder person the way she had, and for calling her such an awful thing. Knot didn't want the apology. "But thank you, Eunice," she said.

Knot was tired of serious looks. And now this nurse was back again with that goddamn blood pressure thing and a goddamn thermometer that had been God knows where. The nurse was wearing her own serious look, too. Writing stuff down on those papers.

"Have you thought about what we discussed, Miss Centre?" the nurse asked.

"Ain't I already tol' you I'm saved?" Knot replied. "I sure do wish you'd let up 'bout that. Shit."

The nurse giggled and said, "Close your eyes, Miss Centre. Let's have a word with God."

"Lord, have mercy," Knot said, rolling her eyes. The nurse put her hand on Knot's shoulder.

"Heavenly Father, we call on you today to ask for healing . . ."

Where the hell is Valley when you need him? She was sure Valley would tell the nurse to do her job and leave.

"In Jesus's name we pray," the nurse ended, "Amen."

"Did Valley come to see me when I was on the machine?" Knot asked. The nurse did not know who Valley was. "The one in the wheelchair. Bald on top, white cornrows 'round the sides and back of his head." The nurse said she hadn't seen him.

The senior living center that Valley lived in was next door to the hospital, separated only by an alley no more than ten feet wide. An orderly had been pushing Valley over to see Knot. He had come just about every day.

"Enjoy the hospital luxury, Knot," he said in response to her wanting to get back to Antioch Lane. "Pretend it's a hotel."

"Bring me some of what I like and we can pretend all you want."

THE NEXT AFTERNOON, when a different nurse pushed Knot back to her room after dialysis, she came back to find Pep there, looking as though she wanted to fight someone. Pep was wringing her long, skinny hands as if they were dishrags.

"You knew Otis Lee was goin' to New York, didn't ya?" Pep accused.

"No," Knot replied. "And good mornin' to you, too."

When Pep arrived home from yesterday's visiting rounds, there had been a note from Otis Lee.

"He got Cedar and Coy with him," Pep relayed. She was angry. She had called Breezy and Fran, she said. The two of them knew nothing about the trip, nor did they know the reason for it. "I know he tol' you, Knot."

"I swear 'fore God he ain't tol' me nothin'," Knot insisted. Pep didn't believe her. Knot could tell.

"I don't believe you," Pep said.

"I don't give a damn what you believe."

"You oughtn't curse like that, being so sick and all," Pep grumbled.

Then Knot asked Pep to lay the quilt over her legs and to set the TV on Channel 3 so that they could watch the soaps. It seemed that Pep had forgotten all about Otis Lee's mystery trip after Knot mentioned Katherine Chancellor.

During the first commercial break, Pep looked up at the TV for a couple of minutes, then she looked at Knot.

"Well, how you feelin'?"

That shoulda been the first thing you said to me.

"The same, I guess." And after a minute: "Thank ya for comin' to check on me, Pep. Hear?"

Pep scooted her chair closer to the hospital bed and rubbed Knot's legs, trying to warm them. The flesh on Pep's used-to-be fat arms swung from side to side.

"But ain't it foolish, Knot?" Pep wanted to know. "What Otis Lee up and done, I mean."

Knot almost agreed with Pep, but then she remembered where she was, lying in the hospital. With Otis Lee getting close to eighty years old, she wondered if maybe he wanted to do something like that—a trip without his wife—while he still could. She shared the idea with Pep.

"I shoulda known you'd side with him," Pep said. She stopped rubbing. "The two of you always *have* sided with one another." Pep looked back up at the TV and folded her arms over her chest.

"Somethin' you need to say?" Knot asked.

"Nope," Pep said. "I rest my case."

"Well, unrest it, and say what you need to say."

Pep looked directly at Knot.

"I ain't got nothin' to say, Knot," Pep said, "'cept for I'm sorry."

There was a time when Knot felt Pep had a lot to apologize for. But Knot and Fran had become so close. And Eunice didn't seem to hate her anymore.

"You all right wit' me, Penelope Loving," Knot said. "I been a pain in yo' ass since I came to this lil town y'all got here."

Pep used a tissue to blot away both their tears.

"You seen Val?" Knot asked. "Been three days. He ain't been here and ain't called."

"He restin'," Pep said. "He'll be all right." She reached through the bed rails and started rubbing Knot's foot.

It was the *He'll be all right* that let her know Pep was lying. Or was it the way Pep had looked off at the TV while she rubbed Knot's foot? She rubbed Knot's foot so hard that it looked and felt as though she were trying to start a campfire.

Valley had suffered another stroke, Pep finally admitted. The doctors had told Otis Lee—since Otis Lee was listed as next of kin—that Valley might not ever come out of the coma.

Until Knot heard the quiet rattling of one of the bed rails, she didn't know she had grabbed ahold of it. The other hand was now a fistful of quilt.

What would Knot do without Valley? Had he been the most dependable friend she had? No. Otis Lee had claimed that title on the day she told him she was pregnant for the first time and that she needed his help. But Knot had been able to tell Valley anything—whatever was on her mind. And as far as she knew, he had never lied to her. Even when she had suspected him of lying, he had generally been telling the truth. Yes, she could say most of that about Otis Lee, almost.

But Valley had never asked her to be anyone other than who she was. Valley never asked her to even try.

"When God gets ready for us to sit down," Pep said, "he sure do know how to make us. Valley had him a good ol'—"

"You said Otis Lee gon' to Queens?" Knot interrupted. And when Pep reminded her that Otis Lee had gone to Brooklyn, Knot said, "Oh. You know Valley's from Queens?" She coughed, and Pep poured water into the teal plastic cup. "Val used to say, 'My mama *had me* in Queens, and *left my ass* in Queens.'"

"He sure can tell a good story, can't he?" Pep said, smiling.

Knot lay thinking about what Valley had told her years ago, about Essie and Otis Lee. Valley swore her to secrecy about it—twice, if memory served her right.

"Otis Lee ever hear from his sister after she was last here?" Knot asked.

"Naw," Pep replied, looking at the TV. "And I don't 'magine he wanted to, either. Otis Lee made peace with all that. She probably long dead by now, anyhow."

Knot could feel her breathing get more and more shallow. For a moment it reminded her of the times she'd given birth to Fran and Eunice. Pep had said to her, "All right. You doin' real good. Now, let's wait for yo' breath to steady for you to push again." Knot was glad that Fran and Eunice had turned out to be good mothers. They had both proven to be far better at mothering than Knot believed she could have ever been to the two of them. Knot was even happier that they didn't have her craving for liquor. If loving Breezy was their only trouble, she counted them lucky. Knot couldn't stand that both her daughters pined for the same man. But they were doing things their way, Knot believed, just as she had. And she figured maybe she'd passed something good along to them after all. They'd be all right.

But what about Essie's secret? If she were going to tell Pep what she knew, so that Pep could tell Otis Lee, now was the time.

"Penelope," Knot said. "Shut that TV off. I got somethin' to say to ya."

With her cane, Pep pressed the button, and the TV screen went black. The only sounds Knot heard were those that came from the hallway. Pep used her cane again to close the door. It closed only halfway.

"What's wrong, Knot?" she asked.

Knot stared at Pep and sang eeny meeny miney mo in her head. Miney mo wanted Knot to break her promise to Valley so that Otis Lee could know his own truth. Otis Lee's sudden trip to Brooklyn had something to do with Essie; Knot had no doubt in her mind about that. To hope that Otis Lee might return from New York with some kind of new peace would be silly. Lately, Otis Lee was becoming bossier and grumpier by the day. Whether he was in New York receiving good news, bad news, or any news at all, Knot believed he'd come home ornery either way, and that would be all right with her. Her faithful Otis Lee.

Knot sang eeny meeny miney mo one last time and it gave her the same answer as before: *No more secrets*, it said. *The longer they're kept, the more hurt they cause when they're set free. Fran and Eunice know their truths. Otis Lee should know his, too, and you're the one holding it.*

Usually, Knot didn't care much for being told what to do, not by miney, mo, or anyone else. But today wasn't a usual day, and Knot wasn't her usual self.

"Knot?" Pep said.

"I'm gon' tell you somethin', Pep," Knot began. "But first, get that book with them naked white people on it and read to me."

TWENTY-TWO

Grateful to have made it to the attorney's office alive—the taxicab driver hadn't seemed to have much regard for speed limits—Otis Lee sighed and offered up a silent *Thank you, Lord*. He asked his granddaughters why cabdrivers drove as though they had only two or three minutes to get to everywhere.

"Time is money up here, Pop," Coy explained.

"I don't understand why folk say that," Otis Lee shot back. He was exhausted and his neck and shoulders ached. "Time is *time*. That's what time is."

Cedar dug into her pocketbook and pulled out the small piece of paper with the attorney's suite number written on it. They were thirty minutes early for the ten o'clock appointment.

"Mr. Roth will be with you shortly," the secretary said. She offered them water, coffee, and tea. Coy had all three, causing Otis Lee great frustration.

"Well," Otis Lee whispered once he was seated between Coy and Cedar, "he must be a nice man."

"Why?" Coy asked. "Because they got free coffee and tea?"

"Don't you see that colored girl sittin' 'bout ten feet in front of us?" Otis Lee said.

"People don't say *colored* anymore, Pop," Coy told him. "Maybe the lawyer's black, too."

"Not with a last name like that, he ain't," Cedar remarked. "I've never met a black person with the last name of Roth."

"Girl, you sound just as stupid," Coy retorted. "What does a name have to do with it?"

"Shut up, Coy," Cedar said.

Otis Lee looked from side to side at his two grown grand-daughters. Cedar, married with two children. Coy, married to herself.

"I 'magine y'all might grow up one of these days."

Coy and Cedar talked about the Manhattan shops they wanted to visit. Otis Lee looked forward to finishing the business right there in Roth's office. He had neither the interest nor energy for shops and boutiques. He did, however, want them out of the hotel room so he could enjoy the television and a long nap.

As it turned out, Roth *was* black. With that shock out of the way, Otis Lee could now concentrate on the business at hand.

"I got a question, sir," Otis Lee said. "Is the money she left in the bank enough to pay me and my grandgirls back for our plane tickets?"

"Indeed," Roth affirmed, and he scratched his goatee. Roth was not tall, exactly. Nor was he short. And though Coy had said Afros had gone out of style, Otis Lee imagined Roth would disagree. He wore tinted spectacles, making it hard for Otis Lee to see his eyes. And his pin-striped navy-blue suit looked as though it had been made just for him. "I've got the most recent statements right here."

Roth spun around in his brown leather chair and flipped through papers on his other desk, the desk with two lamps. When he spun back around, he lay out three pieces of paper in front of Otis Lee.

"Let me go get my grandgirls," Otis Lee said. He used his cane to stand. Roth told him that he would ask Deb to escort them in. He picked up his phone, pressed one button, and less than a minute later Coy and Cedar were there.

"Mr. Loving would like the two of you to see these statements for the certificates Mrs. O'Heeney bequeathed to him."

Cedar picked up two statements, and Coy picked up the third.

"Well, goddamn!" Coy exclaimed. Cedar cursed, too. They were both staring at the statements, flipping them over and over again.

They so much like Knot.

"One of y'all gon' say somethin'?" Otis Lee asked.

"All of this is his?" Cedar said to Roth. The answer was yes. Cedar looked at Otis Lee and told him, "These two statements add up to almost two hundred."

Otis Lee sighed and asked, "Y'all doin' all that cussin' 'bout two hundred damn dollars?"

"Two hundred *thousand*, Pop," Cedar corrected.

"Noooooo," Otis Lee said.

"How much yours say, Coy?" Cedar asked, reaching for the paper in her sister's hand. Coy moved it out of Cedar's reach.

"Twenty-seven thousand and some odd dollars."

Otis Lee looked at Roth, waiting for some sort of correction—anything. He took a deep breath and said, "Great day in the mornin'." And when Roth told Otis Lee that the two houses had steady-paying tenants in five of the six units—no mortgages owed—Otis Lee echoed, "Great day!"

In Roth's car, on the way to see the two side-by-side brownstones on Gates Avenue, Otis Lee thought about the paperwork he had just signed, leaving the two houses to Cedar's twins—and to any children Coy and La'Roy might have. Most of the cash, which would be put away, would be divided between Breezy, Cedar, La'Roy, and Coy; he and Pep would try to enjoy some of it. *We might even spend it!*

"I want mine now," Coy declared.

"Shut up," Cedar said.

When they arrived in front of the houses, Roth gave them a pouch that contained nine or ten keys and copies of papers he needed to hold on to.

"And, Mr. Loving," Roth said, putting his hand on Otis Lee's shoulder, "there's an envelope in there for you. Letters from Mrs. O'Heeney. She wanted me to put them directly in your hand, if I could."

Otis Lee figured the letters were full of "I'm sorrys." He was grateful to her for leaving him something to pass on to his grandchildren and great-grandchildren. But he was in no hurry to open the large envelope and have anyone read to him things he had heard before. *No rush at all.*

BACK AT THE hotel, Otis Lee sat in the high-back chair in the corner of their room and told Cedar and Coy how different houses looked from the way they had in the early 1920s. The house on the right had not belonged to Essie and O'Heeney when he lived there.

Cedar went through the pouch of legal papers, reading everything a second time. Coy was ironing. *She'll lose her mind if she don't get to go shoppin'.*

"You want to open this now or later on?" Cedar asked, holding the large, thick manila envelope that held Essie's letters.

"Later on," he said, and Cedar set it on the desk, next to the Bible.

"Y'all wait 'til I get back to open it," Coy told them. And Cedar told her they would open and read them whenever Otis Lee was ready, whether Coy was there or not. Coy was spoiled rotten, Cedar complained. The two of them exchanged sisterly insults, to which Otis Lee had become accustomed. But today he wasn't in the mood for it.

"Open the damn thing up and read one of 'em," he said.

"Don't pay us no mind, Pop," Cedar said. "We—"

"Open the damn thing up and read it," he broke in. "It's just as well to hear it and get that over with. Then y'all can go where y'all want to and I can get a nap." He rested his head on the back of the chair and looked out the window at Brooklyn's pretty skyline.

Cedar told them that she would read the most recent letter first.

March 19, 1987

Dear Otis Lee,

If you are reading this letter, it means that I have died. I'm sure you'll be surprised to learn that I've hung around this long. I know

I am. But I hope that you will not be surprised that I have left you everything. You may not even want any of it, but I wouldn't have it any other way.

As I've mentioned in the previous letters, I'm sorry not to have told you sooner that I was your mother.

"Say what!" Coy yelled.

Otis Lee shushed her, and he stood to his feet.

"Read that again, Cedar," he instructed. "Slow."

Closing his eyes would ensure hearing it correctly, he thought. The words Cedar had just read had to be a mistake.

Cedar read it again from the top. Essie was his mother, the letter said.

Otis Lee heard very little after that. His memory had taken him back to when he was a young boy, catching bits and pieces of Ma Noni fussing at Rose for having gone along with a lie. Then he was once again a young man standing just a couple of feet from Essie's back stoop. Essie was there, too, with that sweet look on her face.

Otis Lee opened his eyes to find his granddaughters sitting next to him. Cedar had finished the short farewell letter, she said. The letter next in line was dated 1927.

"You want me to keep going, Pop?" Cedar asked. He nodded once, and she read on.

Essie had met Otis Lee's real father—Otis Meachum, a short Negro handyman who worked at the boardinghouse where she lived—soon after arriving in New York City. She had loved Meachum, but their affair was cut short. Essie's looking white had caused more trouble than Meachum was able to handle, the letter said. And not long after their split, Essie discovered she was to be a mother.

Rose had come to New York just before Otis Lee was born in a tenement house in Brooklyn. When Essie found herself struggling to shake off the blues of new motherhood, she begged Rose to take her baby—Otis Lee—back to West Mills, and until she felt able.

Essie had met a group of Negro women who looked like her. And before she knew it, she had fallen into the life she had once been sent to Maine to inhabit: the life of a white woman.

Cedar finished reading the letter and put it back into the envelope.

Maybe Knot was right when she say people don't always need to know everything 'bout everybody.

Cedar rubbed Otis Lee's shoulder. And he knew that if Pep had been sitting there with him, she would have done the same thing. *Essie was my mama. Rose my grandma. Ma Noni my great-grandma.*

"Well, I'll be . . ." Otis Lee mused. Cedar and Coy were looking at him. Waiting. "Life's somethin'. Ain't it, y'all?"

He didn't need Cedar and Coy to reply to know that life was something to marvel at. Life, as Rose and Ma Noni had always told him, was full of surprises—surprises of the good kind, the bad kind, and the kind that had a little of both. Rose had loved and cared for him better than he imagined any mother could. So there was nothing left to do but smile when he thought of how things would have been had she been his real mother.

He looked up at his granddaughters and asked that one of them call Pep. When Cedar handed Otis Lee the phone, he could hear the voices of his neighbors talking in the background.

"Penelope," Otis Lee began. "Essie was my m—"

"I know," Pep said. "I know."

He did not get a chance to ask her how she knew before she was telling him something else, something that made him forget about Essie altogether.

"Knot slipped into a coma today," Pep told him. "Get on back here, Otis Lee. We need ya."

Otis Lee had known many people to go into comas. And none of them had come out. That's what he would have said to Pep if he'd been able to speak. He handed the phone to Cedar, who told Pep they'd be back in West Mills the following evening.

On the road from the Norfolk airport to West Mills, Otis Lee sat in Coy's back seat trying to nap. An hour would be just the right amount of time, he had said when they first got into the car. He closed his eyes but all he saw was Essie. *I'm sorry not to have told you sooner that I was your mother,* she had written. It might have been Cedar's voice that had spoken the words, but when Otis Lee played it over and over in his head, he heard Essie.

Rose. Essie was not the only one who had left Rose. Otis Lee believed that if he had known what Rose had done for him, he would have never gone looking for Essie.

But what about Ma Noni? How was he supposed to feel about her? Was she not the one who had caused it all? Otis Lee wanted so badly to sit with Knot at her kitchen—maybe even with a short drink—and tell her everything he'd learned over the past couple of days, and to hear her say something like, "Well, that's that, I guess." But the shakiness of Pep's voice over the phone had already told him that it would never happen. And for the fourth time since they'd been on the road, Otis Lee pulled his handkerchief from his shirt pocket and wiped away his tears.

The silence was loud on the ride back to West Mills. At one point Otis Lee glanced in the rearview mirror and saw Coy, who was so much like Knot, wiping tears. So he knew that if he were to ask if she was all right, she would probably say yes. Then she would cop an attitude because he had asked.

Cedar had pulled a notepad and a pencil from her pocketbook and was writing.

ANTIOCH LANE WAS lined with parked cars. And Fran's driveway was full. When Coy was about to turn into Otis Lee's driveway, he said, "You might as well take me to Fran's."

"Pop, don't you want to go home for a minute and—"

"Do like I tell ya, Coy," he ordered. "That's what I want right now."

She and Cedar glanced at each other.

"Y'all go on in," he said after they had parked. "Fran probably wants to see ya faces. Go on."

He sat in the car a few minutes longer, refusing to look to his right because that was where Knot's house stood. Because surely there would be a bereavement wreath hanging on her door. The sight of it would shatter him into pieces.

Otis Lee leaned his back against the seat. And much like he had on the day he'd ordered Essie to leave his house, Otis Lee cried. But this time, he wailed.

A FEW WEEKS after Knot had given birth to Fran, he let himself into her house and pulled her out of the bed and out onto the porch. He laid her down in front of the front door.

"Leave me be, goddamnit," Knot said when he rubbed the piece of ice on her face. She had not drunk any water in at least a day, maybe two. He could tell by the smell of her breath and by her chapped lips.

"I can't do that," he said. "I ain't gon' leave you be, Knot Centre. Not like this here. You too special for that. I loves ya."

Knot tried to sit upright and Otis Lee helped her. Finally she had focused her eyes enough to make contact with his.

"You love me?" she asked.

"Course," he replied.

"You ain't gon' stop, are ya?"

"Nooooo," he reassured her.

Knot scooted next to him, and she rested her head on his shoulder. He knew that was the closest thing to a hug he would ever get from her.

It was a warm, pretty day in West Mills.

ACKNOWLEDGMENTS

I am incredibly grateful to the Iowa Writers' Workshop, the Napa Valley Writers' Conference, and the Bread Loaf Writers' Conference for their generous support of my work, and for giving me a chance.

To my agent, P. J. Mark, who guides me every step of the way. A champion. And to Ian Bonaparte, who jumps in wherever needed.

To my editor, Liese Mayer, thank you for loving this project, for asking all the right questions, for your keen eye, and for your patience. And to Grace McNamee, Barbara Darko, and everyone at Bloomsbury Publishing, you are magnificent. Thank you for all you do.

While at Iowa, I learned so much from Ethan Canin, Lan Samantha Chang, Margot Livesey, Rebecca Makkai, and Ayana Mathis. Thank you for sharing your gifts with me. Ayana and Margot were especially giving of their time, feedback, wisdom, and friendship. And how could any of us do anything without the constant care of Connie Brothers, Deb West, and Jan Zenisek? Thank you.

To Elaine Brooks, Geoffrey Minter, Helen Phillips, and Helen Rubinstein, thank you for believing in me.

Many thanks to Mia Bailey, Jamel Brinkley, Marcus Burke, Drew Calvert, Noel Carver, Joseph Cassara, Charles N.

Collier, Tameka Cage Conley, Christina Cooke, Amanda Dennis, Scott Ditzler, Iracema Drew, Jason England, Sarah Frye, Nathaniel Go, Garth Greenwell, Maya Hlavacek, J. M. Holmes, Eskor Johnson, Jade Jones, Sasha Khmelnik, Claire Lombardo, Alex Madison, Magogodi Makhene, Grayson Morley, Melody Murray, Derek Nnuro, Natalie Nuzzo, Regina M. Porter, Ed Roth, William Pei Shih, C. Kevin Smith, Berend ter Borg, Dawnie Walton, Monica L. West, Connor White, Davina White-Elliott, ZZ Packer and her 2017 Napa Valley workshop group, Helena Maria Viramontes and her 2017 Bread Loaf workshop group, and Kim and Robin Christiansen at the Historic Phillips House of Iowa City.

I am so grateful to black writers such as the late Zora Neale Hurston, Toni Morrison, and Alice Walker, who have cleared a path for us.

To Daniel and Alyssa Crouch, Davina and Steve Elliott, and Kevin J. Harrell, thank you for the steadfast friendship over the years.

Had I not been raised village-style, I don't know that I would have been able to write *In West Mills*. Thank you, Betty P. Griffin, Maria "Bebe" Griffin, Nellie "Lil Sista" Mitchell, Maggie Williams, and Eulanda "Landie" Williams, for being there when my parents and I needed you most.

To my aunts Sandra, Gwen, Lynette, DeeDee, Gail, and Wanda, thank you for being some of the strongest black women I know.

To Chanell, Keshia, Shakira, and Davina, thank you for the unwavering encouragement and the constant laughter.

To my big sister Rosalind, thank you for checking in on me regularly.

To Alexus and Treondre Winslow, thank you for coming along and forcing me to grow up. I love y'all.

Last, but certainly not least, I am most grateful for and to my mother, Joan Winslow. It would take another two hundred-plus pages to express my gratitude to you. You and Daddy taught me love, selflessness, and to finish what I start. I love you so very much.

A NOTE ON THE AUTHOR

DE'SHAWN CHARLES WINSLOW was born and raised in Elizabeth City, North Carolina, and in 2003 moved to Brooklyn, New York. He is a 2017 graduate of the Iowa Writers' Workshop and holds a BFA in creative writing and an MA in English literature from Brooklyn College. He has received scholarships from the Napa Valley Writers' Conference and the Bread Loaf Writers' Conference. He lives in East Harlem.

LADIES FIRST

Women Athletes Who Made a Difference

LADIES FIRST

Women Athletes Who Made a Difference

Ken Rappoport

Ω

PEACHTREE

ATLANTA

Published by
PEACHTREE PUBLISHERS
1700 Chattahoochee Avenue
Atlanta, Georgia 30318-2112

www.peachtree-online.com

Printed in October 2009 in the United States of America by RR Donnelly Book
Publishing Services, Bloomsburg, PA

Book design by Melanie McMahon Ives
Photo research by Ana L. Parker

Photo credits: pp. 3, 8, 13, 23, 27, 35, 39, 59, 65, 71, 78, 81, 86, 91, 95, 101, 106, 111,
115, 121, 124—Associated Press/World Wide Sports; p. 44—Al Brodsky; pp. 49,
55—Shirley Muldowney; pp. 131, 138—Orwell Moore.

Cover photos—Associated Press/World Wide Sports, Al Brodsky.

10 9 8 7 6 5 4 3 2

Library of Congress Cataloging-in-Publication Data

Rappoport, Ken.
   Ladies First : women athletes who made a difference / written by Ken
Rappoport.-- 1st ed.
        p. cm.
   Includes bibliographical references.
   ISBN 978-1-56145-338-2 / 1-56145-338-2
1. Women athletes--Biography--Juvenile literature. 2. Sports for women--History--
Juvenile literature. I. Title.

   GV697 .A1R325 2005
   796'.082'0922--dc22   2004026979

For Bernice, my North Star, the light that leads me home

My thanks to Lisa Banim
for bringing me in to Peachtree Publishers,
to Kathy Landwehr for her warm welcome,
and to Vicky Holifield for her professional and sensitive editing.
And, as always, thanks to my favorite editor at home, Bernice.

Contents

INTRODUCTION

In the 1800s, most sports were off-limits to women. People believed that engaging in strenuous sports was just plain unladylike. In addition, they thought that girls' bodies were much too fragile to withstand the rigors of athletics, and their "nerves" or mental capacities were too weak to handle the pressure of competition. When the first modern Olympic Games were held in 1896, the organizers decided that women should not be allowed to participate.

A great many women did not agree with this attitude. More and more of them had already begun to challenge the traditional roles assigned to females; they had worked to gain voting rights for themselves, and they were entering the work force in growing numbers. The time had come to challenge the traditional roles of women in sports, too.

The turn of the century began a new chapter in women's athletics. In the 1900 Olympic Games in Paris, France, eleven women were allowed to participate in tennis and golf. Charlotte Cooper, a tennis player from England, was the first woman to become an Olympic champion.

Pioneering twentieth-century athletes like Gertrude Ederle, Susan Butcher, and Julie Krone proved that sports was no longer a "man's world." Ederle was the first woman to swim the English Channel, Butcher was among the first of her sex to compete in the Iditarod dog sled race through the Alaskan wilderness, and Krone was one of the first important female jockeys.

This book tells the stories of women who made a lasting impact on sports and society. These First Ladies of Sports all defied the general thinking that women are the "weaker sex." With their amazing achievements, they all forged their special place in history.

And they all shared the same qualities that define any great athlete, male or female: courage, perseverance, and dedication.

1
GERTRUDE EDERLE
Against All Odds

Ederle at a beach on Long Island, NY, in 1923

Standing on French soil at Cape Gris-Nez, her heart pounding, Gertrude Ederle surveyed the gray skies and turbulent water. Back in America, a nation waited and wondered. Could she do it?

It was the Roaring Twenties, and a time for great individual expression. Anything went, from flagpole sitters to plucky pilots performing death-defying stunts — and swimmers attempting to cross the English Channel.

But in the 1920s, a female swimmer crossing the Channel seemed to be one of the most outrageous stunts of all. Few people believed the "weaker sex" had the strength or stamina to do it.

Only five swimmers had mastered the Channel up to that point—all men. In 1923, Enrique Tiraboschi had set the world record in 16 hours, 33 minutes. Women swimmers had tried the crossing, but they had come up short time and again. In 1925, Ederle had been one of the failures. Now she was about to try it again.

When Ederle prepared to take the plunge on the morning of August 6, 1926, the treacherous water was rough and choppy, so bad that steamboat crossings were canceled. Nevertheless, nineteen-year-old Ederle was determined to make it across. It was a minimum of 21 miles from the French shore to Dover, England—probably longer on this day. She knew she could be tossed off-course by the rough conditions. But not even she could imagine the harrowing challenges that the Channel would present.

She covered her body with olive oil, lanolin, and lard, a mixture designed not only to keep her warm but also to protect her from stinging jellyfish or Portuguese men-of-war. Wearing a daring two-piece black silk suit with a tiny American flag sewn over one breast, a red rubber cap, and amber-glass goggles, Ederle waited impatiently to make the plunge.

Finally, she shouted, "Cheerio," and dived into the cold, dark water. It was a little after seven o'clock in the morning...

ᏀᎾ

Whether spending summers as a kid at the family's riverside bungalow in Highlands, New Jersey, or paddling around in the Tenth Avenue horse troughs in Manhattan, Gertrude Ederle had always felt comfortable around water.

Gertrude Ederle

Gertrude grew up as a water baby. One could see the Shrewsbury River from their summer home in New Jersey. "Her father would lower her into the water with a rope around her little waist, and she would paddle about and laugh up at him, entirely unafraid," Gertrude's mother said. As a young girl she was a daredevil; she loved to roam the streets of New York or hitch rides on the back of ice trucks.

The third of six children, Gertrude was inspired by her older sister Margaret, a good swimmer, to take up the sport. After years of swimming together, the two joined the Women's Swimming Association of New York.

Gertrude first grabbed national attention in 1922 at a race in the New York area. A total unknown, she finished the 3 1/2-mile Joseph P. Day Cup at Manhattan Beach ahead of fifty-one other swimmers, including U.S. swimming superstar Helen Wainwright and British champion Hilda James.

Ederle, the bashful, broad-shouldered daughter of a New York butcher, was on her way. She spent the next couple of years destroying just about every woman's swimming record in the books—from the 50 yards to the half-mile. She won more than two dozen trophies and set twenty-nine world and national swimming records. She was rapidly becoming a swimmer of international repute. At the 1924 Olympics in Paris, Ederle added to her reputation by winning a gold medal and two bronzes. The next year she was the first woman to complete the traditional 21-mile race from the docks of New York City to Sandy Hook, New Jersey. She was proud to be the first woman to do it, but prouder still to break the men's record with a time of 7 hours, 11 minutes, and 30 seconds. She liked breaking down stereotypes about women and breaking records, particularly those held by men.

In 1925, the coach of the Women's Swimming Association of New York selected Margaret instead of Gertrude to try to swim the English Channel. But Margaret deferred to her younger sister. She knew that "Gertie," as the family called her, was the faster swimmer.

When Gertrude Ederle announced her intention to swim the English Channel, there was hardly an outcry of public support. Even though many people regarded her as one of the world's great swimmers, they just didn't think a woman could accomplish such a feat. Reported the *London Daily News:* "Even the most uncompromising champion of the rights and capacities of women must admit that in contests of physical skill, speed and endurance, they must remain forever the weaker sex."

The newspaper's prediction seemed to be fulfilled when, after nine hours out, Ederle became seasick and overwhelmed by the treacherous currents. Her trainer, Jabez Wolffe, ordered her to quit. She refused and he had to pull her kicking and screaming from the water. Ederle had lost a chance to reach her goal. And her father, Harry, had lost $5,000, the sum he had bet on his daughter to finish.

The irate swimmer dismissed Wolffe. She made up her mind to come back the next year for a second attempt. She found a new trainer, William Burgess, who had swum across the Channel in 1911 after thirty-two attempts. Gertrude's father promised that this time he would not allow anyone to pull her from the water without her permission.

Gertrude Ederle wasn't the only woman with designs to swim the Channel. Three days before Ederle's attempt, Clarabelle Barrett of New Rochelle, New York, was lost in the fog for an hour or so before giving up 2 miles from the French shore. And Lillian Cannon of Baltimore was also getting ready for the swim.

Ederle's second crack at the Channel drew a bit more attention than the first. By now she had become a symbol of the American ideals of courage, spirit, and determination. She signed a contract to tell her story to newspapers. Hardly a day passed during her training period when the press did not mention her or when her words didn't make headlines. "Trudy," as she had been dubbed by journalists, had become a media darling.

Ederle's father made news himself when he bet $25,000 on his daughter to pull off what many thought to be impossible. That princely sum represented the sale of a lot of hamburgers, hot dogs, and cold cuts at the family butcher shop on Amsterdam Avenue. Harry Ederle stood to gain $175,000 with his long-shot bet with world famous insurance company Lloyd's of London.

Bringing glory to the United States and proving critics wrong about female athletes would have been enough

Ederle becomes the first woman to swim the English Channel in 1926.

motivation for Gertrude, but her father provided another incentive. He promised her a "roadster"—a popular car of the day—if she mastered the Channel.

On that blustery August morning in 1926, the young swimmer was ready. She surveyed the bustling scene at Cape Gris-Nez. Two tugboats were going to follow her on her great adventure. One boat carried her father, her sister Margaret, and her trainer Burgess. The other one was full of reporters and photographers.

"Please, God, help me," Gertrude said under her breath. Then she plunged into the surly water.

Burgess had planned for Ederle to drift on the tide for a

good part of the trip, conserving her energy for four hours of hard swimming at the end. The Channel, however, would not cooperate. The water was turbulent, and the strong crosscurrents pulled Ederle around like a limp rag doll. Because of the rough swell, Ederle nearly quit seven minutes after starting. But she swam on, blithely timing her strokes while singing "Let Me Call You Sweetheart." Finally Burgess told her to stop singing so that she could save her breath.

She needed every lungful. The waves pushed Ederle in every direction, at times out of sight of the tugboats and leaving her with "an eerie feeling" that she was stranded at sea. When the tugboats finally caught up with her, the reporters and photographers tried to keep up Ederle's spirits by reading cables from her mother (some of which they made up) and singing another hit tune of the time, "Yes, We Have No Bananas." There may have been no bananas, but there were plenty of sugar cubes, pineapple juice, chocolate, and chicken legs. To help Gertrude keep up her strength, people on the boat extended food to her on a pole. If she touched the boats, her Channel attempt would be nullified.

In the afternoon, vicious squalls kicked up and rocked the tugboats. The water was so choppy that many aboard became ill. Ederle was sick, too. Burgess begged her to quit.

Not missing a beat, Ederle yelled back over her shoulder, "WHAT FOR?"

Courage, spirit, and determination, indeed.

Her body ached as she fought through gales. But she continued with a fierce, almost inhuman dedication. Chew another sugar block. Eat a piece of chocolate. Down another shot of pineapple juice. "About eight hours out I knew I would either swim it or drown."

Day turned into night. The strong currents swept her off her intended course. But Ederle kept going, and now she could finally make out the bonfires on the English shore. Thousands of people had gathered there, waiting to give her a heroine's welcome.

After swimming more than fourteen hours and many miles out of her way, Ederle was feeling the strain. The final 400 yards were brutal, every stroke an agony and every part of her body aching as she headed toward shore.

At last it was down to the final 50 yards.

Flares filled the night sky and a spotlight illuminated the white foam that Ederle was kicking up behind her. Machine-like, she headed toward the shore's promised land.

At 9:40 P.M., she dragged herself onto land at Kingsdown, a couple of miles north of her intended destination of Dover. Thundering cheers went up for Ederle, although she seemed more dead than alive. She keeled over, doubled up by cramps for an hour—too sick to immediately enjoy her magnificent achievement.

What Ederle had done, though, was past human understanding. Not only had she completed the journey across treacherous, life-threatening waters, but she had also—in spite of going an estimated 14 miles out of her way—broken the world record by a full two hours! Her time: 14 hours, 31 minutes.

Suddenly, America had a new sports hero bigger than life. The newspapers were full of praise for this extraordinary woman. Ederle, with her indefatigable spirit, became a legend in her own time. In at least one 1926 poll, she finished ahead of Babe Ruth as the most popular athlete in America.

If all that acclaim was hard for the modest Ederle to believe, even more unbelievable was the hero's welcome that greeted her in New York on her return. Ederle might have been ready for the Channel swim, but she was certainly not ready for this: two million screaming people lined the route for a riotous ticker-tape parade through the city.

Nor was she ready for the numerous stage and screen offers, swimsuit endorsements, and proposals of marriage that followed. Irving Berlin, one of the most popular songwriters in the U.S., wrote a song—"Trudy"—in her honor.

Wholesome. Unspoiled. Thoroughly natural. That's what they wrote about her in the newspapers. All she had wanted to do was swim the English Channel and prove something to the world, and to herself.

"When somebody tells me I cannot do something," Ederle said, "that's when I do it."

She certainly did.

2
Babe Didrikson Zaharias
The Other Babe

Didrikson poses with her trophy at the Miami Biltmore Country Club in 1940.

*I*t's just a publicity stunt. It is difficult and unheard of. But if she succeeds, she will catch the world's attention. The question is: Can Mildred Didrikson pull it off?

Melvin McCombs, her boss at the Employers Casualty Company in Dallas, Texas, believed in her. She couldn't let him down.

In the summer of 1932, hundreds of young women gathered in Evanston, Illinois, for the national AAU track and field championships and Olympic trials.

McCombs had come up with a scheme to get publicity for his firm and his star. He had brought Didrikson to the AAU meet as a member of his company's track team—the only member. She was the entire team!

Other teams had as many as twenty or more athletes.

"I'm going to lick you single-handed," Didrikson announced. To her AAU opponents, it sounded ridiculous. The media loved it: One woman against the rest of the country.

This brash young woman was different. Most females of her time weren't outspoken. They accepted their role as the "weaker sex."

But the word "weak" wasn't in her vocabulary. "My goal," she later wrote, "is to be the greatest athlete in the world." Not the greatest female athlete. The greatest athlete!

In two previous AAU championships, Didrikson had made a strong showing. This time the stakes were higher: a place on the U.S. track team at the Olympics.

At the AAU meet Didrikson entered as many events as was humanly possible. In less than three hours, she raced around the University of Illinois's Dyche Stadium. She competed in both the qualifying heats and finals of each event.

Finish one event, race to the next. At each stop, the officials gave her a few seconds to catch her breath. Then, she was up and running again.

How would this one-woman team measure up?

By the time the meet was over, Didrikson had finished first in five events: the broad jump, 80-meter hurdles, javelin toss, baseball toss, and shot put. She set world records in three of them. And she tied for first in the high jump, giving her more points by herself than any other team in the entire event.

Her total of thirty points had beaten everyone. Her score was eight points better than the runner-up, the Illinois Women's Athletic Club, a squad with twenty-two athletes!

What a one-woman show. What a headline for the newspapers. Gushed the *New York Times:* "The most amazing series of performances ever accomplished by an individual, male or female, in track and field history." She had conquered the best in the United States. Now she was ready to conquer the world.

The meet in Evanston was the start of an unmatched career in athletics. How did it all begin?

Mildred Ella Didriksen's—later changed to Didrikson— parents had come to America from Norway, hoping to find a better life for their family. Soon after they arrived, America slipped into the Great Depression that followed the stock market crash of 1929. Mildred's father, a former cabinet- maker, earned a meager living by refinishing furniture. Her mother took in washing and ironing from the neighbors.

The family was poor. Everyone had to help bring in income. That included Mildred. As a young girl, she picked figs for farmers and did odd jobs for the neighbors.

But even though times were tough, Mildred always found ways to make life fun. When she went to the store, she didn't walk, she ran. She wanted to see how fast she could go. Each day she would try to go faster and faster. She was delighted when she shaved seconds off her run.

Mildred loved to leap over the neighbors' hedges. To make the jumps easier, she asked her neighbors to trim their hedges to the same height, and they were kind enough to oblige. It was better, but some of the bushes were prickly. When Mildred jumped, she tried crooking one leg and extending it higher to avoid being scratched. Her new technique worked. Now she leaped over one hedge after another, hurtling forward, trying to best her time on her way to school.

Later, Mildred would object when people called her a "natural" athlete. There was nothing natural about the hard work she put in to master her skills.

The Didriksen family philosophy was to work hard, play hard.

Mildred's father was a physical fitness fanatic. He built gymnasium equipment for his family and installed it in the backyard of their home in Beaumont, Texas. And he expected the whole family to work out. All the neighborhood kids were attracted to the Didriksens' backyard. At the time Mildred was growing up, girls didn't usually compete against boys. But with four brothers in her own family, she soon learned to compete against them and the neighborhood boys in a variety of sports.

At some point Mildred became known as "Babe." Some say it was because as the sixth of seven children she was the baby of the family; others say it was because she could hit a baseball like Babe Ruth. That explanation seems reasonable: she once hit five home runs in a game.

Babe's athletic talent in high school was apparent from the start. It set her apart from the other students. The boys teased her. Never one to be intimidated, she beat them up when the teasing got too rough. The girls kept her out of their groups. Who wanted to pal around with someone who competed with the boys? Who wanted to be friends with someone who bragged that one day she would be "the greatest athlete that ever lived"?

Her classmates might not have wanted her in their groups at first, but they soon learned to love her on the field. Babe became one of the most popular and respected girls at Beaumont Senior High School. She starred in every girls' sport that was available: basketball, tennis, golf, swimming, and diving.

She was still a high school student when Employers Casualty Company of Dallas came calling. Would she like to join the insurance company and play with the Golden Cyclones? They were one of the nation's top women's amateur basketball teams. Babe was excited. She moved to Dallas with her father's blessing. She went to work as a typist at the insurance company. Her salary of $900 was considered overly generous for the times. But she had no illusions—she knew she had been hired mostly for her athletic ability, not her typing skills.

Babe was an office worker by day, a sports star in her off

time. Her school made special arrangements for her to take final exams and graduate with her high school class. In the meantime, she played sports to her heart's content—basketball, softball, tennis, and swimming. It was in track and field, though, that she really excelled. She competed on the Golden Cyclones' track and field team and participated in three national AAU (Amateur Athletic Union) championships.

Her goal was the Olympics. After her astounding performance at the 1932 Olympic trials in Evanston, she was well on her way to her goal—and she had the nation's attention.

Babe had qualified to compete in five events at the '32 Games. But she was only allowed to enter three. Officials had eliminated the 800-meter run for women from the Olympics. Many people thought such a long race was too hard for women. They believed that women were more fragile than men, not only physically but also mentally. Concluded one national health organization: "Under prolonged and intense strain a girl goes to pieces nervously."

Babe was about to prove otherwise. She brought a cocky attitude to the Los Angeles Olympics. A teammate started to brag about how well she had done. Babe cast a stone-cold glare in her direction. "Oh, I done that, and in half the time."

The outspoken Didrikson was not the most popular athlete on the American squad. When it came time to choose a captain for Team USA, her teammates voted for Jean Shiley. Babe knew Shiley only too well. She had tied Babe in a closely fought high-jump competition at the 1932 AAU meet prior to the Olympics.

The first Olympic event for Babe was the javelin throw. As she unleashed the throw, she felt a twinge in her right shoulder. The javelin landed 143 feet, 4 inches away. Her throw was a world record, shattering the previous record by nearly 11 feet. She had torn cartilage in her shoulder, but won the Olympic title.

Then Babe got ready for the 80-meter hurdle. She had no trouble jumping while racing at full speed. She had perfected her distinct style when leaping over the neighborhood hedges during her childhood days. Now instead of hedges, it was hurdles.

Babe broke the world record in the 80-meter hurdle on her first try. But—hold on—officials announced that she had jumped the gun. She would have to run it over again.

Once again, Babe was off. Once more, she was called back for starting before the gun went off.

On her third try, Babe again pushed off her mark. This time, she wasn't ahead of the gun. She broke her own world record—the one that she had set just moments before—by racing the 80-meter distance in 11.7 seconds. The result stood. Babe claimed her second gold medal of the Olympics.

Next up, the high jump.

Babe faced her rival Jean Shiley for the gold medal. The two athletes presented a dramatic contrast in styles. Didrikson used the so-called "western roll," throwing herself over the bar headfirst. She called it her "men's style." Shiley used the scissor-kick style, going over the bar feet first. It was the classic high-jump technique for women of that day.

Both women cleared the bar at a world record 5 feet, 5$^1/_4$ inches. They had tied again.

The judges met. The decision? They declared Shiley the gold medal winner. They said Babe "dove" over the bar, her head clearing before her body. This technique was not allowed in those days. Using it barred Babe from sharing the gold medal. (She was ahead of her time. In later years, the "western roll" would become the style for all high jumpers.) She was disappointed. She had to settle for second place and the silver. But Babe had medalled in every event she had entered. Her total was now one silver and two gold.

Along with her medals came a barrage of publicity. Flashbulbs popped. Cameras moved in for close-ups of America's newest sports darling. One photo showed Babe posing with Hollywood's handsome leading man, Clark Gable. And Babe loved the attention.

Three Olympic medals in three tries. How was Babe going to top that?

How about playing professional baseball and basketball with men? Touring the country giving billiards and boxing exhibitions? Competing on foot against a racehorse? Doing a vaudeville act? There seemed to be no end to Babe's diverse talents.

Colorful and full of ego, Babe enjoyed boasting that she

could do anything. The media loved it. The audience ate it up. She was the ultimate show-woman and a shameless self-promoter.

Her barnstorming tours made money, plenty of it. She earned as much as $55,000 a year—a staggering amount during the Depression years. She was able to support her parents, send her nieces and nephews through school, and ensure her own future.

When Babe looked to her future, she had visions of being a champion in golf. Why golf? "I'd done everything else," she said.

Skeptics pointed out one problem. She had no golfing experience. A lack of experience might have been a problem for most anyone else, but not for Babe. As she had in other sports, Babe attacked golf with passion.

She practiced six days a week. At times her caddie would stand 150 yards away with an empty golf bag. Babe would chip the golf ball into the bag over and over again. "If the caddie had to move it, she got mad," said Babe's nephew, Dee Didriksen. "I remember her hands would be calloused, and they would bleed..."

Babe's size—a trim 5-foot-7 and 145 pounds—was perfect for golf. She displayed enormous power with her swing. The press referred to her as a "muscle woman." She hated the nickname, yet it was appropriate: she had the strength to outdistance some of the greatest players in the world.

Asked how she did it, the green-eyed Babe usually

responded with a wink, "I just lift up my girdle and let it fly!"

She was soon winning women's amateur tournaments around the country. And putting on exhibitions with stars from the men's game.

Babe would stroll down the green. While other golfers ignored the fans, Babe would stop and chat. She would make wisecracks and joke with them.

"She loved people and people loved her," said women's golfing great Patty Berg.

Not everybody on the golf circuit found her lovable, though. The genteel game of golf had never seen the likes of Babe. She was trash-talking long before it was popular among athletes.

In one pro-am tournament, Babe was paired with golfing great Sam Snead. She stepped up to the tee and hit a long drive. "See if you can beat that poke, Sam," she taunted.

He couldn't.

She was just as hard on the women.

The brash, self-confident Babe would enter the clubhouse and inquire, "Which one of you is finishing second this week?"

It was not surprising that she would try competing with the men at their own game. Babe merely filled out an application and entered the 1938 Los Angeles Open. The operators of the PGA event were thrilled. The tournament had been struggling. It wouldn't hurt to have a celebrity like Babe on the course.

Babe Didrikson Zaharias

Didrikson chips out of a sand trap during a 1947 women's golf tournament in Miami.

As a publicity stunt, the organizers paired Babe with a minister and a former pro wrestler nicknamed "The Crying Greek from Cripple Creek." His name: George Zaharias.

As expected, this odd trio drew the biggest crowds of the tournament. Something happened, though, that was completely unexpected. Romance bloomed on a golf course. Babe and George fell in love. They married later that year.

While Babe's score failed to qualify at that PGA event, it didn't stop her from trying again. In 1944, she failed once more to make the cut. Then in 1945, she finally succeeded! Babe didn't win the tournament, but she made a good showing against some of the best male golfers in the world. And she had broken the gender barrier. She was the first woman to play on the PGA Tour. Here was a great story. But hardly anyone knew about it at the time.

"There was no TV and if you did radio you had to drive to the station," said golf legend Byron Nelson. No cameras followed the Babe around the course. Fast forward to 2003. Think of the publicity Annika Sorenstam, star of the Ladies Professional Golf Association (LPGA), generated. Her bid to play in a men's tournament was shown on TV all over the world.

Actually, without Babe there might not have been an LPGA. Babe wanted to turn pro. But there was no place for her to go. Instead of giving up, she helped to found the Ladies Professional Golf Association in 1947. She became its immediate star, bringing women's golf to the forefront in America.

Babe played in tournaments and tirelessly promoted the sport. She appeared in hundreds of exhibitions. She always had a story or two to tell the press, some of them even true.

She occasionally stretched the truth to make her stories more colorful. Like the tale about outrunning a locomotive, or the one about racing a wild bull.

According to one story, Babe was caught red-handed telling a fib. On a fishing trip during the Second World War, she was asked, for security purposes, to give her date of birth.

Babe Didrikson Zaharias

"Nineteen-nineteen," she said.

"So you were thirteen when you won those Olympic medals, huh, Babe?" said a friend.

Babe smirked.

"Aw, shaddup," she said.

Winning tournament after tournament on the women's tour, Babe was on top of the world. But in 1953, she faced the toughest opponent of her life: cancer. She underwent surgery. About three months later, she was back on the tour and winning once more.

In 1954, despite the spread of the cancer, she racked up five more tour victories. It was her last stand in the spotlight.

On September 27, 1956, Babe died. An entire nation mourned.

She had left an amazing legacy.

The Associated Press named her the greatest female athlete of the twentieth century. Babe tried almost every sport—and very often dominated it. And she did so in a time when women were not supposed to exert themselves in sports. A Hall of Famer in not one, but two sports—in track and field and in golf—Babe destroyed all the "weaker sex" stereotypes. She proved it was okay for women to sweat, grunt, and groan in the athletic arena.

"She brought it to the forefront that women could be athletes, too," said former golfing great Marlene Hagge.

And no one did it better than Babe.

3
SUSAN BUTCHER
The Magnificent Musher

Susan Butcher was making plans for her survival.

Ax, check. Snowshoes and sleeping bag, check.

Enough food and water for the long journey.

And the most important, her dogs: Siberian huskies, powerful allies on the most treacherous trail of all.

Everything was in order. She was ready to start the 1990

Susan Butcher with her dogs in March, 1987

Iditarod Trail Sled Dog Race. Sometimes called the "Last Great Race on Earth," this grueling course was a huge challenge for both man and beast. She was gunning for her fourth Iditarod title.

She grabbed the handlebar and looked over her sixteen dogs. Their bodies were tense, straining, ready to go.

LADIES FIRST

Butcher, clad in a bright red snowsuit, was eager to get started, too. Not that she liked the conditions. The heaviest snowstorm in twenty-five years had hit the area, followed by unseasonably warm weather. A part of the 1,168-mile trail through the daunting Alaskan wilderness had turned to slush.

The weather was not the only concern. Dangerous trail conditions and wild animals could also jeopardize her journey.

Memories of the nightmarish 1985 Iditarod were always with her. After finishing in the top five in several earlier races, Butcher was breezing along on her way to victory. Everything had been going well. Suddenly, without warning, a huge moose appeared on the trail. Wild and out of control, it was headed directly toward her sled!

Before Butcher could react, the crazed animal had attacked the huskies. The harnessed dogs were attached to each other and the sled. They hadn't had a chance against a six-foot-tall, 1,500-pound wild beast. The raging moose went on a rampage. There was blood everywhere in the snow.

Butcher, not thinking of her own safety, had grabbed her ax. She'd struck the moose again and again in an effort to stop the massacre. Suddenly, a shot had rung out. Another dog-sled driver, seeing her peril, had shot and killed the attacker.

But the damage had been done: two dogs dead and thirteen injured. There was no question she was out of the race. Libby Riddles went on to become the first woman to win the Iditarod. But Butcher couldn't worry about having to drop out of the Last Great Race. Her dogs were not out of danger. Grieving, she had *traveled with her wounded dogs to a veterinary hospital. She'd slept on the hospital floor for a week. Despite suffering with an injured shoulder, she'd cared for her dogs until they were healthy enough to go home.*

Butcher tried to shake the terrible images from her mind. She was determined to finish the race first again. Could she become the first woman to win the Iditarod four times?

ᏏᎧ

Susan Butcher had always seemed to be more comfortable with animals than she was with people.

When she was just a little girl growing up in Cambridge, Massachusetts, she hated the city. But she loved the great outdoors. She loved spending time at her family's summer home on the rocky Maine coast. She especially enjoyed restoring a boat with her father and sister, Kate. It was hard work, but it was worth it. Sailing was such fun. Susan never wanted to be in the city again!

And she loved animals—all kinds. Susan's mother came to expect the unexpected—she wasn't even surprised the time she came home and found iguanas crawling up her curtains.

One day Susan received a present: a Siberian husky. The teenager was so excited she went to the library to learn more about huskies. She discovered they are bred to be sled dogs. A year later, she bought another, at which point her mom suggested the house wasn't big enough for both dogs.

Susan, who was always independent, went to live with her grandmother in Maine.

After high school she headed west to Colorado with dreams of raising dogs and living in the great outdoors. There were few places in America more wide open and wild than the Colorado Rockies.

Working with a veterinarian in Boulder, she became skilled in treating animals. Handling dogs was second nature to Susan. A local woman gave her a chance. Soon Susan was training and raising sled dogs. She loved to take them out on training runs, but she was unhappy with the lack of sled dog trails in the area.

"I had to go in a truck to get to trails," she said.

One day in 1975, Susan was reading a magazine about mushers, the people who race sled dogs. An article about a sled dog race in Alaska called the Iditarod caught her eye. She was intrigued. Alaska! At last she had discovered a place where there were thousands of miles of trails.

She made up her mind that she was going to compete in the Iditarod.

The race was named after a trail that mushers took in the early 1900s to bring mail and supplies to Alaskan mining towns. The Iditarod began each year in March in Anchorage—dashing across the Alaskan range, turning west along the Yukon River, and zooming north along the Bering Sea coast into Nome. It took about two weeks to complete. With its frozen rivers, rough mountain ranges,

bleak terrain, windswept coast, and often subzero temperatures, it was no place for the weakhearted. But Butcher was
determined to go.

Four months after arriving in Fairbanks, Alaska, the
twenty-one-year-old made plans to prepare for the Iditarod.
She bought three pedigree dogs. She loaded them into a
truck along with her two cats and food supplies and headed
off into the rugged Wrangell Mountains.

She settled in a small log cabin built in the Gold Rush
years of the early 1900s. There wasn't another human being
around for forty miles. Living in the mountains was hard.
The only water available was in a nearby stream. Butcher
lugged buckets and buckets of water from the stream to her
cabin. For heat, she chopped wood. She hunted and trapped
moose, caribou, and sheep for food. It was not an easy life,
but Butcher was happy. She was able to mush her dogs on
the plentiful trails. She rarely saw another person until the
summer, when she went into Fairbanks to earn enough
money to buy supplies for the next winter.

Butcher signed on for the summer to help with a
University of Alaska project to save the endangered musk
oxen and earned $600.

Although Butcher was happy with her new life, it was
still her dream to race in the Iditarod. Some people considered the Last Great Race a "no-woman's land." Women had
run the race, but no woman had ever won. Men usually had
an advantage when it came to moving the heavy sled up

and down tricky slopes and around trees. When loaded with supplies and equipment, the sleds weighed hundreds of pounds. Mushers needed strong legs to run behind the sleds and push on the uphill stretches.

Butcher was not concerned. Even though she stood only 5-foot-6 and weighed 140 pounds, she was wiry and strong. She felt she could outwork any man.

In 1977, Butcher met Joe Redington Sr., one of the founders of the Iditarod. Redington agreed that she was fit to compete, especially after watching her work in his kennel. Butcher needed two huskies to complete her team. They made a deal: she would train young dogs for Redington in exchange for the two huskies.

Now Butcher needed a company or corporation to back her. It is expensive to enter the Iditarod, and Butcher was broke. She tried to get sponsors herself by going door to door, but wasn't able to raise much money.

Redington came up with a plan to get Butcher in the news. Local television viewers were surprised by what they saw on their screens. There on a frozen lake, Susan Butcher stood with an ax in her hand. In the freezing temperatures, she wore only a bathing suit. After chopping a hole in the ice, she jumped in and emerged smiling. "And this is how a future Iditarod competitor keeps clean," the reporter announced.

The plan worked. The publicity helped Butcher get her first sponsor. In 1978 she entered the race. She became the first woman to finish in the top twenty and in the money.

Susan Butcher

Four years earlier, Mary Shields and Lolly Medley, the first women to compete in the Ititarod, had finished out of the money, eight days behind the winner.

Even though Butcher had finished among the money winners, she was not satisfied.

For three years, she kept improving.

"There are many hard things in life," Butcher said, "but there's only one sad thing, and that is giving up."

She didn't give up. She entered the 1982 race. The race was only one hour old when Butcher ran into trouble. Her sled careened off course and plowed into a tree. The crack-up left Butcher bruised. She checked her fifteen dogs. Four were injured.

Further down the trail Butcher and her team drove into a blinding snowstorm. It was difficult enough to drive against the wind and snow, but now the orange markers set alongside the trail as guides were invisible.

Suddenly, Butcher found herself 10 miles off course. She managed to fight her way back. She reached one of the twenty-four checkpoints on the course where drivers store additional food and equipment. There they can stop and rest or take care of injured or sick dogs. Iditarod drivers are required to take a 24-hour break during the race. But Butcher was forced into a 52-hour stay. A vicious snowstorm stranded her at Shaktoolik, the first checkpoint on the Bering coast.

During the unexpected delay, her first priority was the dogs. She knew the routine: melt down snow for water, feed the dogs, check them over, fix the harnesses. In addition,

Butcher had to chop wood in the face of 80-mile-per-hour winds and 30-foot snowdrifts. She barely had time to catch a little sleep. Despite all this difficulty, she managed to finish in second place.

In the 1984 Iditarod, more trouble. Butcher was racing along a frozen Norton Sound Bay when she heard a frightening noise. The ice was cracking! Suddenly, Butcher and her sled plunged into the dark, freezing water.

Granite, the lead dog, took charge. He pulled with all his might. The other dogs grunted and strained. They struggled to gain a foothold on the slippery surface. Finally, they pulled Butcher out of the water. Her dogs had saved her life! Soaking wet and chilled to the bone, she ran behind the sled for several miles to stay warm. Amazingly, she once again finished second.

The next year, the raging moose spoiled Butcher's plans to become the first woman to win the Iditarod. Having to drop out of the race was bad enough. But sitting by while Libby Riddles became the first female to win the Iditarod made Butcher feel even worse.

"It hurt when Libby won," Butcher said. "But there's more to it than that. I didn't get to race the team I had been working on for seven years. That's what hurt."

Finally, success. She won the 1986 Iditarod in record time. After winning in 1987 and 1988, she became the first person to win the event three straight years.

Butcher won other races, but enjoyed the challenge of the Iditarod most of all.

Susan Butcher nears the finish line of the
1990 Iditarod Sled Dog Race.

She missed winning the championship in 1989. Now it was 1990 and Butcher hoped to reclaim her title.

"All right! Go!" she shouted and squeezed the handlebar. Her powerful team of sixteen dogs was off and running into the Alaskan wilderness.

Because there were seventy mushers, the starting times for the race were staggered. Butcher started as No. 68. But by the time she reached Shaktoolik, she was in the lead. It was close, though. The first three mushers pulled into the area within just eight minutes of each other.

During the race, it is not unusual for dogs to get sick or injured and have to drop out. But suddenly, Butcher had to replace three—including two important lead dogs. One of them was Tolstoy, her favorite. Butcher alternated taking the lead with Lavon Barve and defending champion Joe Runyan.

Butcher had not slept much during the race. Drowsiness and exhaustion are major problems for Iditarod mushers. To wake herself up, she liked to scoop up a handful of snow and throw it in her face.

Her fatigue caused her to imagine things at times. "I'd think I was seeing Tolstoy in the lead," she said.

No, Tolstoy was no longer there, but Lightning and Sluggo, the two new lead dogs, were doing just fine. Butcher took the lead again as she headed along the windswept Bering Sea coastal area—the home stretch—with 270 miles to go.

Butcher's dogs were familiar with the area. She had often brought them there to practice in the wet and windy conditions.

"They know where White Mountain is," said Butcher, referring to the last checkpoint before the final 77 miles into Nome.

Susan Butcher

For the dogs, it was like going home. By the time Butcher's sled reached White Mountain, she was comfortably in front of her closest competitor.

They still had to complete the treacherous crossing of Norton Sound Bay at night. It was 30 miles of sheer ice, and Butcher had not forgotten the experience of 1984 when she almost drowned.

This time, no problem.

As she approached the outskirts of Nome on a bone-chilling, zero-degree day, the word spread around town. The fire siren sounded to alert the townspeople: First musher in!

Students were dismissed from school and ran into the streets in celebration. People emptied out of stores and rushed to Front Street. They didn't seem to notice the frigid temperature. The crowds couldn't wait to get a glimpse of the Iditarod winner. Shouts of congratulations filled the air when they spotted Susan Butcher in her red snowsuit.

Butcher finished the last few yards running alongside her dogs. Once the sled had stopped, she hugged her two lead dogs. Then she embraced her husband, John Monson, a lawyer and fellow musher, who was waiting for her at the finish line. He helped train the dogs and run a kennel near their home in the tiny wilderness town of Eureka, Alaska. In racking up her fourth Iditarod title in five years, she didn't just win—she won with surprising ease. She came in hours ahead of the runner-up.

"This team had power coming out of its ears," Butcher

said with a tired smile. Ice was caked to her eyelashes. She had finished the race in a record 11 days, 1 hour, 53 minutes, and 20 seconds.

Seven of the seventy starters had dropped out. Another was disqualified. Most of the mushers were strung out some 600 miles behind Butcher. They would be hobbling into Nome at various times for at least another week.

For many years dog-sled racing was thought to be strictly a man's domain because of its harsh, unyielding conditions. That is, until Butcher shattered the myth. She showed she was as good as any man running a dog-sled race—in fact, better than most.

Her success sparked the phrase: "Alaska—where men are men and women win the Iditarod."

4
JULIE KRONE
The Horse Whisperer

I t was the last day of the 1993 summer racing season at Saratoga Race Track. Julie Krone climbed aboard her mount, Seattle Way.

One more victory. That's all she needed for the riding championship. The 4-foot-10, 100-pound jockey settled in the saddle, gripped the reins, and squeezed the whip in her right hand.

There had been countless other starts for the thirty-year-old Krone. She was the most successful female jockey in thoroughbred horse racing history. But although she had competed in some 16,000 races, every new start was as

Krone rests for a moment at Monmouth Park Racetrack in 1990.

fresh as the first time. Racing was her passion. It was the only thing she had ever wanted to do.

It explained why she had always bounced back from frightful injuries. There had been enough of those to discourage any rider.

Krone stayed deep in the saddle, waiting for the start of the Saratoga race. The sun splashed on Krone's brightly colored riding gear. The track was dry and the skies were blue—a beautiful day for a race at the historic upstate New York track.

The gates slammed open. They're off!

Twelve sleek, muscular horses shot out of the starting gate and around the track. Krone battled for position with her fellow jockeys. Her face was grim, streaked with sweat and dirt.

Krone stayed behind the leaders for most of the race, pacing her horse. With the race heading into the last turn, Krone found herself behind a wall of thundering thousand-pound animals. The crowd was on its feet, screaming.

As she had done so many times before, Krone was about to make her move for the homestretch run. She tightened her hold on the reins. Suddenly, the jockey on her left steered his horse into her path.

"No! No!" Krone screamed as she stood up in the saddle.

Too late.

The horses collided. Seattle Way buckled, throwing Krone out of the saddle. She flew head over foot and landed hard on her right ankle.

The video replay was scary. As one sports writer described it, Krone looked like "a brightly colored rag doll flopping crazily onto the turf."

She had completely spun over and was sitting on the turf facing back down the track. A horse was heading straight for her! She was unable to move.

"I knew he was going to hit me."

The jockey, Jorge Chavez, tried desperately to steer Two Is Trouble out of Krone's way. The horse was going too fast. His hooves hit hard, striking her in the chest and elbow. Her body did another tumble.

She lay there, not moving. As he looked back, Chavez thought, "Oh, no..."

Krone was barely alive when taken to the hospital. A special protective vest that covered her heart had saved her!

She underwent several operations.

Friends came in to try to cheer her. Fellow jockeys visited, too. Fans wrote letters. But when she went home to rehab at her Jockey Hollow Farm, she was depressed and scared. Scared she could be permanently injured. Scared she would never race again.

☍

Horseback riding came naturally to Julie Krone. She was in the saddle before she learned to walk. Her mother Judi, an equestrian champion, saw to that. "Even before I knew I'd be a jockey, my mom helped prepare me for the work," Julie said.

But she had to grow up first. She lived on a horse farm in Eau Claire, Michigan. Admittedly a "wild kid," she loved the thrill of racing horses. The faster the better.

"If something was dangerous, I didn't care," Krone said. "I valued the thrill a lot more than I valued myself."

Tiny Julie raced horses around the family farm with reckless abandon. She loved performing tricks, even though they were dangerous. With her horse at top speed, Julie stood straight up in the saddle. She jumped fences holding the reins in her mouth!

"It was like going to a rocket launch every day," said Krone's father, Don, an art teacher. "She was always on her pony. She always had some trick to show you. She was fearless."

One day her father found Julie high up in a tree.

"Better look out. You'll fall."

"I already did," Julie answered. "Watch me climb."

Danger was a part of Julie Krone's life. She loved every minute of it.

"I got bit, I got stepped on, I got kicked in the head," Krone recalled. "I got dumped five miles from home; the pony ran back and I had to walk."

Julie was still very much like a young colt herself, still trying to find her legs. When it came to Julie's education with horses, her mother always managed to be around.

Julie loved to compete in horse shows. Her specialty: dressage, the art of training a horse in obedience. When she entered a horse show, she fully expected to win. One year she entered the 21-and-under division at a county fair. She took home the blue ribbon for first place. She was only five years old!

By the time she was a teenager, Julie had already decided

on her future. She and her mother watched the Belmont Stakes on TV when Steve Cauthen was going for the Triple Crown aboard Affirmed. As Cauthen raced across the finish line ahead of the field, Julie turned to her mother and said, "I want to be a jockey." She was fourteen.

One year later, Julie and her mom, now divorced, were on their way to Kentucky. Judi Krone's connections had turned up a job for both of them—walking racehorses around the famous Churchill Downs track.

Julie's experience at Churchill Downs just confirmed what she already knew: Nothing was going to stop her from being a jockey!

Back in Michigan, she hung around fairground tracks and did some riding. Next stop: Tampa, Florida, to live with her grandparents and ride horses.

But when Julie showed up at the front gate at Tampa Bay Downs racetrack, the guards turned her away. They couldn't believe this little girl was old enough to work at the track.

What did she do? She simply went around the back and climbed a fence. She met one of the track's trainers. He liked Julie's spunk and put her on a horse. In just five weeks, Julie won her first race as a professional.

Krone struck up a friendship with Julie Snellings, a former jockey who had been paralyzed in a race.

One day the jockeys gasped as Krone walked out for a race. Krone was not only wearing Snellings's old riding boots and pants. She was actually wearing her colors, too!

Krone rides to a win in the 2003 Breeders Cup race.

Like other jockeys, they were very superstitious. They felt sure that bad luck would follow.

"I'm real superstitious, too," Snellings said, "and it scared me to death that something might happen to her."

"It was no big deal," Krone said of wearing her friend's colors. "I just wanted to change her luck."

Snellings's colors brought Krone good fortune. For the first time in her budding career, she won three straight races.

It was a good start for Krone. But she had bigger plans, much bigger. Tampa Bay Downs was considered minor league when compared to the major tracks up north. She moved to Baltimore. There she could race at the top Maryland tracks like Pimlico, Laurel, and Bowie.

Julie Krone

When she first started, Julie's agent had problems finding mounts for her. Horse owners didn't think that women were strong enough to handle a 1,000-pound thoroughbred.

"Go home, have babies, do the dishes." The fans' voices echoed in her mind. Even though women had been racing horses professionally since 1968, they were still not generally accepted in the male-dominated racing game.

But now Julie was winning—and slowly being accepted. "She was green, but you could see that horses would run for her," said Bud Delp, a top trainer. "She was a natural."

Delp noticed that Krone had a special way with horses.

"She talks to them, she sings to them. She moves her little fingers on their necks and they just run (hard) for her."

And then, just as Julie's career was getting started, it seemed to come to an abrupt halt.

At Laurel she was thrown from a horse. A broken back. Somehow, she found her way back to the track. Finding the winner's circle was another matter.

Julie hit a slump—eighty straight races without a victory. One day on the backstretch, Julie yelled, "I quit! I quit! I quit! I can't stand it!"

Finally, her luck changed again. Working with Delp, she began winning at Pimlico, Delaware Park, and Atlantic City.

But it took some time for Julie to win the approval of the other jockeys. "The guy riders hated her," Snellings said. "They're used to intimidating the girl riders, and here they were getting intimidated by this little girl." Male jockeys eventually learned to respect Krone, and not only for her skill as a rider. She was a battler, too.

She looked so small, sweet, and innocent—but, boy, could Julie pack a punch!

One day during the final moments of a race at Monmouth Park, Julie was heading into the stretch drive. She and Miguel Rujano were neck and neck in a torrid race. Suddenly, Rujano slashed Krone across the face with his whip.

When the race ended, Krone swung out of the saddle, walked over to Rujano, and punched him in the nose. It started a fight that ended when Krone smashed Rujano with a lawn chair.

This was not the only such incident involving Krone and the other jockeys. "Hey, this is a rough game," she said in her familiar high-pitched, squeaky voice, "and you can't let yourself be a victim out on the track."

Soon she would be toasted with champagne. In 1988 Krone became the leading female jockey in history when she rode her 1,205th winner.

By 1993, Julie could boast a long list of riding titles at many of the country's top tracks. She guided Colonial Affair to victory at Aqueduct's Belmont Stakes. It was part of the Triple Crown, the most elusive title in racing. To gain the Triple Crown, a horse has to win the Kentucky Derby, the Preakness in Maryland, and the Belmont Stakes in New York, all in the same year.

Julie was on top of the world in 1993, enjoying one of her

greatest years on the track—until she came crashing down at Saratoga.

The pain of her injuries eventually went away. Julie's thirst for racing did not. In nine months, she felt well enough to test herself on a horse again. She took quiet rides around the family farm. It was nothing like riding a thoroughbred in a high stakes race, but it was a start. One day on a riding vacation, she took a spill. It was her first fall since the Saratoga race. She got up and brushed herself off. She was fine.

"It was good for me mentally," she said, "I was kind of glad to get that fall out of the way. At that point, I knew I was ready to ride thoroughbreds."

Julie was still scared to go back to racing. But it was her great love. Not going back would have been scarier. For five weeks she prepared for her comeback—working and exercising horses. On May 25, 1994, just nine months since her horrific fall at Saratoga, she ran her first race.

Julie didn't win. But she did finish in the money, in third place.

The next day, Julie hopped aboard a horse named Consider the Lily. It was the sixth race of the day at Belmont, a track she knew only too well.

Her horse pounded out of the starting gate and took the lead. Too soon. Julie pulled on the reins. Consider the Lily dropped behind the leaders. She liked to pace her horse—saving energy for the stretch run.

Finally, with 360 yards to go for the wire, Julie was in second place. Time to make her move.

She pushed Consider the Lily. She pulled alongside a tiring Hayley's Abby. She edged in front.

Waving the Flag came up to challenge. Julie pulled away. She booted Consider the Lily home a length and a half ahead of Waving the Flag.

Victory!

Julie hopped off her horse and headed for the winner's circle. She pumped her right hand in the air as admiring shouts from the stands filled her ears. It was far different than the insulting shouts she had once heard.

"Way to go, Julie!"

"Julie, you're back!"

Then she sprinted through the tunnels toward the jockeys' rooms.

It was just another breakthrough for Krone. Not that she paid much attention to her role as a trailblazer. She merely saw herself as just another jockey.

But her numbers measured up to anyone's. Julie was the first female to win a Triple Crown race. When she retired for the first time in 1999, she had ridden more than 20,000 mounts, won more than 3,500 races, and earned more than $80 million in prize money. Those achievements propelled her right into the Thoroughbred Racing Hall of Fame, a first for a female.

Julie would make other comebacks from terrible spills. She would also come back after her retirement.

Why not? If there was a race to be run, Julie Krone wanted to be there.

5
SHIRLEY MULDOWNEY
Driving Into History

*S*hirley Muldowney straps herself into the 8,000-pound Top Fuel dragster that will hurtle her down an asphalt track at more than 300 miles an hour. It is just another day at the track for Muldowney: Drive as fast as possible for one-quarter mile. Fastest car to the finish line wins. Those are the rules of drag racing.

She sits in her dragster, waiting for the race to begin. But is it

Shirley Muldowney in the driver's seat

really Shirley? One really can't tell. The body inside is wrapped from head to toe in a thick, fire-retardant material, topped by a pink helmet. Other than the sponsor's name, all one can see are the eyes peering out.

She's off!

LADIES FIRST

The earth shakes. The grandstands tremble. The noise is deafening, painful to the ears. Then the dragster is off in a cloud of eye-stinging, billowing white smoke. The tires spew black rubber specks like rain from the heavens. The sudden and powerful acceleration sends a vibration through the body, both thrilling and exciting. It is exactly what Shirley Muldowney expects and loves.

It is over in a matter of seconds. By the time the speeding projectile reaches the finish line a quarter-mile away, it needs a parachute to stop. The 24-foot dragster that just moments before was very nearly flying shudders to a halt.

☻☻

V-r-oom!

Shirley Roque put her foot on the gas pedal as the speedometer climbed higher and higher. The noise shook the quiet neighborhoods of Schenectady, New York. The sleek red Corvette with the daredevil petite fifteen-year-old at the wheel roared down Highway 5 at 120 miles an hour.

Suddenly a police siren shattered the summer night air. Roque pulled over to the side of the road.

As it had many times before, the conversation went something like this:

Shirley: Good evening, Officer Barbieri.
Officer: So it's you again. License and registration, please. (A pause.) It's a dangerous game you're playing, young lady.

Shirley Muldowney

But the danger was part of the thrill. Shirley had kept her racing adventures a secret from her parents, too afraid they'd make her quit. She'd sneak out of her bedroom window after her parents had gone to bed, then climb into her souped-up car for another night of drag racing.

Growing up, Shirley had the same problems as most kids. She went to a tough school where she was the target for school bullies. One day she came home from school bruised and battered. She admitted to her father it wasn't the first time. Her father, who had boxed under the name of "Tex Rock," gave her some advice: fight back any way you can.

Shirley never had any problem with school bullies again. By the time she grew up, she had learned never to back down from a challenge of any kind.

"The man gave me the backbone that I needed to survive," she said of her father.

Shirley was not a model student. She cut classes in high school. She didn't hesitate to climb out of a classroom window when the teacher wasn't looking. She often left school and dashed down the street to meet her boyfriend, Jack Muldowney. He's the one who introduced her to speed racing.

"I used to work in a little car-hop restaurant," she said. "Jack Muldowney used to give me a ride home, which was about a mile from the place. But we always took the long route so we could pick up some street races to and from."

It wasn't long before Shirley was racing Jack's car, challenging other hot-rodders. By 1956, when she turned sixteen, she had a learner's permit and a marriage license. Shirley Roque was now Shirley Muldowney.

"Her husband liked to go fast and he built her a car to go a little faster," remembered Shirley's mother, Mae Roque. "It all ended up faster and faster."

Shirley bought her first car for $40. It was a 1940 Ford coupe.

"Jack put a Cadillac engine in it for me," she said. "Guys heard about this and they would come from Amsterdam, Glens Falls, Albany (New York). I'd race them, and when I'd turn around, they'd be going the other way. It was very satisfying."

But Shirley wanted something more. At eighteen, she entered her first organized drag race at Fonda Speedway in upstate New York. And then, Lebanon Valley Speedway.

"The best thing that ever happened was when Fonda and Lebanon Valley opened their doors," Muldowney said. "We realized then what it was to race under supervision. They provided us with a pot at the end of the rainbow."

But the "pot" was not always filled with riches. As a professional race driver, she sometimes wound up with less money than it cost her to race. That didn't bother her, though. She was doing it for the pure love of the sport. Racing was as much a part of her life as breathing.

Drag racing was still in its infancy in the 1950s. The

Shirley Muldowney

National Hot Rod Association (NHRA) had just held its first championship in 1955.

Muldowney, now a mother, wasn't thinking about winning an NHRA championship at the time—just surviving. She did this by picking up a few dollars here and there at local tracks. She also picked up a nickname. One day she noticed that someone had written "Cha Cha" in shoe polish on her car. The signature nickname stuck with her over the years.

Although Muldowney loved racing, she was always aware of the hazards she faced on the track. "If you don't know what you're doing," she said, "you're in a world of hurt."

She knew the "world of hurt" very well. In the early 1970s she started driving the so-called "Funny Cars." She skillfully handled these tricky vehicles, which often jerked violently on the track. Funny Cars had a shorter wheelbase, full bodies, and—most notably—the engine in front.

In 1973, Muldowney was in a terrible accident. The engine of her Funny Car exploded. The front of the car was suddenly engulfed in flames, spewing fire back at Muldowney in the driver's seat. Fire was all around her. When she emerged, she had suffered severe burns.

"It burned the goggles right off my face."

The accident didn't daunt her spirit. Before long she was back on the track. And heading for the real big time—Top Fuel cars.

Top Fuel cars are the elite of drag racing, the fastest cars in the world. They run on the same explosive nitromethane gas used in rocket engines. From a standing start, these cars are capable of reaching speeds over 300 miles an hour in a matter of seconds. Long and sleek, with the engine behind the driver, Top Fuel dragsters resemble an arrow shot out of a bow once the driver hits the pedal.

But everywhere Muldowney turned, doors slammed in her face. Men refused to race against her. The NHRA refused to give her a Top Fuel license. Even after she finally got her license, race organizers rejected her. Fellow drivers and fans made her life miserable.

"Of course it was because I was a woman," she said. "Toughness got me through it."

She was now a single mom and living in Michigan; she had a new racing partner and crew chief, Conrad "Connie" Kalitta. He had a Top Fuel car built especially for her. Cha Cha took to the tracks in 1974 with her shiny, new pink dragster.

Muldowney wasn't there just to make an appearance. And she wasn't there to be a sideshow as the first woman to race in a professional NHRA event. Not on your life. She was there to burn rubber. She was a *racer,* after all, with a fierce drive to win, and win big.

Her determination paid off. In 1976, she stood in the winner's circle at the NHRA spring nationals. Also during that year, she posted the fastest time and speed of any racer. By 1977, she had won enough such events to gain the

Shirley Muldowney

Muldowney competes in a Top Fuel dragster.

overall NHRA title, known as the Winston World Championship. In three short years, this small 5-foot-4 woman who weighed barely over 100 pounds had out-muscled the other drivers. She had become the top drag racer in the world!

A national car magazine voted Muldowney "person of the year." She was named "Top Fuel driver of the year." The U.S. House of Representatives honored her with an Outstanding Achievement Award. She was on top again in 1980 and 1982. Shirley Muldowney was soon to be a house-hold name, thanks to a movie about her life.

She was riding high. It was June 29, 1984, and Muldowney was ready to start the Grand Nationals in Montreal. She had no idea what an ordeal was ahead of her.

The green light flashed and she gunned the motor. She was off! But something was terribly wrong. The rubber started peeling off the tire and wrapping itself around the spindle of the two front wheels. Usually, the rubber just shreds bit by bit and flies back over the top of the car.

"I had a death grip on that steering wheel because I saw it and I watched it and I did everything I could do," Muldowney said.

She hit the button for the parachute to slow down the car. Too late—by that time the rubber had wound so tightly around the wheels, they exploded. Muldowney's car rocketed off the track, slammed into an embankment, and shattered into little pieces. She had been timed at 247 miles an hour just before the crash.

"It was a very freak accident," Muldowney said. "It only took a half-second to disintegrate."

Muldowney was rushed to a Montreal hospital. She spent two months in the intensive care unit. Five months of operations followed, then a year of therapy. Race again? Out of the question. People wondered if she would be lucky enough to just walk again.

Muldowney was left with a stiff limp and was forced to use a cane. She had trouble climbing stairs.

But at least the horrifying accident had some beneficial

effects. Muldowney's mishap inspired the NHRA to set new safety standards. A charity fund was set up to give financial help to injured racers and their families.

Would Muldowney ever come back to racing? How could she in her condition?

How could she not?

"I love racing so much," she said, "I just had to come back."

And so she did. It was just nineteen months after her terrible accident in Montreal. The year was 1986, and Muldowney was making an appearance in an NHRA event near Phoenix. Her pink dragster was waiting for her, glistening in the sun. She needed help to climb into the cockpit. But she did not need any help after that.

Gunning the accelerator, she roared down the quarter-mile track in 5.58 seconds. It was not good enough to catch the winner, but enough to show she had not slowed down.

It took Muldowney three years to win another NHRA event. When she did, she added another chapter to her comeback story. But that was not the final chapter. Later she starred for the rival International Hot Rod Association (IHRA). She set speed records with the help of a crew that included her son, John, and husband, Rahn Tobler.

Fast forward to 2003. At age sixty-two, Shirley Muldowney, champion drag racer and the First Lady of her sport, had hit the heights and also suffered the lows. The sport she loved had very nearly cost her life. After a legendary career that featured three National Hot Rod Association championships, she made her farewell tour on the drag racing circuit. In her dust she was leaving quite a legacy: Shirley had brought more attention to her sport than anyone in history. She had opened doors for women to compete against men in drag racing, much like Janet Guthrie on the stock car circuit known as NASCAR.

By the time she decided to retire from professional drag racing, Muldowney owned just about every women's record. And some of the men's, too. At one time or another she was the fastest driver on the track. For a long time she was at the top of her sport. She served as an inspiration to other daring young women.

Muldowney understood her place in sports history. One day she was driving to an event when she heard two truckers talking on a CB radio.

"As we're driving along the road I heard one trucker say to another trucker, 'Hey, look up on your left because history is driving by you right there.'

"I thought, 'Wow.' I will never forget that one."

6
BILLIE JEAN KING
Serving One Up For Women s Rights

The battle was about to begin.

Excitement filled the air as the crowd waited. Slowly the royal procession entered the arena.

The queen appeared first. She sat on a feathered Egyptian throne. She was held high in the air by broad-shouldered men. She smiled and waved to the crowd.

The king followed. Applause and ripples of laughter ran through the crowd. The king was riding in a Chinese rickshaw pulled by beautiful girls.

King wins the women's singles in Wimbledon, 1973.

The king presented the queen with a sweet treat. The queen handed the king a pig. A live pig! He held the squealing animal up high for the crowd to see.

Cheers and laughter rose again throughout the crowd.

And now it was time for the battle.

Roman gladiators in 73 AD? No, just a tennis match in 1973.

Well, not just a tennis match. This was the so-called "Battle of the Sexes"—in many ways a battle for women's equal rights.

Billie Jean King against Bobby Riggs.

Billie Jean King, the queen of tennis, vs. Bobby Riggs, onetime men's tennis champion.

Riggs had another title: king of the "male chauvinist pigs." Like many men at that time, he showed little respect for the female athlete. At least that was his public side. Billie Jean wanted to prove that female athletes deserved respect. She was fighting so that girls would have a chance to realize their dreams.

So it was on September 20, 1973, that Billie Jean King prepared for a tennis match at the Astrodome in Houston, Texas. It was only an exhibition, but it could be the most important match of her life.

Promoters had pulled out all stops. This show of shows had all the makings of a Roman circus with lots of fun and clowning around.

For Billie Jean King, though, the match itself was not funny. It was very serious. Just a year earlier, the U.S. Congress had passed the Education Amendments to the 1964 Civil Rights Act. Under Title IX of those amendments, federal money would equally support female and male school sports programs. Girls now had an open door to their sports dreams. Billie Jean was worried that a loss to Riggs might cause government officials to rethink Title IX.

Even worse, such a loss might deal a crippling blow to the women's movement.

Billie Jean King

A lot was riding on that one event. Millions of people would be watching. Billie Jean hoped she was up to the enormous challenge.

๑๏

Growing up in Long Beach, California, Billie Jean Moffitt was already marching to her own beat. Girls weren't supposed to play football and softball. Billie Jean did—and she was good at both. At the age of eleven, she fell in love with tennis. She worked at odd jobs to save enough money to buy an eight-dollar racket. Dawn to dusk, she was on the court. The slap of the ball against her racket echoed throughout the park.

Every day Billie Jean would walk seven miles each way to school while her classmates took the bus. Why? She wanted to improve her leg strength.

She was excited about her new sport, but there were things about it she didn't like. She hated the bigotry in the tennis clubs. Her black friends were not allowed to play with her on the courts. Billie Jean also hated the sport's old-fashioned attitudes about women. In 1955, she was playing in a tournament at the Los Angeles Tennis Club. Club officials would not allow her to pose for a group photograph with the rest of the girls. The reason? She was wearing tennis shorts instead of a tennis dress. "If I ever got the chance," she later said, "I was going to change tennis and get away from that kind of nonsense."

But first she had to concentrate on her own game. A friend introduced her to tennis star Alice Marble. Billie Jean was delighted when Marble agreed to coach her. "She was so crazy about tennis," Marble said, "I'd have to lock her in her room to study." By the time Billie Jean was fifteen years old, she was ranked nationally and traveling around the country to tennis tournaments.

Win some, lose some. "I was very erratic when I started playing tournaments," she said. The young tennis player was upset and unhappy when she lost. But she decided to learn from her mistakes. She never gave up.

And then, finally her career began to take off. In 1961, Billie Jean and Karen Hantze Susman became the youngest team to win the women's doubles championship at world-famous Wimbledon in London. They repeated that triumph the following year. And to make her star rise higher, Billie Jean pulled off the upset of the 1962 tournament by beating top-seeded Margaret Smith (later to become Margaret Smith Court).

Four years later, Billie Jean won her first Wimbledon singles championship.

Today, winning at Wimbledon brings riches along with fame. The only riches Billie Jean received were a modest gift certificate and some chocolates.

She was now in the big time—without the big money.

"Being a woman athlete didn't mean much in the sixties," she said. "There was no attention, no support, no structure, no money."

Now married to Larry King, a fellow student at Cal State, Billie Jean was headed for the top of her sport. In 1966, it was one success after another: The Wimbledon singles championship. The singles, doubles, and mixed doubles championships at the United States Lawn Tennis indoor tournament at Chestnut Hills, Massachusetts. The South African women's singles championship in Johannesburg. The North of England singles title.

And, she helped lead the United States to a victory over Great Britain for the important Wightman Cup.

In 1968, the United States Tennis Association (USTA) decided to award prize money for its amateur events. Winning Wimbledon now meant a big payoff. For males, that is. Even though the female stars were contributing more and more to the sport, they were still making just a fraction of what the men were making. Billie Jean King refused to accept that kind of inequality.

And what did it take to make her rebel?

The time: September 1970.
The place: The Los Angeles Tennis Club, the organization that had refused to allow a teen tennis player to appear in a photograph in shorts.
The occasion: The Pacific Southwest Open.
The purse for the men's champion: $12,500.
The total *purse for all the women:* $7,500.

Instead of accepting unequal pay, Billie Jean decided to fight the system. She started her own pro circuit—the Virginia Slims tour.

Seven other players joined her. They believed in the tour, if few others did.

"It was a very lonely time," Billie Jean said. "Tough, disappointing, exciting—we had all those emotions."

Billie Jean tirelessly promoted her new venture. She handed out leaflets at street corners. She gave away tickets in front of department stores.

The Virginia Slims tour's success surprised everyone but Billie Jean. In 1971, she made $100,000—the first female athlete to earn that much from her sport in one year. In 1972, *Sports Illustrated* named Billie Jean King its "Sportsman of the Year." Another first for women.

It was a good time for Billie Jean to make her mark. The feminist movement was fighting for equal rights for women in all parts of society.

More and more women were working as doctors, lawyers, and company executives. What a change from previous years, when most people expected a woman to stay home and raise a family.

Billie Jean was making her presence felt in sports. In 1973, a breakthrough! She won her biggest victory off the court: USLTA officials gave in and decided to award equal prize money for women and men in the U.S. Open.

Meanwhile, Bobby Riggs was dreaming up a scheme. Male chauvinists believed women belonged in the kitchen, not on the court. Riggs saw a perfectly good opportunity to make money by promoting a match between himself and a top female player.

Billie Jean King

King prepares to return a serve at a Virginia Slims Tennis Tournament in 1983.

The fifty-five-year-old ex-champion challenged Billie Jean King to a public tennis match. Her answer: no.

So Riggs played Margaret Smith Court, the top-ranked female tennis player in the world.

Riggs easily won the match. It was such a complete rout, it was known as the "Mother's Day Massacre."

Oh, no, King thought, *now I'm going to have to play him.*

It was up to Billie Jean King to defend the women's honor. This was pressure. Some forty million people would watch the event on TV. It was a record for a tennis match.

When she arrived at the Houston Astrodome, Billie Jean was "scared to death."

She knew how important this match was for females throughout the country. She was the underdog. Yet for every girl and woman, she was the symbol of equality. She just *had* to win.

As fate would have it, the match was played in the very same stadium where Billie Jean's brother Randy, a pitcher for the San Francisco Giants, had often played baseball. When she arrived at the Astrodome, Billie Jean went straight to the locker room. She searched for the locker her brother used when the Giants played the Astros in Houston.

Waiting for the match to begin, she sat alone at her brother's locker. She was sick to her stomach. She felt like throwing up.

But in the silence of the locker room, she suddenly felt calm. She felt her brother's presence. She was ready.

When Billie Jean stepped out on the court, she was wearing a blue sequined dress and blue sneakers.

Flashbulbs popped. Music played. Cheers filled the arena as the two tennis players took their places.

"I had a lot of doubts," Billie Jean said. "I didn't have any idea if I could beat him."

But when she stepped on the court, it suddenly became clear. She knew how she was going to play him.

She had to "run him into the ground." Riggs was nearly twice as old as the twenty-nine-year-old Billie Jean. She believed she would have more stamina.

Billie Jean won the coin toss. Her serve.

In the first set, Riggs moved ahead, 3–2.

But then the rallies became long. Her plan to run Riggs was starting to work. He was tiring.

First set to King, 6–4.

Riggs told a TV courtside announcer between sets: "She's awful quick and swift. I think I have the balls past her and she gets them."

In the second set, it became obvious her strategy was working. Riggs was having difficulty raising his arm, especially after playing the longest game of the match. He was missing his serves.

After Riggs tied it 3–3, King took over.

Second set to King, 6–3.

Families that had never watched women's tennis before were now watching on TV sets in their living rooms. America couldn't believe what was happening.

King took a 4–2 lead in the third set. But she suddenly felt a cramp in her calf. Nerves? Dehydration? Perhaps both.

Riggs was also having problems. His hands were cramping. Timeout for injury. King and Riggs both received massages.

Back on the court. King went up 5–3. She was one point away from victory. But she was struggling. Same for Riggs. It seemed nobody wanted to win.

Finally, Riggs hit one into the net.

It was over.

Game, set, and match to King, 6–3!

King threw her racquet in the air and extended her arms. A feeling of relief swept through her. It was finally over.

An exhausted Riggs jumped the net and extended a hand.

"You were too good," he said.

The court became a mass of surging people. Suddenly, Billie Jean was being crushed by media and fans rushing to get to Riggs. Boxer George Foreman came to the rescue. He walked down out of the stands and battled his way through the crowd.

"Get away from her!" he shouted as he led King to safety.

Back at her hotel, King celebrated. How? She ordered thirty ice cream sundaes.

How sweet it was! All of a sudden, women's tennis was taking off. The revolution was underway. It wasn't long before women's tennis tournaments were being shown regularly on national TV.

Women would soon receive equal pay at major tennis events. By the nineties, prize money on the women's professional tour had reached a stunning $40 million, with more to come.

Without King, it would be hard to imagine female tennis players among the world's top money earners in sports today.

Many others benefited from King's tireless efforts. She not only helped to start the Women's Tennis Association

(WTA), but also a women's tennis league. And a softball league. She seemed to be everywhere at once. Into a new century she continued to work for women's rights, in and out of sports.

"People still come up to me—men more than women—and say, 'Thank you for what you did for my daughter.'"

7
WILMA RUDOLPH
The Clarksville Comet

W ilma Rudolph was waiting.

Waiting to grab the baton…waiting to race into history.

It was the 1960 Olympics in Rome. The American track and field star had already won two gold medals. One more and she would become the first U.S. woman in history to win three golds in the same Olympics.

The AAU awarded Rudolph the James E. Sullivan trophy in 1962.

All she had to do was win the final lap of the 4x100 meter relay race for her team, the Tennessee State Tigerbelles.

Wilma's teammate was running full speed as she completed her part of the race. She reached out to hand off the baton to Wilma.

Trouble.

When Wilma grabbed for the baton, it almost slipped from her fingers. As she desperately struggled to hold on, runners passed her. Finally, she had a firm grip on the stick. By that time, she was in third place behind the German team.

Rudolph took off. Stride by stride, the slender, long-legged runner made up ground. Suddenly, she burst to the front to overtake the other runners. She crossed the finish line by a wide margin over her closest competitor.

The fans were on their feet, roaring. Rudolph had won her third gold medal! She was mobbed by her gleeful teammates. She was overwhelmed with joy and emotion. It was her most satisfying moment on the track.

"Then I could stand on the podium with my teammates, whom I love," Rudolph said, "and we could celebrate together."

◎◎

Coming back to win a race was nothing new for Rudolph. She had overcome numerous hurdles and long odds to become the queen of track. Along the way, she blazed trails for black women in her sport.

At the height of her glory in the '60s, she was known as "the fastest woman in the world." Hard to imagine, considering that as a young girl she was unable to walk.

Wilma grew up in a family of twenty-one brothers and sisters in Clarksville, Tennessee. She was known as the sickly one in the family. Underweight when she was born in

Wilma Rudolph

1940, Rudolph suffered one setback after another. First, double pneumonia, a serious lung disease. Then scarlet fever, which left her housebound. One day five-year-old Wilma woke up and found she had another ailment: her right leg hurt and was twisted inward.

She had been stricken with polio, a crippling virus. It left her limb withered and paralyzed. In the 1940s there was no cure for the disease. Doctors feared Wilma would be severely handicapped for life, or worse, might not survive. They told Wilma she would never walk again. Her mother and siblings thought otherwise.

None of the hospitals near their home admitted blacks. So twice a week, Wilma and her mother boarded a bus for the 60-mile trip to Nashville, the closest city with a hospital that would treat blacks. Well aware that black people were not allowed to ride in the front, they sat in the back of the bus in a crowded section. At the hospital, Wilma took heat treatments and learned how to strengthen her leg with exercises.

At home, Wilma's mother set up a schedule. Each of her brothers and sisters took turns massaging her leg. Three to four times a day, little Wilma, ignoring the pain, would watch her mother and siblings rub her leg. She had to stay at home when her brothers and sisters left for school. School officials would not allow Wilma to attend classes because she could not walk. Someday, she promised herself, she would walk again. Someday, she would be able to join her brothers and sisters in school.

Wilma got around her house by hopping on one foot. She was determined—nothing was going to keep her down. She repeated her exercises again and again each day, no matter how much it hurt. Each day her leg got stronger.

Finally, success! Doctors told Wilma she could walk if she wore a brace. Wilma was overjoyed. She could now join her sisters and brothers in school.

But school was anything but fun. Some of the kids teased her about her heavy steel brace. They made fun of her awkward movements when she walked. Wilma felt miserable. She couldn't even enjoy the sports she loved so much. Wearing the clumsy brace, all she could do was sit on the sidelines and watch everyone else play. Basketball was her favorite. She watched the games hour after hour, longing to step on the court.

Wilma did not give up. At home she continued to strengthen her leg with exercises. She was more determined than ever to walk on her own.

One Sunday she decided to do something daring. Church was already in session when she arrived.

Carefully she took off her brace, steadying herself. Then, with sheer determination, she took her first step forward. She concentrated on one step at a time, placing one foot ahead of the other. Slowly, awkwardly, she walked down the aisle. The church members suddenly became aware of the newcomer. As they stopped to watch, a hush fell over the crowd.

Wilma Rudolph

It was a long walk for Wilma. Step by step, she struggled toward her seat in one of the front pews. Finally, she made it. A wave of relief and exhaustion overwhelmed her as she sat down. The churchgoers were astounded. They believed they had seen a miracle.

Wilma practiced walking without the brace every day. As soon as her leg was strong enough, doctors fitted her with a special high-top support shoe to help her walk without a brace. It was one of the most thrilling moments of her life. At last she was free to play the sports she loved so much. Every chance she got, she was out in the backyard playing basketball with her many brothers and sisters. When the heavy shoe bothered her, Wilma just took it off, tossed it on the sidelines, and played barefooted.

With her long legs, Wilma was able to propel herself through the air. She knew all the moves. She had learned them from watching other kids play on the courts.

Then, soon after Wilma turned thirteen, her doctors pronounced that she was fully recovered. They were amazed. Wilma was not. "'I can't' are two words that have never been in my vocabulary," she said.

Wilma had broken off her physical bonds. Nothing would stop her now. And she had an added motivation.

She hated the way blacks were treated in the South. "I started getting angry about things and fighting back in a new way," she said. "I think I started acquiring a competitive spirit that would make me successful in sports later on."

She turned her anger into an edge. She took to the basketball court with a positive fury, playing harder, jumping higher, and running faster than anyone. She seemed to be trying to make up for lost time.

Wilma went out for basketball at all-black Burt High School in Clarksville. In no time, the little girl who once couldn't even walk without a brace was playing high school basketball. Not only playing, but *starring*. In one season Wilma scored 803 points in twenty-five games. It was a record for girls' basketball in the entire state of Tennessee.

It was not Wilma's ability to put the ball through a hoop that attracted Ed Temple, though. The famous track and field coach at Tennessee State liked the way Wilma ran. He was impressed by the way she sprinted down the track with her long-legged stride. By now Wilma was also a track star winning regularly at the local and state levels.

Temple felt Wilma was special. He was not surprised when she qualified for the 1956 Olympics in Melbourne, Australia. And he wasn't surprised when she brought home a bronze medal for helping her U.S. team to third place in the 400-meter relay.

Wilma was only sixteen, still a high school student. She had grown to nearly six feet. Gangly, with long arms, long legs, and a rail-thin body, she earned the nickname of "Skeeter"—short for mosquito. She was "always buzzing around," said her high school basketball and track coach, Clinton Gray.

Temple wanted Wilma for his team, the famed

Wilma Rudolph

Tigerbelles. Long before she graduated from high school, Wilma's destiny had been set: she was going to Tennessee State on a scholarship. She hoped to add to the legend of the Tigerbelles, one of the great black powerhouses in women's track and field.

Wilma threw herself into track with enthusiasm. Temple loved everything about this devoted runner. He was constantly amazed by her composure. Between races, Wilma took short naps. On the track, she was relaxed and in control. Often she was so far ahead in a race that she slowed down to shout encouragement to her teammates who were further back in the pack.

Not everything went smoothly for Wilma at Tennessee State, though. She missed the entire 1958 season because of illness. In 1959 she was forced to bow out of a meet between the United States and the Soviet Union because of a pulled muscle. In 1960 she became violently sick after having her tonsils removed. But in spite of the setbacks, Wilma qualified for the 1960 Rome Olympics along with other Tigerbelle track and field greats.

Temple was worried that Wilma was pushing herself too hard. When she twisted her ankle in practice the day before her opening race, she didn't let it stop her. She just put ice on the ankle, taped it, and went out to run the very next day.

Wilma survived the three qualifier heats in the 100-meter race. Then she didn't show up for the finals.

"We went crazy," Temple said. "Finally, we found her asleep on the rubdown table in the warm-up tent. Asleep!"

Wilma woke up and won. One gold down.

"After I won the 100...I wondered if my mom and dad were watching because when I left home we didn't have a television. But they were OK. They were able to see me win and see me get on the stand."

Temple worried less about the 200-meter race. It was Wilma's best event.

Rudolph wins gold in the Summer Olympics in Rome, 1960.

Wilma Rudolph

She won. Gold medal number two was hers.

The other Tennessee State runners hadn't had much success individually. They were entered as a unit representing the United States in the 400-meter relay race.

In this race, each member of a team of four runs 100 meters before handing the baton off to the next. Rudolph would run the final lap as the "anchor," usually reserved for the fastest on the team. She was eager for another win, but she wanted the gold medal for her teammates as much as for herself.

"Get me the baton," she told Lucinda Williams, Martha Hudson, and Barbara Jones.

They did. The rest became history.

The first woman to win three track and field golds in one Olympics, she was now a huge international star, adored by millions. Everybody wanted to meet and touch the twenty-year-old woman they called the "Black Gazelle." Some wanted more. A brash fan stole her shoes while she was making her way through a sea of fans in Rome. Wilma stayed in Europe for a while. She gave speeches. She competed. She met the Queen of England.

Back home, Wilma was greeted by cheering crowds. In Louisville, Kentucky, she rode in a pink Cadillac along a parade route. Sitting next to her was her friend Cassius Clay, the Olympic boxing champion who would later be known as Muhammad Ali.

The most important moment of all might have been Wilma's final stop back home in Clarksville.

In her honor, the city had planned a parade and banquet—for whites only. Rudolph was angry. She told the planners she would not appear unless blacks were allowed to attend. They bowed to her wishes. Perhaps for the first time in the history of Clarksville, blacks and whites were together at a public event.

Wilma Rudolph had won a victory for equal rights for blacks. She had always hoped to make a difference. This was only the start.

Her widespread exposure as a celebrity brought new prestige to black women in sports. She paved the way for other great ones to follow.

"I don't think people realize how big an influence Wilma Rudolph had on black female athletes," said Bob Kersee, husband of track star Jackie Joyner-Kersee. She called Rudolph her idol.

Rudolph made a difference in other ways.

When she retired from track in 1962, she became the U.S. ambassador of goodwill to French West Africa. She formed a nonprofit organization to help underprivileged children. She remembered when she herself had been an underprivileged child.

She also remembered how her family's loving support had helped her fight for a better life. Now as a mother, teacher, and coach, it was only right that she would do the same for others.

8
JOAN BENOIT
SAMUELSON
Marathon Woman

On a warm summer morning in Los Angeles, Joan Benoit Samuelson waited to start the biggest race of her life.

It was a historic moment for women in the 1984 Olympics. For the first time, they were running the marathon in the Games.

"This is the dream," Samuelson said. "This is the first women's Olympic marathon."

The gun sounded. The race was underway...

Benoit poses at her home in Freeport, Maine.

Samuelson got off to a fast start. With short, rapid strides, her heels kicking high, she widened the gap. By the 3-mile mark she had surged in front by a large margin.

What was she doing? Marathoners are supposed to pace themselves. They are supposed to save their strength for the long haul. It seemed she would tire herself out long before the race ended.

She hesitated and thought, "This is the Olympic marathon, and you're going to look like a dodo leading for halfway, and then having everyone pass you."

It seemed like a miracle she was running at all. Three weeks before the Olympic trials, she was forced to have arthroscopic knee surgery. Somehow, she had managed to make it back to run in the Olympics. Not just another race, but a grueling 26-mile marathon.

As it was, Samuelson was running against a far tougher opponent than a field of world-class female runners.

She was battling prejudice.

Most of the people—largely men—who controlled the world of track and field believed that women were not capable of running long-distance races. So-called "experts" thought if a girl ran more than a mile, she would do herself permanent harm. Wrong. And Samuelson was determined to prove it by winning the marathon at the 1984 Olympics in Los Angeles.

෧෨

Skiing actually came first in Joan's life. It was the natural thing to do during the long, snowy winters of Cape Elizabeth, Maine. Joan was only in third grade when she entered her first race. Skiing halfway down the bunny slope, she was really excited. And she won. "You could see the exhilaration on her face," said her father, Andre Benoit.

In 1974, when Joan was a sophomore in high school, she broke her right leg while slalom racing.

Joan Benoit

The bad news: She had to wear a cast on her leg for ten weeks. When the cast came off, her leg needed exercise. Joan went to the track and started running.

The good news: She found that she loved running as much as skiing.

A year earlier, track and field officials had decided to allow girls to run the mile for the first time. "But if you ran a mile, you couldn't run any other event with the exception of the relay," Joan said. By the time she was a senior, she was running the mile in 5 minutes and 15 seconds! That was only about 45 seconds over the *world* record for women—4 minutes and 29.5 seconds.

But what would people think about a high school girl running long distances? Joan didn't worry about that. "I decided that if I believe in myself, and I'm happy doing what I'm doing, I'm going to go for it."

Long-distance running wasn't Joan's only sport. She also competed in tennis, basketball, and field hockey, a popular women's sport played on grass. But it was as a long-distance runner that she would find her place in sports history.

One day before a field hockey game at Bowdoin College, Joan ran a half marathon. When she showed up to play hockey, she was in bad shape. Joan could barely run above a trot. The coach was not happy. Joan wasn't going to play, not in that condition.

Joan quit field hockey after the season to concentrate on running. She went south and enrolled at North Carolina

State. It had one of the country's top track and field programs. There was one problem.

"I'm a Yankee," she said. "I missed Maine. I missed the ocean."

Back to Bowdoin College. And back to long runs in the pine-filled Maine woods. Joan decided to prepare to run in the famed Boston Marathon. She completed her first marathon in Bermuda in 2 hours, 50 minutes to qualify for the Boston race.

Joan was a senior at Bowdoin, an unknown in the world of marathon running. Her experience was limited. Winning the Boston would mean instant celebrity and worldwide fame.

It was only eight years before in 1971 that women were first officially allowed to run in the Boston Marathon. Before that, there were women who made headlines by running the race on their own, against the wishes of Marathon officials.

Bobbi Gibb unofficially became the first woman to finish the Boston Marathon. Hiding in the bushes in a black bathing suit, Bermuda shorts, and a hooded sweatshirt, Gibb took off after the race started and finished ahead of two-thirds of the male runners. In 1967, Katherine Switzer applied to run in the Boston Marathon under the name of "K. V. Switzer." The Boston Marathon officials gave her a number, unaware that this applicant was a female. About four miles into the race, Switzer was recognized as a female and chased down by an official, who attempted to pull off the number signs pinned to her sweatshirt. Switzer's boyfriend fought back the official, allowing Switzer to finish the race.

Joan Benoit

Now it was the night before the 1979 Boston Marathon. Joan bunked with a friend and ate lots and lots of pasta. "I slept on a mattress on a floor the night before the race," she later said, "and I remember literally rolling into bed feeling stuffed."

While driving to the race, Joan was stopped by a huge traffic jam. So what did she do?

"I just got out of the car and ran through the woods," Joan said. "I must have bushwhacked two miles to the start. I remember thinking, 'I hope I didn't warm up too much.'"

Wearing her college shirt and a Boston Red Sox cap, Joan pulled off the upset of the racing season. She not only won the famed Boston Marathon, she did it in an American record of 2 hours, 35 minutes, and 15 seconds.

It was exciting at first. She made all the headlines. Her phone rang night and day.

"I hated the publicity," she said. "I hated it so much that I seriously considered giving up running so I would be left alone."

Joan considered herself just another resident of Maine. She preferred the quiet life: trapping and cooking lobsters, knitting wool sweaters, and making preserves.

But racing was a hunger that could not be denied. She picked up her pace with a variety of races—two-mile, 800-meter, 10,000-meter, half marathon, and marathon—often setting records.

The demands of marathon running are staggering. Joan had to work through constant pain. Sometimes after a race

Benoit wins the Olympic gold medal for the women's marathon in 1984.

she could not walk for several days. She needed surgery to repair problems with her heels. But she refused to let pain keep her away from the track. No sooner would she peel off the casts than she was back on a bicycle, pedaling with all her might. "Of all the people I have ever coached, she is the most tenacious," said coaching friend Bob Sevene.

In 1983, Joan won the women's division of the Boston Marathon in world-record time—2 hours, 22 minutes, and

Joan Benoit

43 seconds. By the mid-1980s, Joan was regarded as one of the best female marathoners in the world.

After years of doubt that women could run long distances, the Olympic organizers had no choice but to add the marathon for women in the Games.

Now Joan had to make a choice. She had a good idea how much media attention would be focused on the winner. "It was very difficult for me, and I thought, 'I don't know if I can hold up under that again.' Then I decided that I could."

Just a few weeks before the Olympic trials, Joan was forced to stop practice. Waves of pain flooded her right knee. She needed immediate surgery.

No one was sure how long it would take Joan to recover. She put the Olympics on hold. She worked furiously in rehab. A week before the Olympic trials, she still could not walk. Joan kept working. She didn't give up. By the time of the trials, Joan was ready. And she won, gaining a spot on the Olympic team.

She went home to train. She had looked forward to the Olympic marathon for so long, she could hardly believe it was finally a reality. "It took about a month for it to sink in," she said.

Joan was one of the favorites. The field included the eleven fastest women in marathon history. Among them: Norwegian great Grete Waitz, who had won the New York City Marathon five times.

The women were off and running at the 1984 Games in Los Angeles!

೦೦

The marathon pace had seemed slow to Joan. A lone figure in a white painter's hat turned backwards, she moved ahead of the group. Would she have enough strength to keep up the pace for the full 26 miles?

"I had promised myself I would run my race and nobody else's," she said. No one followed her pace. The other runners thought she was going to burn out before the end of the race, and they would catch her easily. Even the TV commentators were concerned when they saw Joan all by herself so early in the race.

At the 7-mile point, Joan continued her rapid pace. Her lead widened.

By the ninth mile, she was nearly a minute ahead of the field. By the fifteenth, she was almost two minutes ahead.

Waitz made a bid to overtake Joan in the last third of the race. Too late. Joan's big early lead was too much to overcome.

Cruising ahead of the field, Joan saw the huge Los Angeles Coliseum looming ahead. She headed toward the tunnel that would take her into the arena and to a date with immortality.

"Before going into that tunnel," she recalled, "I somehow heard or sensed the crowd inside coming to its feet."

As she entered the tunnel, she was suddenly shrouded in darkness and solitude. Her pounding feet echoed in the eerie silence. She was running toward the light.

Then, a tired thought—the kind that happens when you're so exhausted all you want to do is lie down, curl up, and go to sleep: "I could hide in here and not come out the other side."

Joan Benoit

Of course Joan was not about to hide. Not after long hours of work for the biggest race of her life. Not after her amazing comeback from a knee injury.

She thought: Once you leave this tunnel, your life will be changed forever.

She burst into the arena amidst the roars of 77,000 people. They had been watching her progress on the stadium TV scoreboard and now were cheering wildly as she came into view.

Joan took off her hat. She grabbed an American flag from someone and took her final lap around the track. Only then did she allow herself to smile—a wide, broad smile that said everything.

Her time of 2 hours, 24 minutes, and 52 seconds had wiped out her competition.

Joan was well aware of what she had accomplished.

As the winner of the first Olympic women's marathon, she had achieved the greatest victory of her life—not only for herself, but for women everywhere.

9

SONJA HENIE
The Ice Queen

Henie poses after winning the gold at the Winter Olympic Games in 1932.

She dared not make one mistake.

Sonja Henie, two-time Olympic champion and nine-time world champion, was nervous as she waited to skate onto the ice at the 1936 Games.

She faced the toughest battle of her career. A new challenger was waiting to unseat her as the best figure skater in the world.

In the compulsory figures, Henie had barely managed to win over English skater Cecilia Colledge. It was the closest anyone had come to toppling the Norwegian great.

Henie was entering the free skating competition barely clinging to her lead over Colledge. There were whispers throughout the *crowd: would there be a new champion?*

Dead silence greeted Henie as she skated onto the ice at the Ice Stadium in Garmisch-Partenkirchen, Germany. She was in danger of defeat. How would she respond to the challenge?

∾

It had all started in Norway, the "Land of the Midnight Sun." A little girl named Sonja Henie dreamed of becoming a ballerina. And she did. But she danced on ice, not the stage.

Henie lived in Oslo, the capital of Norway. The country is called the "Land of the Midnight Sun" because it dips into the Arctic Circle, near the top of the world. During the summer, the sun shines all day and most of the night. During the winter, there are only a few hours of daylight, and snow for as far as the eye can see.

The Henie family was rich and owned a lodge outside of Oslo. There, Sonja skied everywhere she could. The charming blue-eyed little girl loved the rhythm of skiing. She loved the feel of the skis, the movement across the packed snow, the wind in her blonde hair. Skiing taught her balance, a skill that would later help her when she became a skater.

Sonja also loved to dance. She studied ballet with Love Krohn, the man who had taught famous ballerina Anna Pavlova.

One Christmas Henie received ice skates. Well, not exactly skates—just a pair of blades she could clamp on her shoes. On her first try, Henie fell on the ice. She fell again. But she would not give up. She found she loved skating more than anything.

After just one year, she won her first figure skating competition. Only seven, she had taken the first steps toward an amazing career: the Pavlova of the ice.

To her skating, she applied the lessons learned from her favorite sports and activities: Balance and rhythm from skiing. Flexibility and graceful moves from ballet.

But Sonja ran into a problem. In those days women skaters wore long skirts to keep them warm in the subzero temperatures of the Norwegian winters. When Sonja went out on the ice wearing the customary long skirt, the wind whipped the skirt between Henie's legs and tossed her in different directions. She couldn't do her fancy new routines.

Her mom came to the rescue. She cut the skating skirt short, above the knees. Then she had another idea. She sewed a border of fur around the bottom of the skirt so it would not blow back or flop around. The problem was solved. Happily, Sonja could now dance on ice.

With her daring new costumes, Henie changed the look of women's figure skating. She was the first to wear silk tights, short white skirts, and white skating boots. They would become her trademark and the talk of the skating world. She was nicknamed "The Girl in White."

But the "Girl in White" could also be the girl in red, or blue, or green.

Not satisfied to stay with the same image, Sonja

constantly tried out new styles. Whenever she took to the ice, she brought the fashion world to skating. She made sure she was dressed for the occasion.

A fellow skater recalled: "The other skaters were in sweaters and skirts. She would show up in a green satin dress with a hat perched on her head at the perfect angle. She never wore the same outfit twice."

The costumes were spectacular, but that wasn't the only thing that made Henie stand out. The main reason she drew so much attention was the way she skated.

At the age of ten, when most kids are enjoying their summer vacations, Henie was hard at work. She went to London to take ballet lessons. With the help of Oscar Holte and other top Norwegian skating instructors, Henie began applying these ballet moves to her skating routines.

Up until then, figure skating hadn't been all that exciting. The women's competition consisted mostly of a boring routine of "figure eights." Skaters were judged on their accuracy as they retraced a path on the ice that resembled the number 8.

The audiences and judges were startled when Henie performed. This skater was different and daring. She jumped higher, spun faster, and lasted longer on her turns than anyone else they had ever seen.

Henie had so many different kinds of spins, it was hard to keep up with them. Would you believe it? Nineteen kinds of spins. Whirling around as many as eighty times. She kept

Henie executes a difficult leap in St. Moritz, Switzerland.

viewers on the edge of their seats. She wove a story with her dance movements in her routines. Onlookers were stunned by her agility, energy, and athletic ability.

It had taken a lot of courage for Henie to introduce these colorful dance routines into her ice exhibitions, particularly her jumps. Jumping was generally considered "unfeminine" at the time.

Imagine winning the Norwegian ladies skating title at the age of ten. That is just what Henie did. Only a young girl, she was already famous in her own country.

What next? How about the Olympics?

Henie created a lot of excitement when she entered the Olympics in 1924 at the age of eleven. She was much younger than any of the other skaters there. When she stepped on the ice at Chamonix in the French Alps, she introduced her new style of skating. Her routine was so different, no one was ready for it. The jumps, the spins, the creative dance routines—all new.

No, she didn't win. But it made everyone stop and think. A new era had begun in figure skating, and a tiny eleven-year-old girl was leading the way.

She won the world figure-skating championship at the unlikely age of thirteen. It would be the first of ten straight world titles, from 1927 to 1936. She won an Olympic gold medal in 1928, then again in 1932.

Then came the 1936 Olympics and the biggest test of her career.

In the free-skating competition, the outstanding English skater Colledge performed before Henie and had the crowd of 11,000 cheering continuously. Henie knew she would have to give her best to beat her opponent.

Once she was on the ice, her nervousness disappeared.

Dressed in a carefully designed white and violet costume,

Henie skated brilliantly. She started with a program of difficult figures and the crowd was with her. Wild cheers followed each routine. She executed a stunning double Axel
Paulsen jump, ending in a graceful split. Henie had never
skated with more mastery. Her championship was no longer
in doubt. She won her third Olympic gold medal.

Olympic triumphs were not enough for Sonja. She had
other ambitions. She wanted to be a movie star.

At the time, Fred Astaire was the most famous dancer in
Hollywood films. Henie said she "wanted to do with skates
what Fred Astaire does with dance."

All of Hollywood had to admire Henie's boldness.
Darryl F. Zanuck, head of Twentieth Century Fox, had seen
her in an ice show, and he was impressed. Would she like a
part in a movie musical? No, she said. She wanted to *star* in
her own movie. And she demanded that she be paid like a
star. Never mind that it was her first film. Zanuck, one of the
most powerful men in Hollywood, bowed to the wishes of
this strong-minded 5-foot-2 skater. *One in a Million* and *Thin
Ice,* her first two American movies, were box-office hits.
Henie was on her way.

During her film career, she shared billing with some of
Hollywood's top leading men. Her movies always had a
happy ending. And they always featured Henie's dazzling
ice-skating routines. She had turned Olympic gold into a
sensational career on the silver screen. She became one of
the highest-paid movie stars in the world.

There's no telling how many little girls in America fell in

love with ice skating because of Henie. It's possible that young Tenley Albright was one of them. She later became the first American woman to win the world championship and Olympic gold.

When Henie wasn't making movies, she could be seen in her traveling ice show—another first for a figure skater. From 1937 to 1952, Henie toured with her famed "Hollywood Ice Review," playing to sellout crowds. Fans clamored for the Sonja Henie souvenirs sold in the arena lobbies, especially the sparkling costume jewelry pins featuring Henie's image. The audiences usually went home with smiles on their faces.

One time, however, the audience didn't go home happy. Just before the show was about to start, a strange sound came from the stands. Suddenly, the bleachers collapsed, sending hundreds of spectators falling over each other and crashing to the ground.

Everyone rushed to help the victims. A little while later, a stage manager asked Henie, "Shall we start the show now?"

Henie had no intention of going ahead with the show. Instead, she spent the night at the hospital visiting the injured.

With the show, movies, and product endorsements—from fake fur bonnets to face cream—Henie became a money-making machine long before it became the style for athletes. At one point her fortune was estimated at close to $50 million. She was the richest athlete in the world in her time.

Sonja Henie

She was never far from the ice—her first love. When she died in 1969 at the age of fifty-seven, Henie left many fans in mourning. She also left a special legacy.

"She made skating something that every little girl wanted to do," said longtime coach Frank Carroll. "She changed the face of skating. There will never be anyone like her."

Henie's story rivaled fiction. It had everything, including a Hollywood ending.

10
ALTHEA GIBSON
The Jackie Robinson
of Tennis

From the ghetto to greatness.

From the hard concrete pave-
ments of Harlem to the grass
courts of Wimbledon, brushing
elbows with royalty.

Was Althea Gibson dreaming?
Was she really at Wimbledon?

It was the summer of 1957. The
place, London, England. The tennis
fans at the All England Championships at Wimbledon were excited.
There was a buzz in the crowd. The
Queen was coming! The Queen was
coming! It was a historic first.

Gibson celebrates her victory in the national
women's singles championship in 1957.

It was not the only first that day. Gibson was gunning for the
singles championship. The historic first? Gibson was black.

The day was steaming hot, over 90 degrees. Gibson walked on
to the court wearing an all-white outfit, shorts and a divided skirt.

She was nervous as she faced her opponent, fellow American Darlene Hard.

Gibson had worked long and hard for this moment. She took a deep breath and the match began.

☯

Althea Gibson was born on a farm in South Carolina. The farm failed, and when Althea was three her family moved to West 143rd Street in the mostly black Harlem section of New York City.

Life was not pleasant for Althea. She hated school, but she wasn't happy at home either. Deathly afraid of her father, she often stayed at friends' houses. Sometimes to avoid going home, this little girl rode the city's subways all night long.

When Althea was nine, her life changed. One day barricades went up on her street. No traffic allowed. Her block had been selected by the Police Athletic League as a "play area."

There were games everywhere. Althea played basketball, football, and paddle tennis, as well as the popular New York street game of stickball. And she was good at every sport she tried. For the first time, she was having fun.

When the Athletic League sponsored a competition among all the play streets, Althea won her first medals. She was unbeatable in paddle tennis. One day a supervisor handed Althea a present: a pair of used tennis rackets.

With a tennis racket and her amazing talent, thirteen-year-old Gibson was on her way. Someone mentioned Gibson's name to Fred Johnson, a pro at the New York Cosmopolitan Tennis Club, one of the top all-black tennis clubs in America. "You really have to see this kid. She's amazing!"

Johnson took a look. He liked what he saw. Gibson was a natural. He took her away from the crowded, noisy streets of Harlem, and there in the quiet and private surroundings of the tennis club, he became her teacher. Tall, athletic, and quick on her feet, Althea was a fast learner. Within one year, she was a champion in the American Tennis Association (ATA). It was the beginning of a long string of ATA championships.

A champion, for sure. But still a *black* champion.

The ATA had been formed for African American players because they were not allowed to play in events sponsored by the all-white United States Lawn Tennis Association (USLTA). Tennis had long been the territory of rich white society. What chance would an underprivileged girl have, and an underprivileged *black* girl at that?

Help was on the way. Hubert A. Eaton Jr. and Robert Johnson, two black doctors, felt that Gibson's talent was too great to waste. They had a plan. They were going to make her the Jackie Robinson of tennis.

Robinson had broken the color line in baseball in 1947. The two doctors thought Gibson could do the same in tennis. But there was a catch: Althea would have to leave home. She would have to live in the South, play tennis, and work on her high school diploma.

Althea was frightened to leave the North. Boxing great Sugar Ray Robinson gave her some advice: "No matter what you want to do, you'll be better at it if you get some education." She decided to go.

It was in North Carolina, far from her friendly neighborhood of Harlem, that Gibson discovered racism in its most terrible form.

When she went to a movie theater she was told that she had to sit in the balcony.

When she boarded a bus she was told she had to sit in the crowded back, even though there were empty seats in front.

She couldn't use most public bathrooms or go to restaurants because they were for "whites only."

That was the unfriendly atmosphere that Gibson faced in the South. She was treated like a second-class citizen. She felt sick, as if she had been punched in the stomach.

"You have to be black to understand the nastiness, the stares, the silence," said Eaton.

Gibson refused to give up her dream of becoming a great tennis player. She poured all of her energies into the sport. And she improved her schoolwork. She remembered the advice the great Sugar Ray Robinson had given her about education.

She finished high school and went to Florida A&M University. It took her only three years to earn a degree in health and physical education. She found a job teaching. Amazing—the little girl who had played hooky from school in Harlem was now a college professor!

By this time, she was also the best African American women's tennis player in the country. But even though she was a star in the ATA, the doors of the highly regarded USLTA were still closed to her.

Tennis legend Alice Marble came to the rescue. Marble, who was white, protested Gibson's exclusion from mainstream American tennis. She challenged the tennis association to allow Gibson to face the country's best players. Prodded by the famed and well-respected Marble, the association had no choice but to allow Gibson to play in its events.

In 1950, twenty-three-year-old Althea Gibson became the first black player, man or woman, to compete in the national championships at Forest Hills, New York. Gibson did not win the title, but that competition was the start of many "firsts" for her in tennis:

In 1951, she became the first black, male or female, to play at Wimbledon.

In 1955, she was the first black to be sent on a goodwill tour of Southeast Asia with other top American players.

In 1956, she won the French Open for her first major singles title, another first for a black player.

Winning on the court was one thing. Beating bigotry was quite another. At most matches Gibson sat on the bench next to the tennis court, all alone. No one bothered to talk to her. The white players avoided her.

Gibson makes a return in a 1956 Wimbledon match.

Except at the French Open.

"My coach noticed she didn't have a partner for the doubles, and I didn't have a partner for the doubles," said Englishwoman Angela Buxton. "...I said, 'Why not ask Althea if she'd want to play with me.'"

Buxton teamed up with Gibson to win the French Open doubles title. Then they won the doubles title at Wimbledon.

Althea Gibson

It was a banner year for Gibson in other ways. In 1956, she swept through the tennis world like a tornado: She won the singles championships in the Pacific Southwest tournament. She earned the Pan American, New South Wales, South Australian, Italian, and Asian titles. She was runner-up in the U.S. Nationals.

Gibson's goal now was to be the first black to win at Wimbledon. In 1957 she competed only on grass to get ready for the tournament. She was so focused on Wimbledon that she refused to defend her title in the French Open, which was not played on grass.

At Wimbledon, she was at the top of her game. In the semifinals against British favorite Christine Truman, she crushed her opponent with alarming ease.

Then came the Wimbledon final against Hard, a tough opponent with a strong net game.

ꙮ

Gibson was all over the court. With successful volleys, her nervousness disappeared. She slammed shots to Miss Hard's backhand with such speed that her opponent could only weakly respond. She moved quickly to the net to stop Hard's volleys. Miss Hard shook her head as her errors mounted. First set to Gibson, 6–3.

Gibson was steady and in control. Keep the ball in play and wait for the right shot. In the second set, Gibson's serves jumped quickly off the fast grass court. Hard was having trouble handling the serves. Second set to Gibson, 6–2. The match was over in less than an hour.

"At last! At last!" Gibson said after winning the Wimbledon singles championship.

The Queen came down from the royal box to present the big gold serving dish trophy to the first black tennis player ever to win at Wimbledon.

"My congratulations," the Queen said to Gibson, handing her the trophy for winning the championship at the historic tennis court.

⚭⚭

Gibson's booming shots, strong play at the net, and brilliant athleticism was the talk of the tennis world. Following another victory in the Wimbledon doubles, she returned to New York for a celebration. She rode in a ticker-tape parade down Broadway. Newspapers and magazines were full of interviews and photos of this new tennis sensation. Everywhere Gibson played, she broke ground as the first black in the tournament. But while the door was opening for Gibson in sports, it was still closed in other parts of American society. In some parts of the country, the welcome sign was not always out for blacks, tennis star or not.

A hotel once refused to make reservations for a group that wanted to honor Gibson at a luncheon. Sorry—no blacks allowed.

When Gibson later broke the color barrier in women's

golf, she faced similar problems trying to integrate that sport. While playing in the Ladies Professional Golf Association (LPGA) tournaments, she was not allowed to use the whites-only clubhouse facilities. Gibson was forced to change her shoes in a parking lot!

Just a couple of months after Gibson's first championship at Wimbledon, a high school in Arkansas became the center of attention in the nation. Little Rock was a big test case in the South for the newly passed integration law. Blacks could now go to the same schools as whites. At least that's what the law said. The governor of Arkansas thought differently. He called up the Arkansas National Guard and sent them to the school. With bayonets drawn, soldiers turned nine black students away from the doors of Central High School. The battle for civil rights was beginning in big cities and small towns across the United States.

At the same time, Gibson continued to rule women's tennis. The U.S. championship followed Wimbledon in 1957. She won both titles again in 1958. She starred for the United States in the famed Wightman Cup series with Great Britain in 1957 and 1958. The Associated Press voted her Female Athlete of the Year for two straight years.

Suddenly, Gibson made a shocking announcement: she was retiring. Despite winning eleven major titles in three years, she could not earn a living from playing tennis. It would be many years before tournaments would begin to award prize money.

She found jobs that paid. She gave tennis exhibitions. She appeared in movies. She sang on TV and made a recording. Gibson played on the women's pro golf tour. And she taught tennis. Still, she had a hard time supporting herself. She eventually dropped out of the public's view.

The next African American woman to win at Wimbledon was Venus Williams in 2000. Venus received $650,000. Match that against the mere trophy that Gibson received for her win in 1958.

It had been a long, hard road, and Gibson's career ended much too soon. She said she was not consciously trying to be a pioneer. She thought of herself as just "a tennis player, not a *Negro* tennis player." But Gibson had opened the door for other black players, both male and female. Among them: Arthur Ashe, Zina Garrison, and Venus and Serena Williams.

In 1988, Althea Gibson presented her Wimbledon trophies to the Smithsonian Institution's National Museum of American History.

"Who could have imagined?" she said at the ceremony. "Who could have thought? Here stands before you a Negro woman, raised in Harlem, who went on to become a tennis player...and finally wind up being a world champion, in fact, the first black woman champion of this world."

This was a dream for Althea Gibson, all right. A dream come true.

11
NADIA COMANECI
The Perfect Gymnast

I t was the first night of the 1976 Olympic Games.

The name repeated by everyone was Olga, Olga, Olga.

Everyone knew about Olga Korbut. She had dazzled the crowd and the judges at the 1972 Olympics.

Her back-flips had turned her sport upside down. Suddenly, gymnastics had become a dynamic sport requiring speed, power, grace, and charm.

Korbut was the first to bring worldwide attention to gymnastics.

Comaneci stands before her perfect score in Montreal.

Now, four years later, the fans were expecting to be wowed by the Soviet Union's star once again.

Hardly anyone had noticed another name on the program: Nadia Comaneci.

Who was Nadia? Just fourteen years old, she was relatively unknown outside of Europe. This gymnast was the mystery element at the 1976 Montreal Olympics.

"I was coming from someplace nobody knew," Nadia Comaneci said.

Nadia was from Romania, a small country in Eastern Europe. She stood just about five feet tall and weighed 86 pounds. The Romanians were the youngest gymnastics team in history to enter the Olympic competition.

Did Nadia and her teammates have a chance against Olga and the powerful Soviet Union team?

ꙮꙮ

The story had begun years earlier in a kindergarten in Romania.

Two little girls were jumping and doing ballet steps in the playground. They caught the eye of Bela Karolyi, a local gymnastics coach.

Such energy! Karolyi was excited. He contacted Comaneci's mother. The next thing little Nadia knew, she was in gymnastics classes.

The Comaneci household was never the same. Nadia practiced her moves at home, using the couch to cushion her fall. Jump, jump, jump…crack! Another couch on the trash heap. Several couches later, she was still going strong.

"I run, run, run and take off and fly." That was her dream. She discovered she could do this much easier in a gym. She fell in love with gymnastics.

"I loved being in the air and how it feels, how it feels on your body."

She soon turned into one of Karolyi's hardest working pupils. At the age of seven, she competed in Romania's National Junior Championships and finished thirteenth.

As a present, Karolyi gave her a doll. The doll reminded her not to come in thirteenth again. She didn't.

"She always had a very strong personality, and she always was an achiever," Karolyi said. "She was going to do anything to be the best."

One year later, she won the National Junior Championship.

Nadia had the talent. But talent is never enough. It is the hard work and a willingness to sacrifice that makes a champion.

After school she trained rigorously for three to four hours every day. One day a coach walked into the gym. He watched Nadia complete six 20-second routines in a row. "She wasn't even breathing hard or missing a move on the sixth one," he said.

Nadia's habit was to repeat workouts as many times as possible. That built up her endurance and strength. At the same time, she learned to concentrate on the task at hand.

The years of sacrifice and hard work paid off. The same year Nadia won the National Junior Championship in 1971, she took first place in her first international competition. At age eleven, she became the national champion of Romania.

Then, at age thirteen, Nadia had a surprise for the gymnastics world. At the European Championships, she upset Lyudmila Tourischeva—the outstanding Soviet gymnast who had won the individual championship at the '72 Olympics. Nadia now held the European All-Around Championship title. By 1976, she was ready for her own appearance at the Olympics.

In Montreal, the young Romanian gymnastics team faced fierce competition from the Soviets. Nadia would be competing against champions like Tourischeva and Korbut, but she was well prepared.

In 1972, television had recorded the emotional Korbut's tears and triumphs. In 1976, the media was expecting more great things from Korbut and her impressive Soviet teammates. Olga, with her outgoing personality, was still the crowd favorite as the Olympics began. Nadia was just the opposite. Pale-faced and solemn, she rarely smiled.

Thanks to Korbut, gymnastics had a show-biz quality. Huge crowds attended the gymnastic sessions daily.

The team competition came first. The Romanians were to begin with the balance beam, an event requiring perfect balance and precise movement. This was one of the most difficult ways to start the competition.

It didn't seem to bother Nadia—she scored a 9.9 on a scale of 10.

On to the uneven parallel bars. In this routine, the gymnast leaps from one bar to another—suspended in midair for one thrilling, breathtaking moment.

Nadia Comaneci

The other gymnasts had completed their first-round routines. Nadia was last. Generally in gymnastics, the team superstar performs last. And what a performance it was.

The plan was to psyche the judges with startling new gyrations and an energetic, athletic performance. With her pigtails tied in red and white ribbons, the lithe Nadia attacked the uneven bars. She performed the compulsory pattern with surprising ease. Acrobatically, she swung down from the higher bar and lashed her pelvis to the lower bar. She was in complete control. Once around again, in perfect symmetry. And then, a difficult, twisting dismount from the top of the uneven bars: A high arc, featuring a half twist into a back somersault.

Comaneci performs an excellent balanced jump.

The landing complete, she arched her back like a ballerina's, her arms outstretched to receive the ovation of the crowd.

The routine was so physically taxing that it seemed inconceivable that someone had accomplished it.

Everyone in the arena awaited the judges' score. Nadia and her teammates were stunned.

A perfect 10!

It was a first in Olympic history. It had baffled the computer experts. How would they show a 10 on the scoreboard? The computer wasn't programmed for what was an "impossible" score. "Because of the gasps around the arena, I looked around and saw the 1.00 on the scoreboard and didn't understand what was happening," Comaneci said. But when the crowd saw the 1.00 flashing on the scoreboard, they knew. Suddenly the fans were on their feet, cheering. This time, Comaneci—the girl who never smiled—extended her hand, waved and smiled. Millions of television viewers around the world tuned in for the second night of the team competition. It was billed as the battle between Nadia and Olga.

Could Nadia make history again?

Korbut opened with a strong performance on the uneven bars, her favorite. She repeated her now-famous risky back flip off the high bar to squeals of delight from the audience.

Her score: 9.90.

Comaneci didn't seem flustered. She calmly mounted the dangerous balance beam. She flipped and twisted, drawing oohs and aahs from the crowd.

Another perfect 10 from the judges.

Unbelievable. Nadia had done it again. A perfect 10!

Korbut was struggling. Comaneci was surging. She received a 9.85 in the floor exercise, another 9.85 in the vault.

Back to the uneven bars. The capacity crowd of 16,000 at the Montreal Forum waited to see Nadia's performance. The only sounds heard were hundreds of cameras clicking as she made her incredible moves.

Would the tough international judges who had never given a 10 before in any previous Olympics give two perfect scores on the same night? And to the same gymnast?

Utterly impossible, everyone thought.

Front flips…twists…a dramatic dismount.

Her performance was flawless. The score flashed on the board: 1.0.

Nadia had done it again! Her third perfect 10.

The upstart new kid on the block from Romania was stealing the spotlight from Korbut. Nadia came close to stealing the team gold medal from the Soviets. Because the score is based on overall team performance, the Soviets won the gold. Nadia and her teammates won the silver.

But Nadia remained the center of attention that night. The crowds applauded and cheered, forcing Nadia to come back twice on the floor. She smiled and waved at the adoring fans.

The fourteen-year-old was taking everything in stride. Everyone seemed more excited over her history-making achievement than Nadia. Her reaction was typically calm: "I was really glad and I felt really good. I think I've done well."

Next challenge for Nadia: the individual competition. Despite her three perfect scores, she was still looking for the gold. The winner of the individual events would not only take home a gold medal but would also be recognized as the best all-around female gymnast in the world.

Comaneci was young, so young. This was her very first Olympics. She was going to perform on the biggest athletic stage in the world. And she was facing incredible competition from Olympic veterans who were several years older.

Comaneci was an athlete unafraid of dangerous moves. But could she beat the world's best for her first Olympic gold medal?

"She has no fear," said Bela Karolyi, her coach.

"She can block out the whole world," another coach said. "It's just her and the apparatus." Her power of concentration was never more apparent than that night at the 1976 Olympics.

She rarely watched other performances. She kept herself busy with warm-up exercises. She chalked the bar for her own routines.

Before going through her exercise she stood in front of the apparatus for what seemed like an eternity. Everything had to be perfect. Was the crowd quiet enough? Was the bar chalked up enough? Were her feet and hands in the right position?

A standing-room-only crowd of 18,000 filled the Montreal Forum. Anticipation was high as the thirty-six all-around finalists walked into the arena. Everyone was waiting. Would Comaneci be able to handle the pressure? Would one of her daring somersaults or double twists produce a fall? Would she be able to score another history-making 10?

She was registered in four events in the individual competition—uneven parallel bars, balance beam, vault, and floor exercises.

In 1976, the winner of the all-around individual title was determined by average scores from both the team and individual competitions.

Comaneci was eligible for a medal in all four events in the individuals.

On the uneven bars, she charged into new territory with front flips and twists and a spectacular dismount. It took imagination and nerve. The dismount was eventually named after her. It's known as the Salto Comaneci dismount. Her routine on the bars was seemingly so reckless that one Olympic official said it should be banned.

The tough international judges had little choice.

The judges' decision: a perfect score.

The balance beam?

Another 10.

Also, Nadia scored a 9.85 in the horse vault and a 9.9 in the floor exercise.

Comaneci won the Olympic gold medal as the top all-around gymnast in the world! Korbut finished a disappointing fifth.

Before the Olympics were finished, Comaneci was awarded two more perfect scores. Her grand total: seven.

Comaneci won three gold medals in Montreal. She added two more at the Moscow Games in 1980. From 1976 to 1984 she won an astounding twenty-one gold medals in Olympic and world championship competition.

Now she seemed to have it all—fame and admiration. But she was not happy. Her country was under oppressive Communist rule. The people were not free like they are in the United States or other democratic countries.

So Comaneci made the biggest leap of her life. She escaped from Romania in 1989. Her destination: America, land of the free. Bela Karolyi, her old coach, had defected earlier.

Time has not dulled her fame. In a 1999 poll of international journalists, Comaneci was voted the Top Female Athlete of the Twentieth Century.

What's more, her historic feat in Montreal may never be topped.

"I think she's the best gymnast the world has ever known," said Frank Bare, executive director of the United States Gymnastics Federation.

Nadia would never again be an unknown.

12
MANON RHEAUME
Manon the Warrior

All alone.

A female warrior waits to meet the enemy.

Her name is Manon Rheaume.

Dressed in armor, an iron mask shielding her face, she glances at the weapon by her side.

She is preparing herself mentally for the challenge ahead of her. She is on a quest to do what has never been done.

Manon Rheaume at a 1992 news conference.

Feelings of excitement rise from the pit of her stomach as she visualizes the battle. Alone, surrounded by ice, she must use her weapon, her skill, her arms, her legs to defend her fortress.

The enemy will try to invade using a missile flying at great speeds. She must stop the missile at all costs, or lose the battle.

The battleground is a hockey arena. Rheaume is a goaltender. She is about to make history as the first female to play in a men's professional hockey game. It is the highest level of hockey—the National Hockey League.

September 23, 1992. Rheaume stands waiting with her Tampa Bay Lightning teammates behind her to take the ice. A near-sellout crowd of 8,223 fills the Florida State Fairgrounds Expo Hall for the exhibition game against the St. Louis Blues.

Will she embarrass herself? Will she let her team down? She's feeling the pressure and her nerves are starting to jangle. Is she just there as a publicity stunt? Are they right? Is she too small, too fragile to play at the top level? Rheaume has been in many high-pressure hockey games before, but never against this kind of competition. She will face blazing shots at 100 miles an hour. And the game will be quicker—much quicker than anything she has been used to.

This game would be faster, rougher, and more violent. Her calm exterior doesn't show the nervousness that is slowly enveloping her.

The organ music breaks into her thoughts. Then, the announcement:

"Ladies and gentlemen, YOUR Tampa Bay Lightning!"

And there she is, leading her team out on the ice to the thunderous cheers of thousands.

As starting goaltender, the warrior takes her place in the net and awaits her first shot…

Manon Rheaume

Breaking barriers was nothing new for Rheaume.

She had been playing goalie since she was five years old. She lived in a small Canadian town outside of Quebec City. At first she played against her older brothers.

"When I was young, in our house downstairs, we put up a goal and a net," Rheaume said. "I would dress up in all the equipment and they would shoot on me."

Rheaume learned all about hockey. The game is played on the ice. The players can skate backward or forward at incredible speeds with equal skill. They use long sticks with broad blades to move an object called the puck up and down the ice. The three-inch puck is round and made of hard, black rubber. It resembles a big frozen Oreo cookie without the cream in the middle. In the National Hockey League, it can travel at speeds up to 100 miles an hour.

As the last line of defense, the goaltender is the most important player on the ice. With a blocker and a big-bladed stick, it is the goaltender's job to stop the opposing team from shooting the puck into the net. Sometimes the goalie uses parts of his body to block the puck.

The goalie is well padded from top to bottom, wears leg shields and a metal helmet with a mask to protect against serious injury. This doesn't mean the goaltender will be safe.

Goalies are bumped. Run into. Run over. And that is only the beginning. They face grave dangers from speeding skaters—and speeding pucks. Goaltending is the most dangerous position in hockey.

Manon Rheaume waits her turn to take the ice as goaltender.

Rheaume's father was a tough hockey coach. He never spared her feelings. She learned to be strong and resourceful. She would never be a crybaby. She would never be a quitter.

Manon played many sports, but hockey was her passion. She grew older. There weren't many opportunities for girls to play hockey. She played against the boys.

Rheaume was a really good player. Sometimes better than the boys. That posed some difficulties when she played on boys' teams.

"Parents were jealous and thought their little boys would make it to the NHL," Rheaume said, "so they thought I didn't deserve the chance to play."

Rheaume thought differently. She continued to practice

and play like her hero, all-star goaltender Patrick Roy, a Montreal native. She copied Roy's "butterfly" goalie style: dropping to his knees and spreading his feet sideways to cover more area of the net.

She took her game to the Canadian Major Junior Hockey League. This league is a steppingstone to the NHL for teenagers—teenage boys. The competition was considered too tough for a girl.

Too tough for most girls. Not for Rheaume.

She was the first female to play in Canada's top amateur league. Her team: the Trois-Rivieres Draveurs.

Game time. Manon the Warrior strapped on her battle gear. She took her place in the net for the Draveurs.

She tensed for a shot. The speeding puck came at Rheaume at eye level. Before she had a chance to react, it slammed into her mask. She reeled backwards from the impact.

Suddenly, she saw blood. A cut had opened near her right eye. Somewhat dazed, she steeled herself, ready to play. She refused to leave the game.

Finally, the blood took its toll. Her vision blurred. She couldn't see. She was forced out of the game.

"My mask looked like it had been in a car accident," said Rheaume, who received three stitches.

The team doctor said that most other goaltenders would have dropped to the ice after receiving such a blast. Yet Rheaume continued to play.

At the time she was on the Draveurs, Rheaume was also playing for Canada's national women's team. In 1992 she led the Canadians to the gold medal at the world championships in Finland. The gold medal attracted attention.

Phil Esposito, general manager of the Tampa Bay Lightning, sent Rheaume an invitation. "Try out for the Lightning," he challenged.

Unbelievable. An impossible dream.

The 5-foot-6, 135-pound Rheaume would be the first female to compete in one of the four major professional sports: major-league baseball, football, basketball, and hockey.

The challenge was out there. The question was, should she accept?

Did she really have a shot at making an NHL team? Or would she be just a publicity stunt, a circus sideshow?

Should she accept the challenge? The pressure would be enormous.

Finally, she said yes.

"I decided I didn't want to look back in ten years and be sad that I didn't go to Tampa Bay," Rheaume said.

The twenty-year-old Rheaume showed up at the Lightning training camp. So did the media. She was like a rock star in skates. In one eleven-day period, she did a hundred interviews!

"I'm having a hard time relaxing and getting good sleep," she said.

Manon Rheaume

She didn't receive, nor expect, any favoritism just because she was a female. Lightning coach Terry Crisp told it as it was:

"The guys out there are all trying to make a living. They can't afford to pull up on their shots. And in the heat of the battle, nobody is going to take time to decide if it's a guy or a girl in the net. She's just a goaltender."

That was fine with Rheaume. She felt she was there for more than just the publicity.

"I don't face 100-mile-an-hour shots everyday and I don't have bruises everywhere on my body to have publicity," she said.

A hamstring and groin injury couldn't stop her. She played through agonizing pain as she blocked blazing shots.

Training camp was tough. Players were cut. But after the first few weeks she was still there.

"I haven't been an embarrassment," she told reporters.

The impossible dream came true. Rheaume would start in the exhibition game against the Blues.

Now the historic moment had come. Rheaume didn't have long to wait for her first shot. Just 40 seconds into the game at the Florida State Fairgrounds Expo Hall, Rheaume stopped a slap shot for her first save.

"It was important to stop it," she said. "After that, I relaxed. I wasn't so nervous."

Then she stopped another shot, kicking the puck away with her right leg pad.

But another shot got by her.

"It was a bad goal," she said. "But even good NHL goalies give up bad goals."

Rheaume soon had a chance to redeem herself. One of the Lightning players broke a rule and was sent to the "penalty box." This gave the Blues a "power play," meaning they had one more skater on the ice than the Lightning. Tampa Bay was playing "shorthanded," a scary situation for a goalie.

☯

The Blues have the puck. Here they come, steaming down the ice, steaming toward the goal that Manon is guarding. Manon tenses. Suddenly a player breaks free right in front of her. He has Manon at his mercy.

He pulls his stick back for a hard shot. He fires toward the upper right side of the net.

GOAL!

But just when it seems certain the puck is going to fly into the net, Rheaume slides across the goalmouth to snare the shot with her glove.

NO GOAL!

The crowd goes wild. The scoreboard flashes the words in capital letters: AWESOME, AWESOME!

☯

With Manon's help, the Lightning had killed the Blues' power play.

Manon gave up a goal before leaving at the end of one period. The game was tied at 2. She had faced nine shots, made seven saves.

"She surprised me like she surprised everyone," said Tony Esposito, the Lightning's director of operations and a Hall of Fame goaltender.

The performance convinced the Lightning to offer Manon a contract with its top minor league team in Atlanta. Over the years she had moderate success while playing on different levels of professional hockey.

Then it was back to the Canadian women's national team and an appearance in the 1998 Olympics. Another goal realized. The Canadians went on to win the silver medal.

By then Rheaume was the most famous female hockey player in the world. She had shown the way for other women like Hayley Wickenheiser, the first female to score a point in a men's professional hockey game.

"When you have a dream," Rheaume said, "you want to go after that dream."

Manon Rheaume had become a legendary warrior.

13
THE ALL-AMERICAN RED HEADS
A Team of Their Own

HE PINCHED ME! HE PINCHED ME!" the redhead screamed, pointing at the opposition basketball player.

The referee's shrill whistle split the air. Five redheads suppressed giggles as an amused audience witnessed the drama on the basketball court.

The All-American Red Heads in the 1950s

"Foul, most foul," the referee declared.

An embarrassed male player stood there, protesting.

"She pinched ME!" the player insisted. No one was listening.

The redheaded basketball player stepped to the line to shoot her foul shots—on her knees! The spectators chuckled.

Down went the player. Up went the basketball.

Score!

One more time.

Score again!

Everyone laughed and cheered.

The All-American Red Heads had come to town.

ꔰ

In red, white, and blue uniforms, this remarkable women's basketball team packed gymnasiums in small towns and drew crowds to big city arenas.

Red, white, and blue—and razzle-dazzle.

They were many years ahead of their time. They blazed a trail for women's basketball long before it became nationally popular in the eighties and nineties.

Before colleges started seriously supporting women's sports, thanks to the Title IX legislation in 1972, there were the Red Heads.

Before the U. S. women's team won a gold medal in the Olympics of 1996, there were the Red Heads.

Before Sheryl Swoopes, Rebecca Lobo, and Lisa Leslie made headlines playing in the Women's National Basketball Association, there were the Red Heads.

The All-American Red Heads

The All-American Red Heads paved the way.

And what a show they put on!

The crowds had never seen two girls dribble four basketballs at one time. They were amazed when a Red Head bumped the basketball into the hoop with her head.

And just as amazed when a Red Head stood on her head and shot the basketball into the hoop with her feet. Or balanced two basketballs on her knees.

It was fun, fun, fun.

Sure, they could do tricks, but they could also play some serious basketball. Make no mistake, they had "game." They were skilled professional basketball players as well as entertainers.

They played mostly men's teams under men's rules. And they usually won. What a blow for the male ego!

"A lot of times, the men came in expecting a bunch of girls they could push around," Mickey Childress said. "But we were in good condition."

Childress played for the Red Heads in the 1960s. "Our first quarter was pure basketball," she said. "We wanted to show the public that we knew how to first of all play basketball."

The rest was pure entertainment.

The Red Heads were a long-running hit, too—lasting for a full fifty years, from 1936 to 1986.

"We like to think we helped women's basketball stay alive when the colleges weren't playing our game," Childress said.

೦෨

It had all started in Missouri in the 1930s. The setting: a beauty parlor. The main characters: two beauticians.

They happened to be on a basketball team sponsored by the beauty parlor. They also happened to be redheads. And so, the idea for a prank.

They convinced their teammates to join in. What did they do? They shocked the fans.

When they walked out on the basketball court for the game, the crowd saw red. Redheaded guards. Redheaded forwards. A redheaded center. Every single player on the team had dyed her hair red.

They were walking advertisements for the beauty parlor they worked for, and a big hit with the fans.

Come out and see the Red Heads play!

The prank was so successful, the following year the "Missouri Red Heads" were touring and attracting big crowds. C. M. Olson and his wife, Doyle, the beauty parlor owners, had founded an American original.

Every season was an adventure for the Red Heads. It was the 1940s, just before World War II. The Red Heads were visiting the Philippines. Suddenly, the State Department issued a warning to leave as quickly as possible. For a while, the girls seemed to be stranded. A cattle boat came to their rescue, and they were escorted out of the area by a Navy minesweeper. In the 1940s, many of the team members left the road to work in airplane factories and support the war effort.

AAU All-Americans began joining the team. The team was renamed. The *All-American* Red Heads were born.

In 1955, coach Orwell Moore bought the team and moved the Red Heads to Caraway, Arkansas. He operated the franchise with his wife Lorene, a former player, until the team's last year in 1986.

Childress was a freshman in high school in Gate City, Virginia, when the Red Heads came to town. Basketball was her first love. When she saw the fun and the skill on the court, she knew right then that's what she wanted to do.

So she approached the coach after the game. "I want to play for the Red Heads," the bold teenager said.

The Red Heads' coach condescendingly patted her on the head. "If you keep practicing, maybe you will someday."

Childress now had a dream to follow. She starred in high school, where she broke a Virginia school record for points in a game. She later played for the University of Tennessee.

Childress's heroics attracted attention. An offer came from the Red Heads: two hundred dollars a month plus expenses.

"It wasn't a great deal of money," Childress said, "but to play basketball and get paid for it was the greatest thing to come down the pike."

A hard worker, Childress was not going to go unprepared. She trained all summer with an NBA player.

"I thought I was in great shape," she said.

She had second thoughts when she started training with the Red Heads.

The workouts were strenuous and intense.

"About the third morning after I got there, I had no idea that everything you owned could be sore at one time—including my eyelids.

"When we got up and finally got dressed and got to the door, the station wagon had already left for breakfast. It was a long time to lunch and a lot of activity left. As we stepped outside our motel rooms, there lay a jump rope for everyone."

It made Marine boot camp seem like a walk in the park.

Things didn't change during an exhausting barnstorming season, which started in the fall and ended in the spring.

Traveling in a station wagon on a trip covering thousands of miles, they would play some 200 games. They played in a variety of cities, on college campuses, Indian reservations, and military bases. They took on American Legion teams, Lions Club teams, high school graduates.

For a full half century, a variety of Red Head teams—sometimes as many as three at a time—barnstormed around North America.

What a whirlwind! Childress's days were spent on the road in the team's old green station wagon—three in the front, two in the middle, three in the jump seat.

Every once in a while, the station wagon would make an "R and R" stop. Rest and recreation? No, roadwork and more roadwork. The players would race each other—wind sprints between telephone poles with cries of "Go, girl, go!" ringing into the air.

There were snowy, freezing days. When the station wagon got stuck, the Red Heads piled out and pushed. One time after a game in Vermont, a car window had frozen in the down position. As the Red Heads pulled away from the arena, some pranksters fired snowballs through the window. Laughing and covered with snow, the Red Heads finally made their getaway.

The trusty old station wagon was a key player in the Red Heads' travels.

"We put our luggage on top. In the wintertime a tarp went over the top. No one wanted to be the last one to put her suitcase on top. That meant you had to put the tarp up."

The Red Heads had to wash their own uniforms.

"They were heavy," Childress said. "And I played many times in a cold, wet uniform that just didn't get dry between games."

But the overall experience was wonderful for Childress, as it was for hundreds of other Red Heads.

In 1959, Ella Cross was a Tennessee teenager who had only played half-court in high school. That year the Red Heads recruited her, and she was called to join the team on the road.

The basketball game was already underway when Cross finally arrived in Poplar Bluff, Missouri. She was

The All-American Red Heads with coach Orwell Moore in 1955

exhausted following her 560-mile journey. Exhausted, yes, but not too tired to play.

Ella soon had her first taste of professional basketball action. It was midway through the first quarter when the coach sent her into the game.

The teenager felt lost, and it wasn't only because she was so far from home.

"Can you imagine being introduced to five redheaded girls and trying to remember their names?" Cross recalled of that night. "I didn't know who could shoot. I didn't know who to throw it to. So I just shot it."

The nineteen-year-old from Oneida, Tennessee, made quite a debut. She scored 27 points for the All-American Red Heads.

The All-American Red Heads

Cross had never done any fancy ball handling. She quickly learned to juggle three balls, shoot free throws with her back to the basket, and spin the ball on her fingertips.

Shooting from unusual positions was normal for the Red Heads. A favorite was the "Old Piggy Back Play," where one player climbs onto the shoulders of another and drops the ball in the basket.

The play had been dreamed up by a pair of early Red Head stars—Gene Love and "Stubby" Winters. Love, 6-foot-4, was nicknamed "Careless Love," after a popular song. Winters was only 5-foot-4, but she didn't let her short stature hamper her performance.

As a matter of fact, it worked to her advantage when the Red Heads put on their famous "Dribbler Through Act."

Love, a center, sets up with her back to the basket, legs planted wide apart. Winters grabs a pass from a teammate.

Dribbling the ball with an opponent in pursuit, she ducks through Love's legs and goes for the basket. Her opponent tries to follow. Big mistake. He is trapped by Love's long legs.

Winters has an easy basket.

And the bounce goes on…

Fast forward to 1999. The Women's Basketball Hall of Fame opened in Knoxville, Tennessee, and some seventy-five Red Heads walked through the door. They were there to be honored as a team with other women's basketball greats. Among them: Senda Berenson, "The Mother of Women's Basketball," who first established the game at Smith College in the 1890s; Nancy Lieberman, first woman to play in a men's professional league in the 1980s; and Ann Meyers, who was invited to training camp with the Indiana Pacers of the NBA, although she never played a game.

"We had a reunion at the Hall of Fame," Mickey Childress said. "We had members of the first team and members of the last team. You cannot imagine the family we were."

Among the early Red Head greats attending the Hall of Fame opening were Charlotte Adams and Red Mason.

So what did they do? They entertained. The Red Heads started doing their old tricks with a basketball.

"The Red Heads had everybody, including the vendors, out dancing," Childress said.

Walking through the Hall, the Red Heads spotted a familiar friend: an old, green station wagon with "Moore's All-American Red Heads" imprinted on the door. Once discarded in an Arkansas field, it had been brought back to life, a reminder of days gone by for a group of female pioneers.

They may have been born with blonde, brunette, or black hair, but in their hearts they would always be Red Heads.

CONCLUSION

By the early 1900s women were pushing harder and harder against the boundaries society had set for them, and in 1920, they finally won the right to vote. Female athletes continued to push, too, breaking down people's stereotypes about women in sports.

During World War II, women pitched in. They came out of the kitchen and into a man's world. They managed businesses; they drove trucks. They worked in factories, building airplanes. Then they flew them, transporting supplies all over the globe. They did everything but fight.

At home they helped to keep up morale by filling in for the male athletes who had been called to the battlefield. While the All-American Red Heads were drawing crowds to basketball arenas all over the country, women were pitching, catching, and hitting on the baseball diamond as part of the All-American Girls Professional Baseball League.

During the fifties and sixties, women athletes like Althea Gibson and Wilma Rudolph not only opened the door for other young black women in sports but also used their celebrity to bring public attention to the struggle for civil rights.

In 1972, Title IX of the Education Amendments Acts was passed, prohibiting all schools and universities that received federal funds from discriminating on the basis of sex. Women's college sports expanded during the next few years, and girls gained more and more opportunities to play sports at a much higher level. Women, once excluded from the Olympics, were making their presence felt at the Games, showcasing their amazing physical skills and attracting worldwide attention. Female superstars in sports such as tennis and gymnastics were idolized by both men and women across the country.

Through the last decades of the twentieth century, female athletes continued to break new ground by competing at high levels in many sports that had been dominated by men. Women ran the marathon. Women jockeys took honors in the most prestigious races. Committed and hardworking females kept breaking gender barriers in sports. Some of these remarkable women are listed below:

ꗁ 1953: Toni Stone, first woman to play baseball in the Negro League

ꗁ 1978: Janet Guthrie, first woman to complete the Indianapolis 500

ꗁ 1985: Libby Riddles, first woman to win the Iditarod dog sled race in Alaska

Conclusion

⚙ 1985: Lynette Woodard, first woman to play for the Harlem Globetrotters

⚙ 1986: Nancy Lieberman, first woman to play in men's professional basketball

⚙ 1989: Julie Croteau, first woman to play NCAA baseball

⚙ 1992: Lyn St. James, first woman to compete in a men's professional racing league

⚙ 1997: Ila Borders, first woman to play in a men's professional baseball game

⚙ 2002: Katie Hnida, first woman to play in a Division I college football game

The women in this book weren't necessarily trying to be trailblazers.

All they wanted to do was participate in a sport, and play it as well as they possibly could. But these First Ladies of Sports, with their courage, perseverance, and dedication, have not just become a part of sports history, they have made a lasting contribution to society.

These women are all winners who made a difference.

BIBLIOGRAPHICAL NOTE

Along with personal interviews, I used a number of newspaper and magazine sources to research this book. I relied most heavily on the Associated Press, *Chicago Tribune, Los Angeles Times, New York Times, Washington Post, Sports Illustrated,* and *Sports Illustrated for Kids.* I also found helpful the Current Biography Yearbook series available in most libraries, as well as some of the leading internet sites.

If you want to learn more about these athletes and other women in sports, you may find the following books of interest.

Althea Gibson, by Tom Biracree

America's Champion Swimmer: Gertrude Ederle, by David A. Adler

Babe: The Life and Legend of Babe Didrikson Zaharias, by Susan E. Cayleff

LADIES FIRST

Female Firsts in their Fields: Sports and Athletics, by Ann Graham Gaines

Figure Skating to Fancy Skating, Memoirs of the Life of Sonja Henie, by Michael Kirby and Scott Hamilton

Joan Samuelson's Running for Women, by Joan Benoit Samuelson and Gloria Averbuch

Letters to a Young Gymnast, by Nadia Comaneci

Manon: Alone in Front of the Net, by Manon Rheaume and Chantal Gilbert

Outstanding Women's Athletes: Who They Are and How They Influenced Sports in America, by Janet Woolum

Riding for my Life, by Julie Krone and Nancy Richardson

Shirley Muldowney's Tales From the Track, by Shirley Muldowney and Bill Stephens

Sports Hero, Billie Jean King (Sports Hero Biographies), by Marshall Burchard and S. H. Burchard

Susan Butcher and the Iditarod Trail, by Ellen M. Dolan

Wilma Rudolph (Black American Series), by Tom Biracree

Winning Ways: A Photohistory of American Women in Sports, by Sue Macy

Women's Sports: A History, by Allen Guttman

ABOUT THE AUTHOR

ongtime sports writer KEN RAPPOPORT is the author and coauthor of dozens of books for young readers and adults, including VILLAINS: THE BAD BOYS AND GIRLS OF SPORTS, TALES FROM THE TAR HEEL LOCKER ROOM, and biographies of Wayne Gretzky and Shaquille O'Neal. Ken has written about the NCAA basketball championship, minor league baseball, college football rivalries, and numerous teams and their players. He received a national award from *Writer's Digest* for a profile on St. John's basketball coach Lou Carnesecca.

At the Associated Press, Rappoport covered every major sport out of New York for thirty years and was the AP's national hockey writer for fourteen years. He covered the World Series, NCAA Finals, Olympics, and Stanley Cup playoffs, among other events.

Ken lives in New Jersey.

6/14/18 -0